O

DEEP BLACK:
DEATH WAVE

DEEP BLACK:
DEATH WAVE

Stephen Coonts
and
William H. Keith

Quercus

First published in Great Britain in 2011 by

Quercus
21 Bloomsbury Square
London
WC1A 2NS

A CIP catalogue record for this book is available
from the British Library

ISBN (HB) 978 0 85738 520 8
ISBN (TPB) 978 0 85738 521 5

This book is a work of fiction. Names, characters,
businesses, organizations, places and events are
either the product of the author's imagination
or used fictitiously. Any resemblance to
actual persons, living or dead, events or
locales is entirely coincidental.

Printed and bound in Great Britain by Clays Ltd, St Ives Plc

10 9 8 7 6 5 4 3 2 1

To Dr. Martin H. Greenberg,
who loves stories and storytellers

DEEP BLACK:
DEATH WAVE

PROLOGUE

The man stood on the rugged volcanic spine of the island, staring west into the sunset. At his feet, the ground dropped away sharply, leveling off eighteen hundred meters below in the green rectangles of banana plantations and tiny, tourist-oriented villages before reaching the ocean five kilometers away, where the piercingly blue waters of the Atlantic crashed endlessly against rock and black sand.

At his back, a drilling derrick towered against a cloud-crowded sky, the harsh, steady grinding of the drill head shattering the idyllic peace of the place. A large white sign in Spanish proclaimed the area off-limits to tourists, a special reserve for the Scientific Institute of Geological Research.

He called himself the Jackal.

That nom de guerre wasn't original, of course. Another man, a Venezuelan revolutionary, had carried that name many years earlier, before he'd been betrayed and sent to prison. Ibrahim Hussain Azhar had declared himself to be the new Jackal—"al-Wawi" in Arabic. He'd first taken that battle name when he'd led the band of Mujahideen that hijacked an Indian Airlines jetliner to Kandahar in 1999. Among the prisoners freed by India in exchange for the hostages had been his brother, the cleric Maulana Masood Azhar.

This new Jackal drew himself up a bit taller as he recalled the thunderous cheers of ten thousand exultant Muslims in Karachi when the freed Maulana Azhar had addressed them. *I have come here because this is my duty to tell you that Muslims should not rest in peace until we have destroyed America and India*, he'd proclaimed.

The Azhar brothers had gone on to create the Jaish-e-Mohammad, the Army of Mohammad, in 2000. This group, based in the rugged mountain fastness of northeastern Pakistan, was dedicated to freeing the embattled state of Kashmir from India—but Ibrahim never forgot that the true, holy cause of militant Islam extended far beyond merely local politics, beyond the geopolitical concerns of borders and governments. India was the enemy of Pakistan, yes—but behind India were the far greater enemies of all of Islam: Israel and the despised United States of America.

When *those* enemies were swept away by the hand of Allah, the supreme, the powerful, the lesser foes of India and Russia would scatter and run like dogs.

Almighty God would reign supreme over a world at last cleansed of capitalism, of Western decadence, of Hindu polytheism, of Christian blasphemy.

A world under Sharia law, ruled by Allah alone, with Mohammad as His Prophet.

AYNI AIRFIELD
SOUTHWEST OF DUSHANBE
TAJIKISTAN
WEDNESDAY, 1452 HOURS LOCAL TIME

f I were a two-kiloton nuclear weapon disguised as a suitcase," Charlie
Dean said with a nonchalance he did not feel, "where would I hide?"

"The cloakroom of the U.S. Capitol Building?" his partner replied over their radio link.

"Actually, I'd like to find the damned things *here*, Ilya. If they
make it to D.C., it's too late."

Charlie Dean stood on the tarmac of an apparently deserted military airstrip, which shimmered beneath a harsh midafternoon sun.
Sweat prickled at his spine beneath the khaki uniform blouse, the heat
dragging at him, sucking the energy from his body.

He decided, yet again, that he was really getting too old for this
sort of thing. A former U.S. Marine, he'd served in the Gulf, and later,
before Bill Rubens had asked him to join Deep Black's Desk Three,
he'd worked with an independent intelligence service in Afghanistan.
The heat reminded him of those deployments.

Dean didn't look the part of one of the National Security Agency's
Deep Black senior field operators, though that, of course, was the idea.
He was wearing the uniform of a wing commander in the Indian Air

Force, the equivalent of an American lieutenant colonel, with his skin and hair dyed dark to give him more of a subcontinental look.

"Hey, Charlie!" The voice of his partner sounded in his ear. "I'm picking something up over here."

He could see the other man thirty yards away, standing next to a battered Russian-made ZiL-131 truck parked in the shade beside a shed. Charlie glanced around. No one else in sight. He started walking toward the other Desk Three operator.

His partner was Ilya Akulinin, sometimes called Sharkie, a reference to the English translation of his family name; when friends called him Ilya, it was with the proper Russian pronunciation, with the accent on the "ya." His cover for this op was that of a major in the Russian Air Force, where pale skin and blond hair were not out of place. He looked the part, and he'd come by that honestly. Akulinin's parents were Russian émigrés, living now in the Little Russia community of Brooklyn, New York.

Their current mission, code-named Haystack, had brought them to Ayni, a military and civil airport just fifteen kilometers outside of Dushanbe, the capital of the Republic of Tajikistan. A few years ago, Tajikistan had struck a deal with New Delhi to turn a dilapidated air base at Farkhor on the border with Afghanistan over to the Indian military. The arrangement had been intended to give India a greater military and political reach in the region, and Tajikistan greater security on its southern border with Afghanistan.

In 2007, New Delhi and Dushanbe had extended the arrangement to include Ayni, outside of Tajikistan's capital. The agreement had been contentious at times. The Ayni base was supposed to be shared in rotation by India, Tajikistan, and Russia—but Russia, displeased with India's recent political accommodations with the United States, had more than once tried to force the eviction of the Indian contingent.

India was still here, however. Plans to complete a natural gas pipeline from Central Asia south to India depended on the region's security and political stability, and India's military bases in Tajikistan were vital to those plans.

Thunder boomed overhead—a pair of Indian MiG-29s circling around to land. Twelve of the fighter jets were based here and at Farkhor, eighty-five miles to the southeast, along with an Indian Army security force.

"Whatcha got?" Dean asked as soon as the MiGs' thunder dwindled into the distance. He spoke quietly, the words little more than subvocalization. The high-tech transceiver imbedded in bone behind his left ear picked up the words and transmitted them via the antenna in his belt.

"He's getting something higher than background," the voice of Jeff Rockman said in Dean's ear. Their transmissions were also being relayed by communications satellite to the Art Room. The code name referred to the Deep Black ops center, located in the basement of the NSA's headquarters building at Fort Meade, Maryland. Rockman was their handler for this part of the op, though Dean knew that the rest of the Art Room crew would be listening in as well—including Rubens, he was sure.

Dean didn't like the real-time communications hookup, which allowed several dozen people to look over your shoulder while you worked. He would grudgingly admit that being able to talk via satellite with Fort Meade could be useful at times, but often it was a royal, high-tech pain in the ass.

"'Something' is right," Akulinin added. "I think this might be the truck."

Walking around to the rear of the vehicle, he jumped up onto the flatbed and moved up toward the cab. "A tarp . . . a big wooden crate. It's empty. We couldn't have gotten *that* lucky. Lots of chatter from the box, though. Hey . . . you people *sure* it's safe to be here?"

"You're getting less radiation right now, Mr. Akulinin," a new voice said, "than you would flying in a jetliner at forty thousand feet." That was William Rubens, deputy director of the National Security Agency and head of the highly secret department of the organization known as Desk Three, the NSA's field operations unit.

"Well, you're up early, sir," Dean said. "What is it back there—five in the morning?"

"Six," Rubens replied. "Nine hours' difference. But who's counting?"

Dean chuckled to himself. Ops in places like China and Tajikistan guaranteed that the micromanagers back home would be keeping graveyard shift hours.

Both Dean and Akulinin wore small but extremely sensitive Geiger counters strapped to their legs just above their ankles, hidden beneath their uniform trousers. The readout was audible only through their transceivers—a faint, rapid-fire clicking that Dean could hear through the implant as he walked beside the truck. By walking slowly across different parts of the airfield, they could pick up minute traces of radioactivity left behind by the shipment they were looking for. They'd already paced through two small storage sheds and a hangar, without result.

An informant in Kazakhstan had told them that their quarry had taken a military truck and headed for Dushanbe, where he would be meeting with persons unknown. This parked truck was the first indication that they weren't on a wild-goose chase.

Akulinin jumped off the tailgate and rejoined Dean beside the cab. Thunder rolled once more across the airfield as one of the twin-tailed MiG-29s boomed out of the east and gently touched down on the tarmac. The Indian Air Force had sixty-nine of the aircraft—known as Fulcrums in the West but called Baaz in India, the Hindi word for hawk.

"So, anybody else shipping hot nuclear material through Ayni?" Dean asked as the rumble died away.

"Negative," Rockman replied over the Art Room channel. "Nobody *official*, at any rate. Check the truck's registration."

Akulinin glanced around to be sure they weren't being watched, then opened the passenger-side door to the cab. Inside the glove box, he found a plastic envelope with various cards and papers. He pulled a card out and glanced at it. "Here we go." He read off the registration number.

"That checks," Rockman told them. "That's the truck checked out to Anatoli Zhernov two weeks ago at the motor pool in Stepnogorsk."

Stepnogorsk was a town in Kazakhstan, nearly a thousand miles to the north. Once, when it had been a part of the old Soviet Union, it had been a so-called secret town, operating under the code name of Tselinograd-25, and had been an important nuclear and biochemical manufacturing site.

"So where's Zhernov now?" Dean asked.

Akulinin had one hand casually resting on the truck's hood. "Engine's cold. He could be anywhere."

"More to the point," Rubens said, "the *shipment* could be anywhere."

"At least this confirms our intel that Zhernov was bringing the shipment here," Dean said. "But who did he meet?" Who was he meeting?"

"If you find Zhernov, find out," Rubens said curtly.

"You bet," Dean replied blithely.

"It might help," Akulinin said as he replaced the registration card in the truck's glove compartment, "if we knew when Zhernov was here. When he handed off the shipment. Is it still here? Did it leave by air? By road?"

"We have our technical assets on it, gentlemen," Rubens said. "In the meantime, you two keep looking for traces there. That could narrow down the field a bit."

"That it would," Dean agreed.

"You can also check the ops log at the Ayni tower," Rubens suggested. "Get a list of all aircraft that have left Ayni for the past, oh, three . . . no, better make it five days."

"I can do that," Akulinin said. "These people are still scared shitless of Russians."

"Besides, your Russian is a hell of a lot better than my Hindi," Dean pointed out.

"Looks like you might get your chance to practice," Akulinin said. "Company coming."

A small party of men, all wearing Indian Air Force uniforms, had just emerged from the base of the control tower and were walking toward them. One wore a group captain's epaulets, making him the equivalent of a colonel.

"We have an ID for you," Rockman's voice whispered in Dean's ear. "That's Group Captain Sharad Narayanan. He could be trouble. He's a relative of India's national security advisor—and he *hates* the Russians."

"You there," Narayanan called in singsong English. "What are you about?"

"Sir!" Dean said, snapping to crisp attention and saluting as the party reached them. "Wing Commander Salman Patel. I am on Air Vice Marshal Subarao's staff." He spoke the phrase in memorized Hindi, then added in English, "I am here to complete a materiel inspection of this base."

The cover story had been carefully fabricated back at Fort Meade, and Dean had papers in his breast pocket to back it up. During the weeks before the op he'd actually gone through a crash course in Hindi. Although Hindi was one of the official national languages of India and by far the most popular, only about 40 percent of all Indians spoke it as a native tongue; English, also an official language, often served as a lingua franca among the diverse ethnic groups of the gigantic and incredibly diverse subcontinent, especially within the military.

"And this?" the group captain demanded, turning dark eyes on Akulinin. Although Russia and India had long been close allies, relations between the two nations had been strained for several years now, as Moscow tried to force Tajikistan to expel the IAF from the Tajik air bases. If Narayanan didn't like Russians, it was probably because of that.

"*Maior* Sergei Golikov, sir," Akulinin said in English, with a deliberately thick Russian accent layered on for effect. "Temporarily attached to Air Vice Marshal Subarao's staff."

"And what are you doing standing around out here?"

The second MiG dropped out of the sky and touched the tarmac, the thunder momentarily making conversation impossible.

"Staying in the shade, Group Captain," Dean replied when the sound dwindled, "while we watch the MiGs land and talk about the possibility of expanding the facilities here at Ayni for the benefit of both India and Russia."

The group captain seemed to relax slightly. The three-way political situation between Tajikistan, Russia, and India was delicate enough that he wouldn't want to get involved, not if his superiors were insisting that the IAF had to work smoothly with their Russian counterparts—and that much of the story was true.

"I . . . see." He snapped something at Dean in Hindi, the words too fast for him to catch.

"He just asked you, more or less, if you were giving away the store," another new voice with a soft lilt to it said in Dean's ear. A number of NSA linguists would be standing by, eavesdropping on Dean's conversations and translating when necessary.

"No, sir," Dean replied in Hindi. "The negotiations are going surprisingly well." His crash course in Hindi had included the memorization of twenty-five useful phrases, everything from "I will need to discuss that with my superiors" to "Can you direct me to the men's room?"

Narayanan barked something else.

"He just asked you where you're from," the linguist told him. "He says you have an unusual accent."

Big surprise there. "I was born in Himachal Pradesh. My parents spoke Punjabi at home."

Again the group captain seemed to relax very slightly. If he had to, Dean could spit back some memorized Punjabi as well, but Narayanan didn't seem interested in pursuing the matter.

"We have had reports, Wing Commander, of terrorist agents covertly on the base, possibly in disguise," Narayanan said in English. "The FSB warned us of an arms deal brokered here involving, shall we say, unconventional munitions. What have you heard of this?"

"Nothing, Group Captain," Dean lied. "*Sir.*"

"There have *always* been reports like this," Akulinin told the IAF officer. "Nothing has ever come of them."

"I hope you are right, Major," Narayanan said. "For all of our sakes, I hope you are right."

The Indians, Dean knew, were pursuing the investigation themselves, as were the Russians, but his orders were to keep Desk Three's investigation carefully compartmentalized from those of both the Indian military and the Russian FSB, hence the lie. The FSB, the *Federalnaya Sluzhba Bezopasnosti Rossiyskoy Federaciyi*, or Federal Security Service of the Russian Federation, was the modern successor to the old KGB, and was riddled with Russian *mafiya* influence, political infighting, and outright corruption. Desk Three believed that those unconventional weapons had been sold by members of the *mafiya*—one of Russia's organized crime families—to an Islamist terror group, using a Tajik criminal named Zhernov as the go-between.

Desk Three wanted to find both the buyer and the consignment without tipping off either the Russians or the Indians and thoroughly muddying the metaphorical waters of the case.

Tajikistan was a former member of the Soviet Union, and the Russians were still very much a part of both government and day-to-day life here. Dushanbe wanted to maintain its independence from Moscow—yet as the poorest of the Soviet Union's successor states, Tajikistan desperately needed Russia to support its economy. Something like half of the country's labor force actually worked abroad, especially in Russia, sending money home to their families.

India wanted to maintain a strong defense against its enemy-neighbor Pakistan and to extend its power into Central Asia, both for reasons of security and to protect its investment in natural gas coming south from Siberia.

As for Russia . . . as always, Russia was the real problem, with factions that sought to restore the old empire of the Soviets, factions seeking to protect the *Rodina* from Islamic revolution or attack, and predatory factions that include organized crime, corrupt politicians, and freebooting military units—and it seems these days that those last three are one and the same.

Dean and Akulinin were threading their way through a minefield.

"Carry on, then," Narayanan said.

"*Sir!*" Dean said, cracking off another salute. The Indian Air Force was closely modeled on the RAF, with the same ranks, conventions, attitudes, and crisp attention to protocol. Akulinin saluted as well, but in a more laid-back manner.

"The man definitely has a stick up his ass," Akulinin said quietly, after Narayanan and his entourage were out of earshot.

"The man is afraid of sabotage," Rubens told him, "either from Russians or from Pakistanis. If he sounds paranoid, he has a right to be."

"Let's see if the tower will show us that flight log," Dean said.

Together, they walked across shimmering tarmac toward the control tower building.

OBHINKINGOW CANYON
CENTRAL TAJIKISTAN
WEDNESDAY, 1535 HOURS LOCAL TIME

The ancient Daewoo Cielo took the next curve at almost ninety kilometers per hour, too fast for the narrow dirt road, sending up a dense cloud of white-ocher dust as it hugged the hillside to the left. Mountains thrust against the sky on all sides, the western fringes of the rugged, saw-toothed Pamir Mountains; to the east, at the bottom of the steep slope in the depths of the valley, flowed the waters of a deep and twisting river. The Tajiks called the river Vakhsh; the Russians used the ancient Persian name, Surkhob, the Red River.

Another curve in the dirt road, and the driver pulled hard on the wheel, bare rock blurring past the left side of the car. The drop-off on the right wasn't vertical; the ground fell away with perhaps a forty-five-degree slope, the hillside punctuated here and there by scattered patches of scrub brush and stunted trees.

The drop was still easily steep enough to kill them all if the dark blue Cielo's driver misjudged a turn and sent the vehicle tumbling down that hill.

The passenger leaned out of the window, staring not down into the valley but behind, through the billowing clouds of dust.

The helicopter was still there . . . closer now. Sunlight glinted from its canopy.

That the helicopter hadn't opened fire on the fleeing automobile was due to one of two possibilities. Either the Russians hadn't positively identified the car yet or they were biding their time, holding their fire until the car could be stopped without sending it crashing down the side of the rocky cliff and into the river below.

"You shouldn't have speeded up," the second passenger told the driver. He spoke Russian with a thick, atrocious accent. "You try to flee, they know you have something to hide."

"Too late," the driver replied, his Russian fluent. He was a rugged-faced Pashtun from Shaartuz, near the Afghan border, a member of the Organization since the days of the Soviet-Afghan War over twenty years before. "They knew who we were when we passed Khakimi. The bastards are *playing* with us."

"The police may have spotted us in Obigarm and called in the authorities," the passenger, Anatoli Zhern, added. For a moment, he lost sight of the pursing helicopter. "Police or FSB."

The second passenger, in the back seat, grunted. "They can't find me here with you," he said. "You need to find a place to let us off. In these mountains—"

"—you wouldn't get half a kilometer before they picked you up," Zhern said, finishing the sentence. He snapped a curved black magazine into the receiver of the AKM assault rifle in his lap. "These hills have no cover, no place to hide. Unless you want to jump down *there*." He indicated the river below and to the right with a jerk of his head.

In the backseat, Kwok Chung On scowled. "Just get me to a place of safety."

Zhern snorted. Kwok was wearing civilian clothing, but he was a *shao xiao*, a major with the PLA, the Chinese military, and he obviously was used to having his orders obeyed instantly and without question.

A lot of good his rank would do him out *here*.

Zhern was a civilian, but he'd fought the Russians in Afghanistan twenty-five years ago, and he knew the importance of discipline. That knowledge had been honed sharper by his devotion to the Organizatsiya, the far-flung Russian *mafiya*. His Russian name was Zhernov, but the Tajiks had acquired the habit recently of dropping the Russian endings of their names in order to display their cultural independence. The president of Tajikistan, Emomali Rahmon, had been born Rahmonov.

He would have to bring that helicopter down.

"Slow down," Zhern told the driver, unfastening his seat belt so he could turn in his seat. "Let them get closer."

The driver slowed somewhat but still took the next curve with a squeal of tires and a spray of gravel hurtling into the abyss along-side. Zhern braced himself against the car's door, leaning through the window. It would be an awkward shot, firing left-handed from the passenger-side window.

The helicopter was closer now, an ancient Mi-8 in Russian Army camouflage. It appeared to be configured as a transport rather than a gunship. Thanks be to Allah, the compassionate, the merciful, for small favors . . .

Not that Anatoli Zhern gave any credence to the faith of his Sunni parents. The Organization took all of his time, all of his focus, a ready source of financial blessings, at least, that surpassed anything the mullahs could attribute to their God.

In Afghanistan, when he'd been a fighter with the Mujahideen, Zhern had once brought down an Mi-8 much like this one. His weapon then, though, had been one of the awesome American Stinger antiair-craft missiles provided by their CIA, not an assault rifle, and he'd been firing from behind a massive boulder that gave him both cover and support, not trying to compensate for the jolts and swerves of a speeding automobile.

Bracing himself within the open window, he took careful aim, then clamped down on the trigger, sending a long, two-second volley spraying toward the aircraft, the AKM's flat *crack-crack-crack* deafen-ing inside the Cielo. He aimed high, trying to allow for the drop of the bullets, but so far as he could tell not a single round hit. The Mi-8 continued drifting closer . . .

Then it shot straight up just as the Cielo rounded another turn, and Zhern lost sight of it. Pulling back inside the car, he fumbled with his weapon, dropping the empty magazine into the foot well and snapping home a fresh one.

The Cielo finished rounding the curve along the side of the mountain and the road straightened once more, the ground abruptly leveling off to either side as they raced across the crest of the hill. The helicopter was *there*, in front of them, hovering ten meters above the gravel of the roadway, turned broadside toward them as its rotor wash stirred up swirling clouds of dust. A muzzle flash flickered in the open cargo hatch door, and geysers of dirt snapped skyward to either side of the car. The windshield disintegrated in slivers of flying glass as the driver lurched back in the seat, blood splattering from face and throat.

Out of control now, the car plunged off the right side of the road, bouncing heavily across open ground that grew steeper, more precipitous, with every lurch and crash. Zhern threw up his arms, covering his face, and screamed. Kwok shouted something shrill from the backseat as more machine-gun bullets sprayed the plunging vehicle.

The Cielo slammed down hard, then rolled, every window shattering. It came to rest on its roof beneath a boiling cloud of ocher dust.

Kwok hung from his seat belt in the back, upside down, blood streaming up his face, his eyes glassy and wide open. Dead, then . . . his neck snapped in the crash, perhaps. Or he might have caught one of the bullets in that last volley.

Dazed and bruised, Zhern could still wiggle through the open window and crawl out into the harsh sunlight. Damn . . . *damn*! Where was his AKM? He'd lost it in the roll, didn't know where it was. Flat on his belly, he reached back through the window, groping for it.

No weapon—but he did find the briefcase and pull it out of the wreckage. He could hear the thunderous clatter of the helicopter coming closer. Blindly, he struggled to his feet and started to run. If he could make it down the slope toward the south, toward the river . . .

Submachine-gun fire rattled, and hammer blows against his back sent him tumbling down the hill. He came to rest on parched, barren dirt, unable to move.

Odd. There was no pain . . .

Within a very short time there was no feeling at all.

A man in civilian clothing walked up to the body moments later, nudging it with the toe of his shoe to roll it over. He squatted, then spent some moments comparing the man's face with the face on a black-and-white surveillance photo. Satisfied that this was Anatoli Zhern and that he was quite dead, the man reached down, retrieved the briefcase, and opened it. After checking through the contents—papers and a computer CD in its plastic jewel case—he snapped the briefcase shut and gestured to the men at his back. "Take him," he said. "Take them all."

"A nice haul, sir," an aide said.

"It was not enough," Lieutenant Colonel Pyotr Vasilyev replied, angry. "They have already made the handoff. We were too late. *Again.*"

The shipment, it seemed, had already been delivered. By now it might already be out of the country and on its way to its ultimate destination, wherever in an unforgiving hell that might be.

Someone—not the Russians, perhaps, but *someone*—was going to pay a very dear price because of that.

2

Twenty miles northeast of downtown Washington, D.C., in a corner of the sprawling grounds of the U.S. Army's Fort Meade
tucked in between the Patuxent Freeway and Route 295, rose the
towering black glass cube of the headquarters building of the National Security Agency. Deep below the structure, behind multiple
security checkpoints and high-tech security barriers, lay the heart of
the agency's direct action operations unit, the Desk Three ops center
known as the Art Room.

William Rubens stood behind Jeff Rockman's workstation, listening in as Charlie Dean and Ilya Akulinin talked with the IAF
sergeant on duty in the control tower office about the airfield's
flight log. The man had been reluctant at first; "Wing Commander
Salman Patel" was not on his list of personnel authorized to see the
log.

The situation was handled easily enough. Dean had the sergeant
phone Air Vice Marshal Subarao's office in Dushanbe directly—in
fact, any call to that number would be picked up by an NSA SIGINT
satellite and redirected to the Art Room. A Hindi-speaking NSA
linguist pretending to be the air vice marshal himself gave the un-

fortunate IAF sergeant a long-distance reaming he would *not* soon forget.

Dean and Akulinin had stood in front of the sergeant's desk for ten minutes, watching him slowly turn first red, then green, and finally a deathly white as he listened to the invective apparently coming from what he thought was the air vice marshal's office. When at last he'd hung up the phone, the unfortunate sergeant had been *most* polite as he rose and ushered the two Desk Three operators into the tower.

There, they'd gone through the listings of aircraft that had landed at and departed from Ayni, not just for the past three days but for the past seven. Reading each line quietly, barely vocalizing as they scanned across page after page, they'd transmitted the entries back to the Art Room for analysis.

Nothing, damn it. *Nothing.*

During the past week, twelve aircraft had departed Ayni, not counting the Indian MiGs based there. All but one had been Russian aircraft; except for Farkhor, all military airfields in Tajikistan were either leased to the Russian military or under joint Russian-Tajik-Indian control, including Ayni. In fact, Russia had been actively opposing Dushanbe's attempt to create its own air force, taking the view that the Russian contingent at Dushanbe was sufficient to protect Tajikistan's airspace.

The single non-Russian aircraft had been the Indian Air Force Antonov An-32 that had brought Dean and Akulinin from New Delhi to Ayni two days ago. That transport was still there, parked at the far end of the runway.

All of the aircraft, Russian and Indian, were accounted for, and all had been well guarded. None had gone on to Pakistan, which was the presumed destination for the shipment. One, an Mi-8 Hip—its NATO code name—had departed two hours ago and flown north, its flight plan listed simply as "patrol," and it was due back at Ayni shortly. It had been three days since any other Russian aircraft had departed the airfield. Desk Three's analysts believed that the shipment had arrived at Ayni only two days ago, probably just ahead of the arrival of Dean and Akulinin.

If the Haystack shipment had not left Ayni by air, either it had to still be there or it had already departed by road.

If by road, it would be on the A384, the single main highway leading from Dushanbe south to the border with Afghanistan. It was a hundred miles, more or less, to the newly built Afghanistan-Tajikistan Bridge, the 672-meter span across the Panj River.

"Why don't you take off and go home, sir?" Marie Telach, the Art Room supervisor, asked Reubens. "Nothing else is going to happen here for a while, and it's been a long night."

Rubens glanced at his watch. Long night or not, he had to go in to give a briefing to the director of the National Security Council in the White House basement at 1130 hours this morning, and he needed to make himself presentable. He'd been up all night and he looked it.

"Not home, no," he said, "but I think I am going up to the office for a while. Give me a yell if anything changes."

"Yes, sir."

He hesitated. "Anything yet on our request to the NRO?"

She turned away, checking a monitor at a nearby workstation. "No, sir. Not yet. But it's only been a couple of hours."

"Okay. Keep me posted. I want to know the instant they come through."

Rubens left the Art Room suite and took the secure elevator to the ninth floor. His office was in Mahogany Row, just down the hall from the office of DIRNSA, the director of the National Security Agency. His secretary wasn't in yet—unlike himself, she kept sane hours, most of the time—and he used his keycard and a code number tapped out beneath a plastic shroud hiding the keypad to let himself in.

His office suite was relatively modest for the altitude but did have a nice view of the morning twilight over the Maryland countryside. Off the main office there was a back room with a cot and a small washroom stocked with the necessary toiletries for those nights when he had to stay on-site.

Rubens was not married—not any longer—and he joked sometimes that no wife would ever be able to put up with his schedule.

It was something of a cliché to say that he was married to his job, but clichés tend to have an element of truth to them, more often than not. He started brewing a pot of coffee, pulled a fresh shirt from the small closet and draped it over a chair, and went into the bathroom to wash and shave.

Operation Haystack had been giving Desk Three fits for two months now, ever since a trusted Russian source had leaked word of the shipment to a CIA officer working out of the American Embassy in Astana, the capital of Kazakhstan. Despite the ongoing turf-war sniping between the CIA and the National Security Agency, Debra Collins, the CIA's deputy director of operations, had approached Rubens and Desk Three for the use of their technical assets in finding and tracking the Haystack shipment.

For the NSA, "technical assets" generally meant spy satellites, electronic surveillance, and SIGINT, or signals intelligence. This threat, however, was both serious enough and credible enough that he'd put eight of his best field agents through special language and culture training, then dispatched them, two by two, to Kazakhstan, Tajikistan, Afghanistan, and Pakistan.

Thornton and Weiss made contact with Anatoli Zhernov in Kazakhstan two weeks ago. They hadn't been able to intercept the shipment, but they managed to get the registration number on the truck he'd taken from a Russian Army motor pool at Stepnogorsk. According to them, the shipment was headed to Karachi, in Pakistan—but Zhernov was an unproven intelligence source, and Karachi could have been merely a clever bit of misdirection.

Once he was shaved and dressed, Rubens took his seat behind his desk and brought his computer online. After he'd typed in his password at the security page, he began paging through classified reports concerning Operation Haystack.

The object of Desk Three's search was not large—a collection of as many as twelve suitcases or similar transport containers each measuring approximately one yard long by half a yard wide and half a yard deep, and each weighing around 120 pounds, a shipment easily transportable by truck or a small aircraft.

"Lebed's suitcases," as they were called within the intelligence community. Alexander Ivanovich Lebed was the Russian nationalist who'd claimed—on the TV program *60 Minutes*, no less—that approximately one hundred of these so-called suitcase nukes, designed to be secretly smuggled into the West in the event of war and used for the nuclear sabotage of key targets such as command and communications centers and transportation hubs, were "not under the control of the armed forces of Russia."

The embarassed Russian government denounce the allegations, of course. Still, the change spotlighted the possibility that rogue elements of the Russian military or the vast underground crime network of the Russian *mafiya* had acquired or sold nuclear weapons, raising the dark specter that some of those weapons might wind up in the hot hands of al-Qaeda or other terror groups.

Each suitcase nuke, according to Russian informants, contained an RA-115 nuclear device built around a Russian 120 mm nuclear artillery shell with a potential yield of between one and two kilotons. Two kilotons wasn't much as nuclear warheads went—the bomb that destroyed Hiroshima had a yield of about sixteen kilotons—but the CIA informant had reported that twelve such devices had been sold by the Russian *mafiya* to Pakistani terrorists just two weeks ago.

Now, apparently those weapons were somewhere in Tajikistan, possibly already on their way to a seaport in Pakistan, almost a thousand miles to the south. Pakistan was facing mounting difficulties with insurgents within its own borders—especially with elements of al-Qaeda and the Taliban hiding out within the nearly autonomous Northeastern Territory. Nuclear weapons small enough to be smuggled across borders in the back of a pickup truck had been added to the mix . . . very small needles lost in a very large haystack.

So far the opposition had been running well ahead of every asset Rubens could bring to bear on the problem.

If his team could find a *mafiya* middleman in Tajikistan named Anatoli Zhernov, they might have a fighting chance.

If they failed . . . even a single two-kiloton mini nuke could destroy the center of a city.

They *had* to find them.

AYNI AIRFIELD
SOUTHWEST OF DUSHANBE
TAJIKISTAN
WEDNESDAY, 1633 HOURS LOCAL TIME

"Okay," Ilya Akulinin said as they stepped out of the control tower building. "Now what?" He sounded worried, which was unusual for the easygoing Russian.

"We continue to check out Ayni," Dean replied. "The nukes *could* still be here, somewhere."

"That seems kind of unlikely," Akulinin replied. "I mean . . . they ship them by truck all the way to an airfield out in the middle of North Bumfuq, then just leave them here?"

"We know the shipment was here," Dean pointed out, "and it's either been transferred to a different vehicle, or it's been stored somewhere around here. If we can't find the nukes, we need to find this Zhernov character."

Akulinin said, "What I want to know is why the Black Cube can't find the missing toys from orbit. I mean—they're spilling radioactivity, right?"

"Yes, but not the right *kind* of radioactivity," Jeff Rockman's voice told them over their communications implants. "The shipment is leaking alpha and beta particles, which is what your detectors were picking up on that truck. Short-ranged stuff. Alpha particles travel only a few inches and can be stopped by the human skin—or even a sheet of paper. Beta particles are more energetic but still travel just a few yards through open air. We'd need a good, strong gamma radiation source to detect it from space."

"We won't get *that* until the bombs are actually detonated," Dean put in.

"So if they pick up a signal by satellite," Akulinin said, "we're already dead."

"Exactly," Rockman told them. "We need to be absolutely certain the shipment isn't hidden somewhere on that base. Whoever bought the shipment from Zhernov might be bringing in an aircraft later."

"Speaking of which," Dean said, pointing, "we've got one coming in now. I wonder why all the excitement."

Several hundred yards away, an Mi-8 Hip transport with Russian military camouflage and markings was gentling in toward the tarmac stretched out in front of the tower. Dean pulled a slim case from his shirt pocket, switched it on, and held it to his eye. The device was both digital camera and telephoto viewer. The push of a button on the case zoomed in on the helicopter as it touched down. The numbers on the tail boom—10450—were prominent in red outlined with white. As the cargo bay door slid open, a number of Russian vehicles moved in. Dean could see Russian soldiers, most of them moving to form a defensive perimeter around the aircraft, crouching down on the tarmac and facing out.

"Are you getting this, Jeff?" Dean asked.

"Roger," the man back at the Art Room console replied. "We have good telemetry and a good image."

"That's the same Hip that left Ayni a couple of hours ago," Akulinin said, peering through his own telephoto camera. "What did they find?"

Through his camera, Dean saw several members of the flight crew manhandling a stretcher out of the cargo bay and into the back of an army truck. It looked as if the stretcher was occupied, but the body had been wrapped in canvas and strapped to the stretcher's frame.

As soon as the first stretcher was loaded onto the truck, a second appeared from inside the helicopter, followed by a third. Dean focused for a moment on the man who seemed to be in charge—a tall blond man wearing the rank emblems of a Russian Army lieutenant colonel. He was giving orders to the soldiers who'd just taken charge of the stretchers. He was holding a briefcase in one hand.

"You have an ID on that Russki officer?" Dean asked.

"Working on it," Rockman replied. "It may take a few minutes to run through the files."

The soldiers climbed back into several of the trucks. The officer entered a waiting automobile, and one by one the vehicles drove away from the grounded Hip, headed north toward the road to Dushanbe.

"Take a look at the Hip's nose," Dean said. "Especially the lower windshield, beneath the pilot. See it?"

"I see it," Akulinin said. "A nice bright white star."

"And bullet holes in the fuselage, farther aft."

"And they brought back three bodies."

"Well, three body bags, anyway," Dean said.

"Got it," Rockman interrupted. "That's Lieutenant Colonel Pyotr Pyotrivich Vasilyev. Russian Special Forces. Currently assigned to Vympel, and with the FSB."

Vympel, also known as Vega Group or Spetsgruppa V, had started off as an elite *Spetsnaz* unit within the First Chief Directorate of the KGB. After the collapse of the Soviet Union, it had been passed to the MVD, but finally transferred to the control of the FSB in 1995. It was now Russia's premier elite unit for counterterrorism and the protection of the state's nuclear assets.

"I think," Dean said slowly, "we'd better find out where that convoy is going and what they have in the back of that truck."

"Our satellite resources are stretched a bit thin," Rockman said, "but we'll put in the request."

Dean continued shooting high-definition video of the departing convoy. "Commandeer a spysat, if you have to," he said.

NSA HEADQUARTERS
FORT MEADE, MARYLAND
WEDNESDAY, 0814 HOURS EDT

For half an hour, Rubens had been going through the reports on Haystack, extracting the necessary files for his briefing session with the NSC later. He was about to patch a call through to the Art Room and see if there was any more news when a chime and a winking red light indicated he had an incoming message. He typed his access code into his keypad and accepted the call. A moment later, the NSA logo appeared on his monitor, then vanished, replaced by the face of Marie Telach, down in the Art Room.

"Yes, Marie."

"The NRO just got back to us, sir."

"Yes? Do we have a confirmed slot?"

"No, sir," she replied. "They're still processing our request. But they *did* pick up an A2TI on 202. They knew we were interested in that AO and passed it up the line."

Interesting. Desk Three had a request in to the National Reconnaissance Office for dedicated time on an 8X satellite pass over Tajikistan. With so many demands for satellite time—from the NSA, the CIA, the DIA and various individual military branches, and even State and Homeland Security—it could take days to reserve a specific pass over a specific AO, an area of operations.

An A2TI wasn't scheduled, though. It stood for "accidental acquisition of a target of interest" and identified something that came up more or less randomly on a spy satellite pass looking for something else entirely.

"Let me see it."

His flat-screen monitor switched to a different scene, an aerial view of a stretch of dusty-looking and arid terrain.

"This was taken by 202 about two hours ago, sir," Marie's voice said. The date and time stamp at the bottom left told him the same thing, along with a set of coordinates.

On the monitor, a blue car appeared frozen in time as it sped along a dirt and gravel road etched out of a hillside. A helicopter, an Mi-8 Hip, appeared to be in pursuit. Three seconds later, the image shifted, showing the same chase. Two more freeze-frame images, and then the helicopter rose suddenly, raced ahead of the speeding car, and descended once again across the road. A moment later, the automobile rounded a curve, then swerved to avoid hitting the aircraft. The car went down the hill and rolled, raising a towering plume of ocher dust. Rubens wasn't sure, but he thought he might have seen debris kicked up by bullets striking the car and the ground around it. The image series froze then and returned to the beginning of the series.

"Is that all there was?" he asked.

"The complete clip was about seventy seconds long. That was the end of it. The satellite moved out of range after that."

That was the problem with satellite imagery. Unless the spacecraft was in a geosynchronous orbit, which kept it positioned above the same spot on the Earth all the time, the satellite would be moving with respect to the Earth, and quite swiftly. The lower the orbit, the faster it was moving, and the shorter the useful hang time above a given target. Geosynch gave satellites a good long look at the target—but was over twenty-two thousand miles up, so far out that it was difficult to get useful resolution.

USA-202 was the first Intruder-class spy satellite launched by the National Reconnaissance Office, or NRO. Originally scheduled for a 2005 launch from Space Launch Complex 37B at Cape Canaveral, a series of technical and political issues, including a new round of budget battles with Congress, had delayed the launch until January 18, 2009.

The Intruder program was designed to offer higher resolution in Earth imagery. It was in a Molniya orbit—a high apogee of 25,000 miles, a low perigee of 300 miles, which gave it extended hang time above the target. Its three-meter mirror, larger than the primary mirror used by the Hubble Space Telescope, had a resolution of just less than four centimeters—not *quite* enough to read the proverbial license plate from orbit, but damned good nonetheless.

USA-202 could deliver clear, crisp images from space, but the satellites of the 8X program were better. Popularly known within the intelligence community as Crystal Fire, the 8X was a class of black follow-on spysats intended to replace the venerable Keyhole program. During the First Gulf War, military commanders in the field had insisted that they needed two things in orbital reconnaissance: real-time imagery and the ability to see a large area—say, all of Iraq—at once. The Intruder program drastically reduced the amount of time necessary for converting raw imagery to useful intelligence available in the AO, yet it was still limited to a relatively narrow field within which to work; Crystal Fire, it was hoped, would provide detailed imagery over a much larger area than had previously been possible. CF-1 had been carried aloft during a shuttle mission late last year; a number of subsequent planned launches had been put on indefinite hold, however, again because of budget debates—which meant it was *very* difficult to get reconnaissance time off of that one bird.

Rubens studied the series of images again, then had Marie halt the series at a frame that showed the Hip hovering above the road in front of the blue automobile. The satellite had shot the image from an oblique angle, perhaps thirty degrees above the horizon, which meant that Rubens could see the side of the Mi-8.

Intruder's imaging system couldn't read license plates, but it easily picked out the serial number on the Hip's tail-rotor boom: 10450.

The analysts, he knew, would have much better resolution on the big screen down in the Art Room, but the detail on his office monitor was still superb. Less than two hours old . . .

"How far are these coordinates from Ayni Airfield?" he asked Marie.

"Seventy-five miles in a straight line," Marie replied. "Closer to eighty or ninety by road."

"This was from Deep One?"

"Yes, sir."

Deep One was Terry Barnes, a friend of Rubens' and a department head at the NRO headquarters in Chantilly, Virginia. He and Rubens had a backroom understanding that let Desk Three bypass some of the mountain of red tape that routinely clogged the communications lines between Chantilly and Fort Meade. Specifically, when Barnes saw something come through that he thought would be of interest to Desk Three, he would pass it along without the usual formal protocols.

"Just what was USA-202 working on when it caught an A2TI?" Rubens asked.

"NRO restricted, sir, but the encrypted ID says it's Agency."

Agency. Not the National Security Agency but the Central Intelligence Agency, the CIA. Each of the NRO's government clients had its own encryption on data transmitted from the NRO; the NSA routinely broke those codes, for practice and to show that they could do it, as much as anything else—they *were* America's premier code-breakers and SIGINT specialists, after all.

Rubens scowled briefly. Although the CIA had brought the NSA and Desk Three in on this op in the first place, they were still playing their little games, competing with the NSA for precious time on the available reconnaissance satellites. The bureaucracy grinds on . . .

The National Reconnaissance Office, which ran the technical end of spy satellite surveillance, provided imaging data to both the CIA and the NSA, among others. This morning, it seemed, while the NSA was trying to get observing time on *any* of the available satellites—Intruder or Crystal Fire—the CIA obviously was running a sweep over the same area and keeping the results to themselves. Presumably, that sweep was part of the same mission, Operation Haystack, searching for the missing suitcase nukes. Rubens wasn't aware of any other situation of particular interest to U.S. intelligence in Tajikistan at the moment.

He decided he would need to talk to Collins about this.

"Mr. Rubens?" Marie's voice said from behind the image of the Russian helicopter.

"Yes, Marie."

"You wanted me to remind you when Ms. DeFrancesca reached her AO."

Automatically, he glanced at his watch, then up at the line of clocks on the wall, each showing a different time zone. It was just past two in Berlin.

"Right, thank you." Yes, there was still plenty of time before his appointment at the White House. "I'll be right down."

STARBUCKS
PARISER PLATZ
CENTRAL BERLIN, GERMANY
WEDNESDAY, 1419 HOURS LOCAL TIME

Lia DeFrancesca always felt a special thrill when she came here. She could feel the pulse of history in this place.

Her bright red fuck-me heels click-clacked across the brick pavement as she walked quickly across the Unter den Linden from the Hotel Adlon. To her left, across the broad, open expanse of the crowded Pariser Platz, rose the Brandenburg Gate, twelve monumental columns topped by a colossal quadriga, the Roman goddess Victoria's chariot drawn by four horses abreast.

Once one of twelve gates through which visitors had entered the city of Berlin, the Brandenburg alone survived. It had been a symbol of the Nazi Party when they'd first come to power, and been one of the few structures still standing in the devastation of the Pariser Platz after the war. In 1961, when the Berlin Wall had gone up, the Brandenburg Gate had been just east of the line, in Soviet-controlled territory. The so-called Baby Wall had blocked East Berliners from the Gate, and the west end of the Pariser Platz itself had become part of the infamous death strip between the East and West sectors of the city. When President John F. Kennedy had visited the city in 1963, the Soviets had hung long red banners from the monument, symbolically preventing him from looking into East Berlin.

But the Berlin Wall had come down in 1989 as cheering crowds filled the Unter den Linden on both sides and met at the top. The Brandenburg Gate had reopened on December 22 of that year, when West German chancellor Helmut Kohl had walked through to be greeted by East German prime minister Hans Modrow. The reunification of Germany, *die Wende*, or the turning point, had swiftly followed.

Today, the Brandenburg Gate was a symbol not merely of Germany but of *Deutsche Einheit*, German unity. In a very real sense, the long and bitter Cold War between East and West had ended *here*.

Lia's meeting this afternoon was a tangible symbol of the capitalist West's victory over the communist East. There, at the southwest corner of an office building overlooking the Pariser Platz, well within the boundaries of what had once been communist East Berlin, was a Starbucks coffeehouse.

Her contact, she saw, was already there, waiting for her beneath an umbrella at a sidewalk table.

The Cold War was over, but now a new and far deadlier war had begun—and the enemy, at least in this battle, was a certain sexist pig named Feng Jiu Zhu.

She took a deep breath. Lia was *not* looking forward to this.

3

William Rubens walked past Desk Three's innermost security checkpoint and back into the Art Room. The huge high-definition monitor covering much of one wall of the chamber above the ranks of workstations and NSA personnel showed a live image blown up to movie-screen proportions, a cluster of sidewalk tables in front of a Starbucks *Kaffeehaus*—a cluster of white tables under gaudily striped, open umbrellas. The scene swooped and jerked with Lia's movements. The image was being transmitted real-time from a tiny camera imbedded in a clump of feathers attached to the front of her stylish broad-brimmed hat. It shifted wildly with each step she took and swung dizzyingly each time she turned her head.

A heavyset Chinese man sat at the nearest table, studying Lia with obvious pleasure. There was nothing inscrutable about that stare as he looked her up and down.

"Is her backup in place?" Rubens asked.

Marie Telach gestured toward a second monitor, a smaller one hanging from a different wall. It showed a still photograph of the Pariser Platz from directly overhead, with each street and building labeled.

"Alabaster is there, on the street," she said, indicating a red flag on the plaza perhaps thirty yards from Lia's position. "Onyx One and

Onyx Two are here—northwest corner of the Aldon Hotel, fifth floor. All three are keyed in and online."

"Good." Alabaster, Rubens knew, was CJ Howorth, currently in training as a field operator with Desk Three. Until recently, she'd been an employee of GCHQ, the British Government Communications Headquarters, and working out of the station at Menwith Hill, in North Yorkshire. GCHQ was closely linked with the American NSA, and with the far-flung Echelon SIGINT system. She was a linguist, a good one, but her sharp thinking and quick action during the *Atlantis Queen* hijacking the previous year had earned her a shot at Desk Three.

Onyx One was James Castelano, former Navy SEAL and an expert marksman. He was on the seventh floor of the Adlon with an M-110 SASS, or semiautomatic sniper system. One of the Art Room wall monitors was showing the image being transmitted live from Castelano's electronic sight—a close-up of Feng's leering face, the crosshairs centered on his forehead. Onyx Two was Harry Daimler, Castelano's spotter.

"Ah! Miss Lau," Feng said, standing awkwardly, bowing slightly and extending his hand. The camera peering down over the brim of her hat showed Lia's hand reach out to be engulfed in Feng's paw.

Lia's cover for this op was that of a Chinese American businesswoman named Diane Lau. This meeting had been set up weeks ago, beginning with exploratory inquiries halfway around the world, in Hawaii. Feng was a big player in an international arms-smuggling operation quite possibly orchestrated by the government of the People's Republic of China itself. Rubens hoped that Feng would offer Lia an advisory position on his staff, a job that would give her a shot at tapping Feng's personal business empire. He was a senior vice president for COSCO, the China Ocean Shipping Company, and that fact by itself meant that Feng was of *great* interest to the NSA.

"It's good to meet you at last, Mr. Feng," Lia's voice said from the wall speakers.

"Please . . . have a seat. Though I must confess I still don't know why you insisted on such a *public* meeting place! The street is such an unlikely place to discuss business!"

"Because it *is* public, Mr. Feng," Lia replied, taking the chair next

to Feng's. "Your phone calls and your e-mails have been most in-
formative. But . . ." The image jiggled slightly as she shrugged. "I
don't know you yet, not personally. You could be *anybody*."

"And a girl can't be too careful," Feng said, his dark eyes twin-
kling. "I *do* understand completely."

His English was excellent. According to his dossier, he'd been educated at Oxford.

"Smooth operator," Marie said.

"The word is 'smarmy,' " Rubens replied. "Have Alabaster move in
a bit tighter."

These next few minutes—Feng's first impressions of Lia—would
be critical.

STARBUCKS
PARISER PLATZ
CENTRAL BERLIN, GERMANY
WEDNESDAY, 1422 HOURS LOCAL TIME

Lia smiled pleasantly at Feng as he signaled a waiter and ordered two
cappuccinos. She'd taken the chair next to the man because the seat
opposite him, which would have been her first choice, might have put
her ridiculous hat into Onyx's line of sight from the hotel, blocking
his shot. She glanced casually up at the window where she knew
Castelano and Daimler were watching. The left half was open, but
she couldn't see them. Thoroughgoing professionals, they would be
set up well back from the window, hidden in shadow, their rifle invisible from the street.

Glancing right, she *did* see CJ—Siege to her friends—dressed in a
green T-shirt and blue jeans, carrying a shopping bag from Peek &
Cloppenburg. Siege was studying a tourist's street map while edging
unobtrusively closer, probably at Rubens' order.

She was glad for the backup. Feng was a thoroughly nasty character.
Formerly a major in the Chinese People's Liberation Army with fif-

teen years' experience in Chinese military intelligence, he was now a high-ranking executive for COSCO, which meant his former connections would still be very much intact. He was known to have underworld connections as well, a working arrangement with one of the more powerful tongs operating out of Hong Kong, and he had a rap sheet that included smuggling, drugs, and gunrunning. His dossier suggested that his weakness was attractive women, with a string of mistresses from Hong Kong to Honolulu to Vancouver to Berlin. He seemed to collect women, though Lia wasn't sure what it was about the man that would attract them.

Perhaps it was just a combination of those most powerful of aphrodisiacs, money and power.

She was dressed this afternoon to entice. The red heels, the short red skirt with the slit up to here, the generous V of exposed cleavage, the smart-looking designer sunglasses, the hat canted across her head at a jaunty angle—all part of the alluring package. Her handlers had designed her look based on careful analyses of six of Feng's recent girlfriends. He liked Americans but seemed to prefer the dark and exotic beauty of Asian Americans, which was why Rubens had asked Lia to volunteer for this op in the first place.

Despite the way Feng kept staring at her chest, however, she knew it was her *brain* that would make or break the deal. According to the employment listing that had first caught Desk Three's attention last month, Feng was looking for an advisor in cultural affairs and public relations, and that was how she intended to sell herself.

Feng glanced up from her chest, and their gazes locked. "So, Ms. Lau. Is this your first time in Berlin?"

"Not at all," she replied truthfully. She'd passed through the German capital several times in the past five years on various missions. "I love this city."

"We have something in common, then." He nodded toward the monument against the western skyline. "The Brandenburg Gate. Magnificent. Though . . . I have to admit that my favorite piece of history connected with it is your President Kennedy giving a speech right over there on the far side of the monument . . . was it 1962?

After the Berlin Wall went up, anyway." He laughed. "'I am a jelly doughnut'!"

"*Ich bin ein Berliner*," Lia said, nodding. "That was 1963. But you *do* know that the whole jelly-filled doughnut thing is an urban legend, right?"

"Lia, what are you doing?" the voice of Thomas Blake said in her ear. Blake was one of the Desk Three handlers and would be running her during this mission. "That Kennedy story is well attested—"

"What do you mean, Ms. Lau?" Feng said at the same time.

"Kennedy was identifying himself with the German people," Lia said patiently. "The story went around—I think it was even in the *New York Times*—about how his use of the indefinite article, *ein*, made it seem like he was calling himself a pastry. In fact, in German the indefinite article is left out when you're talking about someone's profession or place of residence, but it's absolutely necessary when you're speaking figuratively, as Kennedy was. He wasn't literally from Berlin. He was only declaring his solidarity with the city's citizens, in a city divided and barricaded by the Soviets. So '*Ich bin* ein *Berliner*' was completely correct."

"I've heard that people in Berlin don't call themselves Berliners," Feng said. "They reserve that name for jelly-filled doughnuts."

"Not true," Lia told him. "The things are called Berliners elsewhere in Germany, but here they're called *Pfannkuchen*—pancakes, for some odd reason."

"I hope you're sure of your facts, Lia," Blake told her over the communications link. "That's not what it says here." Blake and the other Art Room personnel had access to various guidebooks and reference works, as well as the entire Internet to call upon. If Feng asked her something she didn't know, they would be able to provide the answer in seconds.

But Blake, Lia knew, was wrong. She was relying on a different source, one she trusted.

"So . . . you speak German?" Feng asked her.

"Some," she admitted.

"You seem unusually well versed in the language for an American."

"*Danke*. I'm interested in people, Mr. Feng, and in their stories. Urban legends like that Kennedy story fascinate me, because of what they tell us about people."

"Oh? And what does I-am-a-doughnut tell you about people, Ms. Lau?"

"That too often they jump to conclusions or generalizations, or rely on outright bad information, without checking the source. One of the biggest challenges I face working in PR is cleaning up the mess after someone important puts his foot in it—usually because that someone spoke first and checked his sources later."

The waiter appeared with the cappuccinos Feng had ordered. After he paid the man, Feng's gaze dropped to her chest again, and she leaned forward just a bit, "accidentally" giving him a better view. The idiot could *look* all he wanted—and if he cared more about that than her experience and her brains, so much the better. It just gave her another weapon in her arsenal.

"Diane . . . may I call you Diane?"

"It's Ms. Lau," she told him. "At least for now."

"Don't alienate him, Lia," Blake said in her ear. "You're supposed to be swooning all over the guy."

She ignored the advice. Sometimes it was better to play hard to get, and her legend, the fictitious background created for her by Desk Three, emphasized that she was a hard-nosed professional.

"Of course, Ms. Lau," Feng said, and he smiled. "For now."

Lia glanced down into her cup, then looked up, bemused. The barista had expertly poured the steamed milk to create an incredibly delicate image of two intertwined hearts surrounded by lace. Had that been Feng's idea? Or a misinterpretation of the meeting by the barista? She wondered if Feng had the same picture in his cup, but she wasn't going to lean closer for a look. Instead, she stirred the picture away, then took a cautious sip. The cappuccino was strong and slightly bitter.

"I very much liked your résumé, Ms. Lau," Feng said after a moment. "A double major in public relations and communications from Berkeley, *and* a minor in anthropology. I *like* smart women."

She said nothing, and he pushed ahead. "It says you live in San Francisco. You would be willing to relocate?"

"Yes. Where did you have in mind?"

He sidestepped the question. "The position would require a great deal of travel."

"I'm aware of that. Your interviewer in Honolulu told me as much."

He nodded, smiling. "And you were willing to meet me here in Berlin this afternoon. I appreciate that."

"I travel a lot in the job I have now," she told him. It was the precise truth. "I'm here on business in any case. It seemed like a good opportunity to meet you . . . *personally*."

Again, the truth. When Feng's agents checked up on her, as she knew they would, they would find a solid background for her. Phone calls to any of several numbers she'd provided, including that of her supposed company's HR department, would be answered by people who would swear she worked in the PR firm of Farnum, Pfizer, and Smith.

"Indeed." He took a sip of his cappuccino. "Well, my people in Honolulu would have told you I need a good public relations specialist. But there's considerably more to this position than that. How much do you know about COSCO, Ms. Lau?"

She was well prepared for this one. "I know it's the second-largest dry cargo shipping company in the world. You have a hundred and thirty vessels of over three hundred and twenty thousand TEUs, and over six hundred merchant vessels with a total cargo capacity of thirty-five million metric tonnes, DWT. The COSCO group includes six listed companies and over three hundred subsidiaries, with facilities in over a hundred ports worldwide."

"Nicely memorized, Ms. Lau. Do you know what 'TEU' stands for?"

"Twenty-foot equivalent unit," she told him. "It refers to the standard twenty-foot intermodal containers carried by container ships, by rail, and by truck."

"And DWT?"

"Deadweight tonnage. That's the total weight a ship can carry, including its cargo, fuel, ballast water, fresh water, provisions, passengers, and crew."

"Its displacement, yes."

"No, displacement is something else entirely. That refers to a ship's *total* mass, how much water it displaces when it's fully loaded, which equals the deadweight tonnage plus the weight of the ship's structure itself."

Feng nodded. "Very good. You've obviously done your homework."

"Of course," she told him. She decided to give his ego a tweak, a small one. "After all, it was important that I impress you."

He smiled again. "And you have been quite successful." He sipped his cappuccino, leaning back in his chair. "Ms. Lau, to be quite frank, I need someone beautiful, charming, smart, and extremely, ah, well informed, someone like *you*, in fact, to travel with me as a kind of personal, ah, secretary. I want someone who can inform me of local customs, idiosyncrasies, background culture, language, that sort of thing." The smile faded, and he looked at her intently—looking into her eyes this time. "For instance, if I did this . . ." He held up his hand, thumb and forefinger touching in an "okay" gesture. "What would you tell me about it?"

"That you're fine if you use it in the United States or England. It just means 'okay.' But do *not* use it here in Germany—or in Brazil, or much of Africa, or in parts of Spain or the Mediterranean either, I think. There, it means you're calling someone an asshole." She chuckled. "I read once about a U.S. businessman who'd gone to Rio de Janeiro to work out a business deal down there. Everything was going great, everyone was friendly and happy . . . and then just as they were about to conclude the deal he said, 'Well, okay, then!' And he made the okay sign with his hand like that. The room went cold, and the deal fell through."

He nodded, as if satisfied. "Excellent, Ms. Lau. I think you will work out very well for me. Very well indeed."

"I'm glad to hear it." The okay sign had obviously been a test, as had been the questions about shipping. She wondered if the same had been true with the Kennedy story. Feng might be a sexist pig with a smooth line and a lot of girlfriends, but he had some depth to him, at least. It was possible that some of the testosterone was out there just for show, a means of getting others to underestimate him.

"You are staying over there at the Adlon?"

"Yes, sir." Now that she'd agreed to work for him, he was her boss and she would use the appropriate honorific.

He didn't seem to notice. "I will send a contract over later this afternoon." He considered her a moment longer. "When would you be willing to begin in my employ?"

"Whenever you say, sir. I'm free now."

"No, Diane, I would say you are very, very expensive." He chuckled at his own pun. "And your employers at Farnum, Pfizer, and Smith?"

"This project in Berlin was my last trip for them, sir. I gave them two weeks' notice three weeks ago."

"Ah."

"They know I was going to interview with you today. You can call them and check, if you like."

"I'm sure that's not necessary." He appeared to think about it a moment. "I'll tell you what. I am flying to Spain tomorrow to meet a . . . client. An *important* client. He's Arab, from Pakistan, and it would be *most* useful for me if you could be there to tell me what I need to know about his people."

"Well, I can tell you right now that he's probably not Arab," Lia told him. "Not if he really is from Pakistan. He's almost certainly Muslim, of course—but linguistically he'll be Indo-Iranic, and ethnically he'll belong to one of several groups. Punjabi, Sindhi, Pathan. The Arabs are Semites."

"Well, there . . . you see? You've begun earning your salary already."

"Where will you be going in Spain, sir?"

"To Alicante, and possibly on to the Canary Islands later. I have . . . business interests there."

"Palm trees. Sand. Sun. Bikinis." She nodded. "Such a tough job."

"I beg your pardon?"

"I meant that it sounds like fun."

"Excellent. I'll send a car for you tomorrow." He swallowed the last of his cappuccino. "Until tomorrow, then?"

"Yes, Mr. Feng."

He stood, shook her hand, and walked off, swallowed in a moment by the swirling crowds on the Pariser Platz.

Lia glanced at CJ and saw she'd taken a seat at another table close by. She was still reading her tourist brochure, but Lia heard her voice in her ear as she murmured, "Nice job, Lia."

"Mm-hm," she murmured, then finished her cup, stood, and walked away. It was important to clear the area of operation immediately, especially before she began discussing things with CJ or with Desk Three. There was a distinct possibility, no, a *probability* that, just as Desk Three had been covering the meeting from several angles, one or more members of Feng's operation were watching as well—possibly with long-range shotgun mikes or a tiny listening device stuck to the bottom of the Starbucks table.

You couldn't stay in this job for a week without becoming hopelessly paranoid.

"Where the hell did you get that stuff about Kennedy and the jelly doughnuts?" Blake asked her as she walked back toward her hotel. "We have an archived copy of the *New York Times* here—dateline April 30, 1988—that claims Kennedy screwed up!"

"Check some of your other sources," Lia told him quietly. "Actually, CJ and I were talking about it when we got in yesterday. She knows German, and we happened to be talking about the Kennedy story. So we can thank her."

"Thank you, CJ," Blake said. His voice was touched by just a hint of sarcasm. Lia didn't know Blake well, but she knew he didn't like being shown up in front of others. Too bad.

"Any time, luv," CJ's voice replied.

"Although I sometimes wonder why we're online for you guys when you obviously already know all the answers."

"Just check out the urban legends better, Tom," Lia told him. "Anyway—did anyone listening in get the idea that Feng was putting on a major show for my benefit?"

"What do you mean, Lia?" *That* voice was William Rubens.

"The guy is smart. Speaks perfect English. Educated in Oxford, according to his bio data. The thing about the okay gesture was clearly a test. So were the questions about deadweight tonnage and all. And . . . I don't know. Maybe he didn't have a reason to know about Kennedy and the doughnuts. But his slip about Pakistanis being Arabs was kind of . . . obvious, don't you think? The guy is a high-ranking officer in one of the largest shipping corporations in the world, *and* a major in Chinese intelligence. He should already know stuff like that."

"I think he was surprised Lia knew so much," CJ put in. "Okay, I have two security types sitting at other tables. They just got up and followed Feng. No one's following Lia."

"Good," Rubens said, "but don't relax. There may be others in the area."

"The job offer seems genuine," Rubens said, "although given what we've uncovered about Feng already, we suspect he primarily wants Lia for eye candy."

Lia snorted. "A pretty girl on his arm to impress his customers?"

"Exactly."

"The job offer is for eighty K a year. That's expensive candy."

"He can afford it. COSCO can afford it. Why, Lia? Are you worried?"

"As a matter of fact I am."

"You can still change your mind about this, Lia," Rubens told her. "This op was always volunteers only."

"No," she said, walking past several maroon-jacketed bellhops and through the tall doors of the Adlon Hotel, entering into the magnificently appointed lobby. "Hell, this is exactly the sort of break we were looking for. The guy has me flying to Spain tomorrow, to meet someone he says is from Pakistan. Depending on who this business associate is, it might be our link between COSCO and al-Qaeda."

"Yes, and it also might be a bit *too* neat," CJ put in.

"CJ's right," Rubens said. "Feng's contact in Spain could be perfectly legitimate."

"Well, we'll know tomorrow," Lia said brightly. "Won't we?"

Nevertheless, she wondered just exactly what it was that she was getting herself into.

RUSSIAN MILITARY HOSPITAL
DUSHANBE, TAJIKISTAN
WEDNESDAY, 1825 HOURS LOCAL TIME

Dushanbe was a teeming, sprawling, bustling place.

The name of the city, Charlie Dean had been told, meant Monday— literally "two-Saturday," meaning the second day after Saturday. Originally, the place had been a Monday market village, and there were still extensive bazaars and countless street vendors and stalls that continued the commercial spirit of the place.

Despite the bustle, Dushanbe was a surprisingly *green* city. So much of the Tajikistan countryside was sere and brown beneath barren and rugged mountains, but the center of the country's capital was thickly planted with trees, boasting broad, tree-lined boulevards and numerous parks. The building serving as a military hospital was located on the far side of Rudaki Park, across from the sprawling National Palace and not far from the towering statue of King Ismail Somoni in front of his high, golden crown-capped arch.

The hospital was a dour, concrete structure painted dull red and surrounded by trees, a relic of the Stalinist era. The Russian 201st Motorized Rifle Division was permanently based at Dushanbe. The unit, totaling some five thousand men, had been stationed in the country since before the fall of the Soviet Union, but the main base itself had only been opened in 2004, close by the newly renovated Dushanbe Airport to the southeast. The building near Rudaki Park was actually a much older military base, a satellite medical facility still serving the region until the much newer hospital facilities on the base itself were completed.

Dean and Akulinin had no trouble following the small convoy

from the Ayni Airfield, keeping well back in order to remain inconspicuous. They drove the vehicle they'd checked out from the motor pool the day before, a relatively new Ulyanov Hunter jeep, and dropped onto the convoy's tail on the main drag past the airfield, heading toward the city. Seven miles later, they turned right onto the M41, a modern highway called King Ismail Somoli Boulevard, crossed the bridge over the wide but shallow Varzob River, and entered the city proper just north of the grounds of the National Palace. By that time, they knew they were heading toward the old Soviet hospital and not the newer base on the far side of the city; they found a place to park on Tolstoy Street and navigated the rest of the way on foot. Their military IDs got them past the security desk in the echoing tile-floored lobby. A bored Russian corporal at the information desk pointed out the stairs leading to the basement—and the morgue.

"The place is going to be busy," Akulinin pointed out. "We're right behind them. Maybe we should wait and come back later."

"I'm counting on a crowd," Dean told him. "More confusion, fewer questions."

". . . are break . . . up," Rockman's voice told them, the words blasted by static in Dean's ear. "Do . . . copy?"

Then the connection was lost. Desk Three's personal communications links operated well outdoors, but the basement of a concrete building was something else.

They could hear echoing conversation up ahead. The truck with the body bags had pulled up at the rear of the hospital.

"Vasilyev will be the OIC," Dean told Akulinin. "He'll wonder about me, this uniform, so I'll be the decoy."

"In this part of the world, they shoot spies," Akulinin replied dourly. He was joking, but not by much.

"Won't happen," Dean quipped. "I'm in uniform."

"The wrong one."

Through a set of double doors in a cold and narrow passageway with concrete-block walls, they reached the morgue desk where the duty-watch stander, a junior sergeant, looked up from an ancient, dog-eared *Playboy* magazine.

"*Sudar'!*" the man snapped, suddenly sitting upright and slipping the magazine underneath an open logbook. "*Pajalusta! Pakajiti vahshi bumahgee!*" Dean's Russian was good enough to know the man was asking to see identification.

"We're with *them*," Akulinin replied in the same language, nodding toward the doors beyond the desk as he pulled out his Russian Army ID and flashed it.

"*Da, Meior,*" the man said, glancing first at Akulinin's ID card, then at Dean's. If he was curious about what an Indian Air Force wing commander was doing in a Russian military morgue, he gave no sign. "*Veeryod!*"

Pocketing their IDs, Dean and Akulinin walked up to the pair of swinging doors, marked KEEP OUT in Russian, and pushed through—

—and were immediately stopped by a Russian senior sergeant with Vympel patches on his uniform and an AK-74 assault rifle. "*Stoy!*"

4

Halt!"

"Is Podpolkolnik Pyotr Vasilyev here?" Dean asked, putting a singsong Indian accent into the Russian words. The Vympel soldier blinked and lowered his AK a fraction.

"Who are you?" he demanded.

"This is IAF Wing Commander Salman Patel," Akulinin told him, "and I am Major Golikov. We are on Air Vice Marshal Subarao's staff, and we need to speak with Colonel Vasilyev *immediately*!"

"I . . . that is . . . he . . ."

"*Stand at attention when a superior addresses you!*" Akulinin barked.

"Sir! Yes, sir!" The senior sergeant snapped to attention, but with the rifle at port arms across his chest.

"Guard this door, Senior Sergeant. Make certain that no one comes through!"

"Yes, sir!"

Unlike their American counterparts, Russian enlisted personnel were trained *not* to think, to follow orders immediately and unquestioningly. By playing the role of a Russian senior officer, with bluster, anger, and a hefty dose of stage presence, Akulinin forced the non-com into *his* accustomed role—that of an automaton that did not ask questions, did not make waves.

The morgue was a large and cluttered room, with several metal tables under cold fluorescent lights, concrete-block walls lined with filing cabinets, and a central area taken up by a huge refrigeration unit cooling the morgue slabs behind massive, sealed doors. Half a dozen soldiers were gathered around three tables just around the corner of the refrigerator. Lieutenant Colonel Vasilyev was engaged in an intense discussion with a young, blond, white-smocked woman, presumably the morgue attendant.

Dean and Akulinin joined the group, moving unobtrusively into the rear of the group. One soldier glanced at Dean's Indian uniform curiously. Dean grinned back and winked, and the soldier shrugged, then turned away; if the guard at the door had let an Indian Air Force officer in, obviously he was permitted to be there.

Far more often than not, Dean had learned, a person could get into nearly any restricted area without being questioned so long as he *acted* as though he had a perfect right to be there.

"I want these bodies examined thoroughly," Vasilyev was telling the attendant. "In particular, I want them inspected for radiation."

"Do you mean a Geiger counter?" the woman asked Vasilyev. "To scan them for radiation? Or do you want a pathology workup, looking for cellular damage from radiation?"

"Both."

"We do not have Geiger counters at this facility, Lieutenant Colonel," she told him. "As for tissue sampling and microscopy—that requires a pathologist, and Dr. Shmatko is not here."

"Where is he?"

"I don't see that that is any of your concern, sir."

"Young woman, you *will* cooperate with me! Where is this Shmatko?"

She looked angry. "Gone until tomorrow. An autopsy in Tashkent."

"There will be radiation detectors at the air base," Vasilyev told her. "I will have one sent here, with a trained operator. You will send a message to Shmatko and tell him he is needed here at once. Do you understand?"

"I understand, sir—but that won't get the man here one minute sooner. Tashkent is three hundred kilometers away."

"Just *do* it!" Vasilyev looked around, angry. He saw Dean, saw Dean's uniform, and his eyes widened. "What are *you* doing here?"

"Sir! Wing Commander Patel, special liaison to the Russian forces in Tajikistan."

"That tells me who I am about to put under arrest," Vasilyev growled, "but it does not answer my question. *What is an Indian Air Force officer doing in a restricted Russian military facility?*"

"Sir! Group Captain Sharad Narayanan, at the Ayni Air Base, sent me to find you. There are reports of Pakistani infiltrators at Ayni, at Farkhor, and at Dushanbe! He told me to deliver the message verbally, since our electronic lines of communication may be compromised!"

"Pakistanis! *What* Pakistanis?"

"He didn't tell me, sir," Dean replied, "but Group Captain Narayanan is a relative of India's national security advisor. A nephew, I believe. He may have intelligence passed on from the IB that has not yet reached your desk. Sir." The IB was the Intelligence Bureau, India's equivalent of the CIA.

Vasilyev scowled. "You Indians see Pakistanis behind every rock!"

"Yes, sir. The problem is that Pakistanis hiding behind rocks may have nuclear weapons, and they hate India. A certain amount of paranoia is called for, wouldn't you say?"

Dean hoped his Russian was getting through clearly enough. Was "paranoia" really *paranoia* in Russian, a borrowed word identical to the English? He wasn't sure, and down here in the basement he didn't have Desk Three's linguists online to help him out.

He *thought* it was right, though. The word was so quintessentially Russian.

In any case, any minor slipups in grammar, vocabulary, or pronunciation could easily be blamed on the fact that he really *was* a foreigner—one reason they'd created this particular legend for him back at Fort Meade.

As he answered Vasilyev's questions, he glanced past the man's shoulders and across the room at Akulinin. His partner was standing next to one of the autopsy tables, his left hand cupped around an unseen device. No one else was paying him any attention. As they'd planned, while Dean played the decoy, Akulinin was surreptitiously photographing the bodies.

"The IB," Vasilyev said with an unpleasant smile, "is run by naive and easily excited children."

"Sir!" Dean snapped back. "The Intelligence Bureau is *the* oldest and best-established intelligence service in the world!"

It was a somewhat dubious claim, one based on the idea that the IB had been created by Major General Sir Charles MacGregor in 1885 to monitor a possible Russian invasion of India through Afghanistan. Still, the Indians believed it—and the IB *was* widely believed to be one of the five best intelligence services in the world.

"If you say so, Wing Commander." Vasilyev's unpleasant smile widened. "Right now, however, I need to see some identification from you." He nodded at an aide, a captain, who stepped forward, his hand out.

Dean reached into his pocket and produced his wallet, extracting his Indian military ID card, a second card issued by the Tajikistan Military Authority, and a third card giving the phone number of Air Vice Marshal Subarao's headquarters office. Any call going to that number would be rerouted to Desk Three, as had happened to that unfortunate watch stander at Ayni a few hours before.

"Air Vice Marshal Subarao will vouch for me, sir," Dean said, handing the cards over. He reached into another pocket and pulled out a folded-up sheet of paper, covered by close-spaced Hindi characters. "And my orders, sir."

"You will come with us," Vasilyev told him. "You are not the only one around here afflicted by a certain amount of healthy *paranoia*."

"Yes, sir." He was relieved to hear the Russian use that word.

ILYA AKULININ
MORGUE, RUSSIAN MILITARY HOSPITAL
DUSHANBE, TAJIKISTAN
WEDNESDAY, 1910 HOURS LOCAL TIME

Akulinin stepped back behind the shelter of the central refrigerator unit and watched the gaggle of Russian soldiers crowd out through the door leading to the alley at the back of the hospital. One of them had Charlie Dean in tow, practically at gunpoint.

Unfortunately, there wasn't a lot he could do about that at the moment, and, in any case, the mission always came first. *Always.*

The last of the soldiers banged out through the swinging doors, and Akulinin stepped out from his hiding place. As Dean had predicted, they'd paid no attention to him whatsoever once they'd spotted Dean's IAF uniform.

"*Excuse* me," a woman's voice said at his back. "Aren't you supposed to be going with the rest of them?"

He turned and found himself looking down at the pretty, blond morgue attendant. Her hands were on her hips, and her pale blue eyes had a no-nonsense glare about them. Her smock and rubber gloves were smeared with shockingly red streaks of fresh blood.

"Ah, no, actually," he told her. "I'm with . . . a different unit. The 201st. I came along to get some photographs."

"You have authorization, I suppose?"

"Um . . . no, actually. Lieutenant Colonel Vasilyev has it."

"You don't expect me to believe that, do you?"

"Of course." Akulinin glanced up at a large clock hanging on one concrete block wall. It was just past 7:10. "You're here awfully late. Are you the night shift?"

"I'm working late, actually," she said. "Lieutenant Colonel Vasilyev phoned me from Ayni and said he was on the way."

He gave her his most radiant smile. "Really? So what time do you get off?"

"You can turn off the charm, Major," she told him. "It won't work.

You still haven't told me who you are or given me your authorization to be here."

He cocked his head to one side. "That is an interesting accent there."

"What about it?"

"It sounds American, actually."

She sighed, took a step back, and began peeling off her gloves. "That's because I *am* an American. Russian American. My parents moved to a place called Brighton Beach in Brooklyn when I was three."

Akulinin started. "Really?" He hesitated. He could get into serious trouble dropping his cover, but he couldn't simply ignore what the woman had just said. "Then you and I might be neighbors," he said, shifting to Brooklyn-accented English.

It was the woman's turn to look startled. "Brighton Beach? *You?*"

"My parents emigrated to the United States in '82. I was born two years later."

"My God!" She shook her head. "What are you doing *here?*"

"I could ask you the same question."

"How can I believe you? This is impossible!"

"Unlikely, yes," he said, grinning. "Not impossible. Brighton Beach is probably the largest colony of transplanted Russians in the U.S. You know the intersection of Brighton and Coney Island Avenue?"

Her eyes opened wider. She nodded.

"Remember the subway/el tracks? They come down in a big curve overhead, right above the intersection . . . right? Q train for local service, the B train for weekday express. And when the train comes through, it sounds like thunder!"

"I used to walk under that overpass on my way to school!"

"Public School 253."

"*Yes!* How did you know?"

"I went to the same school . . ."

For several more minutes, Akulinin dredged up memories of his own childhood in Brighton Beach, enough to convince the woman that they had indeed grown up in the same neighborhood. He wondered if he'd ever seen her; she looked to be a couple of years younger, but they might well have attended the same school during the same years, just a few classes apart.

What were the chances of running into her *here*?

He asked her what had brought her back to Russia—and Tajikistan.

"My . . . my parents moved back to Russia when I was thirteen," she told him. There obviously was some pain associated with the memory. "A business opportunity for my father. There was . . . some trouble. Financial trouble. My mother was sick. He got into debt with some very bad people."

"*Mafiya?*"

She nodded. "After my mother died, my father sent me to work with a man he knew, a friend, Dr. Shmatko. He is a pathologist with the Science Academy here in Dushanbe."

"Why?"

"Those men, the ones he owed money? They offered to settle some of his debt if I would go to work for them. Photographs . . . movies . . . to be posted on the Internet, you know?"

Akulinin nodded. He *did* know. The Russian *Organizatsaya* was heavily involved in the sex trade, both prostitution and pornography. White slavery in the twenty-first century, vicious and sick.

"So I came here and trained as a *diener* with Dr. Shmatko."

"*Diener.* A *morgue* attendant?"

She nodded.

"That's horrible!"

"It's not so bad." She shrugged. "My . . . clients don't talk back, and never give me trouble. The pay is . . . not too bad, and Dr. Shmatko is teaching me a lot, so that I can go to school and be a doctor myself one day. But first I hope to save enough to get back to the United States someday. It's . . . life is hard, here."

"What about your father? Where is he?"

She shrugged. The expression on her face, behind her eyes, was heart-wrenching. "I don't know. It's been two years now. I stopped getting letters, oh, two or three months after he sent me away. I think . . . I think . . ."

She was trembling, on the verge of tears.

"It's okay. What's your name?"

"Maria. Maria Alekseyevna. My friends . . . my friends call me Masha."

It was, Akulinin knew, a common Russian nickname for Maria. "I'm Ilya," he told her. "I might be able to help you."

"You still haven't told me what *you're* doing here. You're *not* army, are you?"

"Not exactly."

Her eyes widened. "You're a spy! Who do you work for?"

"I really can't—"

"You're with the American CIA! Right?"

"Something like that." He looked at the corpses on the nearby tables. "I *am* here to photograph these bodies. So . . . are you going to turn me in?"

"Of course not! It isn't every day a girl gets to meet a real-life James Bond! Especially one who grew up in her old neighborhood!"

He pulled out his mini camera and walked over to one of the stainless steel tables. He'd managed to get a shot of one of the bodies earlier, while Charlie was sparring with the Russian officer, but not the others. One of them, in fact, was still anonymously wrapped up in an olive green body bag. He took several more photos of the first two from different angles. The two bodies already removed from the body bags were male Caucasians, still dressed in civilian clothing. Both were heavily tattooed on their arms. One sported a bushy Stalinesque mustache; the other was clean-shaven, his wide-open eyes pale gray against a bright red mask. There was a *lot* of blood, with deep gashes in their faces and arms.

"This one had a bullet wound," Masha pointed out, touching the skull of the mustached man and turning it so he could see. "Left temple. Definitely fatal."

"I . . . see." Akulinin wasn't particularly bothered by death, but the young woman's casual attitude was a bit disturbing.

"Did Vasilyev tell you anything about these guys?"

"No. Just that he wanted complete path workups, and for them to be checked for radiation. I don't know why."

"Well, I can help with that much." Pocketing the camera, he reached down and pulled up the cuff of his uniform trousers, revealing the small radiation counter strapped to his ankle. Unfastening the chrome-colored device, he held it up, peered closely at a switch on the side, and flicked it.

"It was set to transmit data . . . somewhere else. Now it will play what it picks up for us, and record it for transmission later."

Holding the counter like a wand, he passed it over the body in front of him. There was little reaction over the man's face and shoulders, but his hands, both of them, elicited a sharp clattering static from the device.

"Interesting," Akulinin said. He stepped over to the other table, passed the counter over the body, and got the same response.

"What does it mean?" Masha asked.

"That these two guys were handling a leaking crate not too long ago."

"A crate of what?"

"You don't want to know."

"These two are Organizasiya, you know. *Mafiya.*"

He looked at her, surprised.

She touched one blood-smeared arm. "The tattoos." Reaching across, she swiftly unbuttoned the man's shirt and tugged it open. His chest, as well as his upper arms, was a solid mass of intricate tattoos. He could see a rose on the body's chest, a skull, a dagger or sword, delicately interwoven floral designs . . .

"They often start off as prison tats," she told him, "but they also get them to mark advancement within the gang, special achievements, punishments, anything like that. It's a part of the whole culture of the *Vory v Zakone*, the Russian underworld. Someone who knows the language can actually read a man's history with the *mafiya.*"

The second body had tattoos as well.

He frowned. "I'd like to check the third body, too."

"Give me a hand here," Masha said. She was already unzipping the body bag.

Awkwardly, Akulinin helped her, peeling the body bag open and sliding it down. He looked at the man's head and blinked in surprise. "Shit!"

"What's the matter?"

"What the hell is a Chinese doing *here*?"

NSA HEADQUARTERS
FORT MEADE, MARYLAND
WEDNESDAY, 1010 HOURS EDT

Rubens glanced at his wristwatch, confirming what he already knew. "Damn," he said. "I have to go. *Now.*"

"Give our love to the NSC," Marie told him. "I'll call you when we regain signal."

"Do that. I'll be out of touch while I'm in the meeting, but leave me messages and keep trying."

"Of course, sir."

He didn't like leaving now. He was strongly tempted to delegate the NSC meeting to Gene Lenard, his operations director.

Gene was a good man, well able to be Rubens' representative— but the position of deputy director of the NSA was, unfortunately, as much political as it was practical. If Rubens *personally* failed to attend this meeting, the other people present would assume the issues on the agenda were not of high importance to Desk Three or the NSA. Those people included the chairman of the National Security Council, his senior aide, and his longtime political enemy Debra Collins, deputy director of operations at the CIA. If Rubens wasn't there this morning, he could wake up tomorrow and find that the CIA was in charge of Haystack—and he had eight operators on the ground over there right now, two of them out of touch.

If he left *right now*, he should be able to make the meeting in time, allowing for traffic on 295 into town and for the security check at the White House.

"While I'm gone, I want a full workup on Lieutenant Colonel Vasilyev. I want to know where his office is, including architectural plans, blueprints, whatever you can find. Does he have a safe in his office? A computer? Find out."

"Yes, sir."

"I should be back around two, two thirty," he told her.

Rubens checked out through several security desks, picked up his car in the VIP parking area, and threaded his way out of the maze of lots and gates surrounding the towering central buildings of the NSA's Fort Meade complex, long known to insiders as the Puzzle Palace. Canine Road swung him right onto 32 West, and he took the almost immediate cloverleaf onto 295 South, the Baltimore-Washington Parkway. Traffic was light and he hit the pedal, accelerating swiftly past the slower vehicles. Any touch by police radar would trigger a transponder in the car, one that flagged him as having special clearance.

Charlie Dean and Ilya Akulinin would be okay Ruebens mused. Dean was a longtime veteran of the agency, a former Marine sniper who simply never got flustered, who was always in the game. Rubens ranked him as Desk Three's best operator. Akulinin was younger and less experienced. He'd come on board with Desk Three just a year and a half ago, during that Russian *mafiya* affair up in the Arctic, but he was quick, he spoke fluent Russian—it *was* his first language, after all—and he knew the culture. Both men were smart and resourceful, and they got results.

He was more concerned about Lia DeFrancesca. She, too, was a damned good, experienced operator, and her team in Berlin, her on-site backup, was first rate. But the China Ocean Shipping Company was big and it was dirty, an immense commercial giant that was an arm of the Chinese Navy and the Beijing government. Lia wasn't simply up against Feng Jiu Zhu in Berlin. She was squaring off against the government of the People's Republic of China.

COSCO had been involved in illegal gunrunning before.

On March 18, 1996, undercover agents with the U.S. Customs Department and the BATF had accepted delivery of a trial shipment of two thousand fully automatic AK-47 assault rifles from Chinese representatives as a part of a sting operation tagged Operation Dragon Fire. Those weapons had been smuggled into Oakland, California, on board the COSCO container vessel *Empress Phoenix*.

In the history of U.S. law enforcement, there had never been a bigger seizure of fully automatic weapons. The Chinese said that the weapons were for the California street gang market, and that other military-grade weapons were readily available as well, from grenade launchers to Red Parakeet shoulder-fired surface-to-air missile systems.

What the Crips and the Bloods would have done with weapons like *that* was something to ponder.

More recently, the NSA had tracked a COSCO freighter from Shanghai to Karachi, in Pakistan, with a cargo of weapons-related goods. The cargo included specialty metals and electronics used in the production of Chinese-designed Baktar Shikan antitank missiles.

There were plenty of other cases, too.

The NSA had been watching Mr. Feng for almost two years now, turning up a great deal of rather scandalous information about his private life but only hints and whispers about his professional connections. The CIA thought he was clean, though he *was* closely connected with Wang Jun—a senior executive in China's Poly Technologies still wanted for his role in the *Empress Phoenix* affair. Rubens disagreed. Considering Feng's former position in Chinese military intelligence, his reported dealings with people believed to be associated with several Islamic terror groups, including Pakistan's Harkat-ul-Mujahideen and Jaish-e-Mohammad, the Palestinian Hamas, and al-Qaeda itself, the man couldn't *possibly* be clean. If it looks like a duck and quacks like a duck . . .

Contacts within Israel's Mossad were concerned about a Palestinian operation known as Nar-min-Sama, variously translated as Fire of Heaven or, possibly, as Fire *from* Heaven. There was a code name associated with this operation—al-Wawi, the Jackal. Not even the Mossad yet knew who the Jackal was, but believed that he was orchestrating some sort of strike against both Israel and unnamed targets in the West.

There was also the matter of Lebed's suitcase nukes to consider, as well as concerns about nuclear weapons from Iran or North Korea reaching any of a number of Islamic extremist groups.

Feng had recently traveled to Astana, the capital of Kazakhstan, an unlikely, landlocked destination for a high-ranking executive of a maritime shipping company. From there he'd flown to Cairo, where he'd met with several men believed to be associated with Hamas, before going on to Berlin. The NSA had monitored numerous cell phone calls to all of those places, as well as Karachi, Kabul, and Dushanbe.

Connect the dots, Rubens thought, and a rather disturbing picture appeared, one involving transporting something from the heart of Central Asia south to Pakistan's major port, then by ship to the Middle East—Cairo, perhaps, or Israel, or just possibly northern Europe.

That's why Rubens wanted an operator inside Feng's organization, someone who could get a lead on some of these mysterious business contacts of Feng's, and someone who might have the opportunity to bug Feng's computer and phone.

If anyone within the NSA's Deep Black service could handle the job, it was Lia, but that didn't make it any easier for Rubens to walk out of the Art Room at a critical moment in her op.

No, the dots didn't make a pretty picture at all—and Lia and her team might be right at ground zero.

ADLON HOTEL
PARISER PLATZ
CENTRAL BERLIN, GERMANY
WEDNESDAY, 1625 HOURS LOCAL TIME

Lia was sitting on her bed in her hotel room when the knock sounded at her door.

"Sounds like opportunity knocking, Lia," CJ told her.

Lia was alone in her room. CJ was still watching from down on the street, while Castelano and Daimler were in their room up on the seventh floor, but all three—as well as the Art Room crew—were linked in through her communications implant. She was careful of what she said while in the room. Though a sweep earlier had failed to turn up any electronic listening devices, Feng's people might have still managed to bug it.

"Coming," she called out. She'd changed out of her heels, skirt, and low-cut blouse in favor of more comfortable—and practical—clothing: blue jeans, a black pullover, and tennis shoes. Her hat, however, rested on the hotel room desk, its hidden camera set to provide Desk Three with a clear view of the entire room. Swiftly, she pulled her weapon from her open suitcase—a 9 mm SIG SAUER P226 Blackwater Tactical—and tucked it into the waistband of her jeans at the small of her back, tugging the pullover down to conceal it.

She unlocked the door. "Yes?"

It was one of the maroon-jacketed hotel bellhops. "Fräulein Lau?"

"Yes."

"I have two packages for you," he said in passable English. He handed her a manila envelope—that would be the promised COSCO contract—and a small white box tied with red ribbon.

"What's this?" she asked, accepting the box.

"I don't know, fräulein. I was told to give you both of these. And I'm to wait for you to sign something and return it."

"Wait a moment."

Closing the door, she took the envelope back to the desk and opened it. As expected, it was from Feng, three copies of two close-spaced printed pages—more of a letter of agreement than a full-blown contract. She scanned through it quickly, murmuring aloud the pertinent paragraphs for the benefit of the Art Room.

"Looks good and as promised," she said, completing the document. She picked up a pen and signed all three copies. Two went back into the envelope for return to Feng. She looked at the white box for a moment, then decided to wait until she'd given the envelope back to the bellhop.

She opened the door and handed him the envelope and a generous five-euro tip. "Here you go. Thank you."

"*Danke*, Fräulein Lau!"

Lia returned to the desk and picked up the box. "So, is Mr. Feng making a play for me already?" she asked. "Too big for a diamond ring."

"He doesn't strike me as the sort to propose marriage," CJ said. "Are you going to open it?"

"It's also too small to be a bomb," she added.

"But not too small to be a listening device of some sort," Tom Blake said. "Be careful what you say, Lia."

She didn't reply, but she set the package in front of her hat, directly beneath the camera, and began opening it.

A moment later, she pulled the contents out and dangled them for Desk Three's inspection. "Oh, my."

There was a handwritten note inside the package. *For the beach tomorrow*, it read, and it was signed *Jiu Zhu*.

"Are you actually going to wear that?" Marie Telach asked.

"What is it?" CJ said. "I'm blind out here, you know."

"A bikini," Lia said. "A very *small* bikini." She frankly had her doubts that she would fit into that top. It was electric blue, what there was of it, three triangles of rather sheer blue cloth with black borders and some spaghetti-thin black string.

"It's too small to hide a listening device, at least," she said. "Too small to hide much of *anything*."

"Another fine item of female apparel from Testosterone Fantasies Are Us," Marie put in. "You're not actually going to wear those postage stamps in public, are you?"

"I'm not sure yet," Lia said. "I'll have to see if this sort of thing is in my new job description."

In fact, she knew, in a sense it was, since keeping Feng happy—being "eye candy," as Rubens had described it—was as precise a description of the job as was possible.

She knew one other thing, too. If this was supposed to be her working outfit, she was going to have a hell of a time hiding any SIGINT devices inside—to say nothing of her P226.

5

O h, God, no," Masha said, taking several halting steps backward.

"What's the matter?" Akulinin passed the radiation counter over the Chinese man's body. There was no response—or very little. A few clicks that might represent normal background radiation, but nothing like the hiss of static that the other two had shown, even on his hands.

So . . . this one had stayed back while the other two had gotten their hands dirty. Had he been the one in charge? Or had he just not been involved with the actual transfer of radioactive materials?

"The radiation on those two . . ."

"Don't worry," Akulinin told her. "It's not enough to make you sick or anything." *I just hope the Art Room knows its stuff*, he added to himself.

"You don't understand," she said. She looked desperate, and scared. "Those men who were here a few minutes ago, Vasilyev . . ."

"What about them?"

"They're FSB! That means they're part of an antiterror unit, or maybe nuclear security, and they were after these three."

"Yeah . . . so . . ."

"So I'm not *stupid*, Ilya! Those two people were handling nuclear material of some sort, and they're *mafiya*! *That* one"—she pointed at the Chinese man—"if *he's* involved, this must be big. International. Big enough, even, to bring in the American CIA?"

She was quick on the uptake.

He indicated the gray-eyed corpse, "This guy was a *mafiya* middleman," Akulinin told her. "We think he was selling stolen mini nukes to an Islamic extremist group, maybe al-Qaeda, maybe someone else, a Pakistani terror organization. I don't know why the Chinese guy is here."

"Don't you understand? Vasilyev will be back soon with a technician to check the bodies for radiation. They're not going want to let word of this get out. Stolen nuclear weapons? That makes the Moscow government look *very* bad. If they think I know too much, they . . . they're not going to let me go!"

"It's okay, Masha," Akulinin said. He was thinking fast. It was a breach of operational security, but in for a penny—

"It is *not* okay!"

"Look, you said you were trying to get back to the States, right? Maybe I can help."

Her eyes widened. "What? Really? That would be—"

"I'm going to need to clear some stuff with my superiors, but at the very least we can get you out of *here*."

The immediate problem was how. Dean and Akulinin were supposed to exfiltrate across the border into Afghanistan when their part of the op was over. Bringing along a civilian woman they'd just happened to pick up along the way was definitely *not* a part of the plan.

"People who get on the bad side of the FSB," she said, "they . . . they disappear."

Akulinin nodded. The *Federalnaya Sluzhba Bezopasnosti* had a bad rep both for being thoroughly corrupt and for being unnecessarily brutal in the prosecution of their duties. Most Russian civilians were terrified of them, and with good reason. There were reports of *mafiya* extortionists within the FSB shaking down small business owners, of ex-military and ex-KGB thugs kidnapping people and holding them for ransom.

"I know," he said. "That's not going to happen to you. I promise you." He stooped over and reattached the radiation counter to his ankle. "Listen, have you tried the American Embassy here in Dushanbe? I'd think they could help you."

"No. My parents surrendered their American citizenship when they came here . . . and mine, too. And I would need money, *lots* of money, for a plane ticket, and proof I had relatives or a job in America." She shook her head. "They wouldn't help me."

"It depends on who you talk to, Masha. I have . . . friends. They should be able to swing something." He saw a pad of notepaper on a desk nearby, and a pen. He walked to the desk and wrote out an address in clear block Cyrillic letters. "Do you know where this is?"

"Adkhamov Street? It's in the eastern part of the city. About, oh, five kilometers from here."

A long way for her to walk. "Do you have a car?"

"No . . . but there's good bus service."

"Where do you live?"

"Prospekt Apartments, on Karamova. Perhaps a kilometer and a half."

"I want you to go home, pack whatever you need to bring with you—a small suitcase, no more. Then get to this address."

"What is it?"

"A safe house. You'll buzz the intercom at the front door, and when a voice answers, you'll ask them *Net li oo vahs luchshi comatih?*"

She looked puzzled. "Do you have a better room?"

"Right. It's a code phrase. They'll let you stay there, no questions asked. I'll come by later."

"Wait! Where are you going?"

"I have to see about rescuing my friend."

"Who? Oh! The Indian Air Force officer?"

"The same. He's in a lot of trouble right now."

"You . . . you know they probably have men watching the hospital outside. If they see you leave . . . or me . . ."

Damn, she was right—and he should have thought about that. He wasn't thinking clearly, and that could spell disaster for operators in the field, especially when the carefully crafted script had just been thrown out and they were ad-libbing it.

"I know. Masha, look. I'll see what I can do about getting you out of the building and on your way. Then I have to take care of my friend. But I *will* come back for you. You . . . you're just going to have to trust me."

"I . . . I do. It's just . . ."

"Just what?"

"Why are you doing this? Why are you helping me this way?"

"Let's just say I really liked the way you stood up to Vasilyev a little while ago. And you were willing to help me. Besides . . . what are the chances of two kids from Brighton Beach meeting up *here*, of all places, eh?"

"Thank you, Ilya." She stepped forward, stood on tiptoe, and kissed him. After an awkward moment, he put his arms around her and hugged her close.

"Well, well," he said as they stepped apart. "What was that for?"

"For helping me get these cadavers into the refrigerator," she said, all business again.

"I beg your pardon?"

"Well, I don't want to just leave them here in the open to start decomposing! Dr. Shmatko thinks better of me than that." She began opening refrigerator doors, pulling out a morgue slab from each opening.

With a rueful shrug, Akulinin began helping her move the bodies.

ALLEY OFF RUDAKI AVENUE
DUSHANBE, TAJIKISTAN
WEDNESDAY, 1935 HOURS LOCAL TIME

They'd taken Dean out the back door to one of the cars parked beneath a pool of illumination from a security light in the alley behind the hospital. Vasilyev had told a soldier to put him in the rear seat and keep him there, then got into another vehicle just ahead, where he appeared to be making a phone call.

His guard was outside the car, leaning against the wall. The window was rolled down, but the man was far enough away that Dean could say, "I'm back. Did you miss me?"

He spoke quietly, barely vocalizing at all, but he knew the sensitive microphone would pick up the words and transmit them to a communications satellite and back to the Art Room.

"We hear you, Charlie." It was Marie Telach. "What the hell happened?"

"No reception in the basement," Dean said. He kept his replies terse. "I'm being held by Vympel personnel . . . decoy."

"We still don't have a signal on Ilya. Is he with you?"

"Negative. Ilya's in the morgue. Still free, far as I know. I'll keep you informed."

"We copy, Charlie. Uh-oh. Hang on."

"What's going on?"

There was a long pause. "Your friend Vasilyev just put a call through to Subarao's office. We had a 'secretary' talking to him. Now . . . okay. Sudhi is talking with him."

Dr. Sudhi V. Anand was the Desk Three linguist for Hindi and several other Indian dialects.

"Have him give the SOB a good reaming for me," Dean said.

"Copy that."

"Listen, I used the story of possible Pakistani agents loose in Dushanbe and other bases, maybe spying, maybe working to screw the Indian-Tajik treaty. I used the name of another IAF officer—Group Captain Narayanan, at Ayni. I told him Narayanan had sent me to warn him about the threat personally."

"Thanks, Charlie. I'll pass that on to Dr. Anand's monitor."

"Hey . . . Hindu!" the guard outside asked in Russian, leaning closer. "What's that you're mumbling? Who are you talking to?"

"I'm praying," Dean replied in the same language. "I'm calling upon my ancient and powerful gods to make sure that your commanding officer sees the error of his ways."

From the rear seat of the vehicle, Dean could see the back of Vasilyev's head as he spoke on the phone. The way the man's head was jerking back and forth, it looked as though angry words were being exchanged.

Still, Subarao was the equivalent of an army major general, and Vasilyev was a mere *podpolkovnik*, a lieutenant colonel. The Russian might not like Indian nationals, but he wouldn't risk insulting a high-ranking foreign general in Tajikistan's capital and creating a *truly* international incident.

At long last, Vasilyev got out of the vehicle, slammed the door hard, and walked back toward Dean's car. He looked . . . subdued. Angry, too.

"Okay, Charlie," Telach told him. "Dr. Anand says he read Vasilyev the riot act. He backed your story about rumors of Pakistani saboteurs. Vasilyev doesn't like it, but he should let you go now."

"Copy."

Vasilyev reached the car and jerked a thumb over his shoulder. "Out of the vehicle."

"Did you call Air Vice Marshal—"

"I don't need a *foreigner* to tell me my business," Vasilyev snapped. "I have other sources." The way he spat the word *inostranyets*, foreigner, made it sound like an obscenity.

"Sir! I was simply following orders."

"Next time you decide to follow orders, stay out of restricted military areas! It would be . . . unfortunate if you were shot. Your death might create an incident."

"Yes, Lieutenant Colonel."

"Get out of here, and don't let me see you around my city again!"

"Yes, Lieutenant Colonel. Thank you, sir."

Dean hurried down the alley, as if he half expected to be shot in the back. He knew Vasilyev's type well enough—a bully who enjoyed abusing his power over others, whether under his command or in the civilian population. He was just glad the Vympels hadn't decided to search him. The radiation counter on his ankle would have been difficult to explain, as would the folding camera-binoculars in his pocket.

He crossed Rudaki and headed for Tolstoy Street. Ilya would meet him at the car when he was finished getting the pictures.

"C'mon, Ilya, c'mon!" he muttered. "What's taking you so long?"

LOBBY, RUSSIAN MILITARY HOSPITAL
DUSHANBE, TAJIKISTAN
WEDNESDAY, 1954 HOURS LOCAL TIME

Akulinin reached the top of the basement-level steps and peered through the glass in the doors opening into the hospital lobby. Through the small window, he saw a bored-looking attendant at the information desk, but there was no one else in sight. "Come on, Masha," he called over his shoulder. "It's clear."

Maria came up the stairs behind him. She'd shed her white lab coat and rubber gloves and was now wearing blue jeans, a green shirt, and flat-heeled shoes.

A burst of static sounded in Akulinin's ear. "Ilya!" Jeff Rockman's voice called. "Ilya, do you copy?"

"Right here, Jeff. I hear you."

"Where the hell have you been?"

"Cut off down in the basement," Akulinin replied. "I'm back on the street level now. Still in the hospital, about to enter the front lobby."

"Who are you talking to, Ilya?" Maria asked.

"Remember those friends I mentioned?"

"Who's that with you, Ilya?" That was Telach's voice.

"Long story, guys," he said. "I'm going to need your help here. First of all, I have some data to upload."

He pulled out his camera and touched a control on the side. Next he reached down, touching another button on the radiation counter strapped to his leg. The devices began uploading their recordings to a communications satellite.

"We're receiving," Rockman said after a moment. "Nice shots . . . if a bit morbid."

"The bodies are the ones Podpolkovnik Vasilyev brought back on the helicopter," he told the Art Room. "I'm thinking the clean-shaven Caucasian looks a lot like our contact, Zhernov, though his face is cut up and bruised so badly, I'm not sure. The rad counts are being transmitted in the same order as the pictures. I'd be *very* interested in knowing who the Asian guy is."

"We're running the photos through the ID database now," Telach said. "Now . . . who's that with you, and why? We can hear her over the open channel."

"First things first, Marie. Do you have a fix on Charlie?"

"They let him go about ten minutes ago. He's on his way back to your car."

"Excellent." That gave them some additional options. He wasn't happy about turning Masha loose on the streets of Dushanbe if the FSB might be looking for her.

"And who is your little friend?"

"Maria Alekseyevna. Distressed foreign national, Russian citizenship. But she's an American."

"O-kay. How can she be a foreign national *and* an American?"

"Look, we can go into the history later. What's important is she helped me on the mission just now, and there's a good chance that the opposition is going to be interested in her, understand? I need to get her to the safe house—then get her out of the country."

"We'll have to see about that," Telach said. She did not sound like she approved. There was a certain air of "wait until your father gets home" about the way she said it.

"Is the boss there?" he asked. Might as well face the music right away.

"No, he's not. But I imagine he'll want to talk with you when he gets in."

"I'm sure. I . . . wait a second."

"What do you have, Ilya?"

Two Vympel soldiers had just entered the hospital's front door and taken up sentry positions on either side of it.

"Possible trouble."

He turned, about to lead Masha back down the stairs, but he stopped when he heard a hollow thump—a door banging open—echoing up the bare stairwell. Far below, he could hear voices, someone shouting, demanding information. *"G'deh devochka?"* he heard. "Where is the girl?" It sounded like Vasilyev's voice.

He heard another voice—the junior sergeant with the copy of *Playboy* stationed outside the morgue doors—but couldn't make out the words. The man would be pointing to the stairs, however. He'd seen them go that way just moments before.

"Tell Charlie to bring the car south on Rudaki," Akulinin told the Art Room. "Tell him there are two of us, we're on the run, and the black hats are in pursuit! We'll be going south, on the east side of the street, and we'll meet him there!"

"Roger that. We're patching through to Charlie now."

Another boom from downstairs, closer now. Vasilyev and his troops were entering the stairwell, starting up the steps toward the first landing.

"Ilya!" Masha cried.

He gathered her close with his arm. "Trust me!" he said fiercely. "Just play along, okay? And whatever happens, *smile!*"

She nodded as he punched through the double doors in front of them and swept her with him into the lobby. The two soldiers looked up at the noise and began unslinging their rifles.

Akulinin laughed out loud, grinning broadly as he jogged directly toward the soldiers, his arm still tight around Masha's waist. "This is going to be great!" he called out in Russian. "A night on the town you will *not* forget!"

The soldiers brought their rifles to an uncertain port arms. They would have been expecting to see the woman alone, would not be expecting to see a Russian Army major accompanying her.

"Stoy, sudar'!" the one on the left called.

"Stand aside, soldier," Akulinin said, still laughing as they got closer. "I'm taking the most beautiful girl in the world out to dinner . . . then dancing and drinks at the Pamir Club . . . and after that . . ." And he kissed her.

He *kept* kissing her as he strode between the two soldiers, pushing through the hospital's front doors. He was counting on his psychological advantage, on surprise and embarrassment to get them through the doors.

"*Meior!*" one of the soldiers said. "Please halt—"

"Go to hell!" Akulinin said, laughing again.

"Stop that girl!" Vasilyev shouted from the stairway door. "Stop *them!*"

Then they were through the doors and running down the concrete steps in front of the red-painted hospital. It was dark outside now, with only a little glow from the fading twilight, and pools of light beneath the streetlamps. Taking Masha's hand, Akulinin swung left and started racing down the sidewalk.

"*Stoy! Stoy! Slushaisya eelee ya budoo strelyat!*"

Obey or I'll fire.

Traffic was fairly heavy on Rudaki Avenue, a four-lane city street. They needed to get across to the other side—and civilian traffic would make the bad guys cautious about opening fire. Swerving suddenly right, he dragged Masha into the street, thankful that she was wearing sensible shoes. Headlights flared to their left, dazzlingly bright, and a horn sounded, a long, piercing blare. A northbound car slammed on its brakes and screeched to a halt, stopping close enough that Akulinin's free hand slammed down on its hood.

A gunshot cracked from behind them . . . followed by a second shot, and fragments of pavement stung Akulinin's leg. So much for the traffic making the soldiers cautious. At least they hadn't opened up with automatic weapons. Those shots had sounded like a 9mm pistol, probably Vasilyev's. The range was a good thirty yards, against moving targets and uncertain lighting. They had a chance . . .

Akulinin dragged Masha past the halted car, weaving left to put its headlights between them and the gunmen. The car accelerated—he heard the driver screaming obscenities at them—and he swerved right once more, twisting between the lines of oncoming traffic.

Almost across the last lane, headlights flared to the right, and another horn sounded. This time, screeching brakes were followed by a heavy thud as the driver swerved into a tree beside the road. Another car piled into the rear of the first. More horns sounded—the beginnings of a traffic jam.

But they'd made it! They ran onto the grass beyond the curb, a strip thickly planted with large, old trees. Another shot banged out from the hospital steps, this one a deeper, flatter crack that sounded like an assault rifle being fired single-shot. Akulinin heard the snap as the bullet passed somewhere overhead and behind; another shot, and this time the round punched into the trunk of a nearby tree, close enough to fling splinters at them. Turning behind the tree, they ran flat out, racing south now, on the east side of Rudaki.

"Charlie is almost at the car," Jeff Rockman said in his ear. "Just a few more minutes."

"Copy!" Akulinin was panting, out of breath. Dean would be teasing him about spending more time on the obstacle course back home.

"Ilya!" Masha said. She sounded like she was in better shape than he was. "Don't you have a *gun*?"

"Not with me," he told her. A Russian officer would not have checked out a sidearm from his armory unless he was engaged in some duty that required one, and if he'd had to submit to a search, he would have had trouble explaining why he was carrying a concealed weapon.

Besides, Hollywood notwithstanding, field agents only rarely went armed in the real world. Spies were looking for information, not firefights, and depended on getting in and getting out without being noticed. If you got into a gunfight, your mission had failed.

Another rifle shot from behind, from beyond the blaring horns in the street, and Akulinin bit off a curse. He wouldn't say this op had *failed*, exactly, but the getaway was proving to be a little noisier than planned. Horns began blaring somewhere behind them. The bad guys were crossing Rudaki.

"Charlie's at the car," Rockman told him. "Two minutes!"

"Tell him to get his ass in gear!" Akulinin replied. "We've got a small army chasing after us, and we're under fire."

"We've picked up radio calls in your area," Marie Telach said. "Colonel Vasilyev is calling for backup, and he's calling in the local police and the VV."

Dushanbe had its own police force, of course, but there were MVD internal troops in the region as well; Russia's Ministry of Internal Affairs still maintained a presence in most of the countries that had arisen from the now-defunct Soviet Union. The *Vnutrenniye Voiska Ministerstva Vnutrennikh Del*, usually abbreviated VV, was a paramilitary force similar to the U.S. National Guard.

"Copy."

"He's also calling in a GNR," Telach said. "The guy sounds *pissed*."

"Well, it's nice to be popular . . ."

GNR was *Gruppa Nemedlennogo Reagirovaniya*, a police rapid-response group assigned to the local region. They were calling out the equivalent of a SWAT team.

"Okay, Ilya." It was Rockman again. "We have a little problem."

"Just what I wanted to hear."

"Dean can't reach you. Major traffic jam. We have a satellite map up of your part of the city, though, and we're tracking you. We're going to reroute Charlie onto another southbound road. I want you to look for a street or an alley going off to your right."

"I see one just ahead, yeah. Doesn't look like a good part of town."

"Duck down that alley, going east."

"Copy that."

Akulinin and Alekseyevna turned and jogged down the alley. He was tired, fighting to get his second wind. On the street behind them, he could hear the two-toned ululations of police sirens converging on the area.

The tree-lined boulevard of Rudaki Avenue was clean, bright, and almost parklike. Less than a block to the east, however, the cityscape turned dark, with a dilapidated and abandoned factory, piles of rubble, and a distinct lack of streetlights. When the Soviet Union had collapsed in 1991, Tajikistan had almost immediately fallen into a nasty civil war. Non-Muslim minorities had fled the country, rival gangs and militias had carried out widespread ethnic cleansing, and most of the cities had been devastated. Deaths in the war were estimatcd at fifty thousand, and over a million people had fled the country as refugees.

Six years later, Emomali Rahmonov—or Rahmon, as he styled himself nowadays—had engineered a cease-fire with his rivals, and the country had begun to rebuild. Even so, large stretches of Dushanbe, off of the main thoroughfares and business districts, still showed the ravages of brutal civil war.

They slowed down as the darkness deepened. There was light enough, however, to see gang signs scrawled on deteriorating walls, and piles of garbage in the alley ahead.

"Where are we going?" Masha asked. "It's not safe."

"Safer than behind us," he told her. "My friend is going to meet us somewhere ahead."

Several shadows stepped out into the alley ahead. *"Behist!"* someone shouted. By the uncertain light, Akulinin could make out a scarred, bearded face and the gleam of a knife.

"Ya nee panimayu," Akulinin said in Russian. "I don't understand."

"It's Tajiki," Telach whispered in his ear. "A form of Persian. He just told you to stop."

"Well, well," the scarred man said in thickly accented Russian, holding up the knife. "We have a fucking Russian Army officer! And what is this?" He leered, exposing a prominent gap in his front teeth. "A pretty little girl!"

Two other men had emerged into the alley behind the first. Akulinin heard one say something to the other in Tajiki, and then they both laughed. One was holding a length of pipe, the other another knife.

Maybe he *should* have brought a weapon.

"Back off," Akulinin told him. "We're not looking for trouble."

"Sometimes you find it anyway, *neh*? Or it finds you!" Gap-tooth gestured with the knife. "I want your money, pretty boy. Your cards and papers. *And* that uniform! Military stuff fetches well on the black market!" He grinned at Masha. "As for you . . . I think we'll take you as well. We can show you a good time, yes?"

"Please—" Masha said.

"How long 'till Dean gets here?" Akulinin muttered. He was still holding Masha's hand, and he gave it two quick squeezes, hoping to communicate *get ready.*

"Coming down the street in front of you, right to left. Thirty seconds!"

The smallest of their three assailants was on the left, the one with the pipe. He looked young, probably a teenager. Hell, they *all* looked young, even bearded Gap-tooth. Akulinin took two steps closer, snapped out his free hand, and slammed it open-palmed against the pipe-wielder's shoulder. The blow caught the kid by surprise and knocked him off balance, sending him stumbling back against the thug beside him.

Akulinin turned, shoving Masha ahead and through the sudden opening in their assailants' line. "Run!" He shouted in English, then added, *"Skaray!" Quickly!*

Akulinin's training with the NSA had included long hours of martial arts at the Farm, as the CIA's Camp Peary training center near Williamsburg, Virginia, was popularly called. He knew both Tae Soo Do and the U.S. Army Combative System, a streamlined synthesis of several martial arts forms. Pivoting, he brought his right foot up and snapped it around in a roundhouse kick hard to the falling kid's kneecap.

Gap-tooth screamed and lunged forward, jabbing with the knife. Akulinin countered with a wrist-breaker lock, kicked his right ankle, and slammed him to the pavement.

Then Ilya ran after Masha. He'd only disabled one of the thugs— the kid was on his back shrieking, cradling a broken kneecap—but the idea was to get away, not to let himself get bogged down in a street brawl. Besides, more shouts and whistles were sounding from the west end of the alley. The police were closing in.

The two fugitives ran as hard and as fast as they could, their footsteps echoing off bare brick walls. The alley opened onto a larger north-south street, and Akulinin led Masha diagonally across, then turned south. Seconds later, headlights flashed, and the boxy Ulyanov

Hunter squealed to a stop beside them. Akulinin clambered into the backseat, Masha into the front.

Then Dean squealed the tires as he accelerated down the street.

Behind them, Lieutenant Colonel Vasilyev burst out of the alley, pistol in hand, breathing hard.

He was just in time to glimpse the number on the vehicle's license plate.

6

DUSHANBE, TAJIKISTAN
WEDNESDAY, 2014 HOURS LOCAL TIME

So, are you going to introduce me?" Dean asked as he drove the Hunter south.

"Masha, this is my friend Charlie Dean," Akulinin said in English. "Charlie? Maria Alekseyevna. She works in the morgue."

"*There's* a conversation stopper," Dean said. "I remember you, Ms. Alekseyevna. You were telling Vasilyev where to get off."

"Call me Masha," she said.

"You speak excellent English."

"She's from Brighton Beach, Charlie! Tell him, Masha!"

"It's true. I grew up in Ilya's old neighborhood!"

"Remember the Royal Pizzeria, right there under the Brighton Avenue tracks?"

"I *do*."

"Sounds like old home week," Dean said dryly. "Ilya? Better break out the weapons."

"Got 'em right here." A foam-filled aluminum case hidden under one of the seats held two Makarov PM semiautomatic pistols and several full magazines. The weapons were the Russian equivalent of the Walther PP series but would not shout "foreign spy" if they were found in a search. Dean heard the snap-click of a magazine being inserted and a round being chambered.

Akulinin handed him one, butt first. "Round chambered, safety on," he said.

Dean pocketed the small weapon. It wouldn't be much in a fire-fight, but anything was better than nothing. "So, Masha," he said. "What are you doing here?"

Masha filled Dean in as they drove, telling him about her family's move back to Russia, her father sending her to Dushanbe, and how she'd worked for Dr. Shmatko now for two years.

Dean caught Akulinin's glance in the rearview mirror. "Sharkie, this is *so* against regs."

"I know—but we can't leave her for Vasilyev, can we?"

"No. No, we can't now."

"Sharkie?" Masha asked.

"It's the name," Akulinin told her, rolling his eyes.

"Ah! *Akula*. Shark."

"You're quick," Dean said.

"Charlie," Jeff Rockman said, interrupting. "They're throwing out a cordon. Roadblocks on Rudaki at the Medical Institute in the north, at the university in the south. They've already blocked off the bridges over the Varzob, west of you, and they're putting units out on Mirzo Tursunzade to the east."

"Talk me through it," Dean said. "I've got a major drag crossing just up ahead."

"That's in front of Dushanbe University. Turn left."

"That'll take us back to Rudaki."

"Affirmative."

"They have that roadblock in place yet?"

"We're working off a satellite map here, Charlie. We heard them calling for a roadblock in front of the university. Don't know if it's in place yet."

"Well, we'll soon find out."

Traffic was heavy at the intersection with Rudaki, which seemed to be the main north-south thoroughfare through the city. Cars and trucks honked continuously, and a harried-looking policeman stood in the intersection, trying to direct traffic away from Rudaki, which was completely clogged toward the north. The cars in Dean's lane inched ahead.

"Masha," Akulinin said, leaning forward from the backseat, "we're not going to be able to go back to your apartment for your things. Vasilyev will have your records checked to learn where you live. Guaranteed he'll soon have some interior troops on the way there in case you show up."

"That's okay, Ilya. There's nothing there I *need*."

"Good."

The line of cars moved ahead a few more yards toward the intersection, then halted again as several police cars worked their way through the congestion, blue lights flashing. Dean described the scene ahead.

"Turn right if they'll let you," Rockman told him. "That'll put you south on Rudaki, past the university."

"Okay . . . here we go. I'm signaling . . . he's waving me through . . ."

They made the turn. Ahead, in front of the main entrance to the university, more policemen were moving cars to block traffic, and Dean could see one man in an army camouflage uniform holding an AK assault rifle.

"Shit. They've got us blocked. Okay . . . wait a second . . ."

The street was utter chaos, with halted vehicles and shouting drivers. To the right, however, was a broad walkway, crowded with pedestrians, flanked by trees. Dean hauled the steering wheel over and accelerated, bumping up onto the sidewalk. Pedestrians scattered, some shaking fists or gesticulating as Dean nudged ahead through the crowd. The soldier shouted something unheard in the din as he unslung his rifle. More pedestrians scattered, and Dean put his foot down on the gas, sending the right-side wheels jouncing up onto the broad concrete steps in front of the main university building. A crowd of students spilling out of nearby dormitories appeared to be cheering.

The soldier let loose with a burst of full-auto gunfire, but it was aimed high, up into the air. Dean swerved past a clump of huge trees and bumped back onto the street, which, south of the roadblock, was nearly deserted.

He floored it as another burst of gunfire snapped after them. A white star appeared high on the rear windshield as a round struck the metal frame above it and ricocheted. Another round smashed Dean's drivers-side mirror. On the right, he spotted the Dushanbe Fire Station, painted a startlingly bright shade of pink but with more traditionally red trucks parked inside the open bays.

"Passing the firehouse on my left!" Dean called. "Turning left!" He swerved the Hunter across oncoming traffic and ducked into a side street.

"That's going to take you into a residential district, Charlie. A maze of narrow streets, lots of twists and turns. We'll guide you . . ."

Dean decided that just maybe there actually *were* times when having your boss looking over your shoulder and micromanaging the situation was a good thing. With Rockman following his progress on the map back at the Art Room and guiding him through the warren of narrow streets and alleys, he could pay attention to the driving. The Art Room was also able to keep him up-to-date on police calls and radio reports, the signals picked up by one of the NSA's SIGINT satellites and transmitted back to Fort Meade for translation and analysis.

They *might*, just possibly, get away with this . . .

NATIONAL SECURITY COUNCIL BRIEFING ROOM
WHITE HOUSE BASEMENT, WASHINGTON, D.C.
WEDNESDAY, 1131 HOURS EDT

Rubens walked into a room dark with mahogany paneling and plush carpeting, dominated by a long, massive conference table, and found one of the last remaining openings. He noticed Debra Collins' glance from across the table as he took his seat. He nodded at her, but she ignored him, turning instead to watch George Francis Wehrum taking the podium at the front.

Some of the people there were NSC staffers. The rest were a mixed lot of military officers from the Joint Chiefs and personnel from the NRO, the Department of Intelligence, the CIA's Operations Directorate—that was Collins and the aide seated beside her—and the Department of Energy. The session this morning was a planned briefing by several U.S. government intelligence agencies for the NSC's Presidential Advisory Staff.

"Ladies and gentlemen, thank you all for coming." Wehrum was chief aide to ANSA, the advisor on national security affairs. His boss hadn't arrived yet but was expected momentarily. "We have several important briefs on the agenda this morning. It's going to be a long session. I will remind those present that information discussed in this room should be restricted to Top Secret and below."

The National Security Council was comprised of about one hundred staff members working in one of the basement levels of the White House, a labyrinthine fortress with security almost as vigilant and as uncompromising as it was for the Puzzle Palace—with ID checks, a retinal scan, and a stroll through a brand-new backscatter X-ray scanner that could electronically peer through both clothing and hair.

Technically, the NSC was chaired by POTUS, the President of the United States, and its statutory attendees included the vice president, the secretary of state, and the secretary of defense. The senior military advisor was the chairman of the Joint Chiefs of Staff; the intelligence advisor was the director of national intelligence.

The meeting this morning, though, didn't rate attendance by such high-ranking luminaries. Its purpose was strictly to serve as a session for presentations by various intelligence groups, briefing ANSA on several key situations or operational deployments.

Most of the people at the table were well known to Rubens, but at least there was now a new ANSA. The previous advisor on national security affairs had been Debra Bing, an unpleasant woman with political and personal power agendas that had often conflicted with a clear understanding of the information provided by the intelligence community. She hadn't been fired so much as promoted sideways; she was over at Foggy Bottom now, working for the secretary of state.

Rubens could not imagine a better move for the woman.

The new ANSA was a retired Marine four-star general, John L. James. The President's appointment of James had been a real shock to Beltway insiders; the current POTUS was *not* seen as a friend of the military. Speculation and outright gossip held that James was nonconfrontational, had no personal agenda or strong ideological leanings, and could evaluate ideas dispassionately whether they came from the left or the right. Historically, the NSC had often been blocked or sidelined in the rough-and-tumble politics required to gain and hold the President's ear.

James was well respected by nearly everyone in town and was known as a team player. With the secretary of state, the secretary of defense, the director of central intelligence, and the President's chief of staff all battling with the NSC for presidential access, it would take a no-nonsense combat veteran as well as a diplomat to thread the labyrinth of Washington's halls of power. Hell, the guy was a former commandant of the U.S. Marine Corps. If anyone could handle the job, *he* could.

Rubens knew a number of U.S. Marines, both active duty and retired. Charlie Dean was one. He wondered if the President knew just what he'd signed on for by appointing one as his advisor on national security.

"All rise," Wehrum called from behind the podium. A moment later, General James strode into the room, followed by several aides and accompanied by Rodney C. Mullins, a congressman from New York and a prominent member of both the House Armed Services Committee and the House Permanent Select Committee on Intelligence. Rubens had not been aware that Mullins was going to be present today.

"Sit down, sit down," James growled at the room. He was known to dislike ceremony and protocol. "Sorry I'm late. The Honorable Mr. Mullins and I were held up in an Intelligence Oversight Committee meeting. Mr. Wehrum? What's up first on the dog-and-pony show?"

"Sir . . . the Palestinian crisis. We have a report from the deputy DNI—"

"Let's get on with it, then. What do you have for us, Mr. Scribens?"

Wehrum sounded annoyed by James' bluntness—or perhaps it was by his dismissal of the briefing session as a dog-and-pony show, Pentagon slang for formal prepared briefings designed to please, rather than inform, high-ranking officers or civilians.

Rubens smiled inwardly. It was well known that Wehrum had expected to step into Bing's shoes; she'd been grooming him as the next ANSA throughout most of her tenure, and James' appointment must have been a bitter surprise. He took his seat, however, as Paul C. Scribens, one of four deputy directors of national intelligence, stood and walked to the podium.

It would be, as Wehrum had promised, a long session.

Ruebens wondered if Dean and Akulinin were clear yet, and back in contact with the Art Room.

CHARLIE DEAN
SAFE HOUSE
DUSHANBE, TAJIKISTAN
WEDNESDAY, 2040 HOURS LOCAL TIME

"*Net li oo vahs luchshi comatih?*" Dean asked.

The white-haired woman peering through the cracked-open door looked him up and down, then stared past him at Akulinin and Masha. The crack closed, Dean heard the rattle of the chain lock, and then the door opened again. "Did anyone see you?" she asked in accented English. She was an older woman with gray hair and eyes that might have seen too much. Dean guessed that she might be in her sixties. "Did anyone follow you?"

"Not that we could see," Dean told her. "All the excitement is over in the center of the city."

"Excitement is right. You three have kicked over hornets' nest. Get in, get inside."

They'd parked the Hunter inside a shed behind the Adkhamov

safe house. The woman running the house, Tatyana Konovalova, was a transplanted Russian who'd been recruited by the CIA in Moscow back in the bad old days of the Cold War. When her husband had moved to Dushanbe in the 1980s, she'd come along—and continued sending in reports about Russian troops in the area during the disastrous Soviet war in Afghanistan. Her husband, Viktor, had been a civilian, an engineer working on a pipeline project in Kabul, at least until the Mujahideen had caught him and slowly skinned him alive. She still kept a small altar to the man, with candles flanking his photograph on a table in her small foyer.

She remained on the CIA's payroll, the money brought by a messenger from the U.S. Embassy in town each month. In CIA parlance, she was an agent, meaning a local recruited by a CIA officer. There would be at least one Agency officer stationed at the embassy, Dean knew, but he would be unwilling to get embroiled in an NSA op gone sour. Except for the offer of a place to stay for the night, Dean, Akulinin, and their unexpected tagalong would be on their own.

"Mrs. Konovalova doesn't have access to another vehicle," Dean said. He was sitting alone now, in one of three tiny bedrooms carved out of an attic. Beneath a steeply sloping ceiling, a small bed on rope springs was squeezed in between a wooden box that served as dresser, night table, and lamp stand and the stacks of dusty boxes and piles of paper common to any other attic in the world. It was just past nine. "We're going to have to take the Hunter, and the MVD will have a description and a plate number."

"The Firm has new plates for your car," Jeff Rockman told him. "They'll send them over by special messenger in a few hours. We're also looking at how we can compromise the local LE net."

The Firm—another insider's term for the CIA. Maybe the three of them weren't as alone as he'd thought. "LE net" meant the local law enforcement radio frequencies. The NSA possessed technologies that would allow them to infiltrate the Dushanbe police and MVD radio nets, not only to eavesdrop but also to plant misleading messages or information.

"Any data yet on Maria Alekseyevna?"

"There's not a lot available, but from what we've been able to learn, her story checks out. There was an Alekseyevna family living in Brighton Beach until 2002. Moved to Moscow, where the mother died a year later. No information on the father or the daughter since."

"How about a Dr. Shmatko?"

"A pathologist trained in Moscow. He received a posting to Dushanbe two years ago. It's possible he was a family friend."

"What are we going to do with her?" Dean asked. "We can't throw her to the wolves."

"If you can get her to the Afghanistan border, we'll fly her out when we extract you. What happens to her after that . . ." Dean could almost hear Rockman's shrug over the channel. "Mr. Rubens will have to be brought in. Special provisions might be arranged, but the boss will have to take that up with State."

"She's a good person," Dean said. "She helped Ilya, didn't turn him in when doing so might have earned her some brownie points."

"We'll just have to see how it plays out. First step is to get you the hell out of Tajikistan. I recommend you get some sleep now. You'll be up early."

"We're all over that. Any word on getting quality satellite time?"

"Not yet. We're on the NRO's queue. The boss said he's going to be talking to people later this morning."

"It's taking too long. By now, those suitcase nukes could be any-where."

"I hear you. Oh . . . but you'll want to hear this. The photos Ilya got of those three stiffs in the morgue. We have positive IDs on all of them."

"One of them is Zhernov."

"He was styling himself Zhern at last report, as any good patriotic and anti-Russian Tajik would do. The guy with the mustache was Amirzai Shams, a Pashtun with connections to extremist Muslim factions in Tajikistan and Uzbekistan. Both of them have long records with the Russian *mafiya*. Both had sizable traces of radiation on their hands."

"And the Asian?"

"He's the real puzzle in this mess. Major Kwok Chung On. PLA military intelligence. He was with a Chinese trade delegation in Dushanbe until four days ago, when he disappeared."

"So what is he doing in Central Asia?"

"We've done some checking through our banking connections. Two weeks ago, the State Bank of Beijing transferred one point three billion dollars to a private account in Dushanbe. The size of the transaction raised flags at the Financial Desk."

"I would imagine so." The Financial Desk was the department within the NSA specifically tasked with tracking the flow of large amounts of money throughout the corporate world and across the international community. Identifying accounts used by various terrorist organizations, and freezing their assets, was quite possibly *the* most important weapon available in the long-term fight against groups like al-Qaeda. Follow the money, and you knew who was behind a group or an attack. Freeze or seize the money, and you paralyzed the group, making it harder for them to buy weapons, carry out operations, or provide for the families of suicide bombers.

To that end, the code monkeys working at the NSA had developed a number of CIPs, covert intrusion programs, software designed to infiltrate international banking networks, record transactions, and trace large-scale movements of currency and other assets.

"Who owned the Dushanbe account?" Dean asked.

"We don't know, but the account was emptied four days ago."

"When Major Kwok disappeared."

"Exactly."

"So," Dean said, piecing it together, "Zhern and Shams, either one working with the Russian *mafiya*, transport twelve suitcase nukes from Stepnogorsk to Dushanbe. Kwok withdraws over a billion dollars . . . You know, that's one *big*, unwieldy package."

"Bearer bonds."

"Okay. Kwok takes out over a billion in bearer bonds and uses them to pay Zhern and Shams, and probably another party as well, who takes over the nukes for the next leg in the journey. Kwok stays with Zhern and Shams—"

"We suspect they were driving him toward the Chinese border."

"And Vympel, in the form of Lieutenant Colonel Vasilyev, intercepts them."

"In the mountains about seventy miles east of Dushanbe."

"So . . . who has the nukes now? And where?"

"We don't know the who. Our best guess about where . . . they left Ayni Airfield yesterday, maybe the day before, and are at or beyond the border with Afghanistan by now."

"Why Ayni? They could have flown them out from Dushanbe Airport instead."

"Probably because Dushanbe Airport is solidly under Russian control, with the 201st's headquarters right next door. Political control out at Ayni is divvied up between Tajikistan, Russia, and India. They might actually have felt they had a better chance of smuggling the shipment in and out again at a smaller airfield with divided jurisdiction."

"So . . . what now?" Dean asked. "We still need to find out what happened to the shipment, how they got it out of Ayni."

"Our first requirement is to get you and Ilya out of Tajikistan," Rockman told him. "We were looking at sending in a helicopter, picking you up at Ayni, or maybe someplace in the countryside, but things are too unsettled right now. The Indians have closed down Ayni—rumors of Pakistani terrorist-saboteurs in the area."

"Hm. I wonder how *that* happened?"

"Once you have new plates and registration documents for your car, you can drive out. We'll pick you up at Shir Khan, as originally planned. In the meantime, you need to catch up on your sleep."

"Yes, Mother," Dean said, in the tone of a sulky ten-year-old. Rockman was right, though. He was exhausted—and they would have to hit the road as soon as the plates and other gear arrived from the embassy.

He pulled off the rest of his Indian Air Force uniform and collapsed into the bed.

ILYA AKULININ
SAFE HOUSE
DUSHANBE, TAJIKISTAN
WEDNESDAY, 2110 HOURS LOCAL TIME

Akulinin was nearly asleep when the chirp of a floorboard brought him to full awareness. His hand found the pistol beneath his ancient mattress, and he sat up, peering into the darkness. Someone on the stairs?

The safe house's attic was divided into three side-by-side bedrooms. Akulinin was in the middle room, the one with the stairs going down to the building's second floor. If someone was coming up . . .

He heard a faint tap on the door to the right-side bedroom, then the click of a latch being dropped, the creak of a door opening a few inches in the darkness.

"Ilya?" The voice was a whisper, barely heard.

"Masha?" He kept his voice to a whisper as well.

"I . . . I can't sleep. Can I come in . . . can I stay with you?"

"Of course! Come in!"

He tucked the pistol back into its hiding place. He felt rather than saw her standing next to the bed. He heard a rustle of clothing, and then she was slipping in beside him under the quilt.

He gathered her into his arms. She wasn't wearing anything, and she was crying.

"What is it? What's the matter?"

"Will you . . . will you take me back to America? Back *home*?"

"I can't promise anything," he told her, "but I'll do my very best. At least we can get you away from *here*."

"Away from here would be very, very good."

"You probably shouldn't stay here," he told her after a long, close embrace. "Mrs. Konovalova strikes me as the conservative type. I don't think she would approve . . ."

"Mrs. Konovalova is a fussy old babushka," Masha whispered in his ear. "She won't ever know."

"For a little while, then . . ."

CHARLIE DEAN
SAFE HOUSE
DUSHANBE, TAJIKISTAN
WEDNESDAY, 2135 HOURS LOCAL TIME

Charlie Dean was very nearly asleep when a sound brought him wide-awake. His hand found his Makarov PM beneath his pillow. A careless foot on a loose floorboard?

Squeak . . . squeak . . . squeak . . .

It took him long minutes to identify the sound. It was too regular, too rhythmic to be footsteps on squeaky floorboards. As he shifted in the bed, however, and the bed frame gave a mournful squeak with the movement, he realized what it must be.

Squeak . . . squeak . . . squeak . . .

Hiding the pistol again, he rolled over, his back to the gentle sounds from the bedroom next door. *Just so you get some sleep tonight, Ilya,* he thought.

Soon he was asleep himself.

ART ROOM
NSA HEADQUARTERS
FORT MEADE, MARYLAND
WEDNESDAY, 1235 HOURS DST

Squeak . . . squeak . . . squeak . . .

Jeff Rockman looked up, startled. The sound was coming over Ilya's line. He'd thought Akulinin had taken off his clothes—including his belt-antenna—and left them out of range of his communicator implants when he'd gone to bed earlier. Apparently, his trousers were *just* close enough to pick up the signal from his implant.

"What *is* that noise?" he asked the technician sitting next to him at the console.

"Interference on the tactical channel?" she asked.

"Bozhe moy!" a voice said, a *woman's* voice, speaking low but very clear, as though her mouth were close beside the microphone implanted in Akulinin's skull. *"Kak ya tebya hochu!"*

Rockman exchanged a glance with the tech. He didn't speak Russian, but it was the *way* the woman said it . . .

"Ah! Bistraye! Bistraye!"

Every word coming in over the communications channels of officers in the field was recorded, of course, for later analysis. Rockman had a feeling the analysts were going to enjoy this one.

"Gospodi! Kak mne horosho!"

The Old Man, however, was going to hit the roof.

7

Rubens stood and walked to the podium. The briefing session had been going on now for over an hour without a break. The meeting was supposed to end at one o'clock, and Rubens was the last scheduled speaker. These things were always carefully choreographed.

Now it was Rubens' turn.

"We have a solid lead on twelve of the Lebed nukes," he told the room, with no preamble.

His announcement created a buzz of background conversation. Several of the attendees looked puzzled, but he was prepared for that.

"I'll keep this very brief," he said. "On September 7, 1997, the CBS newsmagazine *60 Minutes* broadcast an interview with former Russian national security advisor Aleksandr Ivanovich Lebed. Here is a portion of that interview."

Rubens touched the audiovisual controls on the lectern, and the screen behind him lit up with Lebed's bland Slavic face.

". . . I'm saying that more than a hundred weapons out of the supposed number of two hundred and fifty are not under the control of the armed forces of Russia," Lebed said. "I don't know their location. I don't know whether they have been destroyed or whether they are stored or whether they've been sold or stolen, I don't know."

"Is it possible that the authorities know where all the weapons are, and simply don't want to tell you?"

"No," Lebed said, his voice flat.

He went on to describe the devices, which he claimed could fit inside large suitcases. The nuclear weapons inside measured sixty by forty by twenty centimeters—about two feet long—and could be detonated, he claimed, by one person with less than a half hour's preparation. They had been distributed among special covert operations units belonging to the *Glavnoye Razvedyvatel'noye Upravleniye*, or GRU, Soviet military intelligence. Lebed claimed he'd learned of the weapons' existence only a few years before, when Boris Yeltsin commissioned him to write a report on the whereabouts of the devices.

Rubens let the *60 Minutes* segment play itself out, then switched off the screen. The room was dead silent.

"Mr. Lebed was national security advisor to Boris Yeltsin from June to October of 1996," Rubens told them. "He was fired during the period of intensive political maneuvering surrounding the hospitalization of Yeltsin for surgery. Two years later, he went on to become the governor of Krasnoyarsk Krai, Russia's second-largest region. In 2002, he was killed in a helicopter crash . . . under somewhat suspicious circumstances."

"Mr. Rubens," Representative Mullins said from the far end of the table, "we in Congress carefully evaluated Mr. Lebed's claims and determined that they were without merit. The Russian government also categorically denied that there was anything whatsoever to Mr. Lebed's rather melodramatic claims."

Rubens considered the congressman for a moment. The man had been intrusive and arrogant all morning, with an attitude indicating that he thought the NSC meeting was purely for his benefit.

Well, perhaps it was. General James' expression suggested that the briefing was largely a waste of time. A dog-and-pony show indeed.

"With respect, Mr. Mullins," Rubens replied carefully, "until now, there really was no useful way to evaluate Lebed's claims. Of *course* the Russian government would deny the weapons' existence.

"It's important to remember that Mr. Lebed's claims were corroborated by Alexei Yablokov, a scientist and former environmental advisor to Yeltsin, and by a former Soviet colonel and GRU operative named Stanislav Lunev. And sources within the Russian government *did* later admit that such devices—built around 105 mm nuclear artillery shells, each containing around fifteen kilograms of plutonium—*were* constructed for the KGB during the 1970s. It was Colonel Lunev, testifying before a congressional hearing on Russian espionage in January of 2000, who claimed that some or all of those nuclear weapons had already been smuggled into the United States, and were either already in place within a number of American cities and key parts of our command-control infrastructure, or they were hidden in caches out in the country, awaiting the order to have them planted. That's not exactly something a government admits to the world."

"Well, that may be," Mullins said. "The U.S. Army had its own SADM project, after all. But I have been assured that these devices have a *very* short shelf life. They would have become inert and harmless years ago."

SADM stood for Special Atomic Demolition Munitions, backpack-portable nukes that could be dropped with Special Forces teams behind enemy lines during a war. The most common had been the W54, a cylinder two feet long and weighing sixty-eight kilograms. Some three hundred of the devices had been a highly secret part of the U.S. arsenal until their removal and disassembly in 1989.

General James leaned over and whispered something close to Mullins' ear. Mullins listened, then looked angry. "General, I was assured that this meeting would offer the opportunity for a free exchange of ideas—"

"And right now, sir, it's Mr. Rubens' turn," James said. "Mr. Rubens? If you would continue?"

"As I was saying," Rubens said, "we can *not* objectively evaluate the claims of Lebed, Lunev, and others. They were politically motivated, and they had both political and personal agendas. I think the point we should be keeping in mind, though, is that if there is even a chance that there are several small, easily hidden nuclear weapons floating around loose out there, we need to take that possibility very seriously indeed.

"Two weeks ago, an informant in the central Asian city of Astana, in Kazakhstan, told Central Intelligence operatives that twelve suitcase nukes stored at a former Russian military facility in the city of Stepnogorsk had been stolen by elements within one of the Russian *mafiya* and been sold to an extremist Muslim group—quite probably the Jaish-e-Mohammad, the Army of Mohammad, in Pakistan."

"What does Pakistan want with Russian nukes?" Mullins said, interrupting again. "Pakistan is a nuclear power already."

"The Jaish-e-Mohammad is operating independently of the Pakistan government, sir," Rubens pointed out. "The two might have congruent goals, especially where Kashmir and India are concerned, but Pakistan can't afford to be seen as officially supporting terrorists."

"India has nuclear weapons, too," Wehrum pointed out. "Pakistan must be as anxious to catch these guys as we are."

"The Islamabad government has assured us of their full cooperation in this matter," the observer from the State Department, Catharine Tognetti, added.

"For whatever *that* may be worth," General James put in. "Go ahead, please, Mr. Rubens."

Rubens gave a wry smile. James was doing his level best to keep the meeting on track. That was no small feat, particularly given the size and number of egos in the room.

"The informant indicated that the weapons were being transported by road south to Karachi, in Pakistan, a journey overland of some eighteen hundred miles. According to this informant, in Karachi the weapons were to be put on board a freighter for transport to their final destination, which he believed to be someplace in the Middle East—most likely Israel.

"The CIA initiated what became known as Operation Haystack, in hopes of intercepting these weapons before they reached Pakistan. They brought the NSA into the operation in order to directly employ our SIGINT and other intelligence-gathering assets for this search."

Rubens could feel Debra Collins' cold stare as he spoke. For several years now, Collins, deputy director of operations at the CIA, had been trying to gain control of the NSA's Desk Three, charging that the NSA's charter did not allow for field-operational intelligence-gathering teams and that units such as Desk Three were in fact wasteful duplicates of the CIA's Operations Directorate. In fact, the vast majority of the NSA's duties *were* limited to signals intelligence, code breaking, and electronic surveillance. That meant spying at long range from satellites and from eavesdropping facilities at places like Menwith Hill in Yorkshire, England, and Misawa Air Base in northern Honshu, in Japan.

However, not all intelligence could be intercepted by antennas from hundreds or thousands of miles away. As computer and communications technologies advanced around the world, the NSA had developed the technical means for tapping those technologies—but often that meant first sending someone in on the ground to plant eavesdropping devices, steal computer passwords, copy software or records from hard drives not connected to the outside world, or otherwise physically hack computer networks.

Hence, Desk Three.

Rubens thought he knew just what it had cost Collins to actually request the NSA's help with this op. She hated admitting that sometimes she needed Desk Three's unique capabilities.

"Just how reliable is this CIA source?" This time, the interruption was from James himself, but it was a good question. Rubens and his superiors within the NSA had debated that particular issue for hours when the CIA's request had first come through.

"You'll need to have Ms. Collins address that particular question, sir."

"Ms. Collins?"

"Intelligence evaluation rated the report as a B-2," Collins said. She didn't look at either man as she spoke.

Within the intelligence community, an intelligence source was given a letter code, from A to F, indicating its reliability, while the likely accuracy of the intelligence was given a number, from 1 to 6. B-2 meant that the Agency's source had been evaluated as reasonably reliable and the information transmitted was considered to be probably true.

"Can you tell us anything about your source?"

"No, sir. There are people in the room who are not cleared for that level of security."

Did she mean Mullins? Or some of the staffers and aides? Most of the people in the room were cleared for security access at *least* at the Top Secret level, but Wehrum had warned them early on to limit discussions to Top Secret and below.

"Two days ago, NSA personnel were deployed to several central Asian nations," Rubens continued. "People on the ground. Their orders were to use various technical assets to find the nuclear weapons, which were to be referred to solely as 'the shipment.' In particular, the CIA's original report suggested that one of the devices might be damaged, that it was leaking small amounts of radioactivity. This left a trail of contamination that could be detected by intelligence operatives on the ground, using small radiation detectors strapped to their persons."

"Excuse me, Mr. Rubens," Mullins said. "I must admit to some small confusion here. It was my understanding that the NSA did its surveillance through electronic means and by satellite. Why in God's name do you need people over there?"

The existence of Deep Black and Desk Three was also classified above Top Secret. The fact that the NSA used sources that included operatives on the ground was not, though the NSA never talked about it. One of the well-known meanings of "NSA" among insiders was *Never Say Anything.*

He wondered if he could use Mullins to build some support for his agency. He didn't yet know where ANSA stood on Desk Three's existence—and he could count on Debra Collins to cut him down when she could.

He remembered, though, that Mullins represented a district with strong connections with aerospace, especially the manufacture of high-grade precision lenses used by Crystal Fire and other optical surveillance satellite programs.

"Sir, you are correct that most of our chartered mission is carried out at long range. Our original mandate was restricted to code-breaking and to SIGINT—signals intelligence. Satellites are vitally important to our mission, and we devoutly wish we had more of them. But some things simply can *not* be tracked from space. Radiation sources, for instance."

Rubens glanced at his watch. "About seven hours ago, one of our teams positively identified a contaminated area on the back of a truck that had been abandoned at a military airfield just outside of Dushanbe, the capital of Tajikistan. This suggests that the shipment had gotten at least that far, a little more than half of the distance from Stepnogorsk to Karachi. Unfortunately, our options for continuing the search are somewhat limited at this point. We've hit a wall."

"What wall?" James demanded.

"We seem to be engaged in a small turf war for limited assets with . . . another agency."

"Damn you, Bill," Collins said, sitting up sharply in her seat.

Rubens held up a hand. "I'm not *naming* the agency," he said, "and I'm not casting blame. We, all of us, have more critical things to focus on than internal territorial disputes. But what is necessary now is free and immediate access to NRO data—specifically targeted imagery from Crystal Fire. Either that, or we need more satellites."

General James looked at Collins. "Is the CIA sitting on data the NSA needs?" he asked.

"We . . . have imagery acquired early this morning from CF-1," she admitted, "but it's still undergoing analysis. Raw data must be . . . processed before it can be disseminated to other agencies."

"Very true," Rubens said, "and I would point out that the NSA possesses absolutely the best technology for carrying out that type of analysis. At the very least, we could be processing the data in parallel with our friends at Langley."

"Which would entail a massive duplication of effort," Collins countered. "It means a colossal waste of available resources."

"With the sheer scale of 8X imagery," Rubens pointed out, "we need to double up on resources just to sift through the data. Remember, we're dealing with a whole new level of satellite imagery here."

He didn't specify that scale, of course, since those parameters carried a classification of above Top Secret. In fact, the data stream from Crystal Fire included real-time streaming video at a one-centimeter-minus resolution across an area of something like half a million square kilometers—a scale and a resolution that *far* surpassed anything in the Intruder program, to say nothing of earlier Keyhole satellites.

"*Mr.* Rubens!" General James snapped. "*Ms.* Collins! I have zero patience for interagency bickering here."

"Yes, sir," Rubens said. "However, given the critical importance of this search, I submit that we do need to cut through some of the red tape and compartmentalization. It's crippling us. I agree that we need to avoid duplication of effort—but right now we have reliable evidence that twelve tactical nuclear weapons are on their way from Dushanbe to the port of Karachi. To get there, they have to travel through Afghanistan—not all of which is under friendly control, I'll remind you—*and* through Pakistan, which, though they've assured us of their willingness to help, is not entirely under Islamabad's control. If we're right, they left Dushanbe yesterday. We need that satellite data before the trail goes ice cold!"

His briefing completed, he stepped back from the lectern. "Questions?"

There were a lot of them.

FORT LEE INN
FORT LEE, NEW JERSEY
WEDNESDAY, 1305 HOURS EDT

She called herself Thea, a name she'd once heard meant "goddess." Cynthia Jane Cramer thought of it as her *professional* name, both when she was dancing and when she was with a john. She watched Jack Pender roll out of bed naked, and put on her most sultry and alluring pout. "You're not leaving *now*, are you, honey?" she asked.

He grinned at her, reached down, and squeezed her left breast affectionately. She managed to smile, to not wince. *Asshole . . .*

"Sorry, babe," he told her. "I need to shave and shower. Got a big meeting with my publisher this afternoon."

"But you make me so *hot!*"

"I'd love to see you again tonight," he told her. "I'll have something to celebrate by then—a fat new book contract!"

As soon as he walked into the hotel room's bathroom and closed the door, she was out of bed. She pulled on her dress and heels and tucked her discarded panties into her handbag. Pender's clothes were lying on the dresser. She began rooting through them, searching. She was *sure* she'd seen him tuck it away in here . . .

There it was. She extracted the magnetic room key from his wallet. She eyed the wallet's other contents for a moment. She'd been warned, but . . .

He had a bit over a hundred dollars in cash and a couple of credit cards. Cards and cash both went into her pocketbook, along with the two hundred those guys had already paid her a couple of hours earlier. Not a bad take for half an afternoon's work, and it was going to get better. She could spend the afternoon maxing out those cards, then drop them on some drunk down in Edgewater, and if they ever tracked the missing cards they'd find the drunk and not her.

A paperback book lay faceup on the dresser, next to Pender's briefcase. The title was *Death Wave: The 2012 Prophecies Fulfilled,* by Vincent Carlylse and Jack Pender. She shrugged. She wasn't much of a reader.

"Hey, honey?" she called out. "I'm gonna step out and get me some cigarettes. But I'll be right back, okay? I wanna wish you good luck for your meeting in a really *special* way!"

"Okay, babe!" he called back from inside the bathroom. "Just bang loud on the door, and I'll let you in!"

Yeah, in your dreams, she thought as she let herself out. Men were so fucking predictable. Give them the adoring puppy look, shake your titties at them, and they'd fall all over themselves. Even when they *knew* you were a whore, they ended up thinking it had to be True Love.

They were waiting for her in the hotel lobby. As promised. Two men stood up as she clicked into the atrium on her heels.

"You have it?" one asked.

She held up the white keycard for the room. "Right here. Room 225. You have the rest of the money?"

One of the men reached into a jacket pocket and extracted a roll of bills. He peeled off three hundred and handed it to her. *"Bintilkha-ta,"* the man growled. It didn't sound like a compliment.

"Whatever," she said. "Nice doin' business with ya."

The two turned and walked toward the elevators. They looked foreign—Arab, maybe, but they *might* be Sicilians with that olive skin. Or Greeks. Thea watched them go, wondering if they were enforcers for the mob. Maybe Mr. Pender hadn't kept up with his payments.

She shrugged. Too bad for him. The goddess walked out into the bright New Jersey afternoon.

She didn't see the third man waiting for her in the parking lot.

NATIONAL SECURITY COUNCIL BRIEFING ROOM
WHITE HOUSE BASEMENT, WASHINGTON, D.C.
WEDNESDAY, 1315 HOURS EDT

"Mr. Rubens," Catharine Tognetti said slowly, "just how powerful *are* these so-called suitcase nukes?"

"We don't know the exact designs, of course," Rubens replied. "In particular, we don't know if the warheads have been fusion-boosted. But our best technical evaluation suggests that each device would have a yield of between one and ten kilotons—that's one to ten thousand tons of TNT.

"The nuclear device exploded over Hiroshima in 1945, by way of comparison, was between fifteen and twenty kilotons. We're not talking about city-busters here. A one-kiloton blast would wreck downtown Washington, D.C., but most of the city would remain more or less intact, except for the windows, maybe. However, these smaller devices also tend to be rather dirty. Lots of radiation, lots of fallout, at least if they're detonated at or above ground level."

The room was quiet after that, as each attendee considered the possibility of a one-kiloton nuclear blast in the heart of an American city.

There were more questions, and some discussion after that, but the meeting finally broke up. Rubens decided he would check in with the Art Room as soon as he got back to street level and could get a signal on his cell phone.

As he was packing up his briefcase, however, he was aware of a movement beside him.

"Hello, Debra," he said, not looking up.

"That was damned unprofessional of you, Bill. You made me *and* the Agency look bad."

He sighed, straightening up and turning to face her. "Debra, you should know me by now. I despise politics, and I do not play these silly turf games. The only thing I'm concerned about here is getting the job done the best, quickest, and most efficient way possible."

"You could have come to me personally," Collins said.

"I submitted the usual requisitions through the usual channels," he told her, "*and* e-mails, *and* phone messages. My people also talked to the NRO directly. The data was Agency-encoded." He smiled. "It seems Langley has been tying up both USA-202 *and* Crystal Fire since yesterday. You were hogging our two best orbital assets. Wouldn't it be better if we shared?"

"There . . . may have been an oversight," Collins admitted. "Or a delay putting your request through. But we were not 'hogging' those satellites, as you put it."

"Of *course* you weren't."

Rubens knew all too well how it worked. There would be no policy, no actual directive put out to exclude the NSA from the intelligence loop—but requests to expedite key requests, clearances, director approvals, and the like might accidentally be left in an electronic in-basket, or conveniently ignored for a few hours while other and more pressing matters were addressed.

Such a delay might give the Agency's analysis teams an extra few hours to develop important intelligence before the NSA had a chance to look for the same hidden gems. And if Agency teams turned up the goodies, it would be the Agency that got the credit—and the funding at the next round of budgetary meetings.

"Don't patronize me, Bill," Collins told him.

"I'm not. Don't *you* play cute political games with me."

"At the director's level, politics is a part of the job description. You know that as well as I do. And the only one playing games here this morning was you, sabotaging me in front of the ANSA to build up your own position."

"Debra, it was not my intent to make you look bad this morning—no more than it was *your* intent to sequester that data. We need access to that imagery, though, and we need it *now*. I have people on the ground over there. Their lives, and the success of this operation, both depend on what we can turn up from those satellites, *especially* Crystal Fire. It is my intent to talk to ANSA personally if I have to—I have his attention now, don't you think? I'll take it to the Oval Office if I have to."

She stared into his face for a long moment, as though testing his resolve. Rubens didn't have direct access to the President, but the President's advisor on national security did.

Then she looked away. "I'll authorize transmittal as soon as we get out of here," she told him.

"Thank you, Debra. *Together* I think we can crack this."

She was already walking away.

FORT LEE INN
FORT LEE, NEW JERSEY
WEDNESDAY, 1319 HOURS EDT

The two men used the stolen keycard to let themselves into room 225. One held an automatic pistol at the ready as the door swung open, but the room's occupant was still in the shower. They could hear the rush of water, taste the steam in the air. Quietly, they walked into the room and moved the desk chair to an open space near the foot of the king-sized bed.

Both wore thin disposable gloves. The one with the keycard wiped it carefully with his handkerchief and placed it on the bureau; then the two of them sat down in the remaining chairs over by the closed curtains to wait.

Soon the sound of the water cut off, and a few minutes later Jack Pender walked out of the bathroom, rubbing himself with a hotel towel. In the darkened room, he didn't see his visitors, not until they grabbed him from either side.

"What the fuck—" he yelled, and then one of the men jammed a rolled-up sock into his mouth. Pinning his arms, they slammed him into the desk chair.

"I am sorry, Mr. Pender," one of the intruders said. He reached into his jacket and pulled out a knife. Pender's eyes opened wide, fixed on the blade, which flashed once in a gleam of light from the curtains at his back. He started to struggle, but the man holding him was strong, too strong, his grip on his wrists like steel. Pender tried to kick the guy with the knife, but the man sidestepped the attempt, reached down, and pulled Pender's left arm from behind his back.

"I really do dislike doing this," the man with the knife said. He dragged Pender's arm forward and down until it was pinned against the chair, palm up. "I actually am one of your big . . . what is the American word? *Fans.* Yes. I am a big fan. It is really too bad you decide to suicide."

The intruder slipped the point of the knife into Pender's wrist and sliced deep, dragging the blade up the struggling man's arm, rather than across. Blood welled up from the sudden wound, dark and slick. Pender screamed through the sock, thrashing violently now, but the big man behind him kept him pinned as the other made a second deep slice up his wrist . . . a third . . .

On the fourth cut, the knife hit the artery, and blood splattered across the unmade bed, across a wall, across white ceiling tiles.

After a time, the intruder began cutting the other wrist; by then, Pender was so weak he could barely struggle.

Ten minutes more, and Pender was no longer moving. The man with the knife felt for a pulse at his throat with a gloved finger, peeled back an eyelid, then nodded. *"Taiyib!"* he said.

They released Pender, letting him slump back in the chair, naked, his arms, legs, and torso sheathed in blood. The killer pulled the sock from the man's mouth, then carefully wrapped the fingers of his right hand around the handle of the knife. When the man let go, the knife dropped from limp, blood-gloved fingers and fell beside the chair. The sock went back on the floor by the bed, next to Pender's shoes. Very carefully, then, the intruders stepped past the body, watching where they put their feet, careful not to step in the blood now soaking into the cheap hotel room carpet. There was a *lot* of blood . . .

They were as careful about footprints as they'd been with fingerprints. Bloody gloves were peeled from their hands and went into their pockets, and they wiped the doorknob clean behind them as they let themselves out.

8

Rubens came awake with a start.

He'd driven back out to Fort Meade as soon as the NSC meeting was over, grabbing a fast-food burger on the way for lunch. He'd spoken with Marie by cell phone, gotten an update on the op in Dushanbe, and learned that Dean and Akulinin were at the safe house—with a stray.

He approved transport for the stray—if Charlie and Ilya were vouching for Alekseyevna, he would do his best to help her—then rattled off a string of orders. He didn't want the boys *immediately* leaving Dushanbe but wanted them to pull a quick black bag job first, and Marie should expect a *large* download over the secure line from the CIA.

Once back at Fort Meade, he decided he *had* to get some sleep. He'd been on his feet now for more hours than he cared to think about, and he'd caught himself nodding at the wheel as he drove up the Baltimore-Washington Parkway out of the city. *Not* good.

So when he'd finally reached his office at a bit past two thirty, he'd pulled off his shoes and collapsed into the cot in the back room off his office, facedown in the pillow.

Thirty minutes later, Ann Sawyer, his secretary, was shaking him awake. "Sir? Sir!"

"What is it?"

"Sorry to wake you, Mr. Rubens, but they say there's something you should see on C-SPAN."

"If this is not the end of the world, Ann . . ."

"Sir, I—"

"Never mind, never mind. I'm coming."

He rolled out of the cot and made his way to the office. Ann had already switched on the monitor mounted within one wall.

He recognized the face of Rodney C. Mullins, giving an address.

". . . that it is *critically* important that we provide timely funding for our surveillance satellite system. As I said before, we have *people on the ground* in places like Astana, Dushanbe, and Karachi, and they cannot do their jobs defending this great nation from the threat of rogue states or terrorists quite possibly *armed with nuclear weapons* if they do not have adequate technical support!

"And so I move, Mr. Speaker, that my amendment to the military appropriations bill be voted on without delay . . ."

Rubens stared at the screen in disbelief. "Jesus fucking H. *Christ!*"

AYNI AIRFIELD
SOUTHWEST OF DUSHANBE, TAJIKISTAN
THURSDAY, 0415 HOURS LOCAL TIME

Charlie Dean took another look around the dark compound, then lay down on the ground.

"Tell me again why this is a good idea, coming back in here like this?" Akulinin asked.

"Because it's the one place in Tajikistan they're *not* looking for us," Dean told him.

"And because Mr. Rubens suggested that you might want to try it," Vic Klein added in their implanted speakers. Vic had taken over the Art Room's part of the mission for Dean and Akulinin at the end of Jeff Rockman's shift some hours ago.

"Right. You ready, Charlie?"

Dean closed his eyes and nodded. "Let's do it." His right hand closed a little tighter around the pen he was holding cupped there, out of sight. He heard the faint crunch of gravel as Akulinin hurried away.

The nap at the safe house had been all too brief. He'd been able to sleep for perhaps two hours before the promised messenger had shown up with new plates for the car and new ID cards and papers, both for the two Desk Three operators and for Maria Alekscyevna. Now, her blond hair tucked up inside a black wig, she was Ruqiya Nazarova, and she was listed as Sergei Nazarov's Tajik wife.

Dean wondered if the Art Room wizards had been aware of Ilya's tryst with Masha a few hours ago when they created their new legends. *Probably* not . . . but with them and their high-tech magic at listening in, you never knew. The two had been back in their separate rooms by the time Mrs. Konovalova had come up the stairs to wake them, and *that* at least had worked out well. Dean had the feeling that the old woman would not have approved.

Or . . . perhaps she would. Her eyes had been sparkling a bit when she'd wished them all safe travels, and it seemed to Dean that she'd been smiling in a knowing and somewhat condescending way at Ilya and Masha as they said good-bye.

Maybe the squeaks had penetrated the floor to her bedroom below.

And maybe the woman didn't mind if two young people found a few moments of escape from a dark and pain-grim world.

Their initial goal had been to drive south as quickly as possible, using back roads to avoid the dragnet thrown up around the city by Vasilyev's forces and by the local police. Besides the new license plates, the Dushanbe CIA resident had sent along a new drivers-side mirror to replace the one that had been shot out earlier, plus a spray can of a tacky adhesive with which to coat the car's body. There was no time to repaint the vehicle's green exterior, but handfuls of dirt scooped up from outside the shed and hurled against the body quickly transformed the dark green Hunter from new-looking to something that had been bouncing around on the arid dirt roads of Tajikistan's mountains for weeks. They couldn't do anything about replacing the car's rear window, but they did brush some dark matte gray paint into the bright white star where the bullet had glanced off glass and metal. It wouldn't get past a close examination, but at night, from a distance of a few yards, the scar was now invisible.

While they'd been detailing the car to give it its new look, Rubens had explained the new plan.

According to various surveillance sources, Lieutenant Colonel Vasilyev had his office in the Ayni Airfield tower building. Analysts going over the footage Dean had transmitted of Vasilyev jumping out of the helicopter had shown him carrying a briefcase—not the sort of fashion accessory normally taken by FSB officers on board helicopters. The NSA analysts were not sure what happened to that briefcase. Dean and Akulinin had not seen it in the hospital morgue. It might have been in Vasilyev's car, or it could have been passed to a subordinate and taken to Vasilyev's office in the Ayni control tower building.

Either way, the chances were good that the briefcase was in his Ayni office now, and Rubens wanted the Desk Three operatives to slip inside and have a look.

They'd returned in the middle of the night to Ayni, a few kilometers southwest of Dushanbe. Getting back onto the base had been simple enough. The Deep Black electronic support unit back at Fort Meade had for the past several hours been busily infiltrating the radio and cell phone calls crisscrossing the airwaves over Tajikistan, adding reports, sightings, and orders designed to confuse the manhunt now under way. In several cases, they'd even used the Internet to modify local police and military records and files. Numerous new reports now had the fugitive vehicle fleeing north on the M34 toward the border with Uzbekistan, while other reports suggested that the fugitives were not two men and a woman, as originally reported, but one man and one woman, the female described as blond, the male as being Pakistani, with black hair and beard.

And so a dusty, travel-worn car with different license plates than were on the fugitive vehicle had entered the Ayni front gate. The bored Indian guards there had looked at their IDs and waved them through. Dean had parked the vehicle in the main parking lot, and Masha had stayed in the back, huddled underneath a blanket, while Dean and Akulinin had approached the control tower.

The building—indeed, the entire base—appeared to have shut down for the night. There were two guards in front of the control tower entrance, however, both of them Russians. Dean and Akulinin had watched them for a moment from behind the corner of a large tool shed a hundred yards from the tower. The windows were probably covered by an alarm system; the only way in, then, was through the front door, directly between the guards.

Now Dean lay on his back behind the tool shed, listening as Akulinin's footsteps receded into the distance. A moment later, he heard shouting—Akulinin barking orders.

He heard multiple footsteps returning, crunching over gravel, running this time. "He's over here, around this corner!" Dean heard Akulinin say in out-of-breath Russian. "I think he's still alive."

"I'm not supposed to leave my post, sir," another voice said.

"Don't worry. We just need to get him to the infirmary."

Dean felt someone standing beside him, leaning over him, felt a cold hand touch the side of his face, then probe for a pulse at his throat. He opened his eyes, looking up into the startled face of a Russian soldier, then snapped his arm straight up, shoving the tip of the pen directly into the man's solar plexus.

The applicator was based on emergency medical injector units—the kind used to autoinject massive jolts of atropine in case of an attack by nerve gas. When the tip hit the man's shirt, the needle fired, sending a dose of a powerful relaxant into his central torso. He opened his mouth to yell . . . but no sound came out, and his knees were already buckling. Dean rolled out from beneath him as Akulinin grabbed him from behind, clamping his mouth shut and lowering the sagging body to the ground.

The neurosuppressive cocktail in that pen would keep the man unconscious for at least six hours. As soon as he was down, Akulinin stepped around the corner and waved at the other guard. "It's okay! The son of a bitch is just drunk! Come give us a hand, will you?"

A moment later, the second guard rounded the corner of the shed, his weapon slung. He barely had time to register the fact that the body on the ground was that of the other guard before Akulinin's arm swept around from the side and slammed the tip of another auto-injector into his chest. The second guard collapsed as swiftly and as silently as the first.

Dean used a small lockpick set to open the simple padlock on its hasp securing the tool shed door. They dragged the Russian soldiers inside, relieved them of weapons, ammunition pouches, and IDs, and left them with their hands and feet bound in plastic zip-strips. Somebody would find them when they finally woke up and started yelling, if not before.

The front door to the control tower facility was unlocked—a somewhat worrisome fact. It suggested that there might be an officer of the watch who made periodic rounds inside the building as well as outside. Since they didn't know his schedule, they would have to work fast.

They'd brought a small leather satchel with them, another present from the embassy. Dean pulled out a small device the size of a paperback book and scanned the door carefully, searching for live wires and circuits hidden in the wood or bricks—an indication that there might be silent alarms or hidden cameras. "Nothing," he whispered.

Akulinin pulled a small black cylinder from the bag and planted it in the dirt next to the door. "Okay," Vic Klein's voice told them through their implant communicators. "Good picture. Go ahead."

Inside, the building was completely dark. They didn't have IR or starlight gear, but the two operators used tiny lights to find their way down a long hall and left, to a suite of back offices, the lights red-hued to preserve their night vision. A search through airport staffing records indicated that Vasilyev's office was number 12; a search of architectural records in Dushanbe had pinpointed number 12 at the end of the dogleg to the left. The door was locked. Another electronic scan showed an absence of hidden alarms. Dean pulled out a slender rectangle of steel the size of a credit card and slid it between the door and the jamb, popping the bolt.

The office had two rooms, an outer room for a secretary and reception, an inner sanctum for the boss. They performed yet another electronic sweep with negative results. Akulinin left a micro camera positioned where it could watch the door, then checked with the Art Room to make sure the device was transmitting. Next the two operatives picked the lock to the inner door and entered Vasilyev's private office.

They left the lights off, unwilling to let them show through the closed blinds at the back of the room and make someone suspicious. Using their red minilights, though, they found Vasilyev's desk, then swept the entire room for electronic signatures. Against the wall in one corner was a four-foot steel safe. Akulinin sat down at the computer and powered it up. Dean moved to the safe.

The safe had been imported from the United States—with a Sargent and Greenleaf Model R6730 locking mechanism—and had been identified as such already in the architectural plans uncovered by Desk Three's long-distance computer snooping.

The lock mechanisms for safes rated for holding classified DoD documents back in the United States were now required to be electronic, using a keypad to punch in the combination. Though more secure against safecrackers employing traditional methods—listening to tumblers fall through stethoscopes or manipulating the lock— electronic locks were actually easier to penetrate using modern computer technology.

This kind of lock was tougher to get past. A three-number combination lock like this one theoretically had 100^3, or one million, possible combinations, though minor imperfections and inefficiencies in the way the numbers lined up on the dial and the way the tumblers worked together in practice reduced that number to roughly 283,000 possible distinct combinations. There were several ways of quickly circumventing such a purely mechanical system, but the NSA operatives didn't have a high-speed hardened tungsten-carbide drill, a thermal lance, or a plastic-explosives shaped charge, and they didn't want to make that much noise and call down base security on their heads.

The CIA resident at the U.S. Embassy had sent along something better.

Called a sonic cracker, the battery-powered device fitted around the safe's dial, the back fitting closely against the surface of the safe's steel door. Dean pressed a button and felt the unit vibrate. It operated by sending a subsonic pulse through the steel and the lock mechanism and listening for echoed returns, a form of sonar that worked through steel and brass instead of water or air. A green LED light winked on at the top of the device. Signal return received.

He rotated the dial ten to the right and pressed the button again. He continued the process, turning the dial farther and farther to the right until he'd finished a complete circuit. Then he repeated the process, turning to the left.

Behind him, he heard Akulinin mutter as Vasilyev's desktop came up. "Vista crap, tee-em," he said. "Are we *trying* to make other countries mad at us by exporting this stuff to them?"

"As long as the back door is there," Dean murmured. He was beginning the third set of combination setups now, as the computer chip inside the cracker stored more and more sonic images of the interior of the lock.

"Let's keep the chatter down," Rubens' voice said over their link. "Just in case you missed a passive recorder."

A passive recorder was an electronic device that could monitor a room, switching on only when there were sounds to be heard—like conversation. The NSA used such devices frequently, utilizing ordinary telephones as the pickups.

Vasilyev wasn't likely to have that kind of technology at his disposal, but it was simply good field operations discipline to keep the conversation to a minimum. The fact that numerous software packages distributed globally had undocumented back doors allowing interested parties like the NSA to peek at password-protected information, such as the movement of large amounts of money through different banking systems, was something the Agency wanted to keep *very* secret for as long as possible.

Dean mentally kicked himself on that one—and Akulinin should have known better than to say more than an absolute minimum. That was the sort of mistake that could kill you in this business.

He wondered if Ilya's judgment had been compromised by the woman.

Had *his*?

He also wondered what Rubens was doing up and in the Art Room. Last he'd heard, the Old Man had been asleep.

Abruptly, a second LED flashed green. The flashing indicated that the chip inside the unit was processing all of the data.

"I've got something here," Akulinin whispered. He plugged a small device into one of the computer's USB ports, then typed on the Cyrillic-alphabet keyboard. "Transmitting," he said after hitting the RETURN key.

"Receiving," Klein said over their implants. "How are you doing, Charlie?"

"Working," he replied. There was no telling how long this part of the process would take. The computer inside the cracker was small but extremely powerful, a product of the NSA's computer research labs, where the joke had it that they were developing both hardware and software that were at least fifteen years ahead of anything yet on the market. By analyzing the patterns of reflected sound waves, it was building up a picture of the wheel-and-gate mechanism behind the safe's external dial, looking for irregularities and imperfections that would sharply reduce the number of possible combinations. A skilled safecracker could do this with a good ear and sensitive fingers, as well as an expert knowledge of a safe's internal mechanism, a process known in the trade as manipulation. The sonic returns in the cracker should be able to play through all possible permutations of the wheels inside and come up with just *one* working combination.

The question was how long that process would take. Depending on the lock, it could happen almost immediately . . . or it might take as long as twenty minutes.

"You might want to hurry things up," Klein told him. "We have an officer of the guard coming up to the front of your building. He's looking around, shining his flashlight. He's looking for the missing guards."

"Just freaking great," Dean subvocalized. He didn't want to interrupt the process. Moving the device affixed to the door meant the internal picture would be rearranged when he tried again, and he would have to start over from the beginning.

"He's trying the front door," Klein said. "He's coming inside."

Dean glanced up at Akulinin, whose face was illuminated by the glow from the computer monitor. "Watch the front office door," he said softly. Akulinin nodded, shut down the computer, and slipped out of the inner office.

More minutes passed. "I can hear him in the hallway," Akulinin's voice said over the link. "He's rattling doorknobs and calling names."

"You'll want to take him out," Klein said. "If he can't find them and sounds an alarm—"

"Wait one," Akulinin whispered. "He's outside . . ."

At that moment, the LED stopped blinking, indicating that the computations were complete. The alphanumeric R27 appeared on the one-line window. Dean turned the knob to the indicated setting and pressed the button. A second alphanumeric, L84, appeared, and after another button-press it was R36. He twisted the handle, and the safe opened easily with a soft thunk.

"I'm in," Dean said quietly. He pulled the sonic cracker off the door and slipped it back into the bag. He shone his light into the interior and saw the briefcase, tucked in beside a sheaf of file folders and numerous papers.

In the outer office, the door opened. *"Mutko!"* a voice called. *"Ignatyev! G'deh vashi—"* The call was abruptly cut short by a heavy thud.

"One bad guy down," Akulinin's voice said a moment later.

"It's clear outside," Klein told them. "If he doesn't report in after his rounds, there may be an alarm."

Dean pulled the briefcase out of the safe. The scanner turned up no indication of an electronic defensive system or lock—it didn't even have a combination lock on it. There was a key-type lock, and no key, but a small pry bar from the bag snapped the hasp open with a single sharp ping.

Papers . . . sheets of something that looked like bank bonds . . . and a computer CD in a plastic jewel case. "Jackpot," he said.

"I've got our friend out here zip-stripped and hidden in the office supply cupboard," Akulinin said. "Let's get the hell out of Dodge."

Getting out proved to be easier than getting in, anticlimactic even. Akulinin retrieved the micro cameras on the way out. There was no sense in leaving obvious clues to the burglary of Vasilyev's office. The guards at the front gate waved them through and didn't even seem interested in recording their departure in a log.

They turned east on the Hissar Road south of the airport and drove five miles to the intersection with the A384, the main highway leading south. A broad, modern bridge spanned the river—it was the Kafirnigan here, the Varzob having joined it a few miles upriver, just south of Dushanbe. There was a roadblock at the north end of the bridge, with several bored-looking militiamen stopping and checking each car. At just past five in the morning, there was little traffic, and the short line of cars and trucks in front of the bridge appeared to be moving through quickly.

"Masha," Dean told the woman in the backseat, "it looks like they're not checking the cars thoroughly—just looking at IDs. Get down on the floor again and cover up."

"With the guns?" The two AKMs they'd taken from the guards were on the floor now, under the dark blanket.

"Yup. Just don't fire one by accident."

"Okay, Charlie. I must say you boys *do* know how to show a girl a good time!"

Dean glanced back to be sure she was completely covered. The various reports out were for either a man and a woman or *two* men and a woman, and keeping Masha hidden would simplify the deception, *if* the guards up ahead didn't give the backseat more than a cursory glance in the darkness.

The vehicle ahead, a battered red pickup truck piled high with baskets, moved on across the bridge. Dean eased the Hunter forward and smiled as the guard with a slung rifle shone a flashlight at his face. A second man stood with an AK-74 at port arms in front of the vehicle; two more, Dean noticed, were standing off to the side, caught in the glare of the headlights, watching, weapons ready.

"Identification," the first man said. He leaned forward, placing his left hand on the Hunter's door. Dean watched him remove his hand and look at it curiously, rubbing the fingers with his thumb. The tacky spray, Dean thought, must still feel sticky.

"That should be 'Identification, *sir,*'" Akulinin snapped in his best tyrannical-martinet tone. "I happen to be an officer in the 201st Division of the Russian Army! My driver is an officer in the Indian Air Force, and we're out in the middle of the *fucking* night searching for Pakistani terrorists! Wake up and pay attention to what you're doing!"

"Sir!" the militia soldier said, the stickiness of the car door forgotten. He straightened up, fumbling with the flashlight, attempting a salute with the wrong hand. "Yes, *sir!*"

Dean showed him the IDs, the new ones sent over from the embassy, since the old were compromised by now. "Have you seen anything suspicious at this checkpoint, soldier?" Dean asked.

"No, sir! But we heard on the radio earlier that the saboteurs have been sighted on the M34 well north of the city . . . north of Anzob." The man's Russian was atrocious, but he seemed most eager to please. Police militia would be poorly trained locals working under the orders of either the Dushanbe government or, possibly, the Russians. They would be more terrified of an angry Russian officer than even of the possibility of terrorists.

"Very good," Dean told him. "We are checking out a report from the south. We'll let you know if we hear anything."

"Yes, *sir!*" He stepped back after a cursory glance at the IDs and waved them through. "Good luck, sir!"

"Sometimes," Akulinin said, grinning as Dean accelerated onto the long bridge, "all it takes is an attitude. Step on the other guy's toes until he apologizes."

"That or frightening him half to death. I think the poor SOB's trousers turned a darker shade of brown when you barked at him."

"Whatever works! We're in the clear now, and Afghanistan, here we come!" He reached back and patted the blanket on the floor behind him. "Come on out, sweetie. It's safe!"

"Afghanistan?" she said uncertainly.

"Afghanistan and a NATO flight out of here!"

"Unless they turn up something for us to track," Dean added. "We're still waiting on satellite data, remember."

He wasn't going to get excited about the end of the journey just yet. Afghanistan was still a hundred to a hundred fifty miles ahead, depending on how you measured the route, at least a three-hour drive, and perhaps more depending on the condition of the road.

He would be a lot happier when they were across the border and safely inside Afghanistan. An *awful* lot could happen in three hours.

9

ART ROOM
NSA HEADQUARTERS
FORT MEADE, MARYLAND
WEDNESDAY, 1925 HOURS EDT

Rubens looked up at the display monitor covering one wall of the
Art Room. At the moment, it was showing the blue-bordered logo
for the National Reconnaissance Office—a green and blue graphic of
the Earth on white, circled by a satellite and its orbit in red.

Rubens yawned. The nap earlier had helped, but he was still dead
on his feet. He hadn't been able to get back to sleep, however. Mullins
had spilled the beans about American operatives in Tajikistan on
C-SPAN, an unconscionable breach of security. Was the guy an idiot,
or did he simply not care? Rubens had gone through the entire speech
twice now. Mullins apparently was grandstanding to get more money
for the companies in his district that manufactured precision lenses
and other parts for spy satellites.

But, while Dushanbe certainly suspected that U.S. operators were
in their territory before, now they *knew*. Rubens had spent the last
couple of hours talking to contacts at the State Department and the
CIA, warning them of the possible political fallout to come.

His people in Tajikistan, Charlie and Ilya, were already on the way
out. Thank God for *that* much, at least. He'd watched until they were

safely across the bridge over the Kafirnigan, then made some phone calls to arrange for the pickup at the Afghanistan-Tajikistan Bridge.

In the meantime, he'd received the word that some preliminary results had come through already from the CF-1 data transmitted that afternoon to Fort Meade from Langley. Despite how tired he was right now, he was eager to see it.

"What do you have for us, Gene?" he asked.

Gene Vanderkamp had come to the NSA from his position at the NRO as a satellite mapping specialist. "Our first pass, Mr. Rubens. As you directed, we concentrated our efforts on certain limited areas. But we've turned up something interesting."

"Let's see."

Vanderkamp used a handheld remote to click the image on the wall, which flashed from the logo to satellite imagery of a huge swath of central Asia, from the dark-brown and glacier-white crinkle of the Pamir-Alai Mountains running east-west north of Dushanbe to the flat desert and irrigated fields around Kunduz, in northern Afghanistan.

"It looks like Google Earth," Rubens said, referring to the popular mapping program available on the Internet.

"Yeah, but we can do things with CF-1 those guys can only dream about."

"I know." The image data was layered in such a way that an analyst could pick any area within the reconnaissance sweep and zoom in on it, revealing progressively more detail and higher resolution. It was the answer to American military leaders who'd wanted a surveillance system that could cover all of Iraq, a region twice the size of the state of Idaho. It required massively parallel computing power to process the imagery on the fly, but that was something at which the NSA's computer center excelled.

Vanderkamp began zooming in on the landscape spread out across the display, using a click-and-drag box to highlight an area, then enlarge it. He was focusing on a region halfway between Dushanbe and the Afghanistan border, near the city of Qurghonteppa. The area as seen from space was intensely green, well watered, and covered with cotton fields. Cotton, Rubens knew, a crop known as "white gold" in this region, had made it one of the more prosperous areas of Tajikistan. The chief opposition party to the current Tajik government was centered in Qurghonteppa—formerly known as Kurgan-Tyube—the third-largest city in the country.

"Where is it?" Vanderkamp said, moving the view around. "Ah! There . . ."

Rubens found himself looking at a helicopter, an NH90 TTH, flying south above the cotton fields. The detail and clarity were amazing. As Vanderkamp zoomed in on the aircraft, Rubens could see the faces of the pilot and copilot behind the bubble canopy, the four blades of the main rotor frozen in midflight with almost no blurring.

A roundel was clearly visible on the helicopter's tail rotor boom, a red ring around a white, with a blue center.

As Rubens realized exactly what he was seeing, his eyes widened. "Son of a bitch!" he said.

NEAR DUSTI,
SOUTHERN TAJIKISTAN
THURSDAY, 0710 HOURS LOCAL TIME

Dean had traded places with Akulinin half an hour ago and was sitting now in the Hunter's front passenger seat, watching the landscape pass. The land around them had flattened out a lot since they'd crossed the Vakhsh River above Qurghonteppa, leaving the A384 and picking up another major highway following the river toward the Afghan border.

They'd passed through Kolkhozabad well after sunrise. The fertile valley of the Vakhsh River was a good twelve to fifteen miles across at this point, walled in between low and barren hills and endless stretches of wasteland. Gora Kyzimchak was the highest mountain visible to the west, and it was a mere twelve hundred feet higher than the river below, a slight elevation on the horizon fifteen miles distant. After the soaring towers of the Pamirs north of Dushanbe, the landscape felt eerily like the southern portions of the American Midwest—the cotton fields of Oklahoma, perhaps.

The border, he estimated, was less than half an hour ahead.

"We'll have units on hand to pick you up at the bridge," Marie Telach told him over the satellite link. "They're en route from Kunduz now."

"Why couldn't they just slip in and pick us up inside Tajikistan?" Akulinin wanted to know. "I know they can't get into Ayni, but a helicopter could set down anywhere in these fields. We could've been at the hotel in Kunduz by now."

"We tried," Marie told them, "but there've been . . . diplomatic complications."

"What complications?" Dean asked. "Not our little party in Dushanbe last night, surely."

"That's a part of it," Marie admitted. "Tensions right now are running *very* high with Russia, Tajikistan, *and* India."

"I thought we were blaming it all on Pakistani terrorists," Dean said.

"Yes, and right now Pakistan isn't real pleased with us, either. It wasn't you guys. A few hours ago, a member of the House Armed Services Committee made a speech in which he mentioned that the U.S. has intelligence personnel on the ground in Tajikistan, searching for stolen nuclear weapons. It was broadcast over C-SPAN, so of course the Russians saw it. They put two and two together . . ."

"Shit," Dean said.

Putting two and two together was what most intelligence work was all about. Seemingly innocuous bits of information from disparate sources—a TV news show here, a newspaper story there, an informant from someplace else—allowed intelligence analysts at Langley, Fort Meade, and Lubyanka Square in Moscow to piece together a much larger, much more detailed picture of what was going on. The shoot-out in downtown Dushanbe, the disappearance of a former American citizen from the hospital, the burgling of an FSB officer's safe at Ayni, and the theft of documents relating to stolen and smuggled nuclear weapons . . .

Yeah, put all of that together with a politician shooting off his mouth on-camera about a covert U.S. operation to find those nukes, and it became quite easy for the opposition to connect the dots. Worse, though, was the knowledge that the Art Room's disinformation campaign would swiftly unravel now. Analysts at the FSB headquarters at Lubyanka would consider it *very* unlikely that American operators in Tajikistan would make a run for the northern border. Islamic terrorists, Pakistani agents . . . sure, they might well be fleeing north to link up with other Islamist underground groups in Uzbekistan or Kazakhstan, but Americans would be headed south. Dushanbe was only about a hundred miles north of the Afghanistan border, a country at least nominally under American and NATO military control.

That was where the FSB would concentrate its efforts to stop them.

ART ROOM
NSA HEADQUARTERS
FORT MEADE, MARYLAND
WEDNESDAY, 2225 HOURS EDT

"You *really* should go home and get some sleep, sir," Marie Telach told him. "You've been on your feet for . . . how long? Almost forty hours straight?"

Rubens frowned at her. "I had a nap earlier, Marie. And I want to see the boys out of Tajikistan. I notice *you're* still here."

"I'm working late tonight."

"Well, then . . ."

She nodded and looked up at the big screen. The CF-1 imagery had been replaced by a detailed color map of Tajikistan, an image also based on satellite photos. A green square marked the position of the Hunter as Dean and Akulinin drove south, plotted by satellite triangulation of the signals from their communicators. Red squares for ground units and triangles for air units swarmed behind them to the north, each accompanied by a small line of alphanumerics identifying it.

The aircraft were being pegged by an AWACS E-3 Sentry flying north of Kabul.

Technically, that Sentry was flagged as an aircraft from Luxembourg, the one NATO member with no air force of its own. The twenty people on board, however, were U.S. Air Force personnel serving with NATO. The Pulse-Doppler radar within the rotating thirty-foot saucer mounted above the fuselage could pick out aircraft at low altitudes as distant as 250 miles—as far north as Dushanbe. With Pulse (BTH) beyond-the-horizon radar, they could spot aircraft at medium to high altitude all the way out to four hundred miles, almost all the way to Tashkent, in Kazakhstan.

The ground targets were being identified by radio and cell phone signals intercepted by SIGINT satellites, passed through the NSA's Torricelli Computer Center, then routed through the Signals Analysis Department. Those positions could only be updated when the vehicle in question called in, but there was a *lot* of chatter over the military and police channels in Tajikistan right now, and it was clear that nearly the entire swarm of vehicles was headed south, converging on the new bridge spanning the Panj River.

"What are those?" Rubens asked, pointing at a close-spaced pair of triangles south of Kolkhozabad. They were the two pursuers closest to the Hunter's current position, just south of the town of Dusti.

"Two Hip-Cs," Telach told him. "Out of Ayni. FSB registries."

They were less than fifteen miles out from the Hunter.

"Patch me through to Dean and Akulinin," he told her.

"Yes, sir."

This was going to be damned close.

SOUTH OF DUSTI,
SOUTHERN TAJIKISTAN
THURSDAY, 0731 HOURS LOCAL TIME

"Charlie? This is Rubens."

"Yes, sir."

"You might want to keep a close eye on your six. We're picking up two Hips coming after you. Range twelve miles. Speed . . . a hundred and twenty knots."

Dean scowled as he turned in his seat, looking out the passenger window at the northern horizon. At a speed of about 140 miles per hour across twelve miles, those helicopters would catch up in something like five minutes, even allowing for the Hunter's high-speed bump-and-jolt down the road.

They'd turned off the main highway in the town of Dusti, less than five miles north of the Panj River and Afghanistan. Their course, however, kept jogging from one narrow dirt road to another as they zigzagged past canals and cotton fields. The river now was just two miles south; the bridge, however, according to the map-readers back at the Art Room, was about eight miles ahead, toward the southwest.

Dean ran the math through his head. The helicopters would catch them long before they could make it across the river.

It wasn't as though they could blend in with the local traffic, either. For the past hour, there'd *been* no traffic. Their pursuers would have a description of the car by now, maybe even a license number, depending on how on-the-ball those guards back at the Kafirnigan bridge had been.

"Turn here," Dean said, pointing. "Left!"

"What are you doing, Charlie?" Telach demanded. "That's not the quickest way to the bridge!"

"We're not going to *make* it to the bridge," Dean snapped back.

"I see what he's trying to do," Rubens added. "Recalculate for him."

"How deep is the river here?" Dean asked. "And how wide?"

"Depth varies with the season," Telach said. "Right now . . . it's about thirty yards wide, around five . . . maybe ten feet deep."

"Masha?" Dean called back to her. "We're going to have to ford a river up here on foot. It might be five or ten feet deep in places, and we'll need to swim. You okay with that?"

"Charlie . . . Ilya . . . *I can't swim!*"

Damn, damn, *damn!*

"You're coming up on a bridge over an irrigation ditch," Telach said.

"I see it," Akulinin replied.

"There's a dirt road on the left just beyond. Take it."

"Right."

"Masha," Dean continued, "you'll have to trust us. We'll work out a way to float you across. Ilya will swim with you. You'll be okay, so long as you don't panic."

"*Float* me? But . . . but . . . we don't have a raft or anything like a life preserver or—"

"*Trust us.*" He scanned the sky behind for the helicopters again, then turned and searched the landscape closer at hand for any type of cover at all. The land here was utterly flat, checkered with fields of cotton, crisscrossed by canals and irrigation ditches.

Even above the roar of the engine, Dean could now hear a faint fluttering sound in the air. Turning in his seat again, he could see the helicopters, two tiny specks just above the horizon to the northeast.

If he could see them, they could see the Hunter. Dean pulled one of the AKM assault rifles they'd taken from the guards at the Ayni tower from the backseat and clicked off the safety. It was possible that the pilots of those Hips would miss seeing the Hunter this far off the main road—it looked like they might be following the highway, in fact but he wasn't going to count on that. The car had been leaving a billowing dust trail since turning off the paved road, and that would make them stand out like a roach on a dinner plate.

"There's the river," Akulinin said. "Ahead and on the left."

"Great!" Dean said. "Get as close to the river as you can manage."

"Right!"

Akulinin swerved sharply left, sending the Hunter off the road and bouncing across a field of cotton plants. Dean lost sight of the helicopters and had to lean far out of the passenger-side window to spot them again. They were closer—and showing a narrower aspect. They'd spotted the car and were headed directly toward them.

"Stop here, Ilya," Dean said. "Everybody out! Bring the briefcase and the black bag."

"And both rifles," Akulinin said. "I think we're going to need them!"

The three of them jogged through the rows of cotton plants, crouched low. Dean could see the water now, less than fifty yards ahead. The flutter in the air was much louder, a thrumming buzz swelling to a pounding *whop-whop-whop* as the helicopters drew closer.

An irrigation canal opened up in front of them, cement walled, three feet deep, a couple of yards wide. *"Into the ditch!"*

A thundering chatter sounded behind them, clearly audible above the pounding of the rotors. Dean turned and looked back; one of the helicopters was hovering a hundred yards from the abandoned car. A door gunner behind a side-mounted 7.62 mm PK machine gun was hammering the Hunter, sending sprays of shattering glass exploding into the air. After a few moments, the gunner began sweeping the cotton plants around the car with gunfire. The other helicopter hung farther back, perhaps half a mile away.

"Reconnaissance by fire," Dean said. "They haven't seen us, don't know we're here. C'mon. Stay low . . . as low as you can get!"

Single file, they made their way down the canal, heading for the river. The water was cold, the bottom thick with mud.

"Okay," Dean told them, calling a halt. "Ilya? You know how to use your trousers as a float."

"Yeah, but we don't have rope."

"Use the antenna wire in my belt." He unbuckled his belt and began pulling it free from the loops. "Art Room!" he called, before the short-range radio link between his implant and the belt transceiver was lost. "I'm going off the air!"

"Charlie!" Marie called. "Wait! What are—"

Then the signal was lost.

Akulinin blinked. Without his belt, Dean was out of communication with the Art Room. Then he nodded, took Dean's belt, and, using a pocket knife, began slitting a seam in the leather, revealing the copper-colored antenna wire inside. Dean started shucking off his uniform trousers.

"What . . . what is this for?" Masha asked.

"Old survival trick," Dean told her. "Ilya will take these pants—they're a fine-mesh cotton fabric—and wire the openings at the ankles shut, tight as he can make them. You two wade out into the water. He slaps the pants onto the surface, waist-down and open, and it traps air in both legs. You stick your head and arms between the legs, and the pants become a life preserver."

"My head between the legs? It sounds like a compromising position."

She was clearly scared, her voice shaking, but if she could make a joke like that, she was a lot tougher than she looked.

"Yeah, but it'll keep you afloat. You hold tight to the waistband, keep it underwater and pointed down, understand? Ilya will be right there beside you to keep you steady, keep you from capsizing it, okay?"

"Yes . . . but where will you be?"

He jerked a thumb over his shoulder. "Those guys are going to figure out that we're not near the car any second now. I'm going to give them something else to focus on. With luck, they won't spot you on the river."

"Charlie—" Akulinin said.

Dean cut him off. "You take care of Masha . . . and get that briefcase back to the Art Room, no matter *what* happens."

"I don't think it's watertight."

"Doesn't matter. Paper dries, and there's that CD in there. Ditch the weapons and the black bag gear in the river, but get that briefcase back to Fort Meade."

"But—"

"*Do it!*"

Akulinin didn't look happy, but he nodded. "Here." He handed Dean an extra magazine for the AKM.

"Thanks. Now get the hell out of here."

Akulinin and Alekseyevna turned away and kept moving toward the river. Dean watched them go for a moment, then reversed direction and started heading back toward the north, following the canal when it took a ninety-degree jog to the right. When he chanced a peek above the edge of the canal, he saw the helicopter was moving off, now, its rotor wash flattening cotton plants in a broad footprint beneath the aircraft. The second helicopter had turned and was drawing closer now as well.

Dean kept moving, running now, bent nearly double as he splashed up the canal in his shirt and briefs, putting as much distance between himself and the others as he could. These canals and ditches ran for miles across the flat riverbed terrain, but he only needed to move about a hundred yards to give Ilya and Masha some breathing space.

He heard the hammer of a machine gun again and chanced another peek. The first helicopter was probing another patch of cotton plants, trying to flush the fugitives into the open.

This should be far enough. Dean stopped, leaned against the side of the ditch, and took aim just above the nearest line of cotton plants. The Hip was broadside on from this angle, the left-side cabin door wide open, the gunner clearly visible at the door-mounted gun. Carefully, Dean thumbed his weapon's selector switch from full auto to single shot and took aim.

Once, in a different lifetime long before the NSA and Desk Three, Dean had been a Marine sniper—one shot, one kill. He still kept his skills honed at the Fort Meade weapons range and during training sessions at the Farm.

It was impossible to judge the windage caused by the down-blast of the helicopter's rotors, but the target was only, he estimated, two hundred yards away. He popped up the rear sight. He much preferred the AKM's sighting assembly to that of the older AK-47. The rear sight was graduated to 1,000 meters in 200-meter increments, and the front sight was narrower, more easily positioned in the sight picture. He brought the gunner onto the 200-meter line on the range scale, then raised the weapon just a touch to allow for the rotor wash. He took a breath, released part of it . . . held . . . and squeezed.

The assault rifle fired, a single short, sharp crack, the recoil slamming the butt back against his shoulder. On the helicopter, the gunner jerked to one side but remained behind the gun. Either he was strapped in—or else Dean hadn't allowed enough for the wash, and the man was reacting to the snap of a bullet close by. He took aim again, following as the aircraft dropped its nose and began to break out of its hover, and got off a second shot.

Then the helicopter was roaring off into the distance. Whether he'd killed the gunner, wounded him, or just scared the crap out of him didn't really matter so far as Dean was concerned.

The other aircraft was moving toward him, nose-on.

Dean ducked back into the canal and started splashing toward the east again. The opposition probably didn't have a clear idea of where he was yet, not unless one of the pilots had happened to see the muzzle flash. A moment later, the oncoming Hip thundered across the canal less than a hundred yards straight ahead. Dean ducked and felt the fringe of the rotor wash sweep over him. The helicopter banked to the left and started to circle.

Had they seen him? Or had they spotted the canal and were circling around to check it out? Either way, Dean needed to get out of the water and hide himself among the cotton plants nearby.

The crop was upland cotton, the most common commercial variety, and was growing a little more than a yard high at this time of the season, with green leaves and no white bolls as yet. By lying flat on his belly, Dean could stay fairly well hidden, at least until they got *very* close.

The helicopter swung back around, coming to a hover directly above the canal sixty yards ahead. A machine gun barked, and a line of geysers spouted up the canal. Then the aircraft moved ahead, probably relying on the military axiom that a moving target was harder to hit.

Dean weighed his options. If he stayed on dry land, he would have to crawl on his belly to stay out of sight. In the water, he could travel a lot farther, a lot faster.

It seemed like a no-brainer.

Rolling back into the canal, he started wading toward the east once more. He could hear both helicopters off to his left and behind him.

Behind him. He turned in time to see one of the aircraft following him right up the canal, coming in low, less than ten feet off the ground. The Hip slewed sharply, bringing its open side hatch into view, the gunner crouching behind his weapon.

Dean exploded out of the water, diving onto the land and scrambling forward just as the PK gunner opened up, sending another line of geysering splashes up the canal. Still firing, the machine-gunner swung his aim away from the canal, firing into the cotton plants above the water.

Rotor wash whipped and slashed at the cotton plants, destroying Dean's cover. Rolling onto his back, he snapped the selector switch to full auto and brought the rifle to his shoulder, aiming into the open cabin door as he clamped down on the trigger.

The AKM thundered in his grip, and he saw ricochets spark from the cargo deck's interior, on the overhead. Still firing, he dragged his aim down, saw the gunner leaning against his PK as he brought the weapon into line with Dean . . . then saw the gunner jerk and twist in his harness as Dean's volley struck home.

He shifted aim to the helicopter's cockpit . . . then remembered how the windscreen of the Hip he'd seen at Ayni had deflected gunfire aimed at it, and shifted his aim higher. Hips were well-armored, but there were vulnerable spots at access hatches in the engine fairings, and the rotor head offered a number of exposed targets—blade pitch control rods, swashplate mechanisms, hydraulic drag dampers, and the reduction gearbox.

He squeezed the trigger again and kept squeezing, draining his magazine in one long volley lasting perhaps two seconds. The AKM ran dry; he dropped the spent magazine, slapped in the spare Ilya had given him, and took aim again.

The Hip was already turning away, though, stumbling in flight as smoke billowed from the rotor head. He could hear the grinding in the rotor mechanism; he'd hit something important. The pilot was attempting to set the aircraft down in the field before he lost control entirely.

Dean broke and ran then, leaping the canal and racing south toward the river. Hip-Cs like these two were primarily used as troop transports, and the odds were good that there were a number of soldiers on both. In a few moments, this field was going to be swarming with twenty or more very angry Russian FSB troops.

Dean wanted to be as far away as possible when that happened.

10

Akulinin's voice was coming over the speaker in the Art Room's ceiling. "Keep going! Kick, Masha! *Kick!*"

They heard the splashing, heard Akulinin's gasps as he breathed between shouted encouragements.

"Ilya!" they heard a woman's voice call, ragged with terror. "Don't leave me!"

"I'm right . . . here! You're doing . . . fine!"

In the distance, they could hear the helicopters.

"I wish we could see," Marie Telach said. On the large display, zoomed in now to show only the area near the Panj River a few miles upstream from the bridge, a single green icon slowly moved in the middle of the river. Two red triangles showed just to the north and farther upstream.

That's where Charlie Dean is right now, Rubens thought. "How long before support gets there?" he asked.

"NATO One-Three is five minutes out," Vic Klein said. "Delta Green One is eight minutes."

NATO One-Three was a flight of German Tornado combat aircraft with Tactical Reconnaissance Wing 51 "Immelmann," deployed to Afghanistan as a part of the NATO force there. Delta Green One was the rescue helo out of Kabul.

"Just . . . hang on to . . . the pants," Akulinin's voice said. "We're—" The voice was lost in a burst of static. Then, "Relax . . . keep kicking . . ."

Radio signals from the implant transceiver were blocked by just a foot or so of water. As long as Akulinin was floating or swimming on the surface, enough of the antenna in the belt around his waist was close enough to the surface that they could still pick up his signal. But every once in a while, he let his legs sink as he either treaded water or stood on the bottom, trying to keep Alekseyevna from floundering.

". . . pants . . . losing . . . air!"

"It's okay . . . almost across . . . I've got you . . ."

This, Rubens thought, *is the worst part of this job. Knowing what they're going through over there. Not able to do a damned thing to help . . .*

"We just lost one of the Hip-Cs," Telach reported. On the screen, one of the two red triangles had winked out. It might have crashed—or it might have simply landed. There was no way the E-3 Sentry's radar could distinguish between the two.

"We have more hostiles inbound," Klein added. "That stretch of riverbank is becoming a war zone."

NORTH BANK OF THE PANJ RIVER
SOUTHERN TAJIKISTAN
THURSDAY, 0807 HOURS LOCAL TIME

Cautiously, Charlie Dean raised his head. One Hip-C had just set down in the cotton field, smoke streaming from its engines and rotor head. The other hovered a few hundred yards off. The rear ramp on the grounded aircraft was open, and Russian soldiers were spilling out.

There was no sense in getting into a firefight with these people. They were unlikely to be willing to cross the river, but they would be beating through the fields looking for him very soon now.

The river was fifty yards to Dean's back. It was time to leave beautiful, mountainous Tajikistan and see what the climate was like south of the Panj.

He turned away and crawled.

KOWL-E BAZANGI
NORTHERN AFGHANISTAN
THURSDAY, 0808 HOURS LOCAL TIME

Gasping for breath, Ilya Akulinin struggled forward, felt mud beneath his feet, and almost shouted his triumph. He had one arm around Masha, who still clung desperately to the half-inflated uniform trousers.

"I feel the bottom, Masha! We made it!"

Masha choked and spat water, then dragged in a ragged lungful of air. Too exhausted to reply, she managed a nod, however, and began kicking even harder.

As they'd entered the river on the other side, Akulinin had pulled his own belt out of his trousers and threaded it through the handle of the briefcase, bucking it to create a loop that he'd slung over his head and one shoulder. The briefcase had floated at first, but about two-thirds of the way across it had begun to fill with river water and now dragged against his neck as it tried to sink. Akulinin stumbled a few feet farther toward the south bank, then held Masha with one arm as he pulled the belt off again and began dragging the half-sunken brief-case behind him.

He'd dropped the black bag with its high-tech burglary kit and the AKM in the river once he'd had to stop wading and start swimming. Masha tried to stand now, thrashing in the water. He reached under her arm and hauled her up and forward, dragging her the last few steps onto the muddy riverbank.

"This is a hell of a way to teach someone to swim," she said.

"Sink or swim," he told her. "It's the only way."

The two of them dropped onto the bank, trying to catch their breath. Akulinin looked back across the river, toward the flat green cotton fields beyond, looking for Charlie Dean, knowing he wouldn't be able to see him.

One helicopter appeared to have landed, but the other was hovering motionless perhaps four hundred yards to the north, its nose aimed directly at the two of them on the south side of the river.

Then the aircraft's nose dipped slightly, and it began to move, flying directly toward them.

"Come on!" he shouted, grabbing the woman's arm. *"Run!"*

APPROACHING THE PANJ RIVER
SOUTHERN TAJIKISTAN
THURSDAY, 0809 HOURS LOCAL TIME

"Sir! There they are!"

The FSB sergeant pointed over the pilot's shoulder, and Lieutenant Colonel Vasilyev raised his binoculars, studying the swampy area just beyond the river. He could see two people at the water's edge, stumbling through the waist-high marsh grass.

Vasilyev slapped the pilot's shoulder. "Move across the river!" he ordered. "We will put troops down to encircle the bastards!"

"Sir! That's Afghanistan over there!"

"Don't give me a damned political lecture! Just fucking do it!"

The helicopter roared south across the Panj.

NORTH BANK OF THE PANJ RIVER
SOUTHERN TAJIKISTAN
THURSDAY, 0809 HOURS LOCAL TIME

"No!" Dean shouted. *"No, you bastards!"*

The airborne helicopter was in motion now . . . not toward Dean, off to the east, but toward the south, toward the Panj River and his friends on the south bank. From here he could see them, two tiny, dark figures at the water's edge.

Kneeling, he raised his AKM and opened fire, sending a long volley toward the Hip-C, continuing to fire until the weapon clicked empty. So far as he could see, he hadn't even hit the aircraft.

He heard bursts of full-auto gunfire, heard the crack of rounds snapping above his head. The troops on the ground were closing in, firing as they moved.

His weapon empty, he dropped it and sprinted toward the river.

The Russian helicopter continued flying south, roaring low over the river, crossing the border into Afghanistan. The Russians were risking an international incident to capture two fugitives.

But . . . why not? This stretch of ground south of the looping, twisting Panj was a desolate wilderness of marshes, bogs, and lakes called the Kowl-e Barzangi. The International Bridge and the village of Shir Khan were a good six or eight miles downriver. The nearest built-up area was the district capital of Kunduz, almost forty miles to the south.

He saw the helicopter in the distance pass low above the running figures, swing around, and settle toward the ground two hundred yards inside of Afghan territory.

KOWL-E BARZANGI
NORTHERN AFGHANISTAN
THURSDAY, 0809 HOURS LOCAL TIME

The Hip-C roared low overhead, its rotor wash slashing at the two of them as they ran. "Down!" Akulinin yelled, and they flopped forward onto the muddy ground. The helicopter slowed, drifting sideways as it turned thirty yards away. Akulinin could see the door gunner standing in the open door just behind the cockpit. The man was actually *grinning* as he pointed at them, calling something to others in the cabin. The ramp in the rear of the fuselage was coming down.

Akulin could read the aircraft registry number on the tail boom, 10450, white numerals outlined in red. The same Hip that had brought the bodies of Zhern and the other two to Ayni. He wondered if Vasilyev was on board.

The first Russian soldiers jumped from the open ramp.

"This way," Akulinin told Masha. If they ran east, trying to work their way around the front of the aircraft, they might be able to stay ahead of the ground troops, at least for a time. If whoever was in command over there was smart, though, he would order the Hip to drop off a few troops at several points in an arc, surrounding them.

Akulinin had never felt so helpless. They had no weapons—not even the Makarov pistols that had originally been issued to him and Dean. Those were back in the abandoned car, an added encumbrance better abandoned at the time.

Capture, he knew, would mean savage beatings and interrogation and imprisonment for both of them, probably rape for Masha, *and he couldn't do a damned thing to stop them . . .*

NORTH BANK OF THE PANJ RIVER
SOUTHERN TAJIKISTAN
THURSDAY, 0809 HOURS LOCAL TIME

Bullets slapped and cracked around him, but Dean kept running, bare, muddy legs pumping as he raced flat out for the river. He reached the bank and kept going, launching himself flat through the air, arms extended, hitting the water in a shallow dive as the soldiers ran after him across the field.

He surfaced swimming. He could hear shouts and gunfire behind him, but he focused all his strength on the swim, all of his attention on the southern bank thirty yards away.

KOWL-E BARZANGI
NORTHERN AFGHANISTAN
THURSDAY, 0809 HOURS LOCAL TIME

"Ilya! I can't go any farther!"

"We've got to! Now *move!*"

The ground was soft and uneven, thick with marsh grass and difficult to walk on, much less run. Akulinin turned his head in time to see the Hip lifting up off the ground, leaving behind four soldiers who were making their uneven way across the marsh toward them. The helicopter drifted forward, searching for another place to set down, a place where the fugitives' flight could be boxed in.

Maybe if they doubled back toward the river . . .

The explosion staggered Akulinin and drove Masha to the ground, a thunderous crash and a ball of orange flame erupting from the helicopter's engine compartment and boiling into the early morning sky. The aircraft jerked sideways, and the rotors snapped free, pinwheeling across the marsh directly toward Akulinin and Masha. Both ducked low and felt the breath of the hurtling blades rush overhead. The Hip slewed wildly and slammed belly-down into the ground. Akulinin caught the harsh stink of jet fuel as the aircraft's fuel tanks exploded, sending a second shock wave racing across the marsh.

"Yeah, you bastards!" Akulinin shouted.

Moments later, a shrill roar sounded overhead as two jet fighters banked sharply above the swamp. He could make out the Iron Cross on the wings—German Tornados.

And as the Tornados' thunder dwindled into the distance, Akulinin heard another sound: the fluttering clatter of a large helicopter in the distance. This one sounded like it was coming from the south, however, not from the north.

Slowly, he raised himself into a crouch, holding the draining briefcase, the looped belt still hanging from the handle. He looked for the Russian troopers on the ground, but saw no one. The wreckage of the Hip was close to where he had last seen them. Maybe the crash and explosion had killed or injured them. Maybe they were crawling for the river . . .

"Ilya?" Marie's voice called in his head. "Ilya, do you copy? Are you okay?"

"Yeah," he managed to say. "Not sure how . . ."

"Two NATO aircraft are in your area now. Do you see them?"

"They've been and gone. I hear a helicopter now."

"That's Delta Green One on SAR. They're coming to get you out. But stay alert. We're tracking more hostiles north of you."

"Copy that," Akulinin said. He helped Masha get to her feet.

They had to get clear of the smoke from the burning wreckage, so the SAR chopper could see them.

"It's okay, hon," he told her. "We're going home."

PANJ RIVER
NORTHERN AFGHANISTAN
THURSDAY, 0810 HOURS LOCAL TIME

Dean dove beneath the surface as bullets struck the river around him. Submerged, he could hear the sharp chirp of the rounds striking the water to left and right, but he kept swimming, holding his breath for as long as he could, holding it until he thought his lungs would explode with the effort, then surfacing again with a gasp.

Gunfire cracked and chattered from the northern bank. He felt mud beneath his knees and hands, felt the riverbed rising to meet him. Blinking, he could see the south bank just a few yards ahead—and he could see a billowing column of smoke, a *lot* of oily black smoke staining the bright blue of the sky.

He didn't dare try to climb the bank. The soldiers were only thirty yards away; several, he saw, had taken a few steps into the river, firing at him wildly. One pulled out a grenade, yanked the pin, and hurled it at him. Dean ducked beneath the water and swam hard; the concussion from the grenade struck him a few seconds later, slamming his chest and his lungs.

He surfaced, gulping air as spouts of water splashed nearby. Submerging again, he swam with the current, letting the flow carry him underwater, dragging him downriver. If necessary, he thought, he could drift with the river for as long as it took to reach Shir Khan, sticking his head up only to grab a quick breath when he couldn't hold it any longer.

He was exhausted already, though, and not sure he could keep moving for that long. Besides, while the Russians across the river appeared to be appallingly bad shots, they might well get lucky—or decide to swim across themselves and pick him up.

He surfaced again, gulping down air. He could hear thunder in the sky. *More aircraft*, he thought, *coming out of the north*.

Great. What now?

The aircraft, two of them flying low and wingtip to wingtip, howled overhead. Dean had just a glimpse of the gray shapes—twin-tailed Russian MiG-29 Fulcrums—but then he blinked and almost yelled out loud because he'd caught just a glimpse of the red, white, and green roundels on the undersides of the wings.

Not Russian! *Indian!* Those MiGs must be patrol aircraft out of either Ayni or, more likely, Farkhor, off to the southwest.

The jets banked above the Panj, circling back to the north. The Russian troops on the northern bank watched them for a moment, then appeared to arrive at a consensus, turning away from the river and jogging back into the cotton fields beyond.

After a moment, Dean crawled out of the water. North, he could see more Russian soldiers, but they appeared to be converging on the downed Hip, the manhunt forgotten.

South, the second Russian helicopter burned in the marsh, while two more jet aircraft made a thundering turn in the sky. He began walking.

Five minutes later, he caught up with Akulinin and Maria Alekseyevna.

"Charlie!" Ilya cried. "You made it!"

A helicopter, a ponderous U.S. Air Force HH-53 Super Jolly, was approaching from the south, easing its way toward the pillar of black smoke.

"Where the hell are my pants?" Dean asked his partner.

NSA HEADQUARTERS
FORT MEADE, MARYLAND
WEDNESDAY, 2312 HOURS EDT

"Delta Green One reports three people on board," Marie Telach said. The stress in the Art Room over the past few moments had been twanging tight. She sounded utterly drained now.

"That's good," Rubens said, nodding. "That's good."

"They are en route now and will be in Kunduz within half an hour."

"I think," Rubens said, "they can make it the rest of the way on their own. I'm going home to bed. I suggest you do the same."

"Sounds like a great idea, sir."

"Before you go, please convey my thanks to the commander of NATO's German contingent. I know they didn't want to engage."

But they had. Thank God.

Although it was widely seen as an American war, Afghanistan was NATO's first combat deployment outside of Europe.

Since December of 2001, the North Atlantic Treaty Alliance had forces in Afghanistan. The embattled country had been divided into quarters. Although a number of NATO nations shared the responsibilities for each sector, and some commands rotated among several nations, the United States had the primary responsibility for the southeast, Canada for the southwest, Italy for the northwest, and Germany for the northeast, including the district of Kunduz. A fifth zone had been established around the capital of Kabul, with primary jurisdiction there belonging to the French.

In the late summer of 2009, German troops at Kunduz, thirty-seven miles south of Afghanistan's northern border, had spotted two NATO fuel tanker trucks recently hijacked by Taliban insurgents. They'd called in an air strike, and a U.S. fighter had been vectored in, destroying both trucks. Ninety people had been killed.

Unfortunately, at least forty of those killed had been civilians—a fuzzy distinction, perhaps, in an insurgency where a Taliban fighter could simply drop his rifle and become an instant civilian . . . but there'd been kids among the dead as well. New rules of engagement had immediately been clamped into place, further hampering the U.S. and NATO troops in Afghanistan. There'd been a lot of recriminations in Germany over the incident and elsewhere in Europe as well, questions about what NATO was doing fighting a war so far from Europe.

The Immelmann squadron commander had not been eager to engage Russian helicopters on the northern border, and it had taken a phone call by Rubens to the four-star U.S. general in command of the entire NATO force structure in Afghanistan to get a pair of Tornado fighter-bombers airborne. At that, the Germans had announced that they would *not* engage unless foreign troops actually crossed the border. Rubens was just glad that they'd decided to follow through. The Germans might yet have waffled or insisted on getting repeated confirmations of their orders. He knew, though, that those German pilots maintained their long-established tradition of hating Russians, *especially* the FSB successors of the old KGB, and suspected that that might have tipped the balance once the Hip-C had crossed into Afghan airspace.

Now NATO and the United States had a genuine border incident on their hands. Russia was going to be furious—but at least now the shooting would take place at embassies and, perhaps, at the United Nations.

At least Dean and Akulinin were safe.

And Rubens, finally, could go home and get some long-overdue sleep.

Except . . .

He looked at his watch, then at the line of clocks on the wall. Almost midnight—but there was one final task that *had* to be done. "Marie? I want a private channel to Mr. Akulinin."

DELTA GREEN ONE
NORTHERN AFGHANISTAN
THURSDAY, 0830 HOURS LOCAL TIME

Ilya Akulinin slumped back in the hard, narrow seat of the Jolly Green, letting the tension, the stress, the fear all fall away, leaving behind only exhaustion. *We made it!* His arm was around Masha's shoulders, and she smiled as he pulled her a bit closer. Charlie Dean sat across the aisle from them, head slumped back, eyes closed. The helo's crew chief had given the three of them blankets and scalding coffee from a thermos. Real lifesavers . . .

"Ilya?" Marie's voice said in his ear. "I'm switching you to a private channel."

"Uh . . . right . . ."

"*Mister* Akulinin," Rubens' voice said a moment later. "Does the word 'tradecraft' mean anything to you?"

Here it comes, Akulinin thought. He'd been expecting this . . . though perhaps not so soon. "Yes, sir," he said. "It refers to—"

"What about the word 'professional?'" Rubens said, interrupting. "I ask merely so that I can be sure you and I are speaking the same language."

Akulinin straightened up, his arm sliding out from behind Masha. She looked at him curiously, and he gave her what he hoped was a reassuring smile.

"Yes, sir."

"You violated tradecraft protocol when you took it upon yourself to rescue a foreign national during the course of an operation."

"But she's—"

"*Be quiet!*" Rubens shouted in Akulinin's ear. Akulinin didn't think he'd ever heard the old man even raise his voice. The effect was startling. "The mission comes first, Mr. Akulinin. The mission *always* comes first. I thought you learned that on your first day of training. You put the mission in jeopardy when you involved Ms. Alekseyevna. That was a direct violation of tradecraft. You then went to bed with her while you were on a mission, and *that* was a violation of professional ethics."

Akulinin's face burned red. How the hell had Rubens found out about that?

For the next two minutes, Akulinin endured the most intricate, meticulous, and savage ass-chewing he'd ever received. Rubens detailed his shortcomings without a single use of profanity, without even again raising his voice, and left Akulinin feeling as wrung-out as a used dishrag.

The helicopter was approaching Kunduz as Rubens ended the lecture. "If you *ever* pull a stunt as lame-brained and unprofessional as this again," Rubens said, "I *will* find another use for you, one where your reproductive drive is less likely to compromise the mission. Perhaps putting you in charge of an electronic monitoring station in Tierra del Fuego where you'll have penguins for company, or possibly a listening post on the Svalbard Archipelego, would cool you off."

Rubens paused, and Akulinin took the opportunity to say, "Yes, sir. It won't happen again, sir."

Rubens paused, then added, "We will make arrangements to fly Ms. Alekseyevna back to the United States. We will interview her here first, of course, but I'll talk to someone at State to see about checking her citizenship status and taking care of the paperwork."

"*Thank* you, sir."

"Don't thank me. Just keep your mind on the mission . . . and keep your zipper zipped when you're on company time. Rubens out."

Akulinin heard a small click as the private channel flipped back to tactical. He sagged, letting out a long, shaky breath.

"Ilya?" Masha asked, looking worried. "What was that all about? You looked like you were in pain."

"Don't ask, *lubimaya*," he told her. "It's going to be all right."

He didn't put his arm around her shoulders again.

KUNDUZ
NORTHERN AFGHANISTAN
THURSDAY, 1330 HOURS LOCAL TIME

Dean stepped out onto the sandbagged balcony and looked down on
the streets of the city—dusty, dilapidated, and teeming with people.
One of Afghanistan's legendary traffic jams had congealed along the
road leading north into Kunduz, and both drivers and pedestrians
were locked in a confrontation that had all the signs of escalation into
a riot.

He hated this country. He hated this *city*. He'd been here before,
once, a decade ago.

Akulinin joined him on the balcony. Dean's partner had seemed
uncharacteristically subdued when they'd arrived here this morning
but seemed to have perked up a bit since. "What's the ruckus?" he
asked.

"God only knows," Dean replied.

At least now he was wearing pants. From Kunduz Airport, the
three of them were driven to the high-walled compound that served as
ISAF command center for the airport. They'd been issued gray German utilities to replace Akulinin's Russian garb and the remnants of
Dean's IAF uniform. They would stay in an officers' barracks here
overnight, they'd been told, and be airlifted out in the morning.
Masha was in women's quarters on the other side of the compound.

From their vantage point, Dean and Akulinin could look out across
a barren field and see the airstrip simmering in the midday heat, a facility now restricted solely to ISAF and humanitarian flight operations.
North lay the edge of the city. Someone in the street was shrieking
imprecations. German soldiers watched the worsening brawl with wary
eyes at strategic points all around the compound but didn't seem otherwise alarmed. They appeared to be taking the riot in stride.

"Looks like a really bad case of road rage," Akulinin observed.

"Yeah, although they usually keep that kind of thing in check
here," Dean said. "You never know whether or not the guy in the
other car has an RPG in the seat next to him."

"You've been here before?"

"Yeah . . ."

"An op?"

"Not with Desk Three. I worked as a contractor with an independent intelligence service for a while before the Agency tapped me."

"No shit? You were chasing al-Qaeda?"

He nodded. "Partly. That was mostly later. At the start, they had me here in Kunduz." He gave Akulinin a wry grin. "I was here for the Airlift of Evil."

Akulinin gave him a questioning look. "Airlift of Evil? Haven't heard about that one."

"Not too many people know about it," Dean replied. "It's not classified or anything . . . but the government doesn't like to talk about it."

"What is it?"

"November of 2001," Dean told him, leaning forward on the sandbag wall. "Just two months after 9/11. U.S. Special Forces were here supporting the Afghan Northern Alliance. Kunduz was the last major northern city held by the Taliban before the Northern Alliance came out on top. They had the city pretty well surrounded, and we *knew* there were a lot of high-ranking Taliban and al-Qaeda leaders trapped here.

"There were also a number of ISI officers in the area, and Pakistan was going berserk, wanting to get them out."

The ISI was Inter-Services Intelligence, Pakistan's equivalent of the CIA.

"Well, the Bush government didn't want to upset the Pakistani apple cart. Pakistan's president at the time was General Pervez Musharraf. He'd signed on as our ally in the War on Terror—but everyone knew he supported the Taliban. And there were a lot of ISI officers who, if they weren't Taliban or al-Qaeda, sure as hell sympathized with them. The ISI personnel in Kunduz had been actively helping Taliban forces against the Northern Alliance."

"Playing both sides of the game?" Akulinin asked. He shrugged. "Common enough in this part of the world."

"Bush and Cheney didn't want to destabilize Pakistan's government, and it wouldn't help if everyone found out that Pakistan forces had been fighting against U.S. troops and their allies in northern Afghanistan. Vice President Cheney arranged a deal with Musharraf. The Pakistanis could send in aircraft and evacuate his people before the Northern Alliance took the city.

"So two Pakistani transports took off out of Chitral and Gilgit. They flew in and out several times over the course of two nights, while hundreds of refugees gathered on the tarmac right over there." He pointed at the distant airstrip. Turning, he looked across the broken ground to the east, then pointed again. "I was up there in those hills," Dean said, "along with an American Special Forces detachment. We watched, damn it, while those planes came and went and came and went. They got hundreds out, maybe as many as a thousand. They rescued the ISI personnel, yes. They also rescued al-Qaeda and Taliban personnel, including, we think, some of the low numbers on the most-wanted list. Our intelligence work in the region was pretty solid, and we were pretty sure they were there. There were also lots of IMU—the Islamic Movement of Uzbekistan. Jaish-e Mohammad, the Army of Mohammad. Maybe others." He held out his hand, palm open. "We had them right *there*." He clenched his fist. "And then we watched them board those airplanes and fly off to safe havens in Pakistan."

"Shit."

"And catching those human cesspools was *supposed* to be the reason we'd gone into Afghanistan in the first place!" Dean said. "The Taliban rulers of Afghanistan were harboring the people—al-Qaeda—who'd carried out the attacks on the Twin Towers and the Pentagon and murdered three thousand of our citizens. We went in to break the Taliban and to capture or kill the leadership of the fanatics who attacked us. And Pakistan just whisked them away, right out from under our noses. My CO wanted to shoot the planes down, but he couldn't get authorization from Washington. They wouldn't believe him that the bad guys, the guys we'd come here to get, were getting away. Or they didn't care."

"So Musharraf double-crossed us?"

Dean shrugged. "Who knows? It might have been him, or it might have been the upper echelons of the ISI, turning a minor extraction of a few ISI officers into a major airlift. The real question is why Musharraf left his people in the country for so long, until they were surrounded and there was no other way out. Some of our people thought that Pakistani intelligence was running its own war against us, to keep the Taliban in power. They didn't want to get caught—but they also clearly didn't want to leave until the last moment possible.

"We know there were hundreds of ISI personnel in Kunduz at the time. And we know that Musharraf wanted the Taliban to stay in power. The rumor around Washington was that we'd threatened to bomb his country back into the Stone Age if he didn't cooperate. So publicly he joined our side in the War on Terror. Privately, he provided safe havens for al-Qaeda. The ISI still tips off Taliban and al-Qaeda enclaves in Pakistan's Northern Territories every time we prepare to send in a missile strike."

"So . . . it's politics as usual."

"*Politics!*" Dean spat the word like an obscenity. "Yeah. Anyway, one Green Beret officer I was working with called it the Airlift of Evil, and the name kind of stuck."

"Muslims stand up for one another," Akulinin pointed out, "at least when they're not trying to kill each other." The riot in the street was getting louder. More men were streaming in from every direction, some of them with weapons. The local NATO forces appeared to be keeping out of it.

"*Look* at them, Sharkie," Dean said. "Each one absolutely convinced that he is right, that God is solely on his side and speaking to him directly . . . and willing to fight to the death—or kill their neighbors or their own pregnant daughters—rather than accept the slightest stain on what they perceive as their sacred honor."

"Not all Muslims are like that, Charlie," Akulinin replied. "You know that. These people out here are still more attached to their tribe than to any weird-ass notion like nation or civilized behavior. They're still barbarians living in the Dark Ages, for God's sake!"

"The problem is that some of those barbarians have nuclear weapons. And they have all of the restraint, all of the sound judgment, and all of the willingness to compromise of a spoiled-rotten four-year-old throwing a tantrum. Damn it, Sharkie, we *have* to find those nukes. If we don't, then sooner or later whoever has them is going to use them."

Police sirens sounded in the distance, but it was clear that the road into the city would be closed for some time to come.

Dean was glad they were already at the airport, that they would be flying out tomorrow. The time he'd spent in this country years ago had been far more than enough.

GCHQ
YORKSHIRE, ENGLAND
THURSDAY, 0905 HOURS GMT

"Overnight intercept here," Cathy Jamison told her shift supervisor. "Text message, and the sender was red-flagged."

"Who do we have?" George Sotheby accepted the printout from Jamison and scanned through it quickly. Masood Azhar? Yeah, that might be something hot.

The Government Communications Headquarters was the arm of British intelligence tasked with providing SIGINT and information assurance to both the British government and the armed forces. With its major facility located at Menwith Hill in Yorkshire, it was the equivalent of the American NSA. In fact, the two organizations worked so closely together that some critics had suggested that GCHQ was little more than an arm of their American counterpart.

That was far from true, but Sotheby was still sensitive to the charge. "We do a *few* things on our side of the pond," he'd pointed out more than once.

Menwith Hill was, in fact, a colossal ear, a collecting station tuning in to the radio waves bouncing through the atmosphere over

Europe. A part of the old Echelon program, it had originally been designed to eavesdrop on the Soviet Union. Nowadays, though, it often listened in on cell phone calls transmitted by satellite from as far off as China.

Or, in this case, south Asia.

The various Islamic militant groups were getting smarter, more canny, more technologically sophisticated. Most of their cell phone calls nowadays were encrypted. What the Muslim fanatics didn't know was that Menwith's American cousins had cracked their current cipher—and they'd shared the key with GCHQ. The cipher was fairly simple, actually, with a cycling round of verses from the Qur'an. Today's key was Sura 24, Verse 2. "The adulterer and the adulteress, scourge ye each one of them one hundred stripes. And let not pity for the twain withhold you from obedience to Allah, if ye believe in Allah and the last day. And let a party of believers witness their punishment."

The theology of hatred. Scourge the bastards and Allah will reward you.

But type that verse into the cryptological software the NSA had lifted from the mullahs at their madrasah in Karachi, and you could listen in on their conversations with perfect clarity. GCHQ's crypto nabobs had already deciphered and translated this one. He read it.

"Interesting," he said. "So the rag heads are bumping off American novelists now? I wonder what that's all about."

"Hard to say, sir."

He handed the sheet back. "Well, pack it off to Fort Meade, then, there's a good girl."

He'd not heard of al-Wawi, the call's recipient, but Azhar was a bigwig with the Army of Mohammad, and anything from him was flagged and shipped off to the NSA.

Their problem. Not his.

11

They called it the War Room.

It was located next door to the Art Room, smaller, a little more crowded, and it was run by Dr. Frederick Bailey of the NSA's Analysis Department. Where the Art Room focused on maintaining lines of communication with the various Desk Three operators in the field, the War Room concentrated on planning and strategy. An IMAX-sized display screen dominated one curving wall of the room, while large monitors at a dozen workstations showed maps, satellite imagery, and aerial views of target regions worldwide.

Rubens entered the War Room and glanced around at the technicians at their workstations. Vanderkamp and Bailey were standing near the main console, discussing some aspect of the data. The big screen behind them displayed at the moment the CF-1 imagery sent over from Langley the previous afternoon. A six-hour clip of the NATO helicopter Gene Vanderkamp had showed him yesterday had been playing here constantly since then.

The clip showed a helicopter with French markings . . . a helicopter operating under NATO auspices out of Kabul.

And it suggested corruption and betrayal on an almost unimaginable scale.

Crystal Fire used a Molniya orbit, a highly eccentric orbit with a period of twelve hours. The physics of orbital mechanics meant that the satellite, moving more slowly when it was farthest away from Earth than when it was in close, would enjoy what was known as "apogee dwell," meaning that it hung over the same part of the Earth for as long as eight hours at a stretch. Molniya orbits originally had been a Russian invention—the name meant "lightning" in Russian—useful for satellite communications far north of the equator. The United States had been using them for spy satellites ever since the 1960s, however.

The twin mirrors used in Crystal Fire—larger than the mirrors used in the Hubble Space Telescope—provided superb resolution even when they were peering down from over eleven thousand miles overhead. There were certain highly classified constraints and limitations dictated by the atmosphere it was peering through, of course, but the shape of each mirror was adjustable by computer control, allowing an enormous increase in resolving power.

Crystal Fire had been hanging in the sky a bit north of Tajikistan for nearly eight hours, from early Monday morning through late Monday afternoon. Its second pass had taken it over the south Pacific, but the third had repeated the path of the first precisely, beginning before dawn on Tuesday morning and lasting until around noon. The information displayed on the big screen now was actually a compilation from both orbital passes, representing a total of some fourteen hours of observation and an astonishing amount of raw data nested in layers within layers of imagery.

"Good morning, gentlemen," Rubens said, approaching Vanderkamp and Bailey. "What do you have on our NATO friend up there?"

"We have a destination, sir," Bailey told him, "and we've backtracked and spotted the transfer."

"Let me see."

Vanderkamp used a remote to black out the big screen, then open it again. The display showed the NH90 Tactical Transport Helicopter flying low over a cotton field. "We missed the departure out of Kabul," he said, "but we have tail boom numbers on that helicopter, and we know it was assigned to the French NATO contingent operating out of Kabul. French roundels. And we have a list of the crew members. They signed out of Kabul on a training flight at oh six forty on Monday—supposedly Kabul to Kandahar and back. CF-1 first picked them up about an hour and fifteen later. This is just west of Qurghonteppa, in southern Tajikistan. About two hundred and thirty miles. The flight took them an hour and a half."

On the screen, the French helicopter slowed and began drifting toward a patch of dirt road slicing through the cotton field. A red pickup truck was waiting for them.

Vanderkamp used the remote to zoom in on the people waiting for the helicopter on the ground. There were five of them, four of them bearded, wearing turbans, and carrying AKM assault rifles. The resolution was just barely too low to allow the faces to be recognizable.

"We're running the faces through E&I," Bailey said, anticipating Rubens' question. Enhancement and ID used high-tech processing models to attempt to identify faces photographed from orbit. It was an art as much as a science, and, depending on the quality of the image, it was an imprecise and unreliable art at best. "So far all we can say for sure is that they appear to be Muslim fundamentalists."

"How do you know that? You catch them on their prayer rugs?"

"No, but they fit the profile. Beards. Weapons. I suppose they could be anti-Russian guerrillas, but since most of those are Muslim fundamentalists as well—"

"Point taken."

"And you can see what they have in the back of the truck."

The contents of the truck's flatbed were covered with a dark tarp, but one of the men jumped up and began untying it. Under the tarp was a single wooden crate, measuring perhaps five feet tall by five wide and six deep.

"We've calculated the dimensions of that crate," Vanderkamp said. "About a hundred and fifty cubic feet. Easily big enough to hold all twelve suitcase nukes. And the truck and the empty crate appear to match what our people found abandoned at Ayni yesterday."

As Rubens watched, the helicopter touched down fifty feet away. One of the Muslims jumped into the cab of the truck and backed it toward the waiting aircraft. A man in a NATO uniform waved his hands from the open cargo bay, guiding the truck in close. The driver got out of the cab, and then everyone climbed onto the flatbed and began pulling smaller crates out of the big one and passing them along, fire brigade fashion, into the helicopter.

"There are twelve smaller boxes," Barnes said. "If those are in fact the missing suitcase nukes, the whole crate would weigh about fourteen hundred pounds. Well over half a ton."

"I wish we could get a radiation scan on that," Rubens mused.

"Can't do it from space," Vanderkamp told him. "Not unless it's leaking gamma rays."

"I know. That's why we have the teams over there." He frowned. "That man, there." He pointed. "Is he Chinese?" It was tough to tell, even at maximum zoom, but there was something about the roundness of the face . . .

Bailey nodded. "Seventy percent confidence on that, yes, sir. And his clothing . . . and the clothing worn by *this* man . . . and *this* one . . ." Two more men were highlighted on the screen. "They appear to match the clothing on the bodies photographed by Mr. Akulinin in the morgue yesterday."

"Zhern, Shams, and our friend Major Kwok of Chinese intelligence."

Two of the men on the ground climbed off the flatbed and into the helicopter. The other three, the three highlighted on the display by Bailey, got into the truck, which drove off a moment later. The helicopter waited until they were clear, then lifted again into the sky.

Rubens began trying to piece it together. "Okay . . . those three and two others drive the truck all the way here from Stepnogorsk. They transfer the nukes to the helicopter. Zhern, Shams, and Kwok then drive back to Ayni and leave the truck there, where our people find it the next morning. They take a car and drive east—possibly heading for the Chinese border—and get themselves killed by Lieutenant Colonel Vasilyev. That all hang together so far?"

"Exactly so," Bailey said. "Major Kwok wouldn't want to risk being linked to the shipment, and perhaps he had reason not to rejoin the trade delegation. They may have been delivering him to the Chinese border, or possibly just to another airfield. We're checking that."

"So . . . the million-dollar question," Rubens said. "Where did the NATO chopper take them?"

"Kabul."

"Kabul? Our intelligence suggested Karachi." The thought of one-kiloton nukes in the hands of the insurgents in Afghanistan wasn't as terrifying as the idea of tactical nuclear detonations in twelve American or Israeli cities, but it was a disturbingly unpleasant possibility nonetheless. Were the extremists capable of destroying their own cities in order to inflict damage enough on the foreigners that they would abandon the country entirely?

It was possible . . . but not, Rubens thought, very likely. If the fanatics had twelve nuclear weapons, even small ones, they wouldn't waste them on Afghan cities. They'd go after places with *much* higher visibility and political import. That was the way of al-Qaeda and the other groups linked with it—they liked big, flashy operations with lots of casualties.

Vanderkamp zipped forward through the imagery. Now the helicopter rested on the tarmac at Kabul International Airport.

"As it happens, sir," he said, "the range of an NH90 is about four hundred and seventy-five nautical miles. That's roughly Kabul to Qurghonteppa and back. Cruising speed of about a hundred and sixty nautical miles per hour. They returned to Kabul at oh nine fifty, had the aircraft refueled and serviced, then took off again at fourteen thirty. Once again, it was listed as a training flight. A Lieutenant Alfred Koch at the controls."

"We lost them before they landed," Bailey said. "We lost apogee dwell at around sixteen hundred hours. But by that time we knew they were heading for Quetta. That's two hundred and eighty nautical miles from Kabul, and about halfway to Karachi."

"Quetta. In Pakistan."

"Yes, sir."

"If the helicopter refueled at Quetta and took off immediately," Vanderkamp said, "they could have reached Karachi by eighteen, nineteen hundred hours Tuesday evening." He pushed a combination of buttons on the remote. "We lost satellite coverage until early the next morning, yesterday morning." He shook his head. "We *really* need more satellites to give us full coverage."

It was an ongoing battle between the country's intelligence services and the politicians who doled out the funding. Three satellites with CF-1's capabilities, in three appropriately spaced orbits, could provide twenty-four hours of surveillance of a given target per day. Unless Congressman Mullins and others got their political way, though, it wasn't going to happen.

And *damn* Mullins for leaking even a hint of Operation Haystack to the world.

Vanderkamp was again zooming in from space, this time coming down on an airport east of a sprawling metropolitan center hugging the coast. The image was being displayed at a considerably sharper angle, however; Karachi had been at the southern limit of the target request for the CF-1 passes, and the satellite's view descended on a slant through a lot more atmosphere. As a result, the image now was blurred. You could still see people, but it was tough even to distinguish whether or not they were wearing uniforms. The helicopter was easy enough to identify, however, by the French red, white, and blue roundel and by the registry number on the tail boom. It was parked in an out-of-the-way corner of Jinnah International Airport, on the outskirts of Karachi.

"This smuggling operation appears to involve not only Muslim extremists but the Chinese, the French, and Pakistan as well," Ruebens said evenly. "Maybe even India and NATO as a whole. At the very least, someone in Tajikistan was being paid to look the other way when their airspace was violated."

"At least now we know where to start looking," Barnes said.

"If we have time." Rubens thought for a moment. "So we know

the weapons *did* make it this far. The question now is, where did they go after this? They had all night to load them onto another aircraft."

"Or a ship," Vanderkamp pointed out.

Inwardly, Rubens sagged. Technology had brought them *so* very far along on the trail of the missing suitcase nukes, but there was no way to follow the shipment further. Karachi was a frantically busy port, with hundreds of flights departing each day, hundreds of ships arriving and departing from the harbor.

"It appears, gentlemen," he said quietly, "that from here on we do things the old-fashioned way."

Bailey looked puzzled. "What way is that?" he asked.

"We're back to Mark-One ears and eyeballs, going up to people and asking them questions."

PLAYA SAN JUAN
ALICANTE, SPAIN
THURSDAY, 1615 HOURS LOCAL TIME

A low, rolling surf broke along the beach—endless, sweeping miles of golden-white sand facing east across the blue Mediterranean. Seagulls keeked and screamed overhead, floating on a warm breeze in a cloudless sky. Lia DeFrancesca tugged a little at the triangle of blue and black cloth covering her pubic delta, making sure it was in place, then strode out of the dressing booth and into the full blast of early afternoon sun. Besides the scrap of bright nylon, she wore a broad-brimmed straw hat and designer sunglasses, beach sandals, and a woven bag holding her street clothes.

She *was* still in touch with the Art Room. Her belt, with its concealed antenna, was still in her jeans, neatly folded in the bag. As long as she was within a couple of feet of it, her transceiver implant should keep her connected with the home office.

"I *do* wish we had a visual on you," Jeff Rockman told her over the link.

"Wish all you want," she told him. "Just don't drool on your keyboard."

"Maybe we can reposition a satellite."

"I'd like to see the authorization request on that one," she replied. Then the banter was gone and she became all business. "Okay. Target acquired. Feng is at a table on a restaurant veranda. Two people with him. One Levantine type . . . dark hair, olive complexion. Could be Lebanese. Could be Arab. The other is a male Caucasian. Light brown hair and a mustache. Northern European, I'd say. Here we go."

"Copy that, Lia. Give us an image as soon as you can."

She walked up to the group, smiling. "Good afternoon, Mr. Feng. I made it, as you can see. Thank you for arranging my flight."

"Ms. Lau," Feng said, looking up, sounding surprised. "I'm delighted you came. But . . . you're not wearing all of my gift."

"And why is it, Mr. Feng, that men never seem to be able to guess a woman's bra size with any degree of accuracy? I *might* have squeezed into what you sent me, but I also like to breathe. Besides . . ." She gestured at the beach, where both men and women were enjoying the sun and sea air in everything from jeans and T-shirts to nothing at all. "Most beaches in Spain allow nudity, or at least permit women to go topless," she told him. "I didn't think you would mind."

"Most certainly not! Western Europeans *do* seem to be somewhat casual about displaying their bodies. At least on the beach."

She chuckled. "I once saw a couple on a street in downtown Madrid, both of them completely naked except for tennis shoes, and that's three hundred kilometers from the nearest beach!"

"I *am* surprised," Feng said, smiling. "Americans tend to be *so* conservative, *so* caught up in body taboos and modesty." He grinned across the table at the dark-complexioned man. "Americans are almost as bad as Muslims when it comes to exposing their bodies!"

"True," she said. "*Most* Americans, at any rate. A few of us are more . . . cosmopolitan."

"I'm delighted to learn that about you, Ms. Lau. Please, have a seat. And permit me to introduce two of my business associates."

The pale-skinned man had come to his feet as soon as Lia

approached the table. "Herve Chatel," he said, extending a hand. "*S'il vous plaît*. With Petro-Technologique."

"*Enchanté*," Lia replied, accepting the hand. The man bowed with gallant flair and very nearly kissed her fingers.

"And this is Makhdoom Hussain Shah," Feng said, introducing the other man, who had remained seated. "An associate with Saudi Aramco."

"Pleased to meet you," she said. The name, she thought, was Pakistani or, just possibly, Iranian. While she understood a fair amount of Arabic, she spoke neither Urdu nor Punjabi, nor did she speak more than a few words of Farsi, so she stuck with English.

Shah grunted in reply and looked away, staring past her at the sea.

Lia took the offered chair, crossing her long legs. The Frenchman was having trouble keeping his eyes above the level of her chest. Shah, on the other hand, seemed uncomfortable, angry, perhaps, at her presence. He wouldn't look at her at all.

Well, a practicing Muslim *would* be offended by her current state of dress . . . or undress, rather. She wondered if this was another of Feng's tests—and who was being tested, Shah or her.

"If you would excuse us," Feng told her, "we were just discussing a drilling project in which COSCO is interested."

"Oh, don't mind me," she told them. She pulled a small compact case out of the woven bag beside her chair and extracted a lipstick, which she proceeded to apply to her lips. "I'm *quite* happy here in the sun."

"Of course." Feng turned to the others and said something in Arabic.

Lia didn't catch all of it, but she thought Feng said something like "This is the woman I told you about."

"Very nice," Chatel said in heavily accented Arabic, still staring at her.

Shah responded with a single word. "*Bintilkha-ta!*" It meant "fallen woman" and was the equivalent of calling her a whore.

"Now, Makhdoom," Feng said, still smiling. "Other people, other customs, other ways of thinking. And she will be useful to me as COSCO expands its operational base. *Especially* in the United States."

"She will he useful to you in your bed," Shah replied. "You do seem to have a weakness for degenerate Western sluts."

"I prefer to think of it as my hobby."

"Nice work, when you can get it," Chatel observed.

Lia was amused by Chatel's interest. Europeans—especially the French—thought of themselves as sophisticated and adult; casual social nudity on the beach or in the hot tub would never fluster them. Judging from his reaction, Chatel clearly wasn't as sophisticated or adult as he might like others to believe, however. He was being careful now to keep his legs crossed.

For her part, Lia wasn't bothered by nudity one way or the other. Skin was skin. It was the person inside who was important, not the packaging.

Lia finished touching up her lips, then set the compact and the lipstick on the table in front of her.

"Okay, Lia," Rockman whispered in her ear. "We have a good shot of Chatel. Rotate the camera just slightly counterclockwise, please."

The men continued speaking in Arabic, more quickly now, and she was having trouble following the conversation. No matter. The microphone inside the lipstick tube would transmit every word they said back to the Art Room for analysis. Casually, she played with the compact, turning it slightly to point a small glass decoration on the lid in Shah's direction.

"Okay, Lia. We've got 'em both. We'll run them through ID and see just who we're dealing with here."

Feng turned suddenly to face her. "I wonder, Ms. Lau," he said in English, "if you would go get us some drinks?"

She considered telling him politely that she was a consultant, not a coffee wench, but decided it would be best not to make waves. "Of course, sir."

"Fruit juice for Mr. Shah. A piña colada for me. And for Mr. Chatel?"

"White wine. Whatever they have."

"And something for yourself, of course," Feng told her. "Have them put it on my tab."

"Yes, sir." She stood and strode off toward the bar at the back of the beach veranda.

She could feel all three men staring at her back as she walked.

ART ROOM
NSA HEADQUARTERS
FORT MEADE, MARYLAND
THURSDAY, 1030 HOURS EDT

Marie Telach looked up at the big screen, where lines of type were appearing letter by letter. The three men on the beach in Spain were continuing their conversation in Arabic. As the transmission came through the Language Department, though, Arabic-speaking personnel were typing the consecutive translation, the words appearing on the Art Room screen, complete with identifier tags.

> SHAH: I do not like this slut here at the table with us, Feng. You risk operational security.
>
> CHATEL: She's harmless, Shah. Take it from me. I do admire your taste in women, Mr. Feng.
>
> FENG: She is pleasant to look at. However, I expect to use her to open certain opportunities for COSCO, once the operation is successfully complete. American men will make concessions to a beautiful woman, where, with a man, they would be sidetracked by trying to compete, trying to show how strong they are. She also has considerable experience in public relations.
>
> CHATEL: I'll bet that's not all she's experienced in.
>
> FENG: That is irrelevant. If she does consent to share my bed, that will be most pleasant. As I said, it is my preferred hobby.

"Are you picking it all up?" Lia's voice said, coming through the speaker in the ceiling.

"Loud and clear," Telach told her. "They're discussing you right now like a piece of meat."

"Let them. Anything useful?"

"Not yet. No . . . wait. They're talking about 'the project' now."

FENG: What progress at the drill site?

SHAH: Slow. Slow.

FENG: You are a week behind schedule. Why?

SHAH: We are drilling through solid basalt, not sediment or sandstone. It takes time.

CHATEL: We've also had to order more replacement drill bits from Dhahran. If they arrive within the next day or two, I expect that we shall be at the five-hundred-meter level by the middle of next week.

SHAH: The Jackal told me to ask you. When can he expect the special packages?

FENG: They are en route as we speak. You tell the Jackal that he must have the boreholes complete by next week.

CHATEL: That will depend on the rock. Basalt is very hard.

FENG: Tell him. (*Strong emphasis.*) If they haven't reached one thousand meters, they'll have to go with what they have.

SHAH: We have also had inquiries from Dhahran. Concerned inquiries.

FENG: About?

SHAH: When Operation Wrath of God is complete, the Saudis will have lost one of their major trading partners. Mr. al-Khuwaytir is worried about the effect on the global economy.

FENG: When Wrath of God is complete, the People's Republic of China will be more than able to step into the vacuum. Mr. al-Khuwaytir should keep in mind that the People's Republic owns over one-eighth of their foreign debt. Have faith in God.

SHAH: Do not mock me.

FENG: I'm not. Do not muddy the water with minor concerns. At this point in time, all of our attention must be focused on completing those boreholes. Your compatriots in Jerusalem are impatient. They want to carry out Operation Fire from Heaven quickly, but they must not, must not, act before Wrath of God is complete. If they do, they risk everything we've worked for. Am I understood?

SHAH: You are understood.

FENG: And there is another matter, Mr. Shah. I received a message early this morning from one of my sources on La Palma. It seems your people have been conducting intelligence work, wet work, in fact, on your own, without clearing it with me first.

SHAH: What do you mean?

FENG: I think you know what I mean. Pender? In the United States?

SHAH: That was necessary. Pender and Carlylse are too close, they know too much.

FENG: Killing Pender called attention to him. That was dangerous.

SHAH: It is not an issue. Pender's death looked like suicide. Carlylse is on La Palma now, according to our sources. The Jackal will take care of him as well, and it will again look like suicide.

FENG: Just so the Jackal knows that he must not call attention to Wrath of God in any way. Pender and Carlylse are unimportant. Their books may even help us in the long run. Do not call undue attention to them, or we could lose the, the psychological effect you are looking for within the Muslim world.

SHAH: The Jackal knows what he is doing, Mr. Feng.

FENG: I hope so. What's the matter, Mr. Chatel? You look unhappy.

CHATEL: I don't know. What you're planning, what we're doing . . . This is a lot bigger, a lot more, uh, far-reaching than you told me when you asked me to help with this. I'm having some doubts.

FENG: We are paying you a great deal of money, Mr. Chatel. We are paying you not to have doubts.

CHATEL: I know, I know.

FENG: And there will be a lot more money when the project is done. A very great deal of money. So do not doubt.

CHATEL: The girl is coming back.

FENG: We'll talk more later. In my room. (*In English.*) Ah! Miss Lau! Thank you.

The conversation turned to more mundane things—COSCO's profit margin and Feng's hope to open new markets in Spain. Telach touched a button on her keyboard, then pulled a printout of the conversation from a printer.

Bill Rubens was going to want to see this, and quickly.

12

Rubens waited as Lieutenant General Alexander Douglas finished reading the transcript. The director of the NSA had agreed to meet with Rubens on impossibly short notice. Rubens had secured the appointment by using the code word "Armageddon" in his request to Douglas' secretary. Using that word meant that the subject of the meeting was nothing less than cataclysmic in scope, was an immediate threat endangering the entire nation, and was supremely credible. During Rubens' eleven-year tenure as deputy director of the NSA and head of Desk Three, the code had been used exactly three times— twice when there'd been solid reports of nuclear weapons smuggled into U.S. ports, and on the morning of 9/11.

They sat at the small conference table in a private meeting room off Douglas' office, with the morning sun filtering in through the tinted windows overlooking the sprawl of Fort Meade and the Maryland countryside. Brigadier General Howard Noelle sat to Rubens' left, the two of them opposite Douglas. Noelle was deputy director of the Central Security Service and, according to the organization charts, the number three man in the Agency.

The CSS had been established in 1972 as a combat support agency within the Department of Defense. While Douglas double-hatted as chief of the CSS, it was Noelle who actually managed the partnership between the cryptologic elements of the various military services and the NSA. Anything coming over Douglas' desk flying the Armageddon flag would sooner or later involve the U.S. military, so it was important that Noelle be present as well.

Douglas adjusted his round-framed glasses and looked up. "Bill . . . this is pretty raw. An overheard conversation in Spain? There's not a lot to go on here."

"This may be the break we're looking for, sir," Noelle said. He'd already read the transcript and discussed the high points with Rubens during their twenty-minute wait to see Douglas. "A solid link between Operation Haystack and a terrorist plan to attack the United States."

"Yes . . . but how? What's the target? According to this, there's a . . . a shipment of something going somewhere, but no indication of where. And we don't know for certain that 'the shipment' is comprised of the missing suitcase nukes."

"Actually, sir," Rubens said, "General Noelle is right. We have a pretty strong case here."

"Would you care to enlighten me?"

"Of course. In the transcript, Feng mentions something called Operation Fire from Heaven. In Arabic, that's *Nar-min-Sama*. We've been chasing that one since our friends in the Mossad tipped us off a couple of weeks ago. We think it may refer to a planned nuclear strike against Israel."

"Yes . . ."

"Feng links that with another operation, *Harakat Radab min Allah*. Operation Wrath of God. Feng is insisting here that Fire from Heaven be delayed until well after Wrath of God is implemented. It sounds like a two-tiered attack."

"Hit one target, then take out the second while the opposition is still reeling from the effects of the first," Noelle put in.

"A diversion?"

"Possibly," Rubens said. "From the tone Feng is taking here, it sounds like two different attacks by two different groups on two different targets, but either the chances of the second will be improved if the other attack is launched first, or launching the second attack too early will give something away, maybe make the first attack less effective."

"It still sounds pretty thin," Douglas said. "We have to know the target."

"Feng also mentions a name, a nom de guerre, al-Wawi. The Jackal."

"Carlos the Jackal? Big-name terrorist in the seventies? Isn't he dead?"

"He's serving a life sentence in Clairvaux Prison, in France, sir. We checked as soon as the name popped up."

The original Jackal had been the rather pathetic, overweight Ilich Ramírez Sánchez, a Venezuelan leftist revolutionary who'd made a name for himself back in the 1970s. *Several* names, in fact. He'd become known as "Carlos" when he joined the Popular Front for the Liberation of Palestine. A British newspaper, the *Guardian*, had nicknamed him "the Jackal" when *The Day of the Jackal*, a novel by thriller writer Frederick Forsyth, was found with his belongings.

In fact, Carlos had fallen far short of the myth-making and hype and was not at all the super-assassin of fiction. His most notorious escapades had been a raid on an OPEC conference in Vienna where three people had been killed, and a later string of bombings in France and Germany. The man eventually had been abducted by his own security guards in Sudan, then turned over to French intelligence, and was now in prison.

"So this is a new Jackal," Douglas said, thoughtful.

"Yes, sir." Rubens opened his briefcase and extracted a file folder, which he opened and passed to Douglas. "This is al-Wawi, the new Jackal. Ibrahim Hussain Azhar. He led a team of Mujahideen in the hijacking of an Indian Airlines A300 Airbus in 1999. The aircraft was taken to Kandahar, in Afghanistan, where it was closely guarded by the Taliban.

"After a standoff lasting seven days, India released three prisoners to secure the Airbus and its passengers. Mushtaq Ahmed Zargar. Ahmed Omar Saeed Sheikh. And Maulana Masood Azhar."

"Azhar?"

"Yes, sir. Ibrahim Azhar's brother. A radical Muslim cleric who went on to found Jaish-e-Mohammad, the Army of Mohammad, in 2000."

"The JeM is just involved with Kashmir, isn't it?"

"Yes, sir, but they've increasingly been taking an international stance. Especially since they bombed the Indian Parliament in New Delhi." That had been in December of 2001.

Kashmir was the disputed territory currently divided between Pakistan, India, and China. Since their original partition in 1947, three wars had been fought in the region between India and Pakistan, the most recent in 1999, and a fourth war had been fought between India and China over the northeastern area in 1962. A number of extremist Muslim groups like the JeM had been created over the years—usually with help from Pakistan's ISI—with the goal of forcing the Indians out of Kashmir and Jammu, the southern portion of the region now controlled by New Delhi.

"The Army of Mohammad has been closely tied to both the Taliban and al-Qaeda since the beginning," Rubens went on. "Especially through the Binoria Madrasah, in Karachi. The message preached there calls for global jihad, claiming it's the duty of all Muslims *everywhere* to join together and destroy both Israel and the United States. Kashmir is just a first step toward an Islamic world state."

"Well, we've heard that before," Douglas said. "There are too many internal differences for the Muslims ever to get their act together and take on the whole world. Shi'ites against Sunnis. Radicals against conservatives. Different interpretations of the Qur'an. It'll never happen."

"Not unless someone comes up with a *really* dramatic demonstration," Rubens observed. "Something that proves how powerful the extremist arm of Islam actually is. Or . . . maybe a high-profile demonstration of how powerful Allah is. I remember there were concerns that there might be a global jihad in the wake of 9/11. That attack, the sheer scope of it, proved the radical extremists could hurt even a giant like the United States."

"The bastards were dancing in the streets from Morocco and Great Britain all the way to Indonesia," Noelle said sourly.

"But the more moderate Muslims, the Islamic mainstream, they didn't join in," Douglas pointed out. "There was no global uprising."

"Which makes me wonder about these operations we've tapped into," Rubens told him. "Wrath of God. Fire from Heaven. Tactical nuclear weapons, maybe planted in a dozen different cities? That kind of widespread destruction might be just the universal rallying cry the extremists are looking for. Something to make *all* good Muslims see that the triumph of the extremists is inevitable. It is God's will."

"Possibly." Douglas didn't sound convinced. He tapped the transcript lying on the desk. "You think Feng is suggesting a timetable when he says the drilling has to be done next week?"

"I'm sure of it."

"Okay. Drilling where? By whom?" He looked at Noelle and chuckled. "We don't have any reports of covert drilling operations on the Mall in downtown Washington, do we?"

"Not that I've heard, sir."

"He mentions drill bits from Dhahran. And these two people he was meeting with, Shah and Chatel. What's their part in it?"

"Shah is a minor executive with Saudi Aramco. That's the largest oil company in the world. And Chatel is a salesman with Petro-Technologique, a French company that provides specialized drilling equipment to, among others, Saudi Aramco. He mentions drilling through basalt, though. You don't generally find oil beneath basalt, sir. That's volcanic rock. You find oil in pockets beneath sedimentary rock, and ocean sediments."

"You think they're drilling holes for suitcase nukes? Underground detonations? Why? Setting the things off on the surface in the middle of a city would be more destructive, I would think. One-kiloton tactical nukes wouldn't make much of a bang at the bottom of an oil well."

"We're still studying that one, sir," Rubens said. "I suspect they have something bigger in mind than just wrecking twelve city centers."

"But you don't know what."

"No, sir. But we *do* have one more clue."

"The writers Feng mentions. Pender and . . . who?" Douglas picked up the transcript and scanned through it quickly.

"Carlylse, sir," Rubens said. "Vincent Carlylse. And Jack Pender."

"Who the hell are they?"

"A writing team. They've coauthored seven books over the past three years. Weird, fringe-element stuff, mostly, but pretty popular. Ancient astronauts, UFOs, the lost continent of Atlantis, stuff like that." He handed another file across to Douglas. "Yesterday, Pender was found dead in a motel room in New Jersey. It looked like suicide, but the police are calling his death suspicious."

"Suspicious how?"

"A few hours after they found Pender, they found a prostitute dead in another motel, a few miles away. Cynthia Jane Cramer. Naked, tied to the bed, and strangled with a length of rope. Looked like one of her johns got too rough. Her purse was there. The cash was gone, so it looked like a robbery, but whoever it was didn't take the credit cards. When the police checked, it turned out that one of the cards belonged to Pender."

"Ah . . ."

"We're exploring the possibility that the bad guys used Cramer to get access to Pender's room. She set him up, stole the credit card . . . and still had it when the bad guys killed her later, just to wrap up the loose ends."

"They killed Pender and made it look like suicide."

"Yes, sir. Pender was more or less successful. A book he and Carlylse wrote together about Atlantis actually hit the bestseller lists, which is pretty unusual for that kind of pseudo-science book—and he was scheduled to appear on a TV talk show broadcast out of New York City yesterday afternoon."

"In other words, he had no reason to kill himself."

"I'm told that between divorces, depression, and alcoholism, writing novels is a pretty high-risk profession—but Pender was doing well. Plenty of money in the bank, and the promise of more to come. Pender and Carlylse had just come out with another hot title, this one on 2012. In fact, he was going to be plugging it on that TV show."

"So how is this guy connected with the Army of Mohammad?"

"We're not entirely sure yet, sir. But yesterday afternoon, GCHQ intercepted an encoded cell phone transmission from Masood Azhar, in Karachi, to al-Wawi. When we ran it through crypto, it said that Pender was dead, and that Carlylse was on La Palma, in the Canary Islands. It also said that Carlylse should be dealt with next."

"Good God. But why two scribblers? Why *these* two?"

"We have an analysis team going through their books now, sir, looking for a motive. Most of their stuff is pretty far out, alien abductions and crap like that. But that newest book, the one they wrote on 2012, might turn out to be the key."

"Really? Twenty twelve. That's . . . all of that doomsday stuff, right?"

"Yes, sir. The end of the ancient Mayan calendar and the end of the world. It sounds apocalyptic enough that al-Qaeda or the JeM might have taken an interest."

"So why kill the authors?"

"We're not sure about that either, yet. In the conversation our operative bugged yesterday, Feng was concerned that their deaths might give away the game. So we're researching their books with that in mind."

Douglas nodded. "I see why you're concerned. Twelve loose tactical nukes, two extremist Muslim operations with apocalyptic code names, and a murdered author who writes about doomsday. And Feng here is talking about next week."

"Exactly."

"What's the Chinese role in all of this?"

"Probably opportunistic. In the transcript, Shah mentions concerns that Saudi Arabia is going to lose a major trading partner.

Looking at the context, that could well be the United States. Al-Khuwaytir is probably Mohammad Sayeed al-Khuwaytir, the Saudi foreign trade minister. Feng points out that the PRC could step into the vacuum. If Wrath of God is designed to cripple the U.S. economically somehow, I can see how the Saudis *would* be concerned."

"No more solid silver Rolls-Royces."

"And another bad stretch for the global economy," Rubens pointed out. "We're just climbing out of one economic crisis. Something on the scale these guys are talking about might put the whole world into a financial tailspin. Again, we're still carrying out the investigation, but we think that Feng was the money man. Best guess? He provided the money for JeM to buy twelve stolen suitcase nukes from the Russian *mafiya*."

Douglas pursed his lips. "Ouch. What do you want from me?"

Rubens looked at Noelle. This was his department.

"When Desk Three gets this sorted out," Noelle said, "we're almost certainly going to need military action. *Fast.* Our people are tracking the nukes at Karachi now." He looked at Rubens. "A freighter?"

"Russian freighter," Rubens agreed. "The *Yakutsk*. Maltese flagged. Destination Tel Aviv."

"The *Yakutsk*. We may need to put a VBSS team on board her."

VBSS was the naval acronym for "visit, board, search, and seizure." It meant a SEAL team taking down a Russian ship and grabbing the nukes on board.

Douglas made a face. "That is *not* going to fly well with the Oval Office."

"No, sir. And that's why the request is going to have to come from your office."

"We can enlist Johnny James," Noelle added. "He's sympathetic to us."

"We'll need to brief him." Douglas arched an eyebrow in Rubens' direction.

"I can handle that, sir. This afternoon, if I can get an appointment."

"Use my priority code for the request."

"Thank you, sir."

"It occurs to me that we have some people here we might want to talk to. It sounds like al-Khuwaytir may be in on this scheme, whatever it is. And your sources in Spain—Feng, Shah, and this French guy, Chatel."

"Already on that, sir. Al-Khuwaytir may be someone for State to look at. But my people in south Asia are checking on both the ship and on other forms of transport out of Karachi."

"Good. Anything to stop us from picking up the three in Spain immediately?"

"Just one thing," Rubens told him. "Al-Wawi, apparently, is the guy running Operation Wrath of God. Right now he's on the island of La Palma, Canary Islands. He's the one we *really* want, and we don't want him tipped off ahead of time. If he disappears, he might take the suitcase nukes with him, and we'll have to start all over from scratch."

"Any ideas?"

"Yes, sir. One of my best Desk Three operators is with Feng now, in Spain. I'm sending her to La Palma this afternoon."

"To save Carlylse?"

Rubens hesitated. "If possible. But Carlylse might lead us to the Jackal. That's our first priority."

"Bait," Douglas said.

"Hate to say it, but yes. I don't know how else to flush al-Wawi into the open without spooking him."

"Well, I'll leave that in your hands, Bill. Keep me up to date. Let me know if anything changes. And I'll let you know what the President says. He may insist on deniability."

"That might not be possible, sir. It is *imperative* that we recover those nukes."

"I agree. But in this business, imperatives aren't always possible."

"I know that, sir. All too well."

HOTEL ALMIRANTE
ALICANTE, SPAIN
THURSDAY, 1725 HOURS LOCAL TIME

Lia DeFrancesca walked into the luxurious, light-filled lobby of the Almirante, holding Feng's arm. She was wearing a brightly colored beach wrap now—she didn't mind going three-quarters naked in public, but only where such exposure would be natural and unremarkable, like on the beach. She wasn't about to emulate the couple she'd seen a few years before in Madrid.

"You know, Ms. Lau," Feng told her as they waited for the elevator to arrive on the lobby floor, "you *could* share my room."

"Why, thank you, Mr. Feng," she replied. "It *is* tempting . . . but what kind of a message would that send to your business associates?"

"How would they know? Besides, they would merely think of me as very fortunate indeed."

"I don't think so." She shook her head. "Mr. Shah has the traditional Muslim scorn for women who expose themselves in public. I'm sure he thinks of me as a 'fallen woman.' If he learned you were sleeping with me, he would be convinced that you are as decadent and degraded as I am."

He looked at her sharply. "How do you know he called you a fallen woman? Do you speak Arabic?"

"No, but I know what *bintilkha-ta* means. And associating with such a person would taint you as well. Unless you're *trying* to scandalize the poor boy?"

He smiled and patted her arm. "I do like . . . how is it you Americans put it? To yank on his rope?"

"His chain. You like to yank his chain."

"Just so."

The elevator arrived; the door slid open. They stepped inside and she pressed the button for her floor, then for his.

"Mr. Feng, I'm delighted that you appreciate my skills and my experience enough to hire me. But I submit that you need to decide just what it is you are hiring me for. As a consultant knowledgeable in foreign cultures? Or as a playmate in bed? The one gets in the way of the other."

"And what would you say if I told you I wanted you for my bed?"

"I would say no, Mr. Feng. I would tell you that I was flattered . . . but no." The elevator stopped at her floor, and she walked out. "Until later, Mr. Feng."

"Very smooth, Lia," Rockman told her over her implant. "I'm not sure how you keep him at arm's length with all the drool on the floor, though."

"He wants me for eye candy," she murmured. "I think the job is just an excuse to show off a pretty woman hanging on his arm."

"Are you okay with that?" Bill Rubens asked.

"Oh, sure. He's putty in my hands."

"You're going to want to wash your hands, then," Rubens told her. "I'm pulling you out."

"Why?" She was genuinely startled. Surprise was followed immediately by a flush of anger. "Mr. Rubens. I *can* take care of myself, you know."

"I know you can, Lia, but we need you in La Palma. The sooner, the better."

"La Palma? Why?"

"Because that's where al-Wawi is. It's also where a writer named Vince Carlylse is about to be murdered by al-Wawi's people. When you went off to get those drinks this afternoon, they were discussing it."

"They're killing writers? Why?"

"We don't know yet, but it's wrapped up with a terrorist op, and it's big."

"Feng wants me to fly with him back to Germany. Shah and Chatel are going to La Palma." She had a new thought. "Shah and Chatel. They're involved with the terrorist op?"

"That's part of what we want you to learn, Lia."

"Feng will be suspicious if I quit now and fly off to the Canary Islands with those two instead."

"We'll take care of your legend, Lia. We want to preserve your relationship with Feng in case we need to penetrate his COSCO operations later. But right now, we can have you on Grand Canary in six hours . . . and it'll be closer to twenty-four if I send someone out from the States."

"You got it."

"I'll send along the file information on the writer, and what we know about the Canaries. We're also sending Ms. Howorth down there. She'll be your backup."

CJ had been left behind in Berlin to wrap up some loose ends there.

"Very well. When do I leave?"

"We have a ticket for you at the counter at Alicante Airport. Your flight leaves in eighty-five minutes."

"Then I guess I'd better pack and get over there." She laughed.

"What's funny?"

"Feng, sir. He's going to be *so* disappointed. Or pissed. I can't decide which."

ART ROOM
NSA HEADQUARTERS
FORT MEADE, MARYLAND
THURSDAY, 1515 HOURS EDT

"What is the ship's position now?" Rubens asked.

Marie Telach checked one of the Art Room displays. "Twenty-three forty-five north . . . sixty-five thirty-three east," she replied. "One hundred three nautical miles southwest of Karachi. Course two two three degrees, speed seventeen knots."

"A week to Haifa."

"Yes, sir."

"And the *Lake Erie*?"

"Still shadowing the target, sir. Ninety nautical miles to the south and on a parallel course."

Rubens frowned at one of the monitors, which showed an aerial view of an aging, plodding merchant ship, tiny against the endless blue of the Gulf of Oman. The image was being relayed from a tilt-rotor Eagle Eye UAV remotely piloted from the *Lake Erie*. The *Erie* was a Ticonderoga-class Aegis cruiser, CG-70, part of the *Constellation* carrier battle group. The CBG had been tasked with following the target freighter without crowding her too closely.

A CIA agent in Karachi had come up with the information that a number of containers supposedly carrying small nuclear weapons had been transported yesterday from Jinnah International Airport to a Russian freighter, the *Yakutsk*, moored on the Karachi waterfront. The agent had been unable to say how many containers had been transferred to the ship, but if the suitcase nukes were on board, even one was too many.

In fact, there was no reason to suppose that the twelve weapons had been split up.

Rubens wondered just how much they could trust the CIA's source. This agent was a young Pakistani named Haroon who'd purportedly been turned after the ISI had arrested his sister and his father a year before, accusing them of being Taliban. Both were still in prison; the State Department was supposed to be making inquiries about the two, a part of the package that had brought Haroon to the U.S. Embassy and the CIA's senior resident there.

It felt convenient to Rubens, and he didn't trust convenient.

Still, the man was the only hard source they had at the moment regarding the whereabouts of the stolen nukes. If they were on board the *Yakutsk*, the United States needed to verify that—and secure them.

If they could get the authorization to do so. The administration was—as General Douglas had pointed out that morning—reluctant to board a foreign ship on a suspicion, *especially* a ship belonging to the Russian Federation. Freedom of the sea was a vital principle in both American and international law. Hell, the War of 1812 had started with the British boarding and searching American ships at sea.

What if the ship couldn't be stopped, and nuclear warheads reached the Israeli port?

Operation Wrath of God. Operation Fire from Heaven.

American targets? Or Israeli?

It scarcely mattered. Millions of people might dic. Those warheads *had* to be found and secured, one way or another.

To that end, he'd already ordered Dean and Akulinin to Karachi, where they would be working with the CIA to get confirmation of Haroon's information.

And there was, perhaps, one other thing he could do . . .

"I'll be in my office, Marie."

"Yes, sir."

He had a phone call to make.

13

It was, Dean reflected, a matter of every spy agency for itself.

When in Tajikistan, the Desk Three operators had had to maintain their covers as foreign military personnel. They couldn't work with the Russian FSB because that organization had been thoroughly penetrated by the Russian *mafiya*. The Tajikistan police and security services were, for the most part, controlled by militant Islamics.

Once across the border into Afghanistan, they'd learned that even NATO had been penetrated somehow, and they'd been less than open with their German hosts. So far as NATO was concerned, Dean, Akulinin, and Alekseyevna were journalists who'd needed rescuing.

Now, less than twenty-four hours later, Dean and his partner were in Pakistan, a nation supposedly dedicated to fighting terrorism and bringing down Islamic militarist fanatics whether they were Taliban, al-Qaeda, or JeM—but the two NSA officers had to maintain their deep cover. Many members of the Pakistani ISI, both in the rank and file and in the leadership, were secretly pro-Taliban, pro-Islamist, or both, and simply could not be trusted. The ISI had scored some significant victories in recent years against the militants, especially in

the case of suicide bombings on Pakistani soil, and yet there continued to be major security leaks, covert operations compromised, and
even high-ranking militant leaders who lived and moved openly within
Pakistan's population, often as revered and respected clerics calling
the faithful to jihad.

Maulana Masood Azhar, the Army of Mohammad's founder and
leader, was a case in point.

Dean and Akulinin moved slowly through the crowd that had
spilled out onto the street from the courtyard of the Jami'ah Binoria
Madrasah—a large and well-known Islamic university located in the
sprawl of northwestern Karachi in the heart of an industrial district
with the unlikely name of Metrovil. The mob was as raucous and
noisy as the riot in the streets of Kunduz that morning; this time,
though, the excitement was being generated by the speech coming
from loudspeakers mounted high up on the madrasah's walls. It was
Friday, the Muslim holy day, and the sermon was being delivered to an
enthusiastic crowd. Dean estimated that several thousand people were
packed into the university's grounds and the surrounding city streets.

"What's he saying?" Akulinin asked as a harsh, nasal voice brayed
from the speakers in Urdu. "He sounds pretty passionate about it."

"The usual rant," Jeff Rockman's voice replied through their implants. "God is merciful, God is just, and God is going to mop the
floor with Jews, fornicators, and Americans."

A fresh burst of cheering arose from the crowd. "These people really eat this stuff up," Dean said.

"This would definitely not be a good time to tell them you guys
are American infidels," Rockman said. "Wait a sec . . . I'm reading
the translation off my screen . . . Okay, now he's saying that the
promised end of days is upon us, and God Himself is going to wipe
America away in a deluge of righteousness . . . He has held back His
hand to give America time to repent, but now the time of merciful
forbearance is past . . . and when the eyes of the faithful behold the
divine hand of God sweeping away His enemies, all of His faithful
will put aside their differences and . . . Jesus, this guy ought to be a
televangelist."

"I think we can do without the running commentary," Dean said. "How far to the target?"

"Twelve meters. And a bit more to your left. He's hanging back, on the very edge of the crowd."

"Copy. I think I have him."

The two Desk Three operators continued to skirt the crowd as the impassioned declarations boomed out, eliciting waves of cheering, chants, and dizzying exultation. The speaker was Maulana Masood Azhar, delivering his Friday sermon from somewhere inside the Binoria Madrasah.

That in itself was interesting. The Pakistani government had repeatedly told the West that they had no idea of Azhar's whereabouts.

Dean didn't speak Urdu; since their arrival in Pakistan yesterday, the two operatives had been reliant on the Art Room's simultaneous translations and on the efforts of Najamuddin Haroon. Even so, the rhythm and power and sheer thunder of the declamations had a mesmerizing quality. Dean was reminded of films he'd seen of Adolf Hitler delivering a speech to a sea of passionately adoring listeners at Nuremburg.

The speech was an assault upon reason itself.

Dean had hoped that by this time they would have been on their way back Stateside. After the debacle in Dushanbe, he'd assumed Rubens would pull them out, turning Haystack over to other field assets. He didn't like breaking off in the middle of a mission, but he'd actually been looking forward to it this time. The riot in Kunduz had reminded him how much he hated this part of the world with its Islamic Nazis, volatile passions, brain-dead bigotry, and blind adherence to unreasoning hatred.

They'd said good-bye to Masha at the Kabul airport yesterday afternoon—she would be flying to the States sometime today—and boarded a NATO C-130, heading south to Karachi and landing at a military airfield just outside the city. They'd been met by the CIA station chief himself and taken to the U.S. Embassy, where they'd spoken with Rubens, eaten, and collapsed into exhausted sleep.

Early this morning, they'd been awakened and introduced to

Haroon. They received new legends, identity cards and papers, local clothing, money, and a new mission.

Their target, they were told, was attending a public sermon by Maulana Azhar, who would be speaking at the Binoria Madrasah this morning.

And there he was.

Alfred Koch stood out in the crowd. Blond and blatantly Aryan, he was still wearing his gray flight utilities, though he'd donned a borrowed *taqiyya* in deference to local custom requiring a head covering for men. Koch had been the pilot of the NATO helicopter that had picked up twelve suitcase-sized containers in a cotton field outside Qurghonteppa and flown them to Karachi. He was leaning against the wall of a shop opposite the madrasah's entrance and seemed to be nodding to the cant and meter of the speech.

It had been relatively easy to follow him. Koch's cell phone used a SIM card with a coded number that could be tracked if you had a sufficiently large antenna in orbit, and the NRO had several SIGINT satellites in the sky with truly large antennae indeed. The NSA had been able to lock onto Koch's phone after tracking his banking records; a deposit of a quarter of a million euros that afternoon at a bank in Karachi had focused the agency's attention on the man. German Luftwaffe lieutenants didn't normally make deposits of that size.

A final burst of invective from the loudspeakers set the crowd into wild and jubilant celebration. A chant had started. *"Allahu akbar! Allahu akbar!"*

God is great.

Dean and Akulinin split up as they approached, sidling in from left and right. Koch seemed unaware of either of them until Dean stepped up on his left, draping his SIG SAUER P226 within the long and loose-hanging sleeves of his *kameez* and pressing the muzzle hard against the small of the German's back.

"What's the matter, Alfred?" Akulinin said in English from Koch's right. "You're not joining in with all the celebrating."

"Was ist?" Koch demanded, eyes widening, then narrowing to slits. He shifted to English. "Who the hell are you?"

"We're accountants, Alfred," Dean told him. "We'd like to have a word with you about that bank deposit you made today."

"I've done nothing wrong!"

"Nothing at all," Dean agreed, "except maybe borrowing a NATO helicopter, and flying proscribed weapons for the wrong people."

Surprisingly, Koch smiled. "You are Americans? CIA? You can prove nothing. You have no legal jurisdiction here."

"What makes you think we're CIA?" Akulinin asked, his voice casual, even friendly.

"You're Americans. The accents . . ."

Dean nudged him with the pistol. "Walk. That way. Nice and easy. You're out for an evening stroll with a couple of friends."

"You *must* be CIA!"

Akulinin grinned, a cold showing of teeth. "Alfred, you've pissed off a *lot* of people, not just the Americans."

"But—"

"*Shalom*, Alfred," Dean said, and he gave the German another nudge with the weapon's muzzle.

By the time they reached the car, with Haroon at the wheel, Koch was babbling, almost pathetically eager to talk.

LA PALMA AIRPORT
SOUTH OF SANTA CRUZ DE LA PALMA
LA PALMA, CANARY ISLANDS
FRIDAY, 0915 HOURS LOCAL TIME

Lia DeFrancesca held on to Chatel's arm as they stepped off the boarding ladder and onto the tarmac of La Palma's airport. "Oh, I *do* hope you're not going to tell Mr. Feng on me, Herve," she said, cooing with her best innocent schoolgirl voice. "He would just kill me!"

"Of course not, *chérie*," Chatel said, and Lia could almost see his white knight's armor gleam in the morning sun. "The man is a boor and a barbarian. He hasn't the slightest idea how to treat a beautiful woman properly."

Chatel's tone of voice indicated that, of course, he himself *did* know how to treat a woman well. The patronizing I-know-best flavor to the words set Lia's teeth on edge.

"It's about *respect*, Herve," she told him. "He was treating me like a piece of meat, like eye candy, putting me on display . . ."

"I know, and it was terrible! But you don't need to worry about that now. I'm sure we can find you an excellent position with Petro-Technologique."

"Thank you, Herve." She gave his arm a squeeze as they walked across the tarmac toward the main airport building. "I am so grateful. The guy couldn't keep his hands off me."

As promised, Rubens had had her on a Spanair flight to Grand Canary by early the previous evening. What she hadn't expected was to be here with Herve Chatel, inspecting his company's operations in the Canary Islands. Shah, thankfully, had remained in Spain, but he was expected to arrive on La Palma later today.

They'd stayed on Grand Canary overnight and caught an island hopper across to La Palma this morning. Chatel had spent most of the morning talking—primarily about himself.

Which was fine, so far as Lia was concerned. She needed to learn all she could about this Frenchman who'd expressed doubt about some aspect of a secret operation involving both Feng and the mysterious al-Wawi. So far, she'd learned that he was a senior vice president for his company, which manufactured high-duration drilling bits for the petroleum industry, that he had more money than God, and that he expected to move up to the position of CEO when the old man retired late next year.

"So, how long are you going to be here in La Palma?" she asked him.

"A few days. I need to check with my people in the field on . . . on a project."

"Really? What project?"

"Nothing you would be interested in, my sweet. I've already

reserved a room for you at the Hotel Sol. You can enjoy the sun and the sea while I go check on my people in the interior. When I return, we shall fly back to Paris, and I'll talk to my human resources people about hiring you as my personal assistant."

Lia had already used her laptop to do some research on La Palma, the outermost of the flattened horseshoe of islands off the southern coast of Morocco called the Canary Islands. La Palma was an arrowhead pointed due south, twenty-eight miles long north to south, seventeen across from east to west. The airport was on the east coast, facing the nearby islands of Gomera and Tenerife; the Hotel Sol was directly opposite, in Puerto Naos on the west coast.

La Palma had been forged in fire, a volcanic island of basalt cliffs and black sand beaches. The rounded northern half of the island was dominated by the Caldera de Taburiente, an imposing ring of mountains that, despite its name, was not itself a volcano. A high, rugged spine of mountains, many of which were volcanic, ran north to south down the island's center, almost impassable in places and dividing east from west. The spine was called Cumbre Vieja, the Old Ridge.

The last volcanic eruption on the island, she'd learned, had been in 1971.

"If you really want me to be your personal assistant," she told him with a small pout, "you might be a little more direct and honest about just what it is you do."

"In time, in time." He looked worried. "For now, all you need to do is be beautiful, and you seem to have that down to perfection."

Well, there would be time to ply him later, and there might be some places she could check here on the island. Something, she thought, just wasn't adding up. If Petro-Technologique and Saudi Aramco were involved in a project on La Palma, it *must* involve drilling, possibly exploratory drilling, and on a fairly large scale. Lia knew about petroleum geology, but somehow a volcanic island didn't seem like the best place to prospect for oil. You found petroleum reserves beneath sedimentary rock—sandstone, limestone, and shale—not beneath a mountain of volcanic basalt.

What the hell were these people playing at?

Yet something was tugging at Lia's memory about La Palma . . . and she couldn't quite pull it out into the light.

CIA OPERATIONS
KARACHI, PAKISTAN
FRIDAY, 1721 HOURS LOCAL TIME

"You," Station Chief Charles Lloyd told Dean, "are a sneaky, under-handed bastard. I *like* that."

"I take it our friend is talking?"

"We can't get him to *stop* talking. Anything to keep us from turning him over to the big bad nasties of the Mossad."

"Well, we got lucky. We wouldn't have had time to break him by conventional means."

Lloyd was leading Dean through the twists and turns of some back passageways, ending in a darkened room where two more CIA officers sat with recording equipment, watching the interrogation through a soundproofed glass window. In the brightly lit room there, Koch sat at a small table, his interrogator opposite with a pen and an open notebook. Koch no doubt guessed that the mirror was a one-way window; it didn't matter. He seemed to be only too eager to co-operate.

"Yeah," Lloyd said, nodding. "Ever since Gitmo and Abu Ghraib, we have to be *nice* when we interrogate the bastards. Read them their rights. Ask them 'pretty please.' Takes forever, and the tough ones just laugh at us."

Dean looked at him sharply. "You sound like you're longing for the bad old days of waterboarding and electric shock."

"Maybe I am. Don't get me wrong. I don't like the idea of torture any more than you do. It . . . it contaminates every organization, every person, who uses it. But how the hell do we break a man who might know where a bomb is planted, a bomb that might kill a dozen school kids . . . or a suitcase nuke that could incinerate the center of a fair-sized American city?"

"Torture doesn't deliver reliable information," Dean told him. "You know that. A prisoner will say anything, *anything*, to make the pain stop. That's how the Inquisition 'proved' that Europe was overrun with witches who blighted crops, ate babies, and had sex with the devil. You need to use psychology, not torture."

"Yeah, yeah. And with what for leverage? The bad guys *know* we're not allowed to rough them up."

"We seem to have done okay with Koch."

"Sure . . . with you and the Russian guy pretending to be Mossad, and hinting that you didn't have to follow the rules. He was practically begging to talk to us after that!"

The man on the other side of the one-way glass certainly seemed willing to talk freely. He'd been given a cigarette and appeared relaxed as he answered the interrogator's questions.

"And when did you get your payoff, Lieutenant?" the interrogator was asking, the voices coming through over a speaker in the ceiling.

"It was in two payments," Koch replied. "Half when I agreed to do this thing, half at Qurghonteppa, when I met the truck with the helicopter."

"And how much were you paid?"

"Half a million euros. Half when I agreed, half when I made the pickup."

"Why didn't you take the money, fly back to Kabul, and turn in the shipment?"

"There was a man with me, a Pakistani. Don't know his name. He flew with me all the way to Karachi. He was supposed to be my liaison here. They never said, but I knew he was also a . . . how do you say? A watchdog. To make sure I carried out my part of the deal."

"Isn't it true you were supposed to be paid even more money once you were in Karachi?"

Koch seemed to hesitate. "Well . . ."

"The Mossad has been tracking all of the financial trails in this case."

"It is true. I was supposed to see a man at Jinnah this evening."

"His name?"

As the questioning continued, Lloyd filled Dean in on what they'd learned already. "Koch was deserting from the German Air Force anyway. Seems he's a member of a German Muslim group promoting jihad in Europe. *Der Volk auf Gott.*"

"He doesn't quite look the Muslim type."

"The VaG is radically anti-Semitic, though they're careful about the invective for obvious reasons. It's popular with the more radical flavor of Islamic immigrants in Germany, and is apparently picking up converts among the good, pure Aryan types as well. Especially in the teenaged population. Koch joined eight years ago, while he was in college in Berlin."

Germany, Dean had heard, possessed the fastest-growing Muslim population in Europe, and at least some of that explosive growth was linked with lingering anti-Semitic prejudices submerged since the Nazi *Götterdämmerung* of 1945.

"So Koch is a Muslim convert?"

"At least in name. The VaG started off as a radical skinhead group in the eighties. More into social protest and riots than worshipping God. In any case, Koch was also planning on deserting from the air force. Apparently a Muslim buddy in Kabul knew that, and got him in touch with the Army of Mohammad in Afghanistan. We're getting a lot of leads there. We'll be following them up for a long time to come."

"So he wasn't planning on flying back to Kabul."

"Nope."

"What was he going to do with that helicopter?"

"Abandon it at Jinnah. The Luftwaffe will be treating it as theft of government property on top of desertion."

"So they'll be taking an interest in our friend there."

"Oh, yes. Big-time. They have people flying into Karachi tomorrow to take him back to Germany for court-martial."

"Does he know that yet?"

Lloyd shrugged. "I don't know. We promised not to turn him over to the Mossad, and that's all he's been concerned about so far. He hates Jews and is terrified of the Israeli intelligence service. Almost paranoid."

Dean nodded. Rubens had sent him a file on Koch before sending him to find the man. Apparently, Koch's anti-Semitism and his pre-military membership in the skinhead gang had been well known back in Germany. There'd even been an entry describing his conviction that Mossad agents had infiltrated the German Luftwaffe.

It had been Dean who'd suggested using the Mossad ploy to pick him up, and perhaps convince him to cooperate. With the black hair and olive skin dye from the Tajikistan deployment, he could easily pass as a Sabra, a native-born Israeli. Mossad had a rep worldwide for being thorough, professional, and as ruthless as they needed to be when it came to preserving their tiny nation wedged in between the sea and nations still determined, after more than sixty years, to exterminate them.

"Are you sure you never knew what was in those containers?" the interrogator was demanding.

"They never told me, I never asked," Koch replied.

"Weren't you curious?"

A shrug. "It was my ticket out of the Luftwaffe, that's all. They were paying me to make a delivery."

"Three-quarters of a million euros is an expensive delivery."

"It wasn't my business to know. I just wanted out of fucking Afghanistan."

On the other side of the glass, Dean asked Lloyd, "Have you asked him about the shipment, about where it went?"

Lloyd nodded. "Several times. He says it was being taken to a ship at the waterfront. He didn't know which one."

"That squares with the intelligence we got from you people."

"The *Yakutsk*, yes," Lloyd said, nodding. "She left yesterday. Is the Navy going to intercept her?"

"That," Dean told him, "depends on the political winds back home. They'd damned well better."

Where, Dean wondered, *do you draw the line? Ships at sea belonging to one nation should never be summarily boarded and searched by the military forces of another;* that *was a principle the United States had signed for in blood.* But what if you had good information that the ship carried stolen nuclear weapons, weapons that would be used against you or your allies, weapons that could kill millions?

Was *torture* ever justified?

Hard questions, and Dean knew he didn't have the answers. He knew if Lloyd had tried to torture Koch, he would have stopped it if he could, and reported him back home.

Yet if the man knew where those nukes were . . .

"Okay," Dean said. "Just so a full report gets back to my people."

Rubens could deal with the ethics of information gathering.

No wonder, he thought, the various U.S. intelligence agencies preferred spy satellites over HUMINT, intelligence drawn from human contacts.

Satellites were *so* much more antiseptic.

HOTEL SOL
PUERTO NAOS
LA PALMA, CANARY ISLANDS
FRIDAY, 1543 HOURS LOCAL TIME

Lia DeFrancesca walked into the hotel lobby, a vast and brilliantly lit space of pillars, skylights, tropical plants, and marble floors. She'd checked into her room and unpacked an hour before and was ready for the next phase of her new assignment.

"*Buenos tardes*," she told the young man at the desk. Her Spanish was rusty but passable.

"*Sí*, Señorita Lau," the man replied. "How can I help you?"

"You have, I believe, a guest here? A Señor Carlylse?"

"Yes, miss," the man said, having checked his computer screen. The shift to English was effortless. "Is there a message?"

"Yes. Please tell him a Miss Diane Lau wishes to speak with him on a matter of *extreme* importance." She thought a moment, then added, "Tell him it is about his book, and about his partner."

That *ought to get a response from him*, she thought.

"I happen to know that Señor Carlylse is out of the hotel at the moment," the man said, typing at his keyboard, "but I shall certainly see that he gets the message when he returns."

"*Mil gracias*," she told him and handed him a five-euro tip.

She left the lobby by ascending a broad set of spiral steps, following a blaze of tropical light filtering down through the skylights. At the end of a long hallway, she walked through a set of glass doors and onto a pool deck.

Beyond the pool, a placid semicircle of aquamarine, she looked out over the far deeper and wilder blue of the ocean.

The west coast of La Palma faced the raw, powerful Atlantic. There were no beaches with tame, knee-high rollers surging up a golden sand shelf. The Hotel Sol was perched atop a cliff extending out over the ocean; from here, Lia looked down the black and rugged face of sheer basalt, a drop at least sixty feet high, directly into the surge and thunder of the ocean surf.

The waves breaking on the rocks below the hotel were easily fifteen and twenty feet high, and the thunder as they crashed into cascades of white spray physically assaulted her senses. Looking up, she stared into the western horizon, knowing that there was nothing but open ocean between La Palma and the coast of Florida, fully thirty-seven hundred miles distant.

North of the Hotel Sol, the town of Puerto Naos lay snuggled up to the ocean beyond a broad beach of black volcanic sand curving away from the rocky point. To the south, the land seemed to rise explosively from the water in sheer vertical cliffs of black rock. The land continued to rise steeply inland, culminating in the green-clad ruggedness of the island's central spine, the Cumbre Vieja.

Those mountains running down the middle of the island loomed massive against the sky. They were oppressive, Lia thought, heavy, threatening to come sliding toward her, sweeping the sprawling hotel into the sea. The land looked alien, otherworldly, and raw, as if the entire island had only recently thrust itself above the seething surface of the ocean.

"Okay," she said, leaning on the safety rail. "Carlylse isn't here, you heard?"

"We heard, Lia," Marie Telach told her.

"If you have a position for him, I can try to find him."

"Our best guess is that al-Wawi hasn't found him yet either," Telach said. "No message intercepts to that effect, at any rate. We suggest that you stick with the original plan, and make contact when he returns to the hotel."

"Any ideas on how al-Wawi is going to try to get to him?"

"Unless he already has a tail on him, the hotel is the likeliest venue. They'll find a way to gain access to his room, and kill him there, out of the public eye. They may try to make it look like suicide. That's how they took out Pender."

"Then my best bet will be to hang around the lobby, try to hook up with him when he gets back," Lia decided.

"So where's your new boyfriend?"

Lia made a face, though she knew Marie couldn't see it. "In his room, getting ready to go check on his project later this afternoon. At least he didn't try to share a room with me like Feng did."

"I don't know, Lia. This one sounds kind of cute."

"Marie, you can have him."

"Missing Charlie?"

Was she that transparent? Her relationship with Charlie Dean was less than deep-serious . . . but it was more than casual, certainly, and right now she *did* find herself missing him.

"How is he?" she asked. Marie wouldn't be allowed to say anything about Charlie's mission, but . . . "How's he doing?"

"He's fine. He's wrapped up his current op, and—" She broke off what she was saying.

"And what?"

"Nothing. He's fine."

She was about to tell me he's getting ready for another op, Lia thought.

She knew that Charlie and Ilya Akulinin were in South-central Asia, chasing some stolen suitcase nukes believed to be in the hands of the Russian *mafiya*. She frowned. Russian *mafiya* and Islamist extremists. A deadly mix.

Please be okay, Charlie, she thought.

She wondered if he might be thinking of her.

14

Dean was thinking about Lia.

Their service with the Agency didn't exactly encourage personal relationships, with good reason. Field operators, especially, had to make decisions, hard ones sometimes, that always, *always* kept the mission first. Ilya had made a major error in judgment by letting himself get involved with the Alekseyevna woman. Dean didn't begrudge his partner a bit of fun or comfort, but it would have been all too easy for Ilya to have made decisions out of concern for Masha's safety, compromising the needs of the op.

Charlie Dean and Lia rarely deployed together anymore. No one had said anything about it back at the Puzzle Palace, but they knew how he felt about Lia. Rubens knew, certainly.

Damn, he missed her.

He sat on a hard, narrow seat in the back of a U.S. Navy MH-60S helicopter, flying southwest across a night-shrouded ocean. Unofficially known as the Knighthawk because it was replacing the venerable CH-46D Sea Knight, the aircraft flew off both aircraft carriers and smaller naval vessels in a multi-mission role that included "VERT-

REP" resupply at sea, search-and rescue, and even combat with its add-on "batwing," or armed helicopter kit. An hour ago, he and Akulinin had boarded the helo at Masroor Air Base, a Pakistani military airfield on the western side of Karachi. The Knighthawk had flown in from USS *Constellation*, somewhere in the Gulf of Oman to the south, refueled, and readied for a flight to USS *Lake Erie*.

Ilya was seated across from him, all but anonymous in his baggy Navy flight suit and helmet. Dean wondered where Lia was right now; the last he'd heard, she was in Berlin tracking down the Chinese connection in this puzzle.

He hoped she was okay.

"So what's the story?" Akulinin asked, shouting to make himself heard above the pounding roar of the Knighthawk's rotors. "They bringing in a Black CAT?"

"Don't know yet," Dean yelled back. "CAT Bravo is being deployed, but that's going to take time. We may have to use assets in place."

Black CAT was the NSA's highly secret Deep Black Combat Assault Team, a specialized unit drawn from active duty U.S. Navy SEAL and Army Delta personnel. CAT Alpha was based in San Diego; CAT Bravo was at the Marine base at Pax River, Maryland.

Getting a twenty-four-man unit with its equipment from Virginia to the Indian Ocean, however, would take at least twenty-four hours, and possibly more . . . and that was *after* they got clearance to go in the first place. Rubens had told Dean earlier that they were still waiting to hear from the White House on a go/no-go decision about the *Yakutsk*. He was trying to pre-position the team, but even that required high-level authorization, and from the sound of it, everyone in Washington right now was playing a round of cover-your-ass.

There was a SEAL detachment with the *Constellation* Battle Group, and a forty-man troop—two platoons—was being flown in from Kuwait. If they got the go-ahead, Rubens might well decide to use the CBG—the "assets in place" Dean had mentioned—rather than wait for CAT Bravo to deploy halfway around the world. One way or the other, though, Rubens wanted Dean and Akulinin present when the *Yakutsk* op went down.

The helicopter lurched, dropping a dozen feet, then gave a heavy jolt. The air was rough this morning, the sky overcast and promising rain. When Dean turned to peer through one of the rectangular windows set in the Knighthawk's port-side sliding door, he saw gray ocean below, and nothing else.

Another half hour or so, he thought, until they reached the *Lake Erie*.

Then the real fun would begin.

HOTEL SOL
PUERTO NAOS
LA PALMA, CANARY ISLANDS
FRIDAY, 1615 HOURS LOCAL TIME

Lia DeFrancesca looked up as the tall, slender man entered the hotel lobby. She checked the photograph currently being displayed on her BlackBerry but already knew that it was Vincent Carlylse—pale and wispy hair, glasses, jutting nose.

And he wasn't alone.

"Target acquired," she murmured, putting away the BlackBerry. The Art Room had sent her the image—from the dust jacket of a recent book—earlier that morning. The woman with him, though, was going to be a complication. "He's with someone, a younger woman."

"A prostitute?" Rockman's voice shot back.

"Now how the hell am I supposed to know that?"

"I don't know. Prostitutes carry big, shiny purses, right? How's she dressed?"

"She looks like another tourist. Slacks, blouse, sunglasses . . ."

"They used a prostitute to get to Pender in his hotel room," Rockman told her. "They might be using the same plot here."

"Wait one. I'm going to make contact."

As Carlylse and the woman crossed the lobby, the desk clerk called out. "Ah! Señor Carlylse! *Hay un mensaje* . . ."

Lia emerged from behind one of the tropical plants. The clerk saw her and bowed. "This lady," he said in English, "wished to speak with you."

"Mr. Carlylse?" she said, extending a hand. "I'm Diane Lau. It is important that I talk to you."

"I see," the writer said, looking her up and down. "Are you a re-porter?"

"Not . . . exactly." She smiled at the woman. "Is this your wife?"

"Why . . . uh, yes. Yes, she is." She looked Spanish, with black hair and olive skin. She might have been a tourist from the mainland, or she could have been a native islander.

"This concerns your books," Lia told him, "and your collaborator, Jack Pender."

"Jack? I haven't seen him in over two months. How is the old son of a bitch?"

"Mr. Carlylse, I need to speak with you alone. Please. It's impor-tant."

He pulled a keycard from his shirt pocket and handed it to the woman. "Why don't you go on up to our room, my dear? Room 312. I'll be along in a moment."

Without saying a word, the woman took the key, gave Lia a dark look, then walked away, her heeled sandals clicking across the marble floor. She was young, no older than her midtwenties, while Carlylse was easily fifty. She *might* be his wife . . . but Lia was will-ing to bet she wasn't. She glanced around the lobby. There were other people there—a man reading a Spanish newspaper, a young couple watching a television monitor. It was just a little too public here.

"Let's step outside," she said.

They stepped onto the outside pool area a moment later. There were several hotel guests here as well, sunbathing on the lounge chairs around the pool, but the wind and the crashing surf would make cer-tain that their conversation remained private. Lia pulled out her wal-let and flashed an ID at the man.

"Just what is it you want to tell me, Miss, um, Ms. Lau?" he asked as they walked past the pool toward the safety railing above the cliff. "You know, the State Department ID card you just waved at me had your photograph on it, but the name wasn't Diane Lau."

"No, it wasn't. Congratulations for actually reading an ID when it's showed to you." Most people just glanced at a proffered ID without really looking at it. "You asked how Jack Pender is. I'm sorry to have to tell you this. He's dead."

"*What?*"

"He was almost certainly murdered in New Jersey early Wednesday afternoon," she told him.

"*Murdered?* Who—"

"We're working on that, but we have evidence that they may want to kill you as well."

Carlylse looked thunderstruck. "Who wants us dead? Did we piss someone off? They could always sue us for libel instead . . ."

"Have you ever written about al-Qaeda, Mr. Carlylse? Or any Islamist terror group?"

"Terrorists?" He shook his head. "This is about *terrorists?* Jack and I . . . we write about *weird* shit, Ms. Lau. UFOs. Atlantis. Not . . . not about terrorists!"

"Let's sit down, Mr. Carlylse," she said, gesturing toward a vacant poolside table beneath a brightly colored umbrella. "I need to ask you some questions."

RUBENS' OFFICE
NSA HEADQUARTERS
FORT MEADE, MARYLAND
FRIDAY, 1225 HOURS EDT

"Come in."

"Mr. Rubens?" Ann Sawyer said, opening the office door. "Miranda Franks."

"Send her in."

An older woman walked through the door, carrying a file folder in one hand.

"Miranda. What did you find?" Rubens asked her. Franks was from the NSA's Research Department.

"We might have found what you were looking for, sir," she said, handing him the folder. "The book isn't out yet, but it *will* be in another week or two. We have a call in to the publisher, to try to get some copies. This gives the overview."

Rubens took the papers and began reading through them. Then he stopped, went back to the beginning, and began reading more carefully.

"Jesus," he said quietly. "La Palma?"

"Yes, sir. There's been a little released on the subject already. There was a Discovery Channel show on it last year. The whole idea is *highly* speculative. Most reputable scientists say it would never happen."

"How sure are they?"

Franks shrugged. "There are impassioned voices on both sides, sir. Like global warming."

"You've certainly earned your pay this week, Miranda. Thank you."

He reached for his phone.

HOTEL SOL
PUERTO NAOS
LA PALMA, CANARY ISLANDS
FRIDAY, 1634 HOURS LOCAL TIME

"So why are you on La Palma?" Lia asked Carlylse.

"A research trip," he told her. "Jack and I—" He broke off. "Damn, I can't believe he's dead!"

"I'm sorry, Mr. Carlylse—and I'm sorry to have sprung it on you like that. But we think the same people might be planning to kill you as well, and it would help us, help us a lot, if you could tell us why."

"I understand."

"So why were you here? Research, you said?"

"Yeah. We were planning a new book on the lost continent of Atlantis."

Lia kept her face impassive. She'd already endured as much of the fabled lost continent as she cared to some months earlier, when she'd been a passenger on board the *Atlantis Queen*, a luxury cruise ship with an Atlantean theme that had been hijacked by terrorists.

Carlylse continued talking, enthusiasm brightening his face. "You see, we, Jack and I, we're convinced that the Canary Islands were once the southern rim of a larger, single island, perhaps the size of Spain. The northern edge would have been opposite the Pillars of Hercules, just as Plato's account claimed."

"Mr. Carlylse—"

"Vince, my dear, please."

"Vince, that's all quite fascinating, I'm sure, but I can't see terrorists being interested in you and Mr. Pender because of your theories about Atlantis."

"No. No, I don't suppose so." He thought for a moment. "Of course, it could be the other book that brought me to La Palma."

"And what book is that?"

"*Death Wave: The 2012 Prophecies Fulfilled*," he told her. "I have an advance copy in my room, if you'd like to see."

"More of the 2012 stuff?" she asked. "The end of the world?"

"Some people think so. In the ancient Mayan calendar, their Fourth Sun ends on the Winter Solstice of 2012."

"What does La Palma have to do with the end of the world?"

"Well, there's a rift, a geological fault line, running right down the center of the island. Some geologists think that if that fault slips, like in a really big earthquake or volcanic eruption, half of the island of La Palma could fall into the ocean."

"A landslide?"

"A *big* landslide. Billions and billions of tons of rock. It could generate a gigantic tidal wave, a megatsunami that could sweep across the Atlantic and destroy everything from Maine to Brazil."

"That sounds a bit more promising," Lia told him. "Go on. I'm listening."

OFFICE OF DIRNSA
NSA HEADQUARTERS
FORT MEADE, MARYLAND
FRIDAY, 1315 HOURS EDT

"You're shitting me," Lieutenant General Alexander Douglas said. "Half the island is going to fall into the sea? I thought that was supposed to be California."

"The theory," Rubens said, "is . . . let's say speculative at best. Most serious geologists discount the possibility completely. They point out that during the last major earthquake on the island, in 1947, the fault didn't slip at all. And there was a volcanic eruption more recently, in 1971. Again, nothing moved. There's some question as to just how deep the surface fault extends, and whether or not it's still active."

"You've done your homework," Douglas said.

"I made some phone calls just now before calling you. The chair of the Geology Department at Georgetown was able to point me in the right direction. He doesn't think there's anything to it."

"But you do?"

Rubens frowned. "Do I think the island is going to fall into the ocean by itself? No, sir, but lots of people do. There was a program on cable a year or two ago about La Palma collapsing and triggering a megatsunami. And Pender and Carlylse wrote a book about it, tying it in with the 2012-end-of-the-world crap. So my question is . . . what if La Palma is the actual destination of those suitcase nukes?"

Douglas's eyes widened. "An underground detonation?"

"Yes, sir. Or several of them, in a chain down the central spine of the island."

"That seems a bit far-fetched, don't you think?"

"Look at the pieces, sir. One of my officers bugged the meeting between Feng and two oil people, one with a French company providing specialized drilling equipment to Saudi Aramco, the other with Saudi Aramco. They talk about having the boreholes ready next week . . . and about concerns in Saudi Arabia about losing a major trading partner. The context of the conversation is that Operation Wrath of God will have an enormous psychological impact on the Muslim world.

"Then one of the oil people goes to La Palma and says he has to check on a project there. I spoke with a representative of Saudi Aramco here in Washington. He says there is no drilling taking place in the Canary Islands, not commercial, not exploratory. He says the geology of those islands is completely wrong for oil."

Douglas nodded slowly. "I think I see where you're going with this. Terrorists explode several nuclear devices at the bottom of boreholes drilled into this fault line on La Palma. They trigger the landslide everybody is dreading. The damage to the U.S. eastern seaboard could be cataclysmic."

"It would be like the 2004 megatsunami disaster in Indonesia, but much, much worse. Millions, perhaps tens of millions, would be killed. Estimates suggest that the tidal wave would be in excess of one hundred feet high when it hit the American coast, and traveling at the speed of a jetliner. Entire cities would be wrecked, made uninhabitable. Highways and rail lines washed away. Washington, D.C., destroyed by the surge coming up the Potomac. Wall Street wiped out. Our economy would be devastated. It would take years to recover. Hell, we might get smashed down to the level of a third-world country.

"It's a force multiplier," Douglas mused aloud. "If the bad guys have twelve tactical nukes, they could cause tremendous damage to twelve American cities. That would be bad, yes, but a one-kiloton nuke won't vaporize a city. At most, it'll wreck downtown, and contaminate the outlying parts with radioactivity. But . . . my God. If they use them to trigger a tsunami, they could wipe out every city from Portland, Maine, to Miami. Dozens of cities ruined. Tens, no, *hundreds* of trillions of dollars in damage . . ."

"It has another advantage for them, sir. Maybe an even more important one."

"What's that?"

"Right now, there's no such thing as global Islam. They're divided between Sunni and Shi'ite, between radical and moderate and conservative. Different interpretations of the Qur'an. Different cultural beliefs. But just think what might happen if a volcanic island explodes and sends a tidal wave crashing into the American east coast. It would seem like a natural disaster."

"The wrath of God."

"Exactly."

"Scientists who investigated the explosion would be able to tell it was man-made. An underground nuclear detonation. There'd be radiation."

"Maybe—but it would be days, maybe weeks, before anybody could get there and start carrying out tests. Ten minutes after the tsunami hit, the entire Muslim world would hear that it was an act of God, and that's what the majority would believe, *and keep on believing*. Moderates would be shouted down. Scientific findings would be rejected as attempts to explain away something that was *obviously* a miracle. The vast majority of the world's Muslims don't agree with the idea of global jihad, but what if they saw a miracle? Moderate Islamic governments from Morocco to Indonesia could fall to the radical militants. Egypt. Jordan. Secular Islamic countries like Turkey. There might be a call for a general rising, a holy jihad to sweep across the non-Muslim world. The radical fundamentalists would take it as a sign from God that *now* is the time to unite the Muslim world and destroy the infidels."

"I find it hard to believe that they'd be able to unite that easily."

"Maybe not—but I'll bet you a month's salary *they* think it's a possibility worth the effort. We know that the Jaish-e-Mohammad is the principal enemy group behind this. Al-Wawi—Ibrahim Hussain Azhar—is JeM, and his brother, Maulana Azhar, has been beating the drum for a united, militant fundamentalist Islam for over a decade now."

"You think the JeM is going to go global? They've been pretty much a regional terrorist group until now."

"Yes, sir, but they also have close ties to both the Taliban and to al-Qaeda. It wouldn't take much to shift their focus from India and Kashmir to the world stage. They might think we'll be so busy cleaning up the wreckage of our cities that we won't be able to interfere if they start settling some scores and ending some boundary disputes. Kashmir. Israel. And there might be some bloody risings in countries with large Muslim populations. England. Germany. France. The Philippines. Even here in the United States."

"You're just full of good news this afternoon, Bill." Douglas sighed. "Obviously you want me to inform the President about this."

"At the very least, we are going to need a detailed reconnaissance of La Palma. We need to see the extent of the drilling and the exact positions of the wellheads. We have an agent team on the ground over there, but they'll be limited in how much area they can cover. We need full, high-res satellite imagery, the sooner the better. And we may need to deploy a CAT, or coordinate with the military."

"An invasion? The Canary Islands are Spanish territory."

"If we need to take the boreholes out, we'll need to do it simultaneously, or as close to simultaneous as we can manage. So we don't warn the others when we take down one. We also need to push harder on recovering those nukes. If we can get our hands on those, the boreholes won't matter."

"We're doing everything we can do. The President is out of the country now. He'll be back Monday."

"Then the Vice President—"

"It's not that easy, and you know that as well as I do," Douglas said heatedly. "Requests of this nature go through the President's personal staff at the Oval Office. *They* decide what is important, what has to be put in front of him immediately. We can flag this Code One Ultraviolet, but I'd damned well better have good justification to do so. And you have to admit that the idea of using tactical nuclear weapons to generate a megatsunami large enough to wipe out the U.S. East Coast is just a tad on the far-fetched side."

"What about the request for military intervention on the *Yakutsk*?"

"We're still waiting to hear." Douglas made a face. "I spoke with the President's personal secretary yesterday. He was not . . . encouraging."

"Okay. Then what about the Saudi foreign trade minister? Our eavesdropping on Feng and his cronies suggested that al-Khuwaytir knows at least something about Operation Wrath of God. Enough to guess that our economy is going to be tanked."

"You know, Bill, it's not exactly politically expedient going up to the representatives of a friendly foreign power and accusing a member of that government of collusion in a plot to flood the East Coast. And he would deny it, of course. It would also tip off the JeM. Let them know that we know."

"There's also Feng," Rubens said. "He may be behind the whole plot to begin with."

Douglas leaned back in his chair. "What the hell does China have to do with this anyway?"

"It may just be opportunism on their part. But Feng did mention something about China holding an eighth of the entire U.S. foreign debt."

Douglas snorted. "You think they're going to foreclose on San Francisco?"

"No, but it would give them a hell of a lot of leverage in the world economy. I could see COSCO picking up some bargains when the stock market collapses."

"Hell, a thing like this could cause the *dollar* to collapse. The economy is still damned shaky as it is."

"Yes, sir. Even if they just bet against us on the Asian markets, the People's Republic could end up making hundreds of billions and coming out of this as *the* leader in the global economy. If they have advance warning about what's going to happen, something everyone thinks is an act of God, yeah, they could clean up.

"We *will* want to pick Feng up, sir—but not before we have the nukes secured. It's vital that we find and secure the nukes first. Otherwise, the bad guys go to ground and take their suitcases with them. We might not be as lucky next time around. When those weapons surface again—"

"I know," Douglas said woodenly.

Rubens passed a hand over his face, trying to think.

"Something you said earlier, Bill . . . about the militant Islamists using this to unite Islam and launch a global jihad."

"Yes?"

"Maybe we could defuse things by stealing a march on them—publicize this thing. If the whole world knew before it happened that they were planning this . . ."

"General, *you're* the one who told *me* how thin this sounds right now," Rubens said with a wry grin. "Again, the terrorists would disappear, and take their toys with them."

Douglas merely rubbed his face.

"We *must* recover those weapons," Ruben said flatly, "even if we have to violate Russian territoriality to do it."

Douglas cleared his throat, then said, "The President's secretary brought up another option."

"What's that?"

"We could hand the responsibility off to the Russians."

"We may have to bring them in at some point," Rubens said, "but—"

"Exactly. 'But.' They're not going to search one of their own ships without damned good reason. Especially in light of the Tajikistan incident."

Rubens nodded. The shoot-down of a Russian helicopter over Afghanistan territory was publicly being played as an unfortunate accident, a tragic helicopter crash on the border between Tajikistan and Afghanistan. Congressman Mullins' unthinking revelations about a U.S. intelligence operation in Tajikistan, however, had sharply chilled relations between Washington and Moscow. The Russian ambassador had already delivered a crisply worded protest to the White House about "wild west shoot-outs" in the streets of Dushanbe, this despite the fact that Tajikistan no longer was a part of Russian territory.

"Moscow denies that there are any missing tactical nukes," Rubens said. "They have their heads planted firmly up their asses and aren't going to extract them now."

Douglas grunted. "The *Constellation* CBG is the closest naval force to the area right now, he said. They're in the best position to board and search the *Yakutsk*."

"Yes, sir. *If* we can get the approval to go in."

"Damn it, get me something harder to go on with this tidal wave thing. I can't go to the President with a wild tale from a mass-market paperback."

"I've already arranged for the Deep Black team on La Palma to do some checking, sir," Rubens told him. "I've also initiated a requisition with the NRO for detailed satellite reconnaissance of La Palma." He spread his hands. "It's all we have going for us at the moment."

"Then it's going to have to do. You and your people have my authorization to do what you need to do . . . *but get me that proof.*"

15

T hat woman isn't really your wife, is she?" Lia asked.

"Um, no," Carlylse admitted. He looked embarrassed. "She's a waitress at a restaurant in Puerto Naos. I met her a couple of days ago, and we kind of hit it off."

"You need to get rid of her."

"Damn, she's been up there in my room for over an hour. She's going to be wondering where the hell I am."

"We think that a hooker gave Jack Pender's room key to some JeM assassins," she told him. "If this is the same sort of setup, someone else could be waiting for you in your room."

"Gem? What's gem?"

"Jaish-e-Mohammad," she told him. "The Army of Mohammad. Thoroughly nasty characters who blow up buses filled with civilians, among other unpleasant things."

"Shit." He shook his head. "But Carmen is *such* a nice girl . . ."

"Sure she is. Let's go up to your room together, and you'll explain to her that the date is off for tonight."

"Uh . . . I gave her my key."

"I'd rather not knock. Get another key from the front desk."

"Yeah, sure." Carlylse seemed distracted, even a bit dazed. He wasn't thinking straight.

On the way up to the room, Lia pulled her P226 from her pocket-book and snapped a loaded magazine into the butt. The muzzle was threaded to receive a sound suppressor, which she screwed on tightly. If this was a setup, it was possible that a couple of JeM assassins were waiting in the room for Carlylse's return, and Lia was taking no chances. At the door to room 312, she stood with her back to the wall, the pistol in both hands, muzzle pointed at the ceiling. "Open it," she whispered, "and then get the hell out of the way."

Carlylse nodded and slid the keycard through the reader. The door clicked open, Carlylse stepped back, and Lia rolled around the corner and into the room.

The woman was in the king-sized bed, naked and half asleep. As Lia spun into the room, her pistol aimed two-handed at the woman, the waitress sat up and shrieked.

Lia pivoted, checking each corner of the room, but the woman had been alone. Now she was out of bed, snatching up stray items of clothing from the floor and bolting for the door, still screaming.

"Damn it, you scared the poor girl half to death!" Carlylse thought about it a moment. "You scared *me* half to death!"

"Grab your things."

"Huh? What do you—"

"If this was a setup, she'll be talking to the assassins as soon as she gets her clothes back on. If it wasn't, she'll be talking to the desk manager, and he'll have security up here in a few minutes. Do you re-ally want to wait here and answer their questions?"

"Um, no." He gave her a hard look. "Look, who are you, anyway?"

"I showed you my ID."

"I saw an ID for someone named Cathy Chung. I *think* the ID was for the U.S. State Department, but I've never seen one of those, so I have no way of knowing if it was real. If *you're* real."

"While you try to figure that out," Lia told him, "grab your suit-case and let's get out of here."

"Look . . . did my ex send you?"

"What?"

"Did my ex-wife send you to screw up my sex life?"

"Art Room," Lia said.

"What?" Carlylse asked, looking puzzled at the non sequitur.

"Here, Lia," Jeff Rockman said in her ear.

"Give me some bio on this guy. Stat."

"Coming right up, Lia."

"Who are you talking to?" Carlylse asked, suspicious.

"My electronic backup," she told him. "Never leave home without them." Rockman began reading a file into her ear. Lia listened a moment, then began repeating select lines. "Okay . . . you're Matthew Vincent Carlylse but you've gone as Vince since high school. You were born in Peoria, Illinois, on May 2, 1972. U.S. Army from 1991 to 1995. Married June Hanson in 1994, but she divorced you twelve years later after being diagnosed with schizophrenia. The voices told her you were sleeping with other women. You started writing after your discharge, and your first book was published in 1998. The book was called *Gray Terror: The UFO Abductors*, and was a minor commercial success—"

"Hey!"

"You met John Pender at a book convention in Atlanta the following year, and—"

"All right Hold it! *Hold* it! What's the point of this?"

"To prove to you that I am a U.S. federal agent with access to a great deal of background information on you. Information that foreign terrorists wouldn't have."

"I don't know. My wife was a foreign terrorist after she was hospitalized the first time. *She* would know all of that stuff."

"And she wouldn't have told me that she was schizophrenic. Her medical records, however, are another matter. Mr. Carlylse, can we *please* continue this discussion in my room? Unless you really want to discuss me with hotel security or a couple of assassins from the Army of Mohammad."

Reluctantly, he began gathering his things.

HAFUN
NORTHEASTERN SOMALIA
FRIDAY, 1940 HOURS LOCAL TIME

The place still hasn't recovered, Ahmed Babkir Taha thought as he walked along the sand through the darkness. *Not completely. I wonder if it ever will?*

Even now, well past sunset, the pounding of hammers could be heard farther up the hill from the beach, as small handfuls of people continued to rebuild. A few lights shone here and there. It was late enough in the year that the wind coming in off the ocean was quite chilly. Unfortunately, it was also dry, with the promise of yet more crippling drought.

God the most merciful had not been merciful to the town of Hafun—Xaafuun, in Somali. Drought, crushing poverty . . . and on December 26, 2004, an earthquake fifty-four hundred kilometers away, off the distant coast of Sumatra, had generated a tidal wave that had swept across the Indian Ocean, wreaking untold damage and killing 230,000 people in eleven countries.

Hafun, a fishing village located on a sand spit just above sea level here at the very tip of the Horn of Africa, had been the population center hardest hit on the entire African continent. Some 280 people had been killed or missing, though only nineteen bodies in all had been recovered. Eight hundred homes had been washed away, the wells poisoned by saltwater, the fishing boats destroyed. The land here was parsimonious, barren, and unforgiving; some families had maintained small plots where they'd grown peas or lentils, but fishing had been the principal local industry. The tsunami had left the local people with nothing.

Picking his way through the darkness, Taha made his way out of the town, following a worn track across the sand toward the ocean, guiding on a small cluster of flickering lights on the beach. The *pound-pound-pound* of hammers, he thought, was a beautiful sound. The sound of rebuilding.

The sound of life.

Since the beginning of 2005, the town had started to rebuild, though this time the structures were rising higher up along the ridge of sand, some five hundred yards from the sea. The people were terrified that the waters would come again. Foreign aid had come to the impoverished area, and UNICEF had been attempting to establish a school for the local children, a school for girls as well as for boys, of all things. While anything resembling a real government in Somalia had collapsed in 1991, this northeastern corner of the country, the Horn of Africa, had stabilized somewhat over the past few years, with an uneasy balance between the Transitional Federal Government, operating out of Ethiopia, and the opposition party, the Alliance for the Re-Liberation of Somalia.

It hadn't been perfect. ARLS antiaircraft guns had repeatedly fired at aircraft bringing emergency food and medical supplies to the region, and the rivalry between the TFG and the ARLS continually threatened to slip back into civil war. Still, it had been a start, a small one, back to sanity and self-sufficiency. The Bars region around Hafun had long traditionally belonged to the Majeerteen sub-clan of the Osman Mahmoud. They were the *true* power here, the true government. Or they had been.

Then the outsiders had come.

With the TFG ruling from next-door Ethiopia, most of south and central Somalia was still held in the grip of various rival Islamist gangs—the most powerful being the Hizbul Islam and the rival al-Shabaab. United African forces—Kenyan and Ethiopian troops, mainly—had been alternately battling and attempting to appease the Islamist militants.

Neither military intervention nor negotiation had made much headway.

He was approaching the camp on the beach now. One of the guards stepped out of the shadows, blocking his way. "In the name of Allah and His Prophet," the man said, "you will halt!"

Man? It was a boy, a child no more than fifteen years old. The AK-47 rifle he held with wavering hands looked nearly as large as he did.

Taha raised his hands chest high, palms out, to show he carried no weapons. "God willing, I am here to see General Abdallah," he said. "He knows me. I've been here before."

The boy seemed uncertain, and Taha felt sick fear prickling at his spine. These people were perfectly capable of shooting a man dead in the street for no reason at all save that they mistrusted him, that they didn't like his looks or his demeanor, that they thought he'd failed to show proper respect.

"I'll take him, Oamar," another voice said. Abdiwahid Eelabe Adow stepped out of the night. "It's all right."

Oamar gave Taha a surly look, then nodded, lowering his rifle, and Taha relaxed slightly. He knew Adow, one of Abadallah's chief strongmen and the cleric of the group. At least Adow wouldn't shoot him on sight.

Adow gestured toward a fire burning in a drum on the beach a dozen meters away. "And what brings you to our humble camp this time, Taha?" Adow asked pleasantly.

"News from Addis Ababa," Taha replied. "A possible target with a fabulously rich payoff."

Adow snorted. "Better than the last few targets, I hope. The Westerners have been guarding their ships more and more closely. Business has become . . . very difficult, of late."

"This one," Taha replied, "is unprotected. God willing, it carries a cargo of great value."

"We'll see. There's the general."

Taha despised the group known as *al-Shabaab*, Arabic for "the Youth." Principally active in southern Somalia and in the capital of Mogadishu, they'd been fighting a bitter war there against the TFG. In recent months, they'd moved into the Hafun area as well, a region long under TFG control and protection. Ostensibly, they'd come with their boats, offering help. In fact, they were pirates, heavily armed raiders who set to sea every few days in hopes of catching one of the fabulously wealthy cargo ships passing through Somali waters. They would board a likely-looking vessel, hold the ship and crew hostage, and demand a ransom from the company or even the country owning the ship.

It was more dangerous than fishing, but *much* easier, and the potential rewards meant inestimable wealth and power for those who succeeded.

General Abdallah, Taha knew, was not a real general. He'd been part of the crew that had seized the Ukrainian merchant ship MV *Faina* in 2008. That vessel had been carrying thirty Russian tanks and tons of ammunition and weapons to Kenya when it was seized. The owners had paid 3.2 million American dollars for the *Faina*'s release—and Taha knew that many of the machine guns and RPG launchers on Abdallah's boat had come from the *Faina*'s hold. His share of the ransom had made him obscenely wealthy by Somalian standards, and he'd used that wealth to buy and outfit a larger boat with which to score even greater successes. It was no secret that Abdallah planned to consolidate his political and military power, carving out his own personal warlord's empire from the northeastern Somali coast.

Adow led Taha into the wavering circle of firelight cast by burning scraps of lumber in a two-hundred-liter drum. Abdallah and several of his chief lieutenants stood there, warming themselves against the chill of the evening. Nearby loomed the ruin of the village's tumbledown salt factory, a shell built by the Italians in the 1930s, long abandoned. Beyond, at the end of a long and rickety pier, Abdallah's boat creaked and thumped with the movement of the surf. Other armed guards moved at the edge of the light, and Taha knew there were more in the ruins. The salt factory had become Abdallah's fortress.

"So, my old friend Taha!" General Abdallah said, looking up from the burning drum with a broad, toothy grin. The looks on the faces of his lieutenants were darker, less open. "What news from our esteemed Ministry of Ports and Sea Transportation?"

Ahmed Babkir Taha had grown up in Hafun, but he'd moved to Mogadishu as a teenager, gone to work for a well-to-do uncle, and eventually been able to get an education in neighboring Ethiopia, in Addis Ababa. With his uncle's import-export firm, he'd traveled as far as Cairo and Damascus, attracted the right attention, and finally been appointed as an assistant undersecretary of the Ministry of Ports and

Sea Transportation within the Somalian transitional government-in-exile. His position gave him access to important information about what ships and cargos were entering Somalian waters.

That was information for which some groups paid handsomely.

"General Abdallah," he said, bowing, then awkwardly saluting. "Your Excellency!" He was never quite sure of the proper protocol when dealing with these people . . . and a mistake, an insult, could be instantly fatal. "Excellent news!" he continued. "A cargo ship will be entering our waters in two days. A Russian ship, the *Yakutsk*. Her cargo is primarily machine parts and tools, but I was given information that she has another cargo on board, a highly secret cargo hidden among the crates of tools. My sources say that it is an extremely valuable cargo. The Russians will pay anything you demand to recover it."

"And what cargo would that be?" Mohammad Fahiye asked. Fahiye, Taha knew, thought that he was a TFG lackey and did not trust him.

There was some truth in that, of course. Taha *did* work for the Transitional Federal Government, certainly . . . though his personal loyalties lay elsewhere. Like most of the locals, he believed that the government-in-exile was weak, a tool of the African Union and other foreign interests.

Then again, al-Shabaab was linked with the foreign al-Qaeda. *Everyone* in Somalia these days had foreign ties.

And in truth, Taha was less a supporter of the TFG than he was an enemy of the fundamentalist Islamic groups like al-Shabaab and Hizbul Islam.

"Tell me about this ship," Abdallah said, his dark eyes glinting in the firelight.

"She is a small and aging freighter, Shanghai to Haifa, with stops in Singapore and Karachi," Taha said. "Twelve hundred tons. Speed less than twenty knots, a crew of twenty-one. There may be small arms aboard, but the ship otherwise is unarmed."

"Allah be praised!" Adow said. "This may be what we've been looking for, my friends!"

Allah be praised indeed . . .

Taha was a devout Sunni Muslim. He believed implicitly in the power, the protection, and the mercy of God.

With that merciful God's help, he would destroy these monsters.

Taha stood quietly as the pirates discussed the news. Adow, especially, seemed eager to go after the Russian ship, but Abdallah was hanging back, suspicious, perhaps, of such an apparently easy target. The foreign, Western navies had made things far more dangerous at sea lately. But as the earnest discussion continued, it appeared that Abdallah might be growing more interested as well.

Take it, Taha thought. *Take the bait!*

"Then this Russian ship with its valuable cargo will be moving up the Red Sea?" Abdallah asked. "There with Allah's help, we will have her."

The militia's leaders burst into cheers and wild cries of *"Allahu akbar!"*

HOTEL SOL
PUERTO NAOS
LA PALMA, CANARY ISLANDS
FRIDAY, 1755 HOURS LOCAL TIME

"You can't stay here," Lia told the writer as he sat down on her bed. "My people are making arrangements to fly you back to the States."

"But . . . I'm not done here."

"Done with what?"

"My *research*!"

"Mr. Carlylse, have you heard a word of what I've been telling you? The JeM wants you dead!"

"Yes, but why? I'm not a threat to anyone!"

Lia shook her head, exasperated. Carlylse seemed to live in a tightly wrapped little world of his own and had trouble seeing beyond his next deadline.

"Look, just tell me some more about this book of yours, the one about 2012 and the tidal wave."

Carlylse fished around inside the zippered outer pocket of his suitcase and produced a paperback book. The cover showed the Capitol Building in Washington, D.C., beneath ominous black skies, with a gray-green ocean wave towering hundreds of feet above the dome. The title, *Death Wave: The 2012 Prophecies Fulfilled*, showed in stark contrast against the dark and lightning-shot clouds.

"You know about the 2012 prophecies, right?" Carlylse asked her.

"Not much. Something about the ancient Mayans, right?"

"Right. The Mayans had a fantastically accurate calendar. They divided up history into four ages, or 'Suns,' each under the light of a different sun god, each one doomed to destruction. We're in the Fourth Sun, the fourth age, now—and it ends in December of 2012."

"And you think that an earthquake on La Palma is going to usher in the end of the world?"

"Certainly the end of the world as we know it. This island, this little fragment of lost Atlantis, is a kind of time bomb. When it goes, hundreds of cubic miles of rock will fall into the ocean and raise a tidal wave nine hundred feet high. Six hours later, that wave will start hitting the U.S. East Coast, up in New England, and by that time the waves will be down to a hundred fifty feet high, and they'll smash over ten miles inland."

"That doesn't sound like the end of the whole world."

"With the United States crippled? Our economy literally washed down the drain? The United States could be reduced to third-world-nation status. The financial collapse would bring down industrial economies all over the world. You'd have the radical Muslims claiming that Allah was ushering in a new age. You'd have hungry populations crossing borders like locust plagues, eating everything in sight. You'd have—"

"I get the picture." She turned the paperback over, read the back-cover blurb, and smiled. "Tell me, Mr. Carlylse, do you actually *believe* the stuff you write?"

"Well," he said, and he sounded sheepish, "first and foremost, I *am* in the entertainment business."

HAFUN
NORTHEASTERN SOMALIA
FRIDAY, 2212 HOURS LOCAL TIME

Taha returned to his home an hour after meeting with Abdallah and his lieutenants. He was still alive—and all praise to Allah for that small fact—and the al-Shabaab pirates had taken the bait.

It was now out of his hands, and in the hands of Allah the compassionate, the Most High.

Taha's home was one of the older buildings, a mud-brick dwelling belonging to his father and his uncle. He greeted his father and mother in the front room, then excused himself as quickly as he politely could to go to the room in the back that served as his bedroom when he was in Hafun.

Here, one wall had been partially broken down by the tidal wave and crudely patched over with lumber and sheets of plywood. It was wet and it was drafty, but it served well enough when he wasn't in Mogadishu or Addis Ababa. He went to the back corner next to the patchwork and began moving aside scraps of wood.

Perhaps, because of what he'd done this evening, Abdallah, Adow, and the rest would soon be gone. He prayed that that would be the case . . .

Like Taha and the others native to Hafun, Abdallah and his al-Shabaab militiamen were Sunni Muslims, but theirs was a different flavor of the holy faith, a faith largely alien to the fishermen of the northern coast, the region known as Puntland. It had been one thing when Abdallah had arrived with his boat, offering to help the fisherfolk of Hafun. It had been something quite different when Adow and other Sunni clerics with the group had begun imposing their beliefs on the locals.

The fact that Abdallah and his people were pirates meant little. Then inhabitants of Hafun made their meager livings by fishing, and everyone knew that more and more Somalian fishermen had been switching over to more lucrative means of earning an income these past few years. It had started innocently enough when some Somalian fishermen had begun boarding and seizing the fishing boats of other nations—Kenya and Djibouti, especially—that were entering Somalian waters to fish illegally. With no working government, no coast guard, no navy to keep the poachers out, the fishermen had begun taking matters into their own hands in order to preserve their own livelihoods.

It had not been long before they'd discovered that they could make far more money by capturing foreign cargo ships or the yachts of rich Europeans and holding them for ransom. That was all simply business, and a means for survival. Taha had done quite well for himself and his family by selling information on foreign ship movements to various pirate gangs.

No, the piracy meant nothing. Al-Shabaab, though, had become a monster.

For over a year now, Abdallah and his people had been terrorizing the inhabitants of Hafun and nearby Foar and Jibalei, implementing the shari'a, religious law, with a brutal, insanely self-righteous fervor. Taha knew well that the path of submission to Allah required sacrifice and hardship. Simply attempting to eke out an existence in Puntland required sacrifice on a daily basis.

But this was something more.

Since their arrival last year, al-Shabaab's clerics had begun enforcing their version of shari'a on the region's female population—ordering families not to allow their daughters to attend the foreigners' schools on pain of death, ordering families to have "the cutting" carried out on all of their daughters in accord with ancient tradition, ordering the wearing of scarves and veils as well as the traditional head coverings to comport with *their* ideas of what constituted proper modesty.

Perhaps the most bewildering of all was the recent ban on bras, seen as "deceptive," and therefore in violation of Islamic law. Beginning in Mogadishu in 2009, al-Shabaab militia gangs had been rounding up women and inspecting them in the streets. Those found to be wearing a bra were publicly stripped, given twenty lashes, and forced to shake their breasts in front of the militiamen after the whipping.

Women found to be wearing trousers could receive forty lashes, the maximum allowed by shari'a, after being stripped and shamed.

What, Taha wondered, could a just and merciful God possibly care about women's clothing when the people were starving to death? The local people couldn't protect themselves, were too poor, too hungry, too demoralized to attempt to flee.

In any case, where could they go?

Even worse was the enforcement of the cutting.

Taha still felt a certain fearful ambiguity about that. The cutting of a girl's genitals when she approached marriageable age had long been sanctioned by Islamic culture and was common across Muslim Africa. What was not well known, however, was that the cutting was not required by the holy Qur'an; rather, it was an outgrowth of local cultures, something likely practiced here long before the Prophet's message had come.

The militants like al-Shabaab and Hizbul Islam claimed that only a rigid adherence to traditional Sunni values and religious law would save the people in the eyes of Allah—and that included everything from proper modesty to the cutting. Taha, however, had seen enough of the world to know that the *interpretation* of Islamic law and custom was different in, say, Cairo, where female genital mutilation was actually against civil law, than it was in a small village on the Horn of Africa.

He'd first begun to recognize the importance of those differences in interpretation when his ten-year-old sister had died in agony from an infection two weeks after she'd undergone the cutting.

Even in Egypt, most women still required their daughters to undergo the ordeal. Lately, though, more and more of the people, especially the younger ones, and especially the women, had been saying that perhaps the foreigners were right—that if the cutting was not enjoined by the holy Qur'an, then it was not necessary. They said that education, even of *girls*, was more important than the blind observance of ancient custom.

The outsiders, the militants from the South, carried a different message, and in Taha's eyes, their message was not religion but an abomination, and Taha was determined to fight them in any way that he could.

Beneath the pile of scrap lumber, he found the radio, carefully swaddled in plastic. The battery was growing weak; he would need to get a new one on his next trip to Addis Ababa, but it should last for the next week or two. He switched the device on, placed the earphones on his head, and picked up the microphone.

"Black Bull, this is Sand Shark," he said, as he'd been trained. He kept his voice low, because he didn't want his parents to know. "Black Bull, come in, please . . ."

16

LA PALMA AIRPORT
SOUTH OF SANTA CRUZ DE LA PALMA
LA PALMA, CANARY ISLANDS
SATURDAY, 1115 HOURS LOCAL TIME

The man walked up to the airport ticket counter, wheeling a single suitcase. Handing his ticket to the woman behind the computer monitor, he gave her a friendly smile.

"Is it on time?" he asked in Spanish. "The flight out to Madrid?"

She looked up at the big scheduling board overhead. "*Sí, señor.* Leaving Gate One at eleven fifty." She made an entry at her keyboard, then asked, "One bag?"

"Just one." He folded up the handle and placed it on the scale platform.

"And did you pack this bag yourself?"

"Yes."

"Did any person unknown to you give you anything to pack?"

"No."

"Has your bag been in your possession at all times since arriving at the airport?"

"Yes."

The woman ran through the usual list of security questions, and the man answered each one. At the end, the woman attached a luggage tag, then hauled the suitcase off the scale and slung it onto the conveyor behind her.

The man watched the bag disappear through a plastic curtain. Security here in La Palma, he knew, was light, the questioning and the checks perfunctory at best. The only flights were island hoppers and a few larger commuter flights to and from the mainland, not the sort of traffic that would interest a politically motivated group like, just for instance, the Jaish-e-Mohammad.

The man had been careful not to fit the typical terrorist profile. He was clean-shaven, wore glasses, and was well dressed, and his papers gave him a Spanish identity. He spoke fluent Spanish, and he'd been rehearsed on current events in Spain—politics and sports especially, just in case someone engaged him in casual conversation.

He looked around the terminal. "Not many people flying today."

"Oh, this is the slow season, Señor Mendoza," she told him with a smile. "Not many tourists yet."

"Tell me . . . has a colleague of mine checked in yet? A Mr. Carlylse?"

"I'm sorry, sir, but I'm really not supposed to discuss the affairs of other passengers."

He gave her his brightest smile. "Of course. But surely you can tell me if he's on the passenger list. I know he checked out of his hotel room last night. I was supposed to meet him here before the flight."

"I'm so sorry, sir. Company regulations—"

"Yes, yes. Security. Well . . . can you tell me, is this the only flight out of La Palma today?"

"Yes, sir. It is."

"Then he must be on it! Thank you. I'll find him on the plane."

"Gate One, sir. Right down there."

"I see it. Thank you."

He walked off toward the gate but turned aside to enter the airport's small boutique area first.

He had no intention of going through the security checkpoint, or of boarding that plane.

RUBENS' OFFICE
NSA HEADQUARTERS
FORT MEADE, MARYLAND
SATURDAY, 1015 HOURS EDT

"It's utter and complete nonsense," Dr. Walden said. "It's not even good fiction."

Dr. Kathryn Walden was a professor of geology at Georgetown University. Brilliant as well as drop-dead gorgeous, she was one of a number of science and academic professionals in a Washington-area network created to provide specialist information to the NSA when necessary. At the moment, she was on the other end of a secure-line video hookup on Rubens' computer.

"*What* is utter and complete nonsense?" Rubens asked. "The tidal wave hitting the East Coast? Or the possibility that half of La Palma is going to shift and fall into the sea in the first place?"

"Both!" Walden hesitated, then went on. "Okay . . . *if* that much rock hit the ocean, and *if* it hit with a high enough speed, and *if* it hit all at once, yes, it could create a megatsunami. *Maybe.* Conditions would have to be just right. But geologists aren't sure that the fracture line at the top of the Cumbre Vieja goes very deep. Most think it's strictly superficial. The important thing is, despite a lot of panicky hype to the contrary, there is absolutely no evidence that any of those rocks have slipped at all since we started watching them."

"But if a landslide did happen, it *could* cause a tidal wave?"

"That's a ridiculously big if—but yeah. It might."

"Three hundred feet high? Traveling ten miles inland?"

"No. Absolutely not." She waved a copy of the book in front of her computer video pickup. "Even if the splash started off as high as these guys claim—and that's saying a *lot*, believe me—it would be down to twenty meters or less by the time it crossed the Atlantic. It *would* get funneled by estuaries and river mouths, so there would be a flood surge up rivers like the Hudson, the Potomac, and the York. Those surges might, *might* reach twenty to fifty meters. But what these guys claim would happen, with killer waves scouring everything as far inland as the Appalachian Mountains . . . that's nonsense."

"Twenty to fifty meters is still bad," Rubens said. "A wave over a hundred fifty feet high and lasting maybe ten or fifteen minutes? That would still kill millions of people if we couldn't evacuate."

"Bill . . . since when did you start going in for off-the-wall pseudo-science? These guys write about UFO abductions, for chris-sakes. They're *kooks!*"

"Oh, I skimmed the book, Katie. I agree with you."

"This whole La Palma thing started a few years ago when the BBC aired a so-called documentary about it, claiming an earthquake or a volcanic eruption was going to throw some hundreds of cubic kilometers of rock into the ocean and trigger a megatsunami. They claimed a hundred million people on the East Coast would be killed."

"Yes."

"After that broadcast, thousands of Americans e-mailed the BBC, worried that they were all going to die and wondering if they needed to move. Thousands of tourists canceled their holiday flights to La Palma. Lots of rich Europeans with vacation homes on La Palma sold their property and left the island. JMC stopped their direct charter flights to the island from Britain, as did the Swiss. German airlines reduced their charter flights by half. If you ask me, La Palma could sue the BBC for damages. The BBC has since issued a partial retraction— what amounts to an apology—saying the threat was overhyped."

"So . . . you're saying there's no danger at all?"

"Not the way that program presented it."

"If none of it is true, why did the BBC air it?"

"Because disasters *sell*, Bill. Parts of the BBC program were re-cycled later by an American cable channel, with the same effect." She waved the book in front of the pickup. "These guys are just taking the pseudo-science scare-stories from that program and recycling it. It's damned irresponsible, coming up with scary fiction and passing it off as science to people who don't know any better. Same with all the tripe written about 2012." She scowled out of the monitor. "Please tell me the government is not taking this seriously!"

"There's been a . . . threat. We're still evaluating it. That's why I called you."

"The government's as bad as the damned insurance companies. It's like the powers that be are *trying* to keep the public in a constant state of terror."

Rubens smiled. "Now you're getting into conspiracy theories."

She chuckled, a grim sound. "The real conspiracy is that the sponsor for that BBC *Horizon* program was a hazard research company—which in turn is owned by a major insurance company. The so-called research company provided the writers with a lot of their data—much of it manufactured. People get scared out of their wits watching this drivel—and they go out and buy more insurance."

"I hope I never get as cynical as you, Katie."

"It's not cynicism, Bill. It's the way the modern world works. Sometimes I think we should scour everything clean with a hundred-meter tidal wave and start over!"

Rubens hesitated, then continued. "You're saying the disaster scenario can't unfold the way it was presented on TV, but that was assuming a volcano or an earthquake was the culprit."

"It would *have* to be something of that nature to shift that much rock."

"I'm going to ask you another question, Katie. I remind you that this conversation is classified."

"I've got clearance, Bill."

"I know you do. We wouldn't be having this conversation otherwise. What about a nuclear explosion?"

That startled her. "What?"

"Specifically, *several* nuclear explosions, probably set off at the bottoms of a number of boreholes along the length of the Cumbre Vieja."

"That . . . would depend on the size, placement, and number of the explosions."

"As many as twelve devices, each releasing approximately one kiloton of energy. Placement . . . we're not sure, but likely at the bottom of some deep oil wells drilled along the Cumbre Vieja, down the center of La Palma."

Walden was quiet for a long moment, her face on the monitor thoughtful. "I don't think I can answer that one for you, Bill."

"Okay . . ."

"If we just compare energy released with energy released . . . no. Absolutely not. The nukes wouldn't even come close."

"An earthquake is more powerful?"

"An earthquake measuring four point oh on the Richter scale releases about one kiloton of energy. We classify a Richter four to four point nine quake as 'light.' It rattles the dishes but doesn't cause any significant damage. Twelve kilotons . . . that would still be less than a five. The earthquake off Sumatra in 2004, the one that caused the big tidal wave that killed two hundred and twenty thousand people around the Indian Ocean, that one was around nine point two, maybe nine point three on the Richter scale, and that translates as a hundred and fourteen *gigatons*—a hundred and fourteen billion tons of TNT."

"My God."

"Exactly. That's the equivalent of over one hundred thousand one-megaton thermonuclear bombs going off together, and that's way, *way* more than all of the nuclear weapons in all of the world's arsenals put together." She gave him a wan smile. "We humans have a long way to go before we can compete with Mother Nature in the raw energy department."

"But you're sounding unsure of yourself."

"Because I am. Most of the energy in an earthquake is wasted . . . unfocused. And when it comes to tidal waves, there are so many variables—bottom depth, the shape of the coastline, things like that. We're also talking about two different ways of generating a tidal wave—by direct transmission of the earthquake energy into the ocean, or by knocking a mountain into the sea and causing a big splash.

"What you're talking about . . . a *precise* application of energy . . ." She shrugged. "It probably all comes down to whether or not there really is a deep fault line beneath the Cumbre Vieja."

"And we don't know if there is one."

"Right. There *is* volcanic activity on La Palma, though the last few eruptions were kind of nonevents. And there *have* been earthquakes, so there could be a fault of some sort under that ridge, something more than the scratch we see on the surface. But we just don't know enough about the subsurface architecture to make a good guess at how large or how deep it might be. That BBC *Horizon* program just went off and declared that the fault was there and that it was quite deep—on the order of twenty or thirty kilometers down, if I remember right—but they were making the numbers up."

"To sell insurance."

"Right. But if people are deliberately planting nuclear charges underground right along that earthquake zone? I have to say . . . I just don't know, Bill. *Nobody* does."

"Might the nukes trigger a big earthquake? I guess what I'm asking is, could twelve kilotons jump-start a hundred gigatons? Or would they have to try for making a really big splash?"

"The jump-start, I just don't know. I'd have to say probably not. As for a big splash? A few years back, a Dutch research group tested the hypothesis that if half of the Cumbre Vieja fell into the Atlantic, it would generate a megatsunami. They used pretty advanced computer modeling. What they came up with was . . . yes, it could generate a big wave if everything worked right, but the wave that hit the East Coast wouldn't be a hundred meters high, like it says in this book. Twenty to fifty meters at most. And it would have to be *very* precise—like a diamond cutter striking a diamond's fracture plane exactly right." She looked thoughtful. "One theory—and it's *only* a theory—is that there's a wall, a kind of curtain of basalt beneath the Cumbre Vieja, running north to south beneath the ridge. The idea is that if there is a fault, lava might have welled up through the crack and solidified into a very hard wall."

"Okay."

"I can imagine . . . well, if someone set off a nuclear explosion on the west side of that wall, a lot of the blast would be reflected toward the west."

"What the military calls a force multiplier."

"Exactly. That might push the whole west side of that ridge up, out, and into the Atlantic very quickly. But that's a worst-case scenario, and it depends on that basalt wall being there. We don't know for sure that it is."

"But it's possible?"

She nodded. "It's possible. There are lots of basaltic extrusions along the top of that ridge—odd-looking rock formations, towers, exposed cliffs, things like that, things that suggest a much larger mass of basalt underground."

"I see. How could we find out if that wall exists?"

"Geological surveys. Ground-penetrating radar, maybe. I happen to know there are a couple of tunnels running through the Cumbre Vieja. I don't think the tunnel engineers encountered anything like a solid wall of basalt. Of course, the tunnels are up at the north end of the ridge. The basalt wall, if it's there, would be farther south, probably."

"Well, thank you, Katie. I appreciate your time."

"Not a problem. But . . . Bill?"

"Yes?"

"When the deputy director of the NSA calls me up and asks about one-kiloton nukes causing landslides and tidal waves on the East Coast . . . I have to ask. Is it time for me to sell my house and move to Denver?"

"I can't discuss the details, Katie. I'm sorry. As I said, there *is* a threat, yes. We don't know how serious a threat it is, but we're evaluating it now. Should you move to Denver?" He smiled. "Probably not. You might want to buy some extra flood insurance, though."

"Georgetown is at an elevation of around forty meters above sea level, Bill."

"Perfect. You may find yourself owning high-priced beachfront property. Thanks again, Katie. I'll be in touch."

PLAYA DE PUERTO NAOS
LA PALMA, CANARY ISLANDS
SATURDAY, 1520 HOURS LOCAL TIME

When Lia saw him walking up the beach toward her, she was furious. CJ had called from the airport hours before, saying she hadn't seen him at the airport, that a surreptitious check of the airport's passenger lists had not turned up his name. Clearly, Vince Carlylse had not gotten on the flight for Madrid as planned, but where he'd gone on the tiny island instead had been a complete mystery.

After walking a couple of miles north along the beach, Lia had turned around and was well on her way back toward the hotel when she'd seen his lanky frame coming toward her across the black sand. He'd stood out. Only a few other people were scattered along the beach, bright splotches of swimsuit colors lying on towels or wading at the edge of the incoming surf. Tourism on the island was light; the beach at Alicante had been packed by comparison.

"What the hell are you doing here?" Lia demanded. She looked at her watch. "You were supposed to be on that commuter flight out of here and back to the mainland over two hours ago!"

"I decided," Carlylse replied with an easy grin, "that I didn't want to go."

"What's the matter with you? Is this some sort of death wish thing?"

"Frankly, Lia, I'm not sure I believe all that stuff. I write fiction for a living, you know. I don't know what your game is . . . but I'm having a little trouble believing in this cloak and dagger stuff, or terrorists out to get me because of the books I write."

She sighed. "So would you believe me if I told you little gray aliens from Atlantis were out to get you instead?"

"*That* I might believe!"

Lia was angry, but she found the anger evaporating fairly quickly. Carlylse, when you thought about it, had no reason to trust her, or to believe anything that she'd told him, in fact.

"You are a world-class idiot," she told him. "Has anyone ever told you that?"

"No, actually. I find your candor refreshing."

"Are you still in the same room at the Sol? The one we switched you to last night?"

The evening before, Lia had asked the Art Room to intercede for her, having them contact the front desk and see if there *had* been a complaint about a woman with a gun. There hadn't been, thank God. A Spanish-speaking handler from the Art Room pretending to be Vince Carlylse had gotten a different room for him at the hotel and the solemn promise that *no one* be told where he now was staying. It was one way to stay ahead of any potential assassins until she could get him on a plane bound for the United States.

"Still there. It does have a better view than the other one."

"*Fuck* the view! We need to get you someplace safe."

"Okay, you're trying to track down these assassins of yours, right? What better way to get them into the open than to use me as bait?"

Eyebrows raised, Lia didn't answer that. Part of the discussion with the Art Room the day before had revolved around exactly that possibility—using Carlylse to flush out al-Wawi. She'd argued that it would be better to get him off the island and back to the United States, suggesting that he would be useful in figuring out just what it was about his tidal wave book that had turned him into a target.

When Lia didn't reply, Carlylse went on, changing the subject. "At least Carmen doesn't appear to have caused a problem with the front desk," Carlylse told her. He sounded almost disappointed. "God knows what she thinks of me now, though."

"You can always tell her I was your crazy ex-wife," Lia told him.

He laughed. "I might just do that."

After getting him a new, assassin-proof room last night, the Art Room had booked him on a local flight out of La Palma back to Madrid. From there, he was supposed to catch a flight to Dulles International. A couple of U.S. Marshals were to have met him in Spain to provide security for the rest of the trip back to the States.

Instead, he was still here. *Damn* the man, and damn his arrogance!

"I should have ridden to the airport with you this morning," she told him, "but I assumed you were an adult, that you could follow some simple directions! I didn't think you needed a babysitter!"

"Look, Lia," he said. She'd told him her real name the night before, a concession to his sharp curiosity. "You might as well know that I don't respond well to the heavy hand of authority. Trying to make me do one thing is a great way to make me do something else."

"Look, do you even understand that we're trying to help you? That you're in danger if you stay here?"

"What are you doing down here with those binoculars? Looking for me?"

"Doing some scouting," she told him.

Unable to do anything about finding Carlylse, Lia had come down to the beach from the hotel earlier that afternoon with a pair of binoculars and had walked slowly north for over an hour, taking time now and again to scan the looming ridge of the Cumbre Viejo looking for signs of activity on the crest. She'd already decided that she was going to need to rent a car and drive up there herself.

"Scouting what? I know the island pretty well. Maybe you could use a friendly native guide."

"Not if you can't follow simple instructions."

"I saw you looking at the mountains up there, though. With your binoculars. What are you looking for?"

"I've heard there are trails and bike paths up there," Lia said. Stopping, she raised the binoculars to her eyes again, focusing on the top of the ridge. The looming slope was thickly forested with what looked like pine trees, but the highest peaks were bare, raw, and volcanic. Directly east of Puerto Naos was Pico Berigoyo, with upthrust slabs of black basaltic rock at the crest some four and a half miles inland and six thousand feet above the beach.

"There are," Carlylse said. "There's something like a thousand miles of trails back there. The one I really wanted to see was La Ruta de los Volcanes. It runs along the whole length of the Cumbre Vieja, past all of those volcanic craters. But it's been closed since I got here."

"Closed? Why?"

He shrugged. "Some sort of test drilling operation. The signs say the area is closed to tourists, by order of the Scientific Institute of Geological Research."

"That's interesting."

"Isn't it? La Palma is pretty much self-sufficient—it doesn't depend on tourism to keep going—but those trail closures must be putting a hell of a bite on their tourist income."

She turned away from him. "Jeff? Did you hear?"

"Yes, I did."

"You might want to check out this scientific institute. Is it here on the island? Or back on the mainland?"

"We're on it, Lia."

"Are your, um, friends *always* listening in?" Carlylse asked her.

"Yup. When I'm on duty, anyway."

"So when are you *off* duty? I'd kind of like to get to know you better. Maybe over dinner?"

"Mr. Carlylse, are you making a pass at me?"

"Of course!"

"My only interest in you is getting you back to the States in one piece. Some of those friends you mention want to talk to you about your book—the one about megatsunamis."

"I won't be able to tell them much that isn't already in the book."

"They'd be interested in your sources, your research. Where you got your information about La Palma and giant tidal waves, that sort of thing."

He chuckled. "Most of that came from a BBC television program a few years ago. *Horizon,* I think the show was called. And there was a disaster program on American cable later about megatsunamis that went into La Palma a bit."

"They'd still like to interview you."

"Maybe you could interview me? Then I wouldn't have to go back to America."

"There are people here who want to kill you, Mr. Carlylse. Doesn't that worry you at all?"

"Not really. So far, the most dangerous person I've seen is you."

She ignored the jibe, raising the binoculars once again. "You've been up there, then?"

"Sure was. Wednesday morning. I rented a car in Puerto Naos, drove up to the village of Fatima, then rented a bike and tried to get up there." He pointed to the left of Pico Berigoyo, indicating another peak. "That's Montaña Rejada."

She looked him up and down. "You're in better shape than you look."

"Thank you *so* much. Anyway, I got to a point just below the top of the ridge when the guards stopped me. They had the path blocked off with yellow tape, and there was that geological institute sign."

"Guards? How many?"

"Two."

"What kind of guards? Spanish Army?"

"I don't think so. Might have been a private security group. They were wearing mostly civilian clothing, but the vests and hats looked military. Canteens. Boots. Maybe military surplus. Otherwise, they were wearing sports shirts and blue jeans, that sort of thing. But they had guns."

"What kind of guns?"

"AK-47s."

"You're sure of that?"

"I've written about military stuff. A little, anyway. Yeah, I'm sure. They were either AK-47s or AK-74s. I'm not sure of the difference. But Russian assault rifles, anyway. They told me I was trespassing and that I should go back down the mountain unless I wanted to be arrested."

"So you did?"

"Not immediately. I rode a little ways back down the hill into a stand of pines, parked my bike, and then looked around a bit on foot. I was curious about those guys."

"What did you see?"

"I saw a helicopter land."

"What? Where?"

He pointed again. "It's kind of tough to see from here, but Rejada Mountain has three volcanic craters, side by side, in a kind of V formation. I was on a bike path just below the rim of the middle crater, maybe a hundred feet from the crest. I saw a helicopter fly up over the top of the ridge from the east side of the island, then disappear down inside that crater."

"What kind of helicopter?"

A shrug. "I don't know. I didn't see any markings. It was pretty big, though, like a transport. I figured they must be using choppers to get all their gear up there."

"Did you see any of the drilling rigs or equipment?"

He shook his head. "No. I heard some of the guards up on the slope above me, so I hurried on back to where I'd stashed my bike."

"I think I'd like a closer look."

"I could take you up there."

She gave him an appraising look. "Maybe. It would *not* be a date. You understand that?"

"Absolutely!" He raised his hand. "Scout's honor!"

"We'll need to check the airline schedules first—and I want to see what this geological research institute is, where it's headquartered. But . . . maybe. If you're still here tomorrow morning."

"It's a date!" He grinned, then saw her expression. "Um, it's a deal, I mean," he amended.

"That's better. Let's get back to the hotel."

"Lia?" a familiar voice said over her implant. "This is Bill Rubens."

She stopped. "Yes? What do you have?"

Carlylse looked at her curiously but didn't say anything.

"CJ just called us. There's . . . a complication."

"What complication?"

"Flight Twelve, the commuter flight to Madrid. It went down about half an hour ago off the coast of Morocco."

"My God!"

"What is it, Lia?" Carlylse asked.

She waved him to silence. "A bomb?"

"No details yet. Officially, the flight is missing. Miss Howorth is in the La Palma Airport tower, however, and tells us the plane went out of radio contact with Agadir Traffic Control at fourteen hundred hours, your time. Until we hear more, we must assume that hostiles have attempted to take out Mr. Carlylse."

"Understood, sir." She grabbed Carlylse's elbow, pulling him forward.

"What?" he said. "What's going on?"

"Shut up," she told him, "and *move!*"

17

CUMBRE VIEJA
LA PALMA, CANARY ISLANDS
SUNDAY, 1115 HOURS LOCAL TIME

The bike ride up from Fatima to the crest of the towering ridge had been both exhausting and exhilarating. The view, certainly, was spectacular, with pine-clad mountains thrusting into the sky ahead, with a panorama of impossibly blue ocean and sweeping green and black coastline at their backs. They'd been pumping away with their bikes in the lowest possible gear for the last mile or so, their legs circling steadily as they barely made headway up the slope.

"We never got much of this sort of thing in Yorkshire," CJ gasped. "I think I've been behind a desk for *way* too long."

"Then it's time you got out and got some exercise," Lia told her. Her own legs were burning, however, with the unaccustomed exertion. She'd passed her physical quals at the CIA's Farm near Williamsburg, an endurance-fitness test that included running for four miles—but that had been two months ago, and she hadn't been doing anything nearly this strenuous since.

"I thought you James Bond types were supposed to be in peak physical shape," Carlylse said. He was panting hard himself, though, and sweating heavily.

"That'll be enough out of you, mister," Lia told him. "You're here strictly on sufferance—and until we figure out what to do with you."

"I can think of several possibilities," he said.

Lia ignored him. He'd been flirting heavily with her, or trying to, since yesterday. She wondered if he was capable of taking anything seriously at all.

CJ was in the lead. "Uh-oh," she said. "Up ahead."

"That's the roadblock," Carlylse confirmed.

"Same guards?"

"I don't think so. Hard to tell."

"Chances are they're a different two. I imagine all tourists look alike to them anyway."

The three cyclists brought their rented bikes to a halt as one of the sentries stepped out in front of them, hand waving them off. Carlylse had been right; they were carrying AK-74s, the updated 5.45 mm version of the older 7.62 mm AK-47. They wore a dirty mix of civilian clothing and army surplus cast-offs, and the beards gave them a less than military appearance. She couldn't see any sign of an identifying badge or patch, and they certainly didn't look like members of a private or corporate security firm.

"Alto," the nearest of them said. *"El camino está cerrado."*

"We're meeting friends," CJ said, also in Spanish. She pointed toward the left, toward the rugged skyline of the caldera on the north end of the island. "Over there. Can't you just let us ride up that way, instead of having to go all the way around?"

"No. The road is closed."

As CJ argued with the guards, Lia looked around, making mental notes. The sign was there, nailed to the trunk of a tree, proclaiming in English and in Spanish that the area was off-limits to tourists, courtesy of the Scientific Institute of Geological Research.

CJ was getting nowhere with the guards. "Come on, CJ," Lia told her. "At least going back it's all downhill."

They turned their bikes and began walking them down the road. Lia heard one of the men make a guttural comment in what sounded like Arabic. The other snickered, then said, *"Bintilkha-ta!"*

Down the road and around a curve, they hid their bicycles behind a tumble of massive blocks of volcanic rock. Carlylse pointed up the steep slope. "That's where I went, up there. That's where I saw the helicopter."

"Let's do it," Lia said.

The climb took them about five hundred feet up a steep slope of loose gravel. At first, they had trees and shrubs to grab hold of and help their ascent, but then they emerged into the open. "Keep low," Lia warned the others, "and when you reach the top, stay flat on the ground. Don't show your silhouette against the sky."

They crawled the last thirty feet, reaching the rim of the crater at last. The crest was topped by scattered boulders and rocks, and they were able to find a spot from which they could peer down into the crater without being seen.

The landscape stretched out below and around them was utterly alien and other-worldly, sere and convoluted, a maze of boulders and broken ground. The crater looked like a tiny piece of the surface of the moon, a perfectly formed bowl of dark gray cinders. A few isolated pines grew inside the crater, but for the most part the caldera below was barren. At the bottom, however, a helicopter rested on a cleared patch of ground off to one side. Nearby were several tents, and at the center of the depression a black derrick jutted forty feet high. Even at a distance of over six hundred feet, the noise was jarring—the roar of a gasoline-powered generator, the pounding of a heavy mud pump, the grinding rasp of the turning drill string.

Lia extracted her binoculars from their case and switched the device on. "Okay, Art Room," she said quietly, raising the eyepieces to her face. "Are you getting a picture?"

"It's coming through perfectly, Lia," Marie Telach replied. "What are we looking at?"

"This is the largest of the three craters that make up the top of Rejada Mountain, the one in the center. I'd estimate the floor at about a hundred and twenty feet below the crater rim." Raising the binoculars, she focused on the opposite rim and checked the numbers appearing at the lower right of the image. "The crater is just over twelve hundred feet across, rim to rim. Siege? What's our altitude?"

CJ was examining a small handheld unit. "Fifty-seven hundred feet."

"Weather is clear, with a low layer of clouds off to the north, at the north end of the island . . ."

Lia continued reading off measurements and observations to the Art Room while panning the electronic binoculars back and forth, transmitting the images through the antenna in her belt. After showing the overall panorama, she zoomed in on the activity on the crater floor.

The helicopter was a Eurocopter EC145, a light utility aircraft used for transporting personnel or small cargos. Lia could see neither markings on its dark-olive fuselage nor weapons.

The drilling tower was positioned at the exact center of the crater. Lia could see half a dozen men working at the tower's base, bare-chested and covered in grime. She wondered if Chatel was among them, then decided the Frenchman was a bit too aristocratic to get his hands that dirty.

Another paramilitary guard with an AK stood a few dozen feet away, watching the work.

"Get us a closer look at the drill pipe, will you?" Telach asked.

"Here you go." Lia pressed a button on the side of the binoculars, zooming in even more. She held it on the central mechanism inside the derrick. The tubing appeared to be hexagonal rather than a cylinder, which surprised her.

"Okay," Telach told her. "That's fine. We need to see the approaches now, if you could manage it."

"I don't see any easy way down there," Lia said over the radio link as she pulled back on the zoom and panned across the crater. "The inner slopes of the bowl are bare gravel, rock, and cinders. I can see one more . . . no, *two* more armed guards on the crater rim opposite from our position. There are poles set up around the drill site perimeter, with what look like floodlights. I suspect the crater walls are pretty brightly lit at night."

She continued describing what she could see for another few minutes. Then CJ tapped her arm and pointed. Another guard was walking along the crater rim, three hundred feet away, but moving slowly in their direction. He was taking his time, his weapon slung, and he appeared bored. They hadn't been seen yet.

"Okay," she told the Art Room. "There's a sentry coming. We're going to move back downslope."

Staying flat against the slope, they alternately slid and crawled down the side of the volcanic cone until they were again within the shelter of the pines. From there, they made their way farther down the hill until they returned to the place where they'd left their bikes.

"What now?" Carlylse asked. "Back to Fatima?"

"No," Lia said. "I think we can follow some of these lower trails along the west flank of the ridge south. I want to see where else they have roadblocks—and to see if they have any more drill sites."

"More pedaling?"

"More pedaling."

"You know," Carlylse said, "you spies are supposed to run around in souped-up Aston Martins and high-tech aircraft, not goddamned *bicycles*, for Christ's sake."

"We'll take that under advisement, Mr. Carlylse. But the agency has had to cut back a lot lately. Budget constraints, you know."

They mounted up and started back down the road.

CIC, USS *LAKE ERIE*
NORTH OF SOCOTRA
GULF OF ADEN
SUNDAY, 1605 HOURS LOCAL TIME

"Good picture," Dean said.

"Ought to be," Captain Morrisey replied. "The hardware cost enough."

Dean and Akulinin stood inside the CIC, the Combat Information Center, of the Ticonderoga-class Aegis cruiser *Lake Erie*, a darkened shipboard compartment every bit as high-tech as the Art Room back at Fort Meade. Large-screen monitors were everywhere, watched intently by Navy enlisted personnel, both men and women, seated at workstation consoles. Captain Morrisey had brought them down a few minutes ago, their security classifications taking them past several checkpoints manned by no-nonsense Marine guards.

The largest monitor display showed a high-def television image, an aerial view of a rust-streaked cargo ship. Her name, *Yakutsk*, could be read on her prow.

"I thought you'd want to see," Morrisey said. He pointed. "It's begun."

Two small wooden boats were approaching the *Yakutsk* from astern, their outboard motors churning up frothing wakes. A crewman on the *Yakutsk*'s fantail appeared to be shouting, though there was no sound with the picture. He was holding an automatic rifle.

"Can we get a closer view?" Dean asked.

"Nothing easier." Morrisey spoke with a technician at a nearby console, and the image zoomed in, focusing on the man on the *Yakutsk*'s fantail.

"What's the range?" Akulinin wanted to know.

"Three miles," Morrisey said.

"Do they know we're watching?"

"I doubt it very much," Morrisey replied. "The Fire Scout is small, and it's stealthy. We could be a lot closer and they'd never see us."

The remarkably high-quality pictures were being relayed from a MQ-8B Fire Scout, a Navy UAV. Dean had watched them launch the craft from the *Erie*'s helicopter deck earlier. The unmanned aircraft looked like an odd mix of helicopter and submarine, with a teardrop-shaped body and the rotors attached to what looked like a submarine's conning tower. The craft was twenty-three feet long with a rotor diameter of just over twenty-seven feet, painted gray and weighing a ton and a half. It carried a sophisticated array of sensors and cameras that let it see in the dark or in bad weather, and was said to be able to zero in on the glowing tip of a man's cigarette from five miles away.

The Fire Scout was the smartest robot in the Navy's inventory, with the ability to take off, patrol, and land on the pitching deck of a ship at sea without help from a human teleoperator. Stealth characteristics gave it a tiny radar profile, and its engine and rotor noise had been suppressed to a fluttering whisper. Wth an endurance of over eight hours, it could silently stalk its assigned target without the enemy even knowing it was there.

The man on the *Yakutsk* suddenly raised his AK to his shoulder and fired a burst down at the water, the picture sharp enough to show spent casings flash in the sunlight as they spun across the deck. A technician in the *Erie*'s CIC panned the image on the big screen to focus on one of the pursuing boats. A man in a ragged T-shirt and jeans had just stood up in the pitching craft, an RPG balanced on his shoulder. In the next instant, there was a puff of smoke from the back of the tube, flaring out over the water, and the warhead streaked toward the ship's fantail.

The technician pulled the view back then, just in time to show the silent flash of the grenade exploding on the *Yakutsk*'s deck. The gunman there pitched backward and sprawled on the deck, dead or badly wounded. The pursuing boats, meanwhile, had drawn up to either side of the cargo vessel's stern, and the men on board were unshipping ladders with hooks on the ends. Dean watched, fascinated, as the men hooked the ladders against the ship's side and began swarming up onto the deck.

"Do you ever get the feeling," Akulinin said, "that it's 1801 all over again?"

"Barbary Pirates," Dean said, nodding. "Only this time they're Somali."

"We beat them back then," Morrisey said. "We could do it again if the damned politicians would let us."

In 1801 through 1805, and then again in 1815, the young United States Navy had fought two wars against the Muslim city-states on the North African coast. Two hundred years later, Somalian fishermen had discovered it was more profitable to hunt for ships both close inshore and in international waters, board them, and hold ships, cargos, and crews for ransom. Most of the vessels targeted had been cargo ships like the *Yakutsk*, though the pirates had also begun capturing yachts and pleasure craft as well. As in the early 1800s, countries were finding out that paying the ransoms encouraged more and more attacks—but the lack of anything like a real government in Somalia meant that there were no courts where captured pirates could be tried, no venue for enforcing international law.

Realists like captain Morrisey, repeated pointed out that shooting captured pirates and sinking their boats would stop piracy in these waters in fairly short order. The international community, however, was unable to embrace what they saw as murder; most European states had long since abolished the death penalty, and summarily executing pirates went beyond the pale. While capital punishment was still legal in the United States, the government was not about to permit executions on the high seas, not when such measures would bring a storm of protest from the comfortable politically correct. So piracy and murder were subsidized and encourage by governments unwilling to meet force with force.

The pirates were all on board the *Yakutsk* now, racing along the decks. There appeared to be about fifteen of them, heavily armed with rifles and RPGs. Dean and the others aboard the *Erie* watched as a bearded man stepped out of a watertight door in the ship's superstructure brandishing an AK assault rifle, only to be shot down by the boarders.

"Is this all going out to the Puzzle Palace?" Dean asked. Their implants and belt antennae didn't work here within the shielded and electronically protected confines of the Aegis cruiser's CIC.

"Absolutely," Morrisey told him. "They're seeing this at the same time we are, with maybe a half-second delay off the satellite."

"Good."

"And Ocean Storm is set to go?"

"Affirmative. The *Constellation* is getting this feed, too."

Dean nodded. All of the pieces were in place.

As the *Yakutsk* had traveled farther and farther west, eventually entering the two-hundred-mile gap between the island of Socotra and the southern coast of the Arabian Peninsula, the carrier battle group shadowing it had begun closing the range. The *Lake Erie* now was just under twenty nautical miles southeast of the *Yakutsk*, while the aircraft carrier USS *Constellation* was about thirty miles from the target. The *Yakutsk*'s radar likely was picking up both the *Erie* and the *Constellation*, as well as the other surface ships of the battle group, but these were crowded waters, with international sea traffic funneling in toward the narrow mouth of the Red Sea. With luck, the *Erie* had been dismissed as another freighter, the *Constellation* as a supertanker out of the Arabian Gulf. Not that secrecy was of particular importance now. The *Yakutsk*'s Russian crew would very soon be learning the truth, as would the pirates attacking them.

"Can we have some more detail there?" Dean asked, pointing toward the cargo ship's deck amidships, just forward of the superstructure. A gun battle had broken out between the pirates and a small group of shipboard defenders.

"Those don't look much like sailors," Morrisey commented. "They don't even look like merchant seamen."

"Probably JeM," Dean said, thoughtful. "Pakistanis riding shotgun on the nukes."

"Makes sense that the JeM wouldn't let such a valuable cargo go unprotected. The Russian seamen don't care if the bad guys get the cargo. It's in their best interests to just surrender and let the ship's owners ransom them."

"How many men in the *Yakutsk*'s crew?" Dean asked.

"About twenty," Morrisey told him.

"Plus an unknown number of Pakistani gunmen. The pirates have their work cut out for them."

"Captain Morrisey?" a sailor said from a nearby console. "We're getting an SOS from the ship."

"Record it, Tompkins," Morrisey told her, "and transmit to both Citadel and Xanadu." Citadel was the code name for the *Constellation*; Xanadu was Fort Meade.

"Aye, aye, sir."

"Okay," Dean said, relieved. "We now have official permission to board that ship."

Permission to board and search the *Yakutsk* for the missing nukes had been repeatedly refused by the White House. Dean didn't know for sure, but he strongly suspected that Bill Rubens was behind this somehow—a hint, a suggestion, in the right diplomatic ear might have gotten the *Yakutsk* noticed by the Somali pirates. If the United States Navy was not permitted to search a Russian cargo ship on the high seas, international maritime law *required* nearby ships to come to the aid of that vessel if it sent out a distress message. Rubens had told him to keep a close eye on the ship from the *Erie*'s CIC and stand by to coordinate a Navy SEAL assault—Ocean Storm—from the *Constellation*.

It was almost as if Rubens had somehow *known* that the *Yakutsk* was going to be attacked by pirates.

"Citadel has acknowledged," Tompkins said, "and requested permission to deploy Ocean Storm."

Dean nodded. "Go," he said.

ASSAULT FORCE OCEAN STORM
NORTH OF SOCOTRA
GULF OF ADEN
SUNDAY, 1612 HOURS LOCAL TIME

The leading chief, Senior Chief Petty Officer Carl Raleigh, came to his feet. "Attention on deck!"

"Okay, ladies!" Lieutenant Commander Edward McCauley said as he walked into the compartment on board the USS *Constellation*. "As you were!" The men took their seats again, chairs scraping and clattering as they settled. "We have the word," McCauley continued. "We are go for VBSS!"

"*Hoo-yah!*" Forty voices shouted back, ringing off the bulkheads of the compartment designated as the SEAL Team squad bay. The men, dressed in black and with their faces painted green, were members of Alfa Troop, SEAL Team Three, headquartered in Coronado, California; their operational area was Southwest Asia, which included the Gulf of Aden. They'd deployed to the *Constitution* from Kuwait two days ago, under orders passed down from SOCOM, the U.S. Special Operations Command. Since that time, they'd been on a constant state of alert, waiting for the order to go.

"The objective of this op is to secure the ship, which is believed to be illegally transporting a number of small tactical nuclear devices. We do not have to worry about finding those devices. That is the job of the NEST people who will be following us in. Our job is to get on board that ship, take down the hostiles, and hold it so the techies can do their thing.

"We are clear to use lethal force. The hostiles on board include Somali pirates and members of a Muslim terror group, the Army of Mohammad. In addition, it's possible that the members of the ship's crew may offer resistance.

"Be very clear about this, people. While we have no wish to cause unnecessary casualties among the ship's crew, while it would be useful to capture hostile personnel for interrogation, this *is* a shoot-first order. If anyone shows a weapon, if anyone offers resistance, if anyone even *looks* like he's going to give you an argument, take him down, and take him down hard! *The* number one objective here is to secure those nukes, not to save lives on that ship, not to take prisoners. You have one order on this op. *Secure those weapons!* Questions?"

A hand went up, and McCauley nodded. "Petroski?"

"I was just wondering, sir . . . is there any chance of those nukes going off?"

"Beats me, Pet. What I was told was that it takes twenty minutes to prep one of these weapons, to arm it and set it off. If they do manage to detonate one . . . well, the good news is we'll never know it, and the bastards won't be able to use them against civilian targets. Other questions? Right. Let's move out!"

"*Hoo-yah!*" The SEAL battle cry rang again from the bulkheads as the men began filing out into the next compartment, the armory, where they drew weapons, ammunition, and various items of special gear. Minutes later, they stepped out into the glare of the afternoon sun above the Gulf of Aden, hurrying across the steel flight deck to the waiting helicopters.

"Now hear this, now hear this," blared from the 1MC. "Commence helicopter operations on the flight deck."

The rotors on the big HH-60H helos began to turn.

ART ROOM
NSA HEADQUARTERS
FORT MEADE, MARYLAND
SUNDAY, 0935 HOURS EDT

On the big main display in the Art Room, Rubens saw the image of the *Yakutsk* being relayed by satellite from the USS *Lake Erie*. The *Yakutsk* was just over 240 feet in length and thirty-six feet wide, with a draft of twelve and a half feet. Her bridge house was positioned amidships, just forward of the single, large stack. There were two tall masts, one aft of the stack, one just aft of the raised forecastle forward. Stays and rigging connected the two masts with one another and with various points on the deck and bulwarks.

Those masts and stays could be a problem.

"The first helicopters are away, sir," a technician reported.

"Good," Rubens said. "What's their ETA?"

"Range to the target is now twenty-five nautical miles. The first helos should be over the target in ten minutes, thirty seconds."

"Very well."

This was where the real worrying began. The SEALs and Navy Special Warfare helicopters were now committed to attack a Russian ship, and the hell of it was that the action probably would not have been approved by the White House. Rubens had set up this scenario to respond to the ship's SOS, a tenuous legal fiction. If this went badly, it would mean an international incident, and Rubens would be forced to resign at best, face criminal charges at worst.

Nevertheless, he didn't see any other way to get the job done.

CIC, USS *LAKE ERIE*
NORTH OF SOCOTRA
GULF OF ADEN
SUNDAY, 1635 HOURS LOCAL TIME

A pitched gun battle was being waged on the decks of the freighter, covertly observed by the shadowing Fire Scout. As the observers on board the *Erie* watched, three more speedboats pulled up, and more pirates stormed aboard. The defenders were being forced forward. RPG blasts ripped across the *Yakutsk*'s forward deck, and bodies sprawled in untidy heaps.

"I hope to hell your boss knows what he's doing," Captain Morrisey said. "If he doesn't, we might be about to start a war with Russia."

"Shit," Akulinin said, "the SEALs board the ship, grab the nukes, and get the hell out. What could *possibly* go wrong?"

"More than I care to think about right now," Morrisey said. "Why didn't they just send in CTF 151 and let them sort this out?"

Since January of 2009, Combined Task Force 151 had been patrolling the Gulf of Aden. Led by the United States with the USS *Boxer* as the flagship, it included vessels from fourteen nations. Many, like China and Russia, were only there to escort their own ships, but the rest, including the American contingent, had been aggressively attempting to suppress piracy in the area. Hampered by bureaucracy and by the pirates' ability to vanish into Somalian coastal waters masquerading as fishing boats, the international force had so far achieved mixed results.

"I think the people back home running this op wanted an all-American force, Captain," Charlie Dean told him. "Fewer complications that way. They probably also think it better to keep the Russians out of the loop for as long as they can. The *Yakutsk* is Maltese-flagged, so the Russians aren't in there escorting her, but if they knew what was about to go down, they would *not* be happy about it."

"I'm not sure *I'm* happy about it," Morrisey said. "But if we bloody some pirate noses, I won't mind one bit."

"I think we can count on that, Captain. Right now, though, my partner and I have to get in there."

"The helo is warmed up and waiting for you," Morrisey told him. "Good luck . . . and don't get yourself shot."

Charlie Dean and Ilya Akulinin left the *Erie*'s CIC, heading aft.

18

The flight of HH-60H Seahawk helicopters came in low and tight, skimming above the oceans low enough that their rotor wash threw up clouds of spray. There were eight aircraft, each carrying five Navy SEALs, each mounting GAU-17/A miniguns in their open cargo doors, and four carrying AGM-114 Hellfire missiles slung from hardpoints on either side. They came in out of the southwest, out of the late afternoon sun. Before the pirates were even aware of the danger, the Seahawks peeled off, sweeping around the *Yakutsk* in a counterclockwise circle.

The flight was divided into two platoons, Alfa and Bravo. Alfa was the assault group, Bravo the reserve. With the airspace above and around the *Yakutsk* suddenly dangerously crowded, Bravo hung back while the four helos of Alfa Group pressed the attack.

Alfa One, the command ship, swung in close, bringing its left side to bear on the cargo ship's forward deck. A second hovered nearby, offering fire support to the first. The port-side door gunner leaned into his harness as he brought his weapon to bear. He pressed the trigger, and a shrill whine filled the Seahawk's cargo compartment, the weapon's six fast-rotating barrels delivering a blistering four thousand rounds per minute onto the target.

The firestorm of 7.62 mm rounds engulfed the step of the *Yakutsk*'s foremast, slamming off the steel deck and splintering the white-painted wood of the mast itself. Ship crewmen and JeM defenders scrambled for cover as ricocheting bullets and finger-sized splinters sliced through the air.

Firing at a rate of better than sixty rounds every second, the door gunner kept his weapon trained on the base of the mast as more and more chunks splintered away. Abruptly, then, the mast broke free just above the base, jumping and leaning sharply to the right. The gunner shifted aim then, sending the stream of slugs into the port-side attachment point for the foremast's stays, hammering at the tiny target until wire rope parted and the shackle broke free.

The loose stay whipped and cracked through the air, and the mast, cut loose at its base, began to topple away from the helicopter, falling over the cargo vessel's starboard side and hitting the water in a cascade of white spray. The gunner had already shifted his aim, targeting a second stay attachment, moving systematically to take out masts and cables that posed hazards to low-approaching helicopters.

On the command helo's cargo deck, one SEAL leaned over and asked Lieutenant Commander McCauley, "Sir! What happens if we punch a hole in one of those nukes? Game over?"

"Nah," McCauley replied. "Not unless they're booby-trapped. But it'll make a hell of a mess, and I wouldn't count on having kids afterward."

"Got one already, sir."

On the forward deck of the cargo vessel, a Somali pirate emerged from the deckhouse carrying an RPG on his shoulder. Before he could take aim, a minigun burst from Alfa Two literally shredded him from the waist down, splashing an ugly red smear across the steel deck next to the savagely torn torso. The man triggered the RPG as he collapsed, the round striking a stanchion nearby and detonating with a flash.

"We have one Papa down, one Papa down," came over the SEAL tactical net. For ease of communications, the people on board the *Yakutsk* were identified as Papas (pirates), as Tangos (terrorists), and as Charlies (crew members). The SEALs would attempt to avoid hitting Charlies, but the Papas and the Tangos were fair game.

The difficulty was in telling them apart in the heat and raw confusion of combat.

On the bridge, high above the deck, a window smashed open on the portside wing, and the flicker of a muzzle flash winked full auto. The SEALs on Alfa One heard a close-spaced pair of loud thumps as rounds struck the Seahawk, but then Alfa Two turned its port-side minigun on the ship's bridge and sent a stream of rounds smashing through the open window. Glass exploded from the bridge, shards sparkling as it fell in the sunlight.

The ship's mizzenmast, rising from the deckhouse aft of the ship's stack, shuddered, then collapsed as Alfa Three hammered at the mast's step, sending it toppling into the sea alongside the ship. The last of the standing rigging parted with the fall, leaving the *Yakutsk* dead in the water, a tangle of masts and rigging off its port side.

"Deck approach is now clear," McCauley called over the tactical channel. "Alfa Three, you are go for deployment."

"Copy, Alfa One."

One of the Seahawks circled around the *Yakutsk*'s port side, turned sharply, and came in across the bow. Hovering above the forward deck, the helicopter hung motionless as a rope curled from the open side hatch and the first Navy SEAL slid down and onto the deck. He was followed by a second man, and a third. The SEALs on deck spread out as soon as they touched down, H&K submachine guns up against their shoulders as they moved. With the last of the five SEALs delivered to the *Yakutsk*'s deck, Alfa Three moved off, to be replaced by Alfa Four. Within the space of a few seconds, five more SEALs fast-roped to the ship's deck.

"Alfa Four element, on deck! Moving!"

An armed man—whether Papa or Tango, it was impossible to tell in the battle haze—appeared on a walkway along the side of the bridge house and was immediately cut to bits by a minigun burst from Alfa One. Alfa Two moved aft, drifting into position, then delivering its five-SEAL payload to the *Yakutsk*'s fantail.

"Alfa Two element, on deck! Moving!"

Alfa One continued to hover alongside the ship, LCDR McCauley directing the attack. At his command over the network, Bravo One moved in then and took up station off the ship's starboard side, flying shotgun as Alfa One moved in to deliver its five SEALs. TM1 Johnson tossed a coiled line out the open door.

"First up!" McCauley yelled. One by one, then, the SEALs grabbed hold of the line with gloved hands and jumped out into wind-blasted space. McCauley went down last, a dizzying descent through the hurricane blast of the Seahawk's main rotor, landing on the open area directly above the *Yakutsk*'s bridge.

He continued to hear radio chatter from the other SEALs as they moved through the ship. "One-three! I'm on the bridge! Two Tangos down, two Charlies down!"

A ladder led down to the port bridge wing, then past the piles of broken glass, a dropped weapon, a torn body in a pool of blood. Inside the bridge proper, the other four SEALs of Alfa One were checking for survivors in cupboards, behind the compass binnacle, inside the tiny head.

"Alfa, Alfa Three-one," sounded in the radio receiver in McCauley's ear. Nearby, two of the SEALs in his element kicked open a door leading off the bridge and found two men cowering inside the ship's radio shack. "Fo'c'sle secure! We have six Charlies, two probable Tangos, tripped and zipped."

"Copy, Three-one."

"Alfa One-one, Bravo One-one," another voice said.

"Alfa One, go," McCauley replied.

"NEST One and NEST Two are inbound," Senior Chief Petty Officer Carl Raleigh told him. "ETA five mikes."

"Copy that," McCauley replied. He glanced around the ruin of the *Yakutsk*'s bridge. Holloway and Yancey had dragged the two men out of the radio compartment and forced them onto their bellies and were now zip-stripping their hands behind their backs. Judging by their clothing and pale skins, they were ship's crew and probably Russians, but in an op like this one you did *not* take chances. "Objective's bridge is secure. Two collaterals."

"Copy bridge secure, Skipper."

McCauley glanced at his watch. Two minutes, fifteen seconds had passed since the first minigun burst, and he'd been on board the ship for fifty seconds.

ART ROOM
NSA HEADQUARTERS
FORT MEADE, MARYLAND
SUNDAY, 0948 HOURS EDT

Rubens watched the battle unfold on the big screen as the images were relayed from an orbiting Fire Scout UAV to the *Lake Erie*, then by satellite back to Fort Meade and the Art Room.

"Objective's bridge is secure," came through on the speaker in the Art Room's ceiling. "Two collaterals."

The minigun fire directed at the bridge must have swept through the compartment like a storm, killing two terrorists and two crew members. Collaterals—collateral damage, meaning civilian casualties—were unavoidable in a fight like this. The SEALs were there to secure the nukes, not rescue the *Yakutsk*'s crew. There would be apologies to the Russian government later, perhaps reparations as well, but the imperative at the moment was to clear the ship of hostiles. The NESTs—Nuclear Emergency Security Teams—were on the way now. The SEAL assault force did not have much time.

This is the tough part of the job, Rubens thought. *Sitting back here in a nice, safe underground fortress playing puppet master, giving orders and watching others carry them out seven thousand miles away.*

"So how do you think this is going to go over at the White House, sir?" Telach asked him.

"Not well." *If there'd been any other way . . .*

"You know we're behind you, sir. Every one of us."

Rubens smiled. "I appreciate that."

But if it came to a sacrifice, to someone needing to put his neck on the chopping block, Rubens would make sure that it was *his* neck, that no one else would go down with him.

The decision—and the deception—had been his, and his alone.

"Alfa, Alfa Three!" A voice called. "We're in the Number One Cargo Hold. Two Tangos down, hold secure! Moving to Hold Two!"

As always when it came to Washington politics, *success* became the best form of validation. If this op off the island of Socotra was a success—if the nukes were found on board and no Islamic militant loony decided to push the button and go straight to paradise in a sun-brilliant flash—the status quo would be maintained. Desk Three would survive, the NSA would survive, even Rubens' career might survive—though *that* wasn't what was important here. Diplomacy would smooth things over with the Russian government, especially since the Russians wouldn't care to admit that suitcase nukes had been stolen from one of their facilities, then shipped by terrorists on board one of their freighters.

If things went wrong, however—if a terrorist *did* manage to detonate the nukes rather than see them recaptured, or even if the NESTs got on board and the nukes turned out not to be there—the diplomatic fallout would be damned near as bad in some ways as *real* fallout might have been, at least in terms of finger-pointing and cover-your-ass recriminations.

Still, Rubens played the cards he was dealt.

The chance to stop an Armageddon-born nightmare was absolutely worth *any* risk to himself, to the agency, to the men now boarding that ship.

FORWARD HOLD
CARGO SHIP *YAKUTSK*
GULF OF ADEN
SUNDAY, 1649 HOURS LOCAL TIME

The enemy was getting closer.

Syed Rehman Ashraf crouched in the darkness, listening to the

approaching enemy. He wasn't sure who they were—American Delta
Force, SEALs, or Marines; British SAS; Israeli Mossad; even Pakistani Black Storks, their Special Service Group. He knew only that
they were deadly, black clad, and silent, shadows descending from the
helicopters onto the freighter's deck who'd proceeded to kill his fel-
low fighters with a ruthless and implacable efficiency. Interception by
a foreign counterterrorist force had always been a possibility in Operation Nar-min-Sama, and the fighters accompanying the weapons
had been prepared to sacrifice themselves in the name of Allah.

That was why Ashraf was here in the near darkness.

The weapons had been stored in the ship's forward hold, carefully
hidden in a wooden crate identical to the crates of machine tools
around it. The hiding place was sheltered by several empty crates
positioned next to a bulkhead; slinging his assault rifle, Ashraf shoved
the empty crates aside, then used a knife to pry open the one he was
after.

He could hear the distant stuttering thunder of helicopters, punctuated now and again by the high-pitched shriek of their weapons.
He'd seen Achmed literally sliced in half by one of those guns, and
was still shaking.

The lid peeled back off the crate, and Ashraf began pulling out
sheets of plastic packing material. Inside were two trunks, aluminum
painted a dull olive drab, with numbers and Cyrillic lettering sten-
ciled on the top and sides. He had to struggle to haul one out and
lower it to the deck. It was heavy—at least thirty kilos—and it hit
the deck with a thud. He froze for a moment, listening. Had the enemy heard?

Apparently not. He heard footsteps on the steel ladder in the next
hold aft. He'd already dogged the watertight door leading into this
hold, however, and jammed a length of pipe into the locking wheel to
keep it shut.

He used a key on a chain around his neck to open the lock on the
trunk.

Ashraf knew nothing about nuclear weapons, save that they were
powerful enough to destroy cities, and that Allah had seen fit to

allow several of them to come into the possession of the Army of Mohammad. The devices had been intended for use against the hated Jews, but that, unfortunately, was not to be. Rather than have the enemy take the weapons back, he would trigger this one, vaporizing ship, helicopters, and the black-clad attackers in a single, brilliant flash of God's light . . .

CARGO SHIP *YAKUTSK*
GULF OF ADEN
SUNDAY, 1653 HOURS LOCAL TIME

The HH-60 helicopter off the *Lake Erie* swung in above the *Yakutsk's* forward deck, hovering low above hatch covers and tangled rigging. The ship was dead in the water, but the seas were high enough to give the vessel an uncomfortable pitch up and down beneath the chopper's keel. "You're good to go, sir!" one of the helo's crew shouted. "Good luck!"

Dean held the descent rope in one gloved hand, gauging his chances of breaking an ankle. He'd fast-roped in his physical quals several months back, but that had been off a stable wooden tower in the pine forests of the Farm. The tower hadn't been drifting on the hurricane blast of its own rotor wash there, and the ground had not been pitching up and down with the rolling sea.

He grinned at Akulinin, gave the Russian a thumbs-up, and stepped backward out of the helicopter as Akulinin tossed him a jaunty salute in reply.

Dean slid rapidly through thirty feet of emptiness and hit the deck with flexing knees, meeting it as it came up with the ocean swell. Rotor wash blasted the ship's forward deck. As soon as Dean was down, the rope went up and the helicopter moved off, slowly circling. Akulinin would stay with the helo, in reserve as team liaison officer if something happened to Dean.

"I'm on the ship," Dean said.

"Copy that," Jeff Rockman said in his ear. "Watch yourself, Charlie."

"Mr. Dean?" a Navy SEAL said, anonymous in his black balaclava. Dean was dressed the same—balaclava, black utilities, Kevlar vest, and combat harness, with an H&K submachine gun harnessed to his side. "This way."

He looked around the ship's forward deck. A small group of men, ship's crew, most likely, lay facedown, hands zip-stripped at their backs, a watchful and heavily armed SEAL crouched nearby. Several bodies—and pieces of bodies—lay elsewhere, in front of the bridge house and near the wreckage of the foremast. There were no signs of fighting, no indication of any ongoing resistance whatsoever. Several SEALs stood or crouched at key spots, where they could command the vessel's deck areas.

"Is the ship secure already?"

"We still have some holdouts below, sir. I'd keep my head down if I were you."

Dean followed, moving aft toward the deckhouse.

In other special ops takedowns carried out on behalf of the Agency's Deep Black programs, Dean had been in charge, at least technically. In the assault on the hijacked cruise liner *Atlantis Queen* a few months before, he'd led an NSA Black CAT assault team, parachuting onto the ship's fantail with the other operatives and leading them against jihadist terrorists holding the ship and its passengers hostage. This time, though, he was definitely a supernumerary, present as Desk Three's eyes, ears, and voice, but a noncombatant rather than a part of the assault team.

It was comforting to have the H&K nonetheless.

FORWARD HOLD
CARGO SHIP *YAKUTSK*
GULF OF ADEN
SUNDAY, 1655 HOURS LOCAL TIME

Syed Ashraf heard a bang at the hatch leading to the next hold aft and began working more quickly. It was fussy, complicated work, removing one sixty-centimeter cylinder from the heavy trunk and attaching it to a shorter, lighter cylinder, matching end to end, and screwing the connections tight with a small screwdriver. The only light in the hold came from a couple of small bulbs up high on the overhead and from emergency lighting panels at the bulkheads. It was hard to see what he was doing, almost like working in the dark.

Back at the training camp in northwestern Pakistan, he'd practiced the operation time after time until he could do it blindfolded. His trainers hadn't told him much about how the assembly worked, but his understanding was that the shorter cylinder was packed with plastic explosives, and when those explosives detonated, they would slam one piece of a heavy gray metal down the length of the longer tube so that it smashed, with a lot of energy, into a second mass of gray metal at the other end. Something about having more than a certain amount of the gray metal all together in one place, he'd been told, would cause the device to explode with far more energy than would be liberated by the relatively small amount of C-4 packed into the shorter cylinder.

For the thing to work properly, the two cylinders had to be screwed tightly together *just* so. If they weren't perfectly aligned, he'd been told, the detonation would be much smaller than expected, and might fail altogether.

Ashraf felt an unpleasant queasiness in his stomach, but he continued working.

ART ROOM
NSA HEADQUARTERS
FORT MEADE, MARYLAND
SUNDAY, 0958 HOURS EDT

"Sir!" Marie Telach called. "We're getting a gamma trace from the ship!"

That sent a cold prickle up Rubens' spine. It meant that someone on board that ship had opened up one of the suitcase nukes.

"How much?"

She pointed at an indicator on her console. "Not much—but higher than background. The Geiger counter you had them put on board the UAV is picking it up."

If alpha and beta particles could only be detected at close range, gamma rays penetrated most common substances, and they did so at the speed of light. While gamma rays would have been present on the truck bed and elsewhere during the Operation Haystack search—gamma radiation was released as part of the decay of alpha particles—they would have occurred in very small quantities, so small that they were lost in the overall count of background.

The radiation detector installed on board the circling Navy Fire Scout was getting a count now high enough to suggest that one of the suitcase nukes had been opened on board the *Yakutsk*, exposing the plutonium-239 inside. Radiation levels weren't dangerous, by any means, but the fact that the Fire Scout was picking up gamma radiation at a range of over a mile suggested that someone had removed the nuke from its suitcase—almost certainly in order to trigger it.

CARGO SHIP *YAKUTSK*
GULF OF ADEN
SUNDAY, 1658 HOURS LOCAL TIME

Led by the Navy SEAL, Dean had just joined Lieutenant Commander McCauley on the *Yakutsk's* bridge. "Welcome aboard, Mr. Dean," McCauley said. Like the other SEALs, he was anonymous in black combat dress and balaclava face mask. "I hope—"

Dean cut the officer off with a sharp wave of the hand as a warning squeal sounded over his comm implant. Someone in the Art Room needed to talk to him right now. "Go ahead," he said.

"Charlie!" Rubens' voice replied. "We're getting a Geiger counter reading from somewhere on board that ship! Best guess . . . someone's prepping a charge for detonation!"

"Copy," Dean replied. His throat was tight, his mouth dry. He looked at McCauley. "They're picking up radiation Stateside," he said. "Someone's getting ready to set off a nuke."

"Shit. Wait a sec—" McCauley touched fingertips to one ear, listening. Someone was talking to him over the SEAL command net. "The hatch leading to the forward hold has been locked from the other side," he said. "One guess where our Tango is playing with his new toy."

"We need to get in there," Dean said, "by any means you have available!"

McCauley touched a switch on the radio strapped to his shoulder. "Bravo One, Alfa Team Leader. We need door-kickers on the forward deck, and we need 'em *now*!"

FORWARD HOLD
CARGO SHIP *YAKUTSK*
GULF OF ADEN
SUNDAY, 1703 HOURS LOCAL TIME

Syed Ashraf completed the final connection, tightening the last screw holding the two major components of the weapon together. Next, he needed to attach the battery, which was in a separate case at the end of the cylinder, threading the bare ends of two copper wires around the battery posts and tightening the connections.

Done.

The trigger was still inside the case, connected to a timer. The detonator planted inside the C-4 charge within the weapon's base could be set off by any of several means—by sending a radio signal to the trigger from a remote control unit, by activating a small LED display timer, or simply by pressing a button with a direct line of sight to the weapon. Any of those would fire the detonator, which in turn would set off the C-4, and that would slam the two pieces of metal inside the cylinder together, and the world would be illuminated by God's holy light.

Only one more step remained—and that was to snap two triple-A batteries into the trigger, which looked like a small TV remote. The batteries were included within a small plastic bag; al-Wawi had thought of every contingency. Ashraf popped the back off the trigger's battery compartment and opened the plastic bag.

The batteries snapped into place, one, two, and he replaced the cover.

Timer set to zero . . . detonator armed . . .

All that remained now was to . . .

CARGO SHIP *YAKUTSK*
GULF OF ADEN
SUNDAY, 1704 HOURS LOCAL TIME

"Fire in the hole!"

Dean crouched lower as a SEAL pressed a switch. Yard upon yard of detcord wrapped around the locks, hasps, and flanges of the forward hold deck hatch went off with a piercing bang, followed a split instant later by the heavier blast of multiple charges of C-4 laid around the hatch perimeter. Bits of metal pinged and shrieked off the side of the deckhouse as the hatch was peeled back, lifted bodily into the air, and spun to one side like a misshapen, square-cut Frisbee ten feet across.

The C-4 and detcord—the "door-kickers" requested by McCauley—had been dropped onto the deck moments before from one of the HH-60 helicopters. Several SEALs wired the explosives to the locked forward hatch, an evolution that had taken less than two minutes. McCauley gave the word, and a SEAL fired the charge.

Now Dean and four Navy SEALs rushed forward from where they'd taken cover in front of the deckhouse, playing out black nylon line behind them as they ran. The open hatch yawned in front of him, a smoky haze still blanketing the deck around it as he stepped over the edge and into emptiness.

The ends of their lines were secured to cleats on the deck behind them, and they fast-roped into the hold, a drop of about twenty feet, letting the rope slide through gloved fingers as they descended.

Dean spun dizzyingly at the end of his line . . .

FORWARD HOLD
CARGO SHIP *YAKUTSK*
GULF OF ADEN
SUNDAY, 1704 HOURS LOCAL TIME

Ashraf lay sprawled on the deck, stunned and bewildered. The sudden blast, the sudden explosion of sunlight spilling into the hold, had taken him completely by surprise, convincing him just for a moment that something had gone wrong, that the weapon had fired accidentally, before he'd had a chance to press the trigger.

As he looked up, he saw shapes, faceless black shadows, gliding down through the light at the center of the hold. The trigger lay on the deck a meter away; his AK-47 was leaning against a crate beside him. For just an instant, he hesitated . . .

CARGO SHIP *YAKUTSK*
GULF OF ADEN
SUNDAY, 1704 HOURS LOCAL TIME

They were coming down approximately in the middle of the hold; as he spun clockwise at the end of his rope, dropping fast, Dean caught a glimpse of a lone figure lying beside a stack of crates against the hold's forward bulkhead. He hit the deck, released the rope, and brought his H&K up, snapping off the safety. From the deck, he could no longer see the figure by the crates.

"*Wakkif!*" Dean yelled, racing forward. "Stop!"

He rounded a stack of wooden crates just as two SEALs above and behind him, still suspended on their ropes halfway down from the open hatch, triggered their H&Ks. A bearded man in a headcloth and fatigues twisted in front of him, trying to bring his AK to bear. The SEALs fired multiple three-round bursts, triggering them so fast they sounded like a full-auto fusillade, slamming the Tango in head and chest, knocking him backward against the bulkhead, blood splattering across steel as he collapsed.

Dean reached him an instant later. "Tango down!" he yelled.

The man was clearly dead, eyes open and glassy. Something like a remote control unit lay on the deck just beyond his reach.

Dean's gaze flicked from the trigger to the recently assembled weapon to the dead terrorist and back to the trigger. A timer display on the weapon read "000." The thing might be booby-trapped, set to go off if he pulled the wrong wire . . . but one thing he could do was scoop up the remote control trigger. The back panel had popped off. He flipped out the two batteries.

The world did *not* vanish in white light, and Dean let out a sigh of pent-up stress.

Then he glanced inside the crate.

"Art Room," he said, as two Navy SEALs came up behind him. "One Tango down, weapons secure."

"Thank God," Rubens said.

"Don't thank Him yet," Dean replied. "We still have a small problem."

"What problem?"

"I only see two trunks here. Unless they're hidden someplace else on board, we're still missing ten suitcase nukes."

19

Hold tight," Rubens told Dean. "The NEST guys will be there in a few minutes."

"Copy that," Dean replied. "McCauley is posting SEALs in each hold. I've just been told that the ship is secure."

"Pass a message to Commander McCauley for me, please," Rubens said. "Under no circumstances are the pirate boats alongside the *Yakutsk* to be sunk. I'm also passing orders to the helicopter gunships that the pirate mother ship not be fired on. Just in case the pirates were able to get the nukes off the freighter."

"Roger that—but it doesn't look like they had time to move anything. Unless there are more crates hidden down here somewhere, the nukes are not on board the *Yakutsk*."

"NEST should be able to confirm that. Meanwhile, I suggest you get out of that hold. Unshielded plutonium is not conducive to a healthy lifestyle."

"Copy."

The Nuclear Emergency Support Team operated under the DOE's National Nuclear Security Administration, providing squads of specialists who could find, evaluate, and disarm nuclear or radiological weapons, whether planted by terrorists or in the aftermath of an accident involving such weapons. Rubens had requested that a number of NEST personnel be flown out to the *Constellation* over the past two days, where they'd been awaiting the word that the *Yakutsk* was secure before going aboard. With them were several tens of millions of dollars of high-tech hardware, from handheld radiation scanners to neutron detectors to X-ray devices used to find hidden weapons.

Their HUMINT from Alfred Koch in Karachi had suggested that all twelve stolen suitcase nukes had been put on board a ship—but it was possible they had been divided up among several ships or, more alarming, that some had been put on an aircraft for a flight to their final destination.

Which the information Lia had developed strongly suggested was the tiny island of La Palma in the Canaries, part of the mysterious project involving an unlikely alliance between the Army of Mohammad and Chinese intelligence.

Rubens picked up a phone from a nearby console and punched in his secretary's number. "Ann? I need you to schedule a meeting for me with ANSA."

"Yes, sir. Tomorrow? Or sooner?"

It was Sunday, though Rubens rarely distinguished weekends from workdays.

"ASAP," he replied. "Today if he's available. Tell him it's Priority Yankee White."

"Yes, sir."

He paused, then added, "Tell him we *will* need a face-to-face with POTUS on this one."

The President of the United States would be back in the Oval Office tomorrow, and Rubens would need to talk with him directly if there was any way to swing that.

It was a meeting he did not expect to enjoy.

CUMBRE VIEJA
LA PALMA, CANARY ISLANDS
SUNDAY, 1515 HOURS LOCAL TIME

Lia called a halt, and the three of them pulled their bicycles off the narrow path. It was midafternoon, with a searing tropical sun beating down on the western face of the Cumbre Vieja ridge. Eight miles or so to the north, the vast caldera of the Cumbre Nueva appeared to be nestled within a spectacular layer of clouds, its rugged peaks protruding above a flowing sea of white.

They'd been on and off the trail for over three and a half hours now, at times walking their bikes across ruggedly inhospitable volcanic terrain in order to avoid stretches of bike trail that had been blocked off by the mysterious Scientific Institute of Geological Research. The tangle of bike trails below the crest of the ridge, however, had for the most part allowed them to find alternate routes, and Lia's implant gave them the equivalent of GPS tracking. The Art Room knew exactly where they were at all times within about half a meter, and could even transmit detailed topological maps based on satellite imagery to Lia's BlackBerry.

So from the cluster of three craters on Montaña Rejada, they'd traveled a mile and a half south to the crater of Hoyo Negro just below the loom of Pico Berigoyo, then along the Ruta de los Volcanes for another half mile to the towering, rounded caldera of Duraznero. Four-tenths of a mile beyond that was Deseada, and beyond that San Martin 1 and 2. The volcanic craters were strung along the top of the ridge like pearls, or snuggled up close high along the western flank, a different crater pocking the black and red soil every half mile or so.

Altogether, it was a straight-line distance of about five miles along the ridge, from the northernmost of the three Berigoyo craters to the Volcán de San Martin in the south. Ten volcanic calderas in all; Lia, CJ, and Carlylse had visited five of them. The others would have required traversing barren, open slopes where they were certain to have been seen. Several times they saw more guards on the ridge above them, and once they were stopped at another checkpoint.

Fortunately, the sentries up along the ridge crest weren't talking to one another, because they were simply warned off a second time. Now they were at the southernmost of the craters, overlooking Volcán de San Martin, less than six miles from the extreme southern tip of the island.

At the bottom of each crater they'd gotten close enough to investigate, they'd seen a drilling derrick, tents, piles of supplies, and teams of men working in the hot sun.

And guards. *Always* guards, grim-looking men with mix-and-match army surplus clothing and AK assault rifles. Lia estimated that there were anywhere from five to ten armed sentries at each drill site; there might be as many as a hundred men guarding the chain of drilling rigs—and multiply that by three to include off-duty troops serving a four-on, eight-off rotation. Helicopters made frequent flights in to the craters from the east—probably the La Palma Airport. They watched as workers off-loaded drilling equipment, water, and reel upon reel upon reel of what looked like electrical wiring.

There was plenty of daylight left, but the bottled water they'd brought along was nearly gone. They would have to turn back soon. Lia wanted to see how far they could push the envelope to get more information, however, and here, at the southernmost drill site, she thought she saw how she could do just that.

They lay among volcanic boulders at the rim of another crater—a black cinder cone on the outside, but a startling red-ocher within the crater bowl. Through her binoculars, she could see Herve Chatel. He was standing near the tents, off to one side of the drilling rig, apparently deep in conversation with someone dressed identically to the guards, including a checkered kaffiyeh. One of the unmarked civilian helicopters rested on a makeshift landing pad nearby.

"Art Room," she said quietly, still holding the binoculars on the pair. "Can you give me an ID on the character in the head scarf talking with Chatel?"

"Working on it, Lia," Marie Telach told her. A minute dragged past. "Okay! Got an ID . . . seventy-percent-plus probable match. That's Ibrahim Hussain Azhar. Pakistani, probably with links to

Pakistan's ISI. One of the founders of the Army of Mohammad, probably with ties to al-Qaeda. He's the one they're calling al-Wawi, the Jackal."

"Show me," she said, pulling out her BlackBerry.

A moment later, her handheld device pulled in a signal from an NSA communications satellite, downloading a photograph of a bearded man in a Jinnah cap, the round fur hat, or *qaraqul*, worn by men in south Asia. She took another long look through the binoculars. It *might* be the same man.

"Art Room," she said. "I'm going to go down there. I'd like to see what my friend Chatel has to say about all of this."

"Lia?" Rubens' voice said in her ear. "I don't think that would be a good idea."

"I have backup," she said. "CJ and Roger will be up here watching every move I make."

"If they decide to kill you, CJ and Mr. Carlylse won't be able to help you. I'm sorry, Lia. I'm denying your request."

"Wouldn't you like some up-close photos of what they're doing? Maybe be able to listen in on Chatel and al-Wawi, to see who's really in charge? There's a helicopter down there. Maybe I can look and see if they've delivered those suitcase nukes."

"The risk—"

"Is a part of the job," she said, interrupting. "This is an absolutely one-in-a-million opportunity that we cannot afford to pass up. *Sir.*"

Rubens paused, perhaps thinking it over. "Okay," he said at last. "Reluctantly, okay. But you keep all channels open and do not antagonize them, you hear me?"

"Yes, sir. I'll play the fluff-head and tell him I'm lost. Herve will get all protective. Won't be a problem."

She stood up, dusted off her jeans, and started down the steep slope into the gaping crater.

"Watch yourself down there," CJ told her.

"Actually, I'll be watching *them.*"

CARGO SHIP *YAKUTSK*
GULF OF ADEN
SUNDAY, 1725 HOURS LOCAL TIME

Twenty NEST personnel had fast-roped to the Russian freighter's deck and spread out through the ship, searching with handheld scanners. Forty minutes later, they'd confirmed Dean's earlier assessment: there were two, and only two, nuclear weapons on board the *Yakutsk*. Those were carefully dismantled to prevent accidents, packed into lead-lined cases, and hoisted away by helicopters dropping lines onto the ship's forward deck.

The four pirate speedboats were also searched, and a SEAL unit had been dropped onto the pirate mother ship a mile to the south after the vessel had displayed a prominent white flag.

Dean and McCauley were on the ship's bridge with the vessel's recently freed captain. He was a small and fussy-looking man named Nuranin who spoke passable English—and he was furious.

"Captain Nuranin?" Dean said. "We are turning your ship back over to you."

"After killing two of my crew? That is so very decent of you, American."

Dean winced and exchanged a glance with McCauley. The butcher's bill had included two dead Russian crewmen and four wounded, out of twenty. The wounded, at least, had not been seriously hurt. Superficial splinter wounds; those miniguns on the HH-60s could send shards and splinters flying for a hundred feet.

There'd also been eight passengers on board—all Pakistanis, so far as Dean had been able to determine, and they'd fought hard when the SEALs had come aboard. Only three were still alive. As for the Somali pirates who'd provided the excuse for assaulting the *Yakutsk*, they'd nearly been an afterthought. Four had been killed by the helicopter gunships, and two wounded; all the rest, twelve of them, had surrendered as soon as the SEALs had arrived.

None of the SEALs had been killed, none wounded. With the exception of the collateral damage to Nuranin's crew, it had been a near-perfect op.

Except that only two of the expected twelve suitcase nukes had been on board.

"We regret the casualties, sir," Dean told the man.

"*Da?* Then you can regret it all you like to the Russian antipiracy flotilla. It will be here any moment."

Dean already knew about the Russian ships, a detachment from the Russian contribution to the international force patrolling Somali waters, though in practice they only escorted Russian ships. Since the *Yakutsk* was Maltese-flagged, perhaps they'd overlooked her.

Or, *just* possibly, they'd deliberately planned on distancing themselves from the *Yakutsk* when she reached Haifa with her deadly cargo. Did the Russians know about the nukes on board? That raised a few terrifying thoughts . . .

That was for the politicians to work out, and the Navy SEALs and the NEST personnel had no intention of being on board when the Russians arrived. According to radar reports, a couple of Udaloy-class guided missile destroyers and the frigate *Gromkiy* were on the way but still three hours off, rather than due to arrive "any moment," as Nuranin claimed.

"There is also the small matter of damage to my ship," Nuranin complained. "My forward hatch blown off, the locking mechanisms destroyed! Both of my masts cut down, the standing rigging destroyed! Bullet holes everywhere! The bridge windows smashed out!"

"Put together a list," McCauley growled at him, "and shove it up your ass!"

"I believe Commander McCauley means . . . submit it to our State Department," Dean added.

"Should I list the cargo you forcibly removed from my forward hold?"

"We have no idea what you are talking about, sir," McCauley said.

"Liars! You were seen sending packaged bundles up to your helicopters! You are as bad as the damned pirates!"

"I think you will find, Captain," Dean said carefully, "that everything on your ship's cargo manifest is still on board."

"What was in those bundles?"

"We have no idea what you are talking about, sir," McCauley said, repeating himself in a manner that suggested he would continue repeating that sentence, word for word, for as long as Nuranin cared to keep asking the question.

"This . . . this invasion means big trouble between your country and mine," Nuranin declared. "You cannot simply shoot your way on board and rifle through my cargo!"

"You're welcome," Dean said. "We're always happy to help distressed seamen of any nation."

McCauley tapped his Velcro-covered watch. "We need to haul ass, sir."

Dean tossed Nuranin a mock salute. "Don't hesitate to call us if you have any more pirate problems," he said, grinning.

"*Padla!*" the Russian spat.

They emerged on the port bridge wing and trotted down the metal ladder to the deck. The sun was setting in a bank of flame-washed clouds off the ship's bow. The helicopters had been circling the ship in shifts, returning to the *Constellation* as their fuel ran low and being replaced by others.

On the forward deck, the three Pakistani prisoners were being readied for their ascent to one of the HH-60s. Their hands were zip-stripped at their backs, they had hoods over their heads, and each had been wrestled into a harness. As Dean watched, a heavy snap-hook was affixed to a D-ring on one prisoner's harness, with a cable reaching from the hook up to the hovering aircraft overhead. A SEAL gave the cable three sharp tugs, and the prisoner was jerked off his feet, screaming as he rose swiftly through the darkening evening sky, his legs kicking wildly.

The captured pirates would be left for the Russian military to handle. The Pakistanis, however, were a priceless windfall for American intelligence. While they were likely the terrorist equivalent of privates rather than officers, and probably ignorant of the overall plan, interrogating them might turn up the names of contacts or leaders, timetables, telephone numbers, the locations of training camps, and details of their operational orders.

As the prisoner vanished into the cargo hatch of the HH-60 overhead, McCauley said, "Officially, there were no survivors."

"What do you mean?"

McCauley shrugged. "We can't very well send them to Gitmo, right?"

"I've already reported to my handlers," Dean said. "These prisoners will be properly and *legally* processed."

McCauley made a face. "What good is it fighting the bastards if we have to let them go?"

"Well . . . that won't happen for a while yet. They'll be questioned, probably at a military base somewhere in Europe." Likely the prisoners would be held at the same facility where they would be working over Koch, or possibly the Israelis would get them. Those two weapons had been aimed at Israeli targets, after all.

It would be cleaner to shoot them here and pitch them over the side. How did you get desperately needed information from people, information that might save tens of thousands of lives, without violating their rights as human beings?

The question had gnawed at Charlie Dean ever since they'd picked up Alfred Koch in Karachi. If there was an answer, it had to do with people losing those rights when they sought to kill people on a monstrous scale. That they did so behind the cloak of religion made it worse, if that was possible.

Charlie Dean was very glad that the decisions were not his to make.

CUMBRE VIEJA
LA PALMA, CANARY ISLANDS
SUNDAY, 1533 HOURS LOCAL TIME

Lia picked her way down the steep inner slope of the crater, cinders and small rocks tumbling away in front of her with each awkward step. As soon as she started down the red-colored slope, the guards inside the caldera saw her and moved to a point directly beneath her, weapons ready, watching her descent expectantly.

She was already having second thoughts about the wisdom of this. If they wanted to, they could pick her off with a single shot. If they let her get to the bottom alive, her survival depended, she realized, on Herve Chatel's goodwill—and, just possibly, on how much influence he had with Ibrahim Azhar, a known terrorist, hijacker, and murderer.

The hell of it was, there was no way for her to change her mind. She couldn't scramble up and out of this crater if those people down there decided that she wasn't going to leave.

The San Martin crater was oddly shaped, an oval a third of a mile long, northwest to southeast, and two-tenths of a mile wide. The crater ridge rose only about fifty meters above the surrounding black, moon-surface terrain; the deepest parts of the crater's interior, however, plunged into shadow over a hundred meters below. The crater's floor was broken and uneven, some places much deeper than others. The helipad and tents had been set up on a relatively shallow, level stretch to the southeast; the drilling derrick rose from the very deepest part of the crater, in the northwest. To Lia's untrained eye, it looked as if the crater was the product of *two* eruptions, creating a single oblong caldera but, most likely, occurring many years apart.

The guards came up to meet her as she neared the bottom of the cinder slope. "You are not permitted here!" one barked in accented Spanish, then repeated himself in even worse English. "You no come here!"

One guard grabbed her arm and yanked her forward. "Hey!" she shouted, playing the outraged tourist role. "Get your hands off of me!"

"What you do, restricted area?" one of them demanded.

Lia turned and looked at Herve Chatel, watching from perhaps fifty yards away. "Herve!" she called. "Herve! It's me, Diane! Call off your dogs, will you?"

One of the guards snarled something in Arabic and struck her in the back with the butt of his rifle, sending her sprawling to the ground. Too late, she remembered that the term "dog" was a deadly insult among Muslims in general and Arabs in particular. She'd meant the phrase colloquially, not as invective.

Shit. A fine cultural liaison I turned out to be, she thought.

Rough hands grabbed her by either arm and hoisted her to her feet, dragging her toward Chatel and Azhar.

"Lia, are you okay?" Rubens' voice said in her ear.

"Yeah," she said through clenched teeth. "Language difficulties."

"Silence, whore!" the guard on her right growled. They dropped her in an untidy heap on the ground.

"Diane!" Chatel said, hurrying forward. "What are you doing here?"

"I was out biking," she told him. She started to rise, and Chatel reached out and helped her stand, brushing the volcanic dust off of her shirt in entirely too familiar a manner. She ignored it. "I was *just* out biking . . . and I saw this cinder cone above the trail. I was up there." She pointed to the rim of the caldera, carefully avoiding that part of the crest where she knew CJ and Carlylse were still watching from under cover. "I was interested in the drilling . . . wondering what they were drilling for. And I saw you." She patted the binoculars, now in their case and slung over her shoulder. "I hadn't seen you since we got here, so I thought it wouldn't hurt if I came down to say hi!"

Azhar joined them, his face dark but otherwise unreadable. "You know this woman?"

"Yes," Chatel said. "She came with me from Spain. She is . . . a friend."

Azhar smirked at that. "I know about your 'friends.'" He looked at Lia. "Didn't you see the postings on the trails? No trespassing."

"I saw one north of here," she said. "At Montaña Rejada. After that, I stayed on the bike trails below the crest of the ridge. Those weren't blocked off."

"You needed to be on the crest trail to get here," Azhar told her.

"I went off-trail," she replied. "I crossed a flat, open stretch of cinders and pine trees, and ended up on the ridge trail. I didn't see any roadblocks."

All of that was the exact truth. They couldn't possibly block off all those miles of twisting bike trail and footpath, not without bringing in an army.

"Are you alone?" Chatel asked her.

"I was riding with a couple of other tourists for a while, but that was a few hours ago." That would explain the presence of her companions if Chatel checked with the sentries that had turned them back at Re-jada.

"I really wish you hadn't come up here, Diane," Chatel told her. "It makes things . . . complicated."

"Why not? You were gone so *long*! I missed you!"

"I would have been back to the hotel tonight. I'll be flying back to Spain tomorrow."

"So . . . what are you doing here, anyway? Drilling for oil?"

"Not inside a volcanic crater," he told her. He seemed uneasy. "This island, these volcanoes, they're all igneous rock, not sedimentary. Not a good place to prospect for petroleum."

"This is part of a research project," Azhar told her. "There is a . . . a danger of the volcanoes on this ridge exploding, of them possibly triggering a massive tidal wave."

"I've heard the theory," Lia told him. "Why all the security? Roadblocks, armed guards . . ."

"These things can be . . . misunderstood by the general public," Chatel said. "It could even cause a panic. People might think that an eruption is imminent if they see us drilling up here."

The explanation actually made sense.

"I was reading a book just the other day about La Palma blowing up and causing a big tidal wave. *Death Wave: 2012*, or something like that."

Chatel made a face. "*That* nonsense again. A bit too sensationalist for my taste."

As they talked, Lia looked around the floor of the crater. In the deeper part, to her left, the drilling derrick ground and chugged. Nearby, she noticed more enormous wooden spools of insulated electrical wire. What the hell was that for?

"So long as I'm here," she said brightly, "can you show me around? I *love* science." She said it in that perky and airheaded singsong that suggested that she probably didn't know the difference between astronomy and astrology.

Chatel exchanged glances with Azhar. "Perhaps later. But you *will* stay with us for a bit, *chère*."

She looked at her watch. "Just so I'm back at the hotel by seven."

"We'll see what we can do." He turned at the sound of rock scraping. Another figure was coming toward them from the direction of the workers' tents.

Lia followed Chatel's glance, her eyes widened, and she bit off a curse. *Shit!*

"Well, well," a familiar voice said. "The elusive Ms. Lau. I was wondering what had become of you."

Feng Jiu Zhu, formerly of Chinese military intelligence, had the cold stare of a venomous snake as he joined them, and he was holding an ugly little semiautomatic pistol.

20

His cell phone vibrated in his pocket, and Rubens fished it from his jacket. The only person who would call him on that phone was his secretary.

"What is it, Ann?"

"You have a one-thirty appointment with ANSA, sir," she told him. "White House basement."

Rubens groaned inwardly. He made a serious error letting Lia descend into that crater, and he didn't want to leave the Art Room. Feng might kill her at any moment.

"I hate to ask it of you, Ann, but is there any chance in hell General James can see me later in the day?"

"I doubt it, sir. He was tight for time as it was, and told me it had 'fucking well better be about Armageddon or worse,' his words, sir. I gather he's going to be flying to London this afternoon."

"Right." Rubens thought hard for a moment. There was nothing he could do for Lia if Feng decided to pull a trigger. He also needed to keep his eyes on the bigger situation. He needed the President to sign off on sending Marines into La Palma, and he wasn't going to get it without ANSA.

He'd already flagged his request to James as Yankee White urgent. You did *not* use such a high-level code without very good and immediate reason. Worse, if he delayed, he would end up talking to Wehrum, James' chief aide, and Wehrum was a political enemy who would block Rubens just for the hell of it.

"Mr. Rubens?" Ann Sawyer asked. "Can I confirm?"

"Yes, Ann. Confirm me for one thirty, WHB." He snapped the phone shut and checked a wall clock. He would have to leave within the next few minutes to be sure he was there on time. "Marie!"

Marie Telach looked up from her console, startled. "Yes, sir?"

"Status on Black CAT Bravo, please."

"They're at Sigonella, sir."

Sigonella was a joint Italian-NATO air base in Sicily, the location of a U.S. naval air station, NASSIG, which served as the hub of U.S. military operations in the Mediterranean. Yesterday, Rubens had ordered a Close Assault Team to fly from Pax River to Sigonella, where it would be closer—about three thousand miles—to the scene of the pirate hijacking in the Gulf of Aden. If something had happened to shut down the SEAL assault on the *Yakutsk*, he'd wanted a second force ready to go in.

Sigonella was also about two thousand miles from La Palma.

The situation on board the *Yakutsk* was well in hand. They wouldn't need CAT Bravo there. "Okay. Tell the CO of CAT Bravo I want his team to deploy to Rota immediately. Have them stay at Readiness Green-One. Second, see what we can do about getting Dean and Akulinin to Rota as well."

"Right away, sir."

"Third, I want your best people monitoring Ms. DeFrancesca at all times. I want to know *exactly* where she is, who she's with, and what's happening. Support her every way you can."

"Yes, sir."

"Next, check whatever records we can snag on flights out of Karachi, Tuesday through Thursday. I want to know how they might have gotten ten suitcase nukes to La Palma, and when."

"Yes, sir."

"Raise Ms. Howorth."

"She doesn't have a comm implant, sir."

"No, but she has a cell phone, and La Palma has a cell network for European tourists. I want her and Carlylse out of there. They can't help Lia, and if the Jackal picks them up they become tactical liabilities."

"Right."

He thought for a moment more. "Okay. There's a major observatory on La Palma, isn't there? Some sort of big scientific facility?"

"Yes, sir. La Roque, up on the north end of the island."

"Have Ms. Howorth see about getting in touch with the public affairs people there, at least for a start. If the JeM is pretending to be a scientific research expedition of some kind, the Jackal might have talked with someone official there—getting permission to put up those roadblocks, to shut down park trails, that sort of thing. She might also talk with the island's *guardia*. I want to know how extensive this thing is—how many people the Jackal has on the island, where they're located, whether they've infiltrated local organizations like the *guardia* or the observatory. Find out who on the island is responsible for watching those volcanoes, and where they're based. La Roque? Or someplace else?"

"Yes, sir."

Was there anything else he could do? There was not, he decided. Everything rested now with ANSA and, ultimately, with the President.

If he could get permission to deploy the CAT to La Palma, he would, but Rota would do for now. Rota was another U.S. naval air station, located across the bay from Cádiz, sixty miles north of the Straits of Gibraltar and just 850 miles from La Palma. That was a two-and-a-half hour flight for a C-130 Hercules.

However, the CAT Bravo team numbered just forty men, too few for a simultaneous assault on all ten drilling sites on La Palma.

For this job, Rubens needed U.S. Marines.

SAN MARTIN VOLCANO
CUMBRE VIEJA
LA PALMA, CANARY ISLANDS
SUNDAY, 1658 HOURS LOCAL TIME

Lia's knee shot up, catching the guard in the crotch. He doubled over, white teeth bared by his grimace, but the other guard, standing behind her, placed his hands on Lia's shoulders and slammed her down onto the folding metal chair.

"Let me go, you bastards!" she screamed, still playing the role of outraged tourist. "You have no *right*—"

"Excuse me, but we have all the right we need," Feng told her. He patted the pistol, now resting in the leather holster on his hip. "So sit still and behave yourself while we decide what to do with you."

Her wrists were handcuffed behind her back. The guard kept his hands heavy on her shoulders, pinning her to the chair.

They'd taken her to one of the tents near the parked helicopter. It appeared to be used for storage, with a number of large crates stacked up in the back and along both sides of the interior. Feng was examining the items they'd just taken from her—a compass, her BlackBerry, the binoculars in their case, her wallet—all laid out on a folding card table. He pulled her ID card from the wallet and looked at it.

"Cathy Chung, U.S. State Department, GS-14," he said, reading it. He flipped it over to check the back. "At this point, I think we can assume this is a false ID."

"You'd better pray it's false," she snarled. "When State gets through with you—"

Feng smiled. "They'll what? Slap me with sanctions?" He dropped card and wallet on the folding card table in front of him, picked up her BlackBerry, and thumbed through several apps. Finding nothing of interest, he opened the binoculars case.

"Very fancy," he said. He held the device to his eyes and pressed several of the buttons on the small control panel on top. "CIA issue?"

"You can get them in any good electronics store back in the States."

"Electronic binoculars? I think not. As a senior executive for COSCO, I have a good understanding of what's available to consumers. Is this how you turn them on?" He stepped to the entrance of the tent and aimed them up at the crater rim. "Yes. Zoom control . . . and is it also a video recorder?"

He continued playing with the button controls. Lia watched him in silence. He was looking at the crater's north rim, not the west, where she'd left CJ and Carlylse, and she hadn't been so amateurish as to have left data in the device's memory. He turned and came back into the tent. "*Quite* ingenious. Does it let you transmit your recordings to a remote site? Possibly by satellite?"

"To my laptop with a cable connection, yes," she lied.

"I assume that's in your room. We'll send someone down there later to retrieve it." He set the binoculars on the table. "So . . . what is it you expected to learn, coming up here like this?"

"I already told you. I was looking for Herve."

"Your taste in men is deplorable. I was most upset when you simply left me in Spain. I thought we'd come to an understanding."

"I got cold feet."

"That . . . or your handlers decided to send you after Mr. Chatel. What did you see in him?"

She thought she saw an opportunity. "Look . . . my name is Cathy Chung, and I *am* with the U.S. State Department. COSCO is on our watch list, you know . . . because of the *Empress Phoenix* affair. My bosses were curious about you, and they *did* plant me on you in order to find out if COSCO was up to no good."

"Indeed? And what did you learn?"

"Nothing. After I met you in Spain, they decided you weren't important. They told me to come home."

"You live in the Canary Islands?"

"No. I decided to take a bit of vacation as long as I was over here, and Herve offered to let me tag along with him to the Canaries." She managed a shrug, despite the weight of the guard's hands still pressing down on her shoulders. "I thought he would be fun, but he disappeared on me as soon as we got to the hotel."

"Mm." He turned and raised his voice. "Mr. Chatel! Would you come in here a moment?"

Chatel entered the tent a moment later. He must have been standing just outside the tent's entrance. "Yes, sir?"

"Ms. Chung here told me she came to these islands with you. Is that true?"

"She was on my flight out of Alicante." A Gallic shrug. "I assumed you'd sent her here on some errand that was none of my business. She didn't come *with* me, however. We didn't even speak—"

"He's lying," Lia said, snarling the words through clenched teeth. If she could get the two of them squabbling with one another, there might be an opening for her, at least a chance to cause confusion enough to help her escape.

"She suggests that the two of you have a relationship. Is that true?"

"Absolutely not." He cocked his head to one side. "She *is* pretty . . . but definitely not my type."

"She is female, which *makes* her your type," Feng said. "But I believe you. You may go."

Chatel left the tent. Feng leaned over her, pinning her with cold eyes.

"I believe you to be CIA, Ms. Chung . . . or whatever your real name is."

"I am *not* CIA—"

"And we will learn the truth, soon enough. What your real name is. Who you work for. What you know about our . . . our operation here. *Everything*."

"Go to hell! I'm telling you the truth!"

"Perhaps you are. We'll soon know for certain, however, one way or another. I have a . . . a specialist flying in. He'll be here tomorrow, and then we will learn *everything* about you that we wish to know."

An interrogation, then, and a professional one if they were bringing in a specialist. With torture? Drugs?

Lia felt very cold, and very much alone.

"Tie her to the chair," Feng told the guard. Reaching out casually, he lightly stroked her cheek. She snapped her head back, pulling away from the touch. He smiled. "And keep a *very* close eye on her. I want two guards in here with her at all times, watching her, two more outside the tent, and two more at a distance, watching *them*. If there is one mouse in the woodpile, there are almost certainly more."

"*Ya m'allmi!*" the guard replied.

Lia hoped that CJ and Carlylse had already gotten back to the hidden bikes and were on their way down the side of the mountain.

"We're with you," the voice of Marie Telach whispered in her ear. "We know exactly where you are, and we'll find a way to get you out of there."

Maybe so—but Marie was thirty-five hundred miles away. Lia wished Charlie was somewhere close by, but he was even farther away than the Art Room, almost five thousand miles if he was still in South Asia.

If she was going to get out of this, she would have to do it on her own.

OFFICE, ANSA
WHITE HOUSE BASEMENT,
WASHINGTON, D.C.
SUNDAY, 1331 HOURS EDT

"So what the hell is so important that you flagged it Yankee White?" General James demanded. "You drag my ass back in here on a Sunday—"

Rubens dropped a file folder on James' desk. "We have recovered two of the Lebed's suitcase nukes," he said. "We know where the other ten are, who has them, and what they're going to do with them. We need military intervention to secure them. *Now.*"

James stared into Rubens' eyes for a moment, then picked up the folder and leafed through the report inside.

"You're suggesting an MEU?" James gave it the in-service

pronunciation, "em-you." The letters stood for Marine Expedition-
ary Unit.

"I believe MEU-26 is in the mid-Atlantic, sir. The *Iwo Jima* strike
group. They could be deployed to La Palma with a minimum of delay."

"FORECON may be the best we can do." He read for another
moment. "You realize this requires presidential approval?"

"That's why I'm here, sir."

"How much time do we have?"

"Unknown, sir. However, one piece of intercepted intelligence suggested that the bad guys were going to have everything ready sometime this coming week . . . and we believe earlier in the week rather
than later. If I had to guess, tomorrow or Tuesday."

"Shit. You're just full of good news, aren't you?"

"That's what they pay me for."

"And you really think these terrorists are able to generate a tidal
wave of this magnitude?"

Rubens shifted uncomfortably. James had immediately highlighted the weakest part of the threat assessment. "There are . . . pros
and cons," he admitted. "We have a lot of good people looking at the
situation. A geology professor over at Georgetown tells me that the
idea of La Palma blowing up and causing a hundred-meter tsunami is
a crock. It would take just the right explosion, triggering a really big
volcanic eruption, and with a *lot* of rock hitting the ocean all at once,
to make a respectable wave. She says that computer modeling carried
out in Holland recently suggests that it just wouldn't happen that
way."

"But?"

Rubens sighed and nodded. "But. Can we take the chance? Do we
gamble the entire U.S. East Coast on those Dutch computer simulations? What if they're wrong?"

"The terrorists obviously think they have something. Otherwise,
they wouldn't use ten suitcase nukes just to make a big splash. They'd
go after cities."

"Exactly. We think there may have been a power struggle inside

JeM over those nukes. The two weapons we've just recovered in the Gulf of Aden were probably the compromise—'okay, we'll give you two weapons to use against Israel, if you let us have the other ten for La Palma.'"

"I'm still not sure I follow that logic," James said. "Sure, if the tidal wave thing works, they have us on our knees. But it seems like a hell of a long shot. They'd be better off smuggling those weapons into ten U.S. cities."

"I think, sir, that they're looking for something more. Not a political or economic victory. A *religious* victory."

"What do you mean?"

Rubens pointed at the folder. "You saw the part about the writer?"

"The guy in New Jersey? Yes." He leafed back through the report. "Here he is. Jack Pender."

"Pender was assassinated by JeM or al-Qaeda killers at a hotel in Fort Lee last Wednesday. It took us a long time, though, to figure out *why*."

"It says here that Pender and another guy—Carlylse—wrote a book about the La Palma megatsunami. Your source in Spain found out that the bad guys had targeted both of them. Maybe they wanted to shut them up."

"Except that the book is already on the shelves and hitting the bestseller lists," Rubens said. "Not only that, the La Palma theory has been circulating for years, ever since the BBC's *Horizon* aired the first program about it back in 2000. And the closer we get to the year 2012, and all of the nonsense about the end of the world, the more we've been hearing about it. Cable TV programs, Web sites—it's all over the place, so much so that Pender and Carlylse jumped on the bandwagon as well. So why slam the barn door shut after the horse gallops out? *Especially* if killing the writers calls even more attention to the book?"

"Point . . ."

"We've had our analysts going over the book, looking for anything that the enemy might not want us to know. And we think we now know what they're worried about."

"What?"

"*Death Wave: The 2012 Prophecies Fulfilled* is about how all sorts of doomsday predictions might come true if La Palma blows up, okay?"

"Yes."

"The collapse of the U.S. economy, widespread destruction of lots of our cities. Pender and Carlylse tie all of that into the Book of Revelation in the Bible."

"Like you said. Doomsday."

Rubens shook his head. "Except that the Book of Revelation doesn't have anything to do, really, with the 2012 garbage, *except* for doomsday."

"I don't follow."

"The year 2012 is when the ancient Mayan calendar runs out. Some airy-fairy New Age types think that means a new age of peace and enlightenment will be upon us, kind of like the Age of Aquarius back in the sixties. Some, including sensationalist writers like Pender and Carlylse, think it means the end of the world. It's the sensationalists who link the end of the Mayan calendar with something completely different—Armageddon and the end of the world as described in the Bible, in Revelation."

"It seems like a reasonable supposition. The end of the world is the end of the world, whether you're Christian or Mayan."

"Or Muslim," Rubens pointed out. "The Qur'an has verses about Judgment Day, and some of them are closely patterned on the Book of Revelation—trumpets sounding, mountains being carried away, that sort of thing. Some of the Hadiths, the sayings of Mohammad, are even more to the point. There's one that says that just before the Day of Judgment, there will be three tremendous landslides, unlike any seen before—one in the west, one in the east, one in Arabia."

"Pender and Carlylse go into some of that in the book, including the idea that in the aftermath of the disaster, a lot of people on the Religious Right in America might think that the Book of Revelation is literally coming true. 'And I saw something like a burning mountain fall into the sea . . .'"

"The Qur'an?"

"No, sir. Book of Revelation, Chapter eight, Verse eight. They suggest that the tsunami might lead to an all-out war between fundamentalist Christianity and fundamentalist Islam, ending in the Battle of Armageddon. What they *don't* say is that Muslims might get the same idea."

"How would killing Pender and Carlylse help the terrorists?"

"We know they were planning another book about a megatsunami and the end of the world. We also know that Pender was about to appear on a TV talk show being filmed in New York City the afternoon he was killed, and that he was going to be talking about end times stuff, how their book might fit in with prophesies about the end of the world.

"The terrorists didn't care if the murder of those two writers gave them more publicity or not. So far as they were concerned, the more people to read it the better, probably. But what they might want to hide was the possibility that a megatsunami on the U.S. East Coast *might be seen by devout Muslims as anything but divine judgment on America*. By selectively putting out verses from the Qur'an and some of the Hadiths, they might convince a lot of Muslims that it was time to rise up against Allah's enemies all over the world. They would have to hide the fact that Islamic terrorists caused the disaster, of course. It would have to look like a literal act of God. I think that what they were trying to hide was, not the book itself, but the possibility that somebody might be crazy enough to create that kind of disaster artificially."

"Do you have any evidence that Pender and Carlylse were thinking along those lines? Talk about an Islamic plot to blow up La Palma?"

"No, sir. Not yet. Pender is dead, and Carlylse is still on La Palma, with one of our operators. We're trying to get him safely back here so we can question him about that." Rubens shrugged. "It's the best we have to go on right now, though. Our analysts have been running themselves ragged, trying to figure out why JeM would try to trigger an eruption instead of just blasting twelve cities. The only thing that comes close to making sense is the idea that JeM hopes to cause a disaster that they can point to and say, 'Look! Allah is wrecking America! It's time to unite and destroy the infidels!'"

"I'm not convinced," James said. "Too many what-ifs."

"I'm not sure *I'm* convinced. But can we ignore the possibility?"

"No, we can't."

"Anyway, whether we think it's plausible or not, there's another consideration."

"What's that?"

"La Palma's population is eighty-six thousand. Setting off ten small nuclear weapons could kill a *lot* of people, whether there's a landslide or not."

"True . . ."

"And the fact remains, we don't know what ten nuclear weapons are going to do to an active volcanic region. Those Dutch modelers were confident that they'd discredited the idea, but we just don't know for sure. I'm told that a powerful earthquake has a *lot* more energy than a nuclear weapon. But if it served as a trigger . . ."

"A detonator. A small charge that sets off a larger one."

"Exactly."

"I assume you realize that the Canary Islands belong to Spain. The President will insist that we consult with them first."

"And I suggest that that would be a very bad idea," Rubens replied. "The bad guys almost certainly got some sort of official authorization to do this, probably under the guise of scientific research. If they find out ahead of time that we're planning an amphibious operation to secure those drill sites, they might set the weapons off early—or even trigger them when our Marines are getting close. We *cannot* afford to tip them off ahead of time."

"There are, unfortunately, military realities . . . and there are political realities." He thought a moment. "Do you know Admiral Ericson?"

"SOCOM? Of course."

"Let's see what we can do through his office in order to pre-position some of our assets."

"Ericson's a good man," Rubens said. He'd only met Charles

Ericson a few times, but he had the reputation of being pragmatic, direct, and no-nonsense, with little patience for bureaucracy and armchair quarterbacking. "What about Foster?"

Jerry C. Foster was the assistant secretary of defense for special operations/low-intensity conflict and intendependent capabilities, the head of a coordinating board within the National Security Council.

"He'll have to be brought in. The Joint Chiefs and the Pentagon, too. But a lot of that can be UNODIR."

Rubens nodded. "UNODIR" was an unofficial military acronym that had crept into common usage within the U.S. Special Forces community over the past couple of decades. It stood for "unless otherwise directed" and had come from the tangled political morass of spec-ops in Vietnam. An officer planning a risky but necessary operation—a recon, say, deep into enemy-held territory—might write an op plan, telling headquarters that it would be carried out *unless otherwise directed* . . . unless HQ came back and told him no. The op plan would then be submitted, but too late for headquarters to call off the op, and too late for enemy agents to tip off the bad guys. It had been, in fact, a common means of sidestepping political micromanagement from the rear.

What James was suggesting, though, went far beyond the scope of platoon-level operations in Vietnam.

"It's our careers on the line, you know," James added. "If you've guessed wrong, they're going to hang us out to dry."

"If I've guessed wrong, at least we won't get wet," Rubens replied. "But if I've guessed right and we don't act, we'd all better be able to tread water for a *long* time."

"Sometimes," General James replied, "I think treading water is what I do for a living."

Rubens knew exactly what he meant.

He'd considered bringing up Operation White Horse with James—a plan, still in development, to get a small team onto La Palma with the explicit purpose of rescuing Lia DeFrancesca. The thought of just leaving her there, to be interrogated and killed by the terrorists, was simply beyond the pale.

However, he also knew that while such a plan could be subsumed into the larger op easily enough, it would be *very* hard to get approval for a rescue op if his request for an amphibious invasion of La Palma was down-checked.

And he was not going to leave his people behind, even if it meant circumventing directives from the White House.

21

*D**amn it, I never should have left her behind.*
Carolyn Howorth stood on the rampart of the tourist observation deck, precariously perched on the edge of the dizzying overlook at the rim of the Caldera de Taburiente. The crater wall fell away beneath her feet, a precipitous fall of over a mile, virtually straight down.

The caldera was a vast mountain ring more than four miles across. Despite what it looked like, Taburiente was not the result of some ancient, colossal volcanic explosion. The formation had begun as a shield volcano, some millions of years in the past, but water erosion had eventually carved it into its current shape. To the southwest, the caldera had been torn open by a river valley, the Barranco de las Augustias, a gap in the mountain wall leading to the Atlantic at the village of Puerto.

The crater-pocked length of the Cumbre Vieja began at the caldera's rim on the far side from where she was standing and ran south from there. Lia was off that way, somewhere . . .

She was beginning to think Rubens and the Art Room had sent her up here as an exercise in busy-work, to keep her out of the way.

To keep her from trying to help Lia.

Carlylse was with her, leaning on the rail and chattering about . . . something, she wasn't sure what.

". . . and the Guanches are obviously descendents of the ancient inhabitants of Atlantis. They're supposed to be related to the Berbers of North Africa, but lots of them had red or blond hair, you know. Of course, all the Guanches are gone now, extinct. The Spanish wiped them out, enslaving them or killing them with smallpox. The last hold-out here on La Palma was King Tanausa, who retreated into the Taburiente Caldera in the early 1490s and turned it into an impregnable fortress. The Spanish got him by pretending to offer a truce, then ambushing him when he came out."

CJ blinked. "What? Who are you talking about?"

"The Guanches . . . the aboriginal inhabitants of the Canary Islands." He grinned at her. "Where were you?"

"Wishing I could get back there and help Lia."

"Ah. Is Lia her real name?"

CJ wasn't sure which of several aliases Lia had been using with this guy. She shrugged and said, "One of them."

"Have you two been working together long?"

"Not really. But . . . she's a good friend."

Officially, CJ was still in training—she didn't have a communications implant yet—but she'd worked closely enough with Lia and Charlie Dean and some of the others to become quite close to them. The camaraderie shared by people who worked in the field together could be incredibly intense.

Watching through binoculars as those guards had dragged Lia into a tent had been one of the hardest moments of her life.

Even harder had been moments later, when the Art Room called on her cell phone and ordered her to get herself and Carlylse out of there.

She'd followed orders, leading the American back down the black-cinder slope to the spot where they'd hidden their bikes. There was nothing she could do. She wasn't even armed, but it hurt like hell to abandon her friend.

Safely back at the Hotel Sol later that evening, she'd had an argument with Rubens on the phone, an argument she lost. He ordered her to come up to La Roque de los Muchachos this morning and talk to the observatory's public affairs people.

La Roque de los Muchachos—the Rock of the Boys—was a pinnacle of the Taburiente Caldera that was home to some fourteen observatories operated by various nations, a part of the European Northern Observatory. The observatory domes were scattered across the northwestern slope of the mountain just below the caldera's rim, looking from here like so many bright white golf balls sitting on the outer slope. The sight had almost made her homesick for Menwith Hill and its cluster of gigantic, spherical white domes housing the ELINT and communications antennae.

Her orders were to talk to the person in charge of the scientific installations on the island, but that proved to be a wild-goose chase. She found a visitors center that supervised tours of the facility, but the observatory headquarters for the Instituto Astrofisica de Canarias, she was told, was located on Tenerife, another island in the Canaries some eighty miles to the southwest.

No one at La Roque de los Muchachos, apparently, knew anything about La Palma's volcanos, or about a scientific institute blocking them off or drilling holes in them. The receptionist at the visitors center suggested she check with park headquarters, which was located in Santa Cruz, north of La Palma's airport. A phone call to a number provided by the visitors center yielded a message in Spanish, telling her the park office was closed.

Dead end.

"You should try to relax, Ms. Howorth," Carlylse told her. "Look at that view!"

Across the gulf of the caldera, an endless sea of white engulfed the eastern side of the island. These were the clouds coming up the ring-wall slopes and spilling over into the crater like a waterfall of white mist. The view was awe-inspiring, strikingly beautiful, a spectacular display of nature . . . and utterly useless to CJ at the moment.

"Relax, hell," she told Carlylse.

"There's nothing you can do," he replied.

"Except watch *you*," she said with disgust. The crash of Flight 12 had gone a long way toward proving that someone wanted Carlylse as dead as his coauthor. Rubens had told CJ not to let him out of her sight, and they'd ended up spending the night together in her hotel room, with him in the bed and her uncomfortably on the couch.

Maybe *that* was why she was feeling so cranky today; she hadn't gotten much sleep. Carlylse snored.

After her futile questioning of the receptionist, she and Carlylse drove up here in a green Fiat Panda, parking at the overlook lot and coming, at Carlylse's insistence, to the tourist observation deck. The overlook, arguably La Palma's most popular tourist site, was fairly crowded, with several dozen tourists either on the sightseeing platform itself or on the path between the platform and the parking lot. She and Carlylse leaned against the railing side by side, watching the spectacular cloud-fall in the distance. Carlylse kept running on about his books on lost Atlantis, past and future, and didn't seem to pick up on CJ's broadly dropped hints that she would *really* rather have a bit of peace and quiet, time to think about what she should do next, about what Desk Three might let her try.

The problem was that her thoroughly old-school British upbringing demanded that she be polite to the twit, that she listen and be attentive, that she—*oh, hell!*

A dark, bearded man dressed like a tourist had just come up behind Carlylse, bumping against him sharply from behind, grabbing his belt, and lifting *hard.*

It happened in an instant; the attacker was bigger and taller than Carlylse, *much* bigger than CJ, likely outweighing her by eighty pounds.

CJ whirled to her right, her elbow coming up. Taller the man might be, but her elbow connected with his nose with a satisfying crunch. Carlylse's attacker staggered back at the blow, still holding Carlylse's belt, dragging him back a step from the precipice before releasing him. As nearby tourists turned to face the commotion, CJ pointed at the man and screamed in Spanish, *"He tried to push me over the edge!"*

Several nearby men in the crowd began closing in on the attacker, who was holding his nose now, his face streaming blood. CJ grabbed Carlylse's hand and ran, dragging him off the sightseeing platform and back up the path toward the car.

"He tried to push *you* over the edge?" Carlylse panted as they slammed the Panda's doors.

She turned the key in the ignition and backed out of the parking space. "There were all those macho Spaniards around. I thought they'd be more likely to help a girl than you."

"Good thinking."

"It seemed—" She was interrupted by a loud crack and the thunk of metal striking metal. Thirty feet away, another bearded man was aiming a handgun at them.

"Get down!" CJ hit the accelerator and spun the wheel, slammed on the brakes, then put the car into drive and floored it once more, tires squealing. A second shot shattered the rear window in a spray of milky shards.

"He's . . . he's *shooting* at us!" Carlylse cried.

"No shit! What was your first clue?"

She turned left out of the parking lot and started down the hill. A glimpse in her rearview mirror showed the gunman sprinting for one of the parked cars.

This could get interesting. The observatory grounds were at the top of a long and zigzagging series of sharp switchbacks up the side of the mountain.

Coming up was the cylindrical Telescopio Nazionale Galileo, the Italian contribution to the ENO. A hairpin to the right took them past the telescope's downhill side, between the Italian facility and the massive silver dome of the Gran Telescopio Canarias. CJ risked a look back over her shoulder. Other observatory domes were strung across the top of the ridge behind them; a single car, a blue Ford Mondeo, hurtled at reckless speed along the road in pursuit.

The road twisted back and forth down the face of the mountain. Ahead, it came to a T-intersection with the main highway. Left was LP-4, the way they'd come hours earlier, leading back to the western side of La Palma; right was LP-1032, which looped around the north side of Taburiente and down to the island's east coast.

Which way? Both roads were treacherous chains of switchbacks down the mountain, but she'd been on the eastern road, didn't know the western circuit at all. Hauling the wheel over, she blew through the stop sign and to the left. Another car coming up the hill swerved off the road, horn blaring.

"Never a cop when you need one," she said conversationally. If she could attract the attention of a local *guardia* or Park Patrol vehicle . . .

Carlylse was clinging to the safety handle above the door with a white-knuckled grip. "My *God*, lady!"

"Would you rather they caught us?"

"I'd rather that you drove on the right side of the road!"

CJ swore at herself. In the excitement she'd reverted to her British driving habits, even though the Panda had a left-side steering wheel. She wrenched the car back to the right. "In a *civilized* country we drive on the left," she said.

She wrenched the car around the next hairpin turn, still racing downhill. The vista ahead and to the left was magnificent, an unending expanse of blue-violet ocean beneath puffy white cumulus clouds and, seemingly directly below the left side of the road, the pine-tree-clad wrinkles of the mountain slope, gradually flattening as they reached out toward the coast. In her rearview, she caught a quick flash of the Ford as it negotiated a twist in the road several turns back.

Calling the Art Room would be useless. There was no help for her out here. Worse, the Ford Mondeo was a heavier, more powerful car than the little Fiat. That *might* be an advantage for her, since more mass meant the driver would have more trouble negotiating the turns at high speed down the mountain. On the other hand, it also meant the other driver could accelerate faster on the straight parts, and if he caught up with them, he would have little trouble ramming them from behind and plowing them off the side of the road.

It was a *long* way down, and their deaths would look like an accident.

The Ford was still far enough behind them, though, that it was only intermittently in view. When she couldn't see it, thanks to intervening terrain, the other driver probably couldn't see them. If she tried to race him all the way to the bottom of the hill, she would lose. If she was going to try to change the equation of the chase, she had to do something *now*.

Up ahead, she thought she saw a possibility.

She tromped down harder on the gas . . .

GREEN AMBER
C-130 HERCULES
300 NMI SOUTHWEST OF ROTA
MONDAY, 1145 HOURS LOCAL TIME

Charlie Dean sat in the cargo compartment of the big Marine Corps transport as it droned southwest across the ocean. Earplugs and his helmet held the thunder of the four big Allison turboprops at bay, and should have given him quiet enough to gather his thoughts—but the truth was he was exhausted and kept drifting off. He'd been on the go now for . . . how long? The last time he'd *really* slept had been on board the *Lake Erie* Saturday night, and reveille had sounded at 0600 Sunday. So thirty-some hours, depending on time zone differences.

He and Ilya had been grabbing catnaps on various aircraft since they'd flown off the *Constellation* in a C-2 Greyhound last night after leaving the *Yakutsk*. The COD—for "carrier onboard delivery"—had flown them from the carrier group to Djibouti, then northwest up the Red Sea to Haifa. From there, a U.S. Air Force C-17 Globemaster III had flown them the entire length of the Mediterranean, setting down at the naval air station at Rota at just past ten that morning, after over twelve hours in the air altogether. They'd gained a free hour flying west from Israel to Spain; they would gain another hour flying to the Canary Islands, which were on Greenwich Mean Time.

Now they were airborne again, an hour out of Rota on board the big C-130 Hercules. They would reach the La Palma drop zone at 1215, local time.

How he was supposed to conduct a parachute drop into enemy territory and carry out a mission on next to no sleep was something of a mystery to Dean—but he knew he would do it. He *had* to.

The bastards had Lia.

Rubens had filled him and Akulinin in during the COD flight north from Djibouti last night. The missing suitcase nukes had almost certainly been flown out of Karachi on board a Pakistan International Airlines cargo flight which had reached Mogador Airport in Morocco sometime on Saturday. From there, privately chartered helicopters had probably flown them out to La Palma, some 460 miles farther to the southwest. The JeM terrorist leader called the Jackal was drilling boreholes down the throats of volcanos on La Palma. Detonate ten small nuclear warheads buried deep beneath the crater-pocked ridge of the Cumbre Vieja, and there was a chance—according to some—that the resultant tidal wave would scour the eastern seaboard from Canada to Brazil.

"Most scientists say that won't happen," Rubens had told him as the Greyhound droned through the night above the Red Sea, "but, then, no one's ever tried setting off nuclear warheads inside a string of volcanos to see what *will* happen. If those blasts serve as a trigger, I'm told they might penetrate the magma chamber beneath the island and generate a megatsunami. Even if they don't, thousands of people are at risk on La Palma itself."

Among those thousands, Rubens had told him, was Lia.

Dean and Lia had kept their relationship discreet over the years, but he knew that Rubens was aware of it, knew he might have guessed, at least, that they were lovers. Such relationships among field officers weren't forbidden, exactly, but neither were they encouraged.

Dean was surprised—and pleased—that Rubens had brought him in on the ad hoc op to rescue Lia. Dean hadn't even known that Lia was on La Palma. Rubens could easily have brought him back to Fort Meade and broken the news to him then.

Then again, maybe Rubens figured that if he did that, Dean would take the Puzzle Palace apart chip by chip.

Akulinin said something, shouting to be heard over the engine roar. Dean still couldn't hear. He removed his helmet and pulled out an earplug. "What?"

"I said . . . we'll get her!"

So Akulinin knew as well. That figured. Dean had kept quiet about his liaison with the Alekseyevna woman.

"I know," Dean shouted back.

They were fitted out for a specops HALO jump—Gore-Tex jump suits and gloves, oxygen tanks and masks, helmets, MA2-30 altimeter, and MC-5 Ram Air Parachutes. Dean carried an M4A1 close-quarters battle weapon with its SOPMOD kit strapped to his right leg. On his left leg was a Marine-modified laptop computer, with a solid-state hard drive that would survive a slam into the ground, or almost anything else short of a direct hit by a 9mm round. All told, he was lugging nearly eighty extra pounds of gear, including ammo, most of it in a release bag strapped to his harness. It made moving awkward, so the two and a half hours on board the Herky Bird would be spent sitting on the hard, narrow fold-up seat.

Dean glanced at the others in their team—twenty Marines from FORECON, the 2nd Reconnaisance Battalion of the 2nd Marine Division, deployed out of Camp Lejeune. They'd flown off the USS *Iwo Jima* somewhere in the mid-Atlantic yesterday and touched down in Rota hours ahead of Dean and Akulinin. Two Marines would approach each of ten volcanic craters; Dean and Akulinin would be traveling with Gunnery Sergeant Rodriguez and Sergeant Dulaney to the southernmost of the calderas.

"Remember," Rubens had told Dean as they approached Rota earlier. "You get to the crater, you look around, but you will *not* attack, and you will *not* attempt to rescue Ms. DeFrancesca until you get specific word from me. Do you understand?"

"Yes, sir," Charlie Dean had said—but he hadn't understood, not really.

"If you go into that crater too soon," Rubens had gone on, "you could spook the bad guys, make them run or, worse, trigger those nukes prematurely. We don't want that to happen."

"No, sir."

"Those Recon Marines will be there to help play this game out in any of several ways, depending on what goes down. They can laser-tag the drilling rigs for a smart-bomb strike. They can pin down the enemy while a larger Marine force gets ashore. Or they can spot for air assets or artillery. We're not sure yet just what we're going to be able to bring in."

Which meant that they were making this op-plan up as they went along, still unsure of presidential support, unsure even if they would be allowed to deploy a small, surgical strike.

A helluva note. One thing was certain, though. He was going to go in and get Lia, one way or another.

And not even nuclear-armed terrorists were going to stop him.

NORTH FACE OF TABURIENTE
LA PALMA, CANARY ISLANDS
MONDAY, 1150 HOURS LOCAL TIME

Ahead lay the tree line. The upper reaches of the Caldera de Taburiente were naked and exposed, but at around two thousand meters altitude and below, the slope became thickly forested, mostly with growths of weirdly surreal Canary Island Pine. CJ took another look over her shoulder. The pursuing blue Ford was hidden for the moment by the hillside.

On the way up this road earlier that morning, she'd noticed that many of the switchbacks were short-circuited by dirt tracks. Evidently, tourists with Jeeps or other four-wheel-drive vehicles liked to take short cuts. Just where LP-4 entered the tree line, one of these tracks left the right side of the road and plunged down a precipitous embankment, cutting a straight but terrifying path down the slope to connect with the lower arm of the switchback.

Howorth slowed slightly, then turned the wheel, swerving off the paved road.

"What the fuck!" Carlylse screamed. The Panda lurched and jounced

over eroded ditches in the track, slowing now until it was inching ahead and down.

The track ran at about a forty-five-degree slope, steep enough that in moments the Panda was well below the edge of the upper arm of the switchback and out of sight of the road. Below, the lower bend in the road ran along the base of the track. CJ edged forward enough to be sure she was out of the line of sight of a driver coming down the road above, and too high up to be seen by a driver around the sharp bend below. A clump of oddly shaped pine trees and several boulders as big as houses provided some additional cover. She was tempted to try to tuck in behind the boulders but decided against that. The ground dropped away in a sheer cliff to the left, near the boulders, and it would be all too easy to strand the Panda—which, unlike the vehicles that had made this track, did *not* have four-wheel drive. Her biggest worry was that leaving the paved road had raised a considerable cloud of dust. It was possible that the assassin would see it and figure out what had happened.

It was too late to back out now, even if she could back up that slope. She eased the little two-door vehicle to a stop, pulled up the parking brake, and held the handle tightly as she gingerly took her foot from the brake pedal on the floor.

The car rocked slightly but then held firm.

"You . . . you're hoping they go past us?"

"They shouldn't be able to see us here," she told him, "but just in case, watch out the back, will you?"

"For what?"

"A blue Ford. A man coming down that hill with a gun."

Actually, that last wouldn't be so bad. If the assassin got out of his car to come down the track, she could roll forward and gain some ground while he scrambled back to the car. But she was hoping—

"There he is!"

"Where?"

Carlylse pointed past her nose, out the left side of the car. She turned her head and glimpsed the blue car flickering intermittently beyond the pines and at the bottom of the escarpment. A moment later, the Ford rounded the last bend and raced past the dirt track below them, accelerating hard out of the turn.

"He didn't see us!" Carlylse said.

"No—but we'll still wait for a moment." Much depended on how observant the assassin was. If he got a clear look at the road in front of him and realized the Panda had vanished, he might put two and two together, turn around, and come back up the hill after it.

A minute passed . . . and then another. CJ put her foot on the brake pedal again and slowly eased off on the parking brake. Carefully, carefully, she started the Panda rolling forward. Rocks skidded and slipped beneath the tires; the car bounced hard and started moving faster than she wanted . . . but then they bottomed hard on the narrow road shoulder below, turned left, and began driving up the hill, headed back toward the observatory entrance.

Ten minutes later, they passed the entrance and started descending once more, now on LP-1032, heading toward the east coast. On the maps she'd seen, the road in this direction was even steeper and more tortuous than the other, but eventually it would bring them out at the coast road just north of Santa Cruz.

After that? She wasn't sure.

She *was* sure that more than anything else, she wanted to get Carlylse safely onto a plane and off this damned island.

She reached for her cell phone.

SAN MARTIN VOLCANO
CUMBRE VIEJA
LA PALMA, CANARY ISLANDS
MONDAY, 1210 HOURS LOCAL TIME

They left Lia tied to the folding metal chair all night, releasing her once in the morning to use the facilities—a bright blue portable construction john positioned a few yards away from the tents. There was nothing in the narrow plastic box that would serve as a weapon, no pieces of wire that she could hide as a lockpick for later, no odds and ends with which she could MacGyver her way out. She stepped out of the john; they led her back to the tent and again handcuffed her before tying her to the chair.

Later, they'd brought her a plate of scrambled eggs and watched her while she ate. At least they weren't going to let her starve.

"What time is it?" she murmured. The two guards were still there, sitting on chairs on the far side of the tent, watching. *Always* watching. Every few hours they were replaced by two others.

"Just past twelve, where you are," Marie Telach whispered in her ear. Back at the Art Room, it would be five hours earlier—about seven in the morning.

She wondered if Charlie was still in south Asia, or if he'd wrapped up his part of the op and flown home.

The interior of the tent was stiflingly hot, with the tropical sun beating down from directly overhead. Would they give her water if she asked for it?

With startling suddenness, Feng threw back the tent flap and barked something in Arabic at the two. They leaped to their feet, slung their weapons and hurried to untie her.

"He told them to take you to the tube," another voice said in Lia's ear. Dr. Fahd al-Naimi was one of Desk Three's language specialists, fluent in both Arabic and Urdu.

Still handcuffed, she was led out of the tent and into the dazzling midday sun.

The small tent city was set up on the floor of the higher and shallower of the two partially merged craters. Walking her between them, the guards led her along a well-worn footpath through cinders and red sand, taking her over a low lip, then down a much steeper path into the deeper, northern crater. The drill was still in operation—she'd heard its grinding all through the long night, punctuated by the clang and clash of metal when the workers swapped out a cutting head or added more drill pipe.

At the floor of the deeper crater, she was led around to the right. In front of her, a round and very black opening gaped in the rock, a tunnel entrance leading down into the rock beneath the higher, southern caldera.

"They're taking me into a cave or tunnel of some sort," she murmured. "South wall of the northern crater."

"Quiet, whore," one of her captors growled. "You talk all you want . . . later."

"We copy you, Lia," Marie whispered. "They're taking you into a tunnel entrance near the drilling rig in the deeper crater."

They walked her out of the sun and into deep shade. The difference in temperature was startling, and she suppressed a small shiver.

"The island is riddled with tunnels and ancient lava tubes," Marie continued, talking, perhaps, just to reassure Lia, to maintain contact with her. "Up in the northern part of the island, they use them to channel rainwater down to—"

Marie's voice faltered, then broke off. Lia caught a few garbled words after that, and then there was nothing but silence.

The walls of the cave were blocking the signals between her belt antenna and the NSA communications satellite overhead.

Lia hadn't realized how much comfort she'd been drawing from the periodic, reassuring voices from the Art Room. As the guards led her deeper into the cool and echoing stone throat of the tunnel, Lia DeFrancesca felt more alone than she'd ever felt before in her life.

22

GREEN AMBER
C-130 HERCULES
APPROACHING LA PALMA JUMP POINT
MONDAY, 1212 HOURS LOCAL TIME

Stand up!" The cargo master barked the order over the intercom from his station at the front of the cargo bay. "Gear check!"

Charlie Dean turned and faced Ilya Akulunin, tugging at various snaps, latches, and D-rings to make sure all was secure, having him turn so he could check his back, and then standing with arms slightly out from his body while Akulinin did the same check-over for him.

"Ready for this, Sharkie?" he yelled.

"Just like in training," Akulinin yelled back.

No, Dean thought. *It never goes the way it does in training . . .*

The rear ramp of the Hercules ground slowly open, and Dean saw dazzling sun-glare off impossibly white clouds below. In some ways, it was good making a HALO jump in daylight; night operations were always a *lot* riskier. On the other hand, they would be coming down near the bad guys' positions in broad daylight.

The rushed timetable, he knew, had been cobbled together because no one knew when the Tangos might have their bombs planted and armed, or when they were planning on detonating them. The smart money said that the ten nuclear devices arrived at Mogador

Airport Friday or Saturday, and that the terrorists started flying them out to La Palma as soon as possible to avoid complications either from the Moroccan authorities or from American or Spanish agents.

If the bombs were already on La Palma, they might already be planted. Marine Task Force Green Amber might be about to fly into a nuclear holocaust.

Colonel Kemper, in charge of the FORECON elements deployed for Green Amber, had argued hard for a night drop, but he'd been overruled. It was more important that the two-man Marine elements be down and in place absolutely quickly as possible than that they come in under the cover of darkness.

Besides, the chances that they would be seen were not as large as might be imagined, Dean knew. This was a HALO jump—the acronym standing for "high altitude, low opening." The C-130 was currently cruising southeast at twenty-six thousand feet; the jumpers would exit the aircraft and free-fall all the way down to six thousand feet before opening their chutes. Their target drop zones along the eastern flanks of the Cumbre Vieja were all at around three thousand feet above sea level. Once they popped their chutes, they actually would be flying in along the mountainside at an altitude well *below* the very top of the ridge, which averaged around fifty-nine hundred feet and in places rose as high as sixty-two hundred. The op planners thought that the Tango sentries patrolling the rims of the volcanic craters wouldn't see individual parachutists in free fall—dust motes against the sky. Even after their Ram Air chutes opened, the Marines might be too far away for the guards to spot them; the actual drop zones were almost a mile from the top of the ridge.

The weather reports were promising. A large mass of cumulus clouds had been moving in with the northeastern trades all morning, their base at around six thousand feet. The jumpers would actually have the clouds as cover for the gliding part of their descent.

While nothing was ever certain in a military operation, especially one with as many variables as this one, the chances were acceptable that the Marines would be able to get to their positions without being seen.

The insertion was the easy part. Ten separate terrorist sites, ten nuclear weapons. The approach, recon, and takedown would have to work perfectly ten times in a row, or people, quite likely a *lot* of people, were going to die.

Dean felt the deck of the aircraft tilt beneath his feet. The Hercules was turning now, coming around to a northerly heading. The Marine Recon jumpers would exit the aircraft two at a time, spaced out along a line five and a half miles long, matching the south-to-north line of volcanos up the center of La Palma. Dean and Akulinin would go with the first two Marines, vectoring toward San Martin, the southernmost volcanic crater.

"First jumpers! Stand ready!"

The rear ramp was fully down now, with sunlight blasting across the slanted exit track. Dean and Akulinin stood just behind the first jumpers, Sergeant Dulaney and Gunnery Sergeant Rodriguez, waiting . . . waiting . . .

A red light above the gaping opening flashed to green, and the jumpmaster yelled, "First jumpers . . . go!"

Dulaney and Rodriguez launched themselves forward, running down the ramp and flinging themselves into the sunlight. Dean and Akulinin were right behind them, hitting the ramp, then diving head-first into sun-brilliant emptiness.

They fell, wind hammering at their torsos, the blast fluttering loose folds of Gore-Tex tight around their outstretched arms and legs. The sheer adrenaline rush of free fall hit Dean as it always did, a sharp, pounding exhilaration that caught at his breath and chest.

The four jumpers drifted slowly apart, turning to orient themselves. La Palma was off to the right and below, spread out against the blue ocean like an immense mottled arrowhead pointed south. Clouds massed against the north and northeastern coastline, blindingly bright in the midday sunlight. Dean could easily make out the island's principal feartures—the vast circular formation of mountains called Taburiente in the north, the straight thrust of the Cumbre Vieja toward the island's southern point. He could see the line of craters down the central ridge, but it took him a moment or two to positively identify his target—San Martin—for there were several other craters around it. Scattered cumulus clouds drifted slowly above their own shadows down the eastern side of the ridge. He made out the clear separation in color and texture between the forested lower slopes of the ridge and the barren, volcanic cinder and rock higher up. He spotted the area designated as his drop zone—among the trees, but in an area more open, less heavily forested than others. The idea was to land somewhere sheltered by the woods but not so heavily overgrown that he ended up stuck in a tree.

He was *very* glad that they weren't doing this at night.

Dean checked the altimeter, which was mounted on his reserve chute in front of him. He was now falling past twenty thousand feet. He'd reached terminal velocity—about 124 miles per hour, or just under eleven thousand feet per minute. That gave him a bit over a minute of free fall; his AAD, or automatic activation device, would open his chute at eight thousand feet above sea level, with his drop zone target at five thousand. One of the dangers of HALO jumps lay in the possibility that a malfunction in the parachutist's breathing gear might cause him to pass out. The AAD made sure his chute would open whether he was conscious or not.

The other jumpers in his team had spread out, with plenty of room between them. They were falling past ten thousand feet now; the ones- and tens-place numerals on his altimeter's digital readout flickered past almost too fast to read. More alarming was the loom of the mountains below and ahead. With arms and legs extended and his back sharply arched, he'd picked up some forward momentum and literally flown toward the island. The city of Santa Cruz was spread along the coast to his left, just north of the single sharp, straight slash of the island's airport runway.

At six thousand feet, his drogue deployed, pulling his Ram Air chute from the pack gently enough to avoid damaging it during the deployment. A moment later, the Ram Air caught hold, the sudden deceleration a sharp jerk against Dean's harness that made it feel as though he'd suddenly grown *very* heavy, then started rising.

He took a quick look up to make sure the canopy had deployed properly—no rips or tears, no "Mae West" twists in the fabric. Everything was working as it should. The canopy itself was neither night-ops black nor traditional white, and it certainly had none of the bright colors popular in sports-jumping. It was a blend of neutral grays in random computer-generated patterns that blended well with sky or with distant vegetation. He was still a good six miles from the crest of Cumbre Vieja, coming in toward the beach at Punta El Lajio. "Chute open and functioning," he reported.

"Copy, Charlie," Marie Telach replied.

It was good to know someone was listening over his shoulder.

He could see the El Lajio lighthouse below, a stark, modernistic white tower with a rounded cap that probably had been intended as futuristic architecture but looked like a tall, skinny grain silo . . . or an enormous sex toy. That lighthouse had been his first waypoint marker for his drop zone approach.

"Going feet dry," he said. "Fifty-five hundred feet and directly above the giant dildo. I have the DZ in sight."

A fifteen-mile-per-hour trade wind out of the northeast had him on course. Ideally, a ground team should have been present to set out signal panels to mark the drop zone, but there hadn't been time to organize that. Rubens had told him that two more NSA officers were on their way to La Palma—one to join CJ, the other to take charge of the writer, Carlylse—but they didn't have any of the equipment necessary for marking one DZ, much less ten. Instead, each parachute team had memorized the rugged silhouette of the Cumbre Vieja, the position of each volcanic caldera, and the general appearance of the designated drop zones on the ridge's eastern slope.

As he got closer, he realized that this last wasn't quite as easy as he'd thought at first. There were a lot of clouds floating above the east side of the island, many of them flowing up against the ridge crest itself. North, the entire northern curve of La Palma appeared to be engulfed in a sea of dazzling white, a solid cloud deck pressing against and spilling into the hollow of the big Taburiente caldera.

The view was spectacular, the interplay of clouds and sea and mountain utterly mesmerizing. He was flying southeast, now, above a tiny village—it *should* be Tigalate—and that road glimpsed through the trees would be LP-132. That was waypoint two, at an altitude of two thousand feet. Beyond, the ground began rising *very* sharply. Directly west now was Mount Deseada, its crest at over sixty-one hundred feet, looming above him. The top was lost in a chain of clouds running down from the north, but he could tell he was already below the peak.

His altimeter read five thousand feet.

Much more quickly than he'd expected, the ground began rising up to meet him. Trees skimmed past beneath his jump boots in a blur. Tugging on his risers, he brought the leading edges of his Ram Air double canopy up, stalling to kill some of his forward velocity. He passed over another village, a cluster of white and brick-pink roofs seemingly imbedded in the steep hillside. That was waypoint three, the town of Monte de Luna, at a mean altitude of twenty-four hundred feet above sea level. He yanked at his right-hand risers, pulling into a sharp right turn, swinging from a southwesterly heading to directly west.

He saw patches of heavy forest interspersed with more open ground. He aimed for one of the thinner regions, which appeared to be riding on a bare-topped shoulder extending east from the mountain.

Treetops skimmed beneath his boots, the ground rising swiftly. He unhooked his drop bag from his hip and let its nylon tether pay out through gloved fingers until it was dangling twenty feet below. His gliding descent carried him over open ground . . . the drop bag struck, and he tugged again on his risers, killing more speed and settling toward the slope.

He touched down at a quick walk, the parachute dumping air and spilling into an unruly mass in front of him. He kept walking, bundling the fabric in with his arms. Fifty feet ahead and to his right, another parachutist touched down. He couldn't tell whether it was Ilya or one of the Marines.

From the drop bag he extracted electronic binoculars, pouches holding ammunition for his rifle, Kevlar vest, combat harness, water and rations, backpack, and a last-minute piece of special gear shipped out the day before from Fort Meade. The jump harness, reserve chute, breathing equipment, helmet, and attachments went into the bag.

The other parachutist was Gunny Rodriguez, but both Dulaney and Akulinin joined them a few minutes later as they trudged up the slope from below. To the east, the falling ground offered a spectacular view of blue ocean, scattered clouds, and the village of Monte de Luna less than a thousand yards away and about nine hundred feet below. West, they looked up . . . and *up* at the slope in front of them, culminating in the peak of the San Martin caldera some fifteen hundred feet higher.

A GPS tracker confirmed they were now just twelve hundred yards from the rim of San Martin. It was going to be one hell of a long twelve hundred yards.

They started walking.

LA PALMA AIRPORT
SOUTH OF SANTA CRUZ DE LA PALMA
LA PALMA, CANARY ISLANDS
MONDAY, 1410 HOURS LOCAL TIME

"Miss Howorth?" the man asked in brisk, no-nonense tones. "Mr. Carlylse?" James Castelano stepped out from behind a pillar. Nearby, on the other side of the entrance to the airport terminal, Harry Daimler pretended to read a newspaper.

"Good to see you again, James," CJ said—and it *was* good. CJ's knees were shaking as she shook his hand. There'd been no way to know if other assassins were waiting for them along the descent off Taburiente, or here at the airport. Being no longer *alone* gave her a tremendous surge of relief. Right now, Castelano looked about ten feet tall, and she was tempted to ask where his white charger was.

"Is this our package?" He gave Carlylse a cold look up and down.

"The very same."

"Are you going to board the aircraft with us now, sir," Castelano asked in a flat voice, "or do we knock you unconscious and carry you on board?"

Carlylse raised both hands. "I'm going with you! Jesus Christ . . ."

"He's not available at the moment, Mr. Carlylse. You'll have to settle for my partner over there instead."

"You're not going back?" CJ asked.

"No, ma'am. I've been ordered to stay with you."

"Is it . . . is it safe?" Carlylse asked. He looked terrified, and CJ could understand why. He was a firm believer in the frailly of life . . . now.

"We flew in on a private plane, Mr. Carlylse, a Learjet 45. It was thoroughly checked before we left Rota, and there are two U.S. Marshals standing beside it on the tarmac now. Yes, it's safe."

"In that case, sir, there is *nothing* I want more than to get off this godforsaken island!"

"We can get your stuff out of your room," CJ told him. "Your computer and clothes and all that. I'm sure they can set you up at Fort Meade with a razor and a toothbrush."

"Thank you. I don't want to lose the laptop. It's got half of my next book on it."

They went through the terminal, and Castelano flashed a card at a security gate that let them all go through. The Learjet was waiting on the far side of the terminal, two tough looking men in civilian clothes standing beneath it.

"Is that your plane?" CJ asked. "You really did arrive on a white charger!"

"I beg your pardon?" Castelano asked, looking puzzled.

"Never mind." CJ had already decided that Castelano and Daimler, with body-builder muscles beneath their touristy bright-print shirts, were lacking in the conversation department and had social skills approximating those of bricks.

"This way, Mr. Carlylse," Daimler said.

Carlylse turned suddenly. "Thank you, CJ. You . . . you saved my life back there a couple of times over."

"Don't mention it," she told him. "That's what we get paid for."

"Well, I appreciate it. And . . . I wasn't *really* that upset by your driving . . ."

She gave him a hug and a quick peck on the cheek. He nodded, then turned and followed Daimler across the tarmac toward the waiting aircraft.

When she'd called Rubens earlier, during the drive down the east side of the mountain, he said, that Charlie Dean, Ilya Akulinin, and a number of Force Recon Marines were on their way, by parachute. As she and Castelano stood in the blazing tropical sunshine outside the terminal, watching Carlylse walk up the boarding stairs, she looked away, toward the west and the southwest, wondering if she would catch a glimpse of them.

That was impossible, of course. She had no idea when they would be arriving. Rubens had not confided anything else about the op, and rightly so. He'd probably been bending security regulations just telling her that they were coming. They might still be on the way from the air base in Spain, or they might already be on the ground.

She did see something unexpected, though . . . an aircraft much closer at hand. It was a big, blue Aérospatiale Puma with a bright red Moroccan flag showing on the tail boom, and the white-letter logo of Marrakech Air Transport, a civilian air charter service. She'd seen two like it yesterday, when the three of them had picked their way across cinder slopes and through puine forests to peer into the ten calderas along the Cumbre Vieja. This one, with a thunderous roar, was lifting off of the southern end of the La Palma runway. As she watched, it hovered a moment, then dipped its nose and turned away, angling toward the mountainous interior of the island.

From this angle, it looked like it was heading straight for the San Martin volcano, just seven miles to the southwest.

She pulled out her cell phone for another call to the Art Room.

GREEN AMBER ONE
EAST SLOPE OF SAN MARTIN
MONDAY, 1422 HOURS LOCAL TIME

"Charlie? Ilya?" Jeff Rockman's voice said over Dean's implant. "You may be about to get company."

Charlie Dean was panting with the effort of the climb. They'd emerged from the pine forest on the slope below the San Martin crater and were in the open now, trudging slowly up the loose cinder scree of the volcanic cone. He stopped, looking up. The crest was still two or three hundred yards ahead, and another three hundred feet above them.

"Whatcha got?" he asked.

"CJ's at the airport," Rockman told him. "She just called in a report. A Moroccan civil helicopter is on its way, headed in your direction."

Dean whirled in place, fumbling for his binoculars—and suddenly he realized that he didn't need them. He could see the aircraft now, between him and the airport, several miles away.

"Take cover!" he called, his voice barely above a sharp whisper. *"Incoming aircraft!"* The others saw the helicopter now as well. It would be over them in less than a minute—and they were well above the tree line, nakedly exposed on the volcano's eastern slope.

Inside his backpack, on the very top, was the special gear from Fort Meade, a tightly rolled bundle of tough, waterproof fabric. He ripped open the closures, unrolling it on the ground. A seven-by-seven blanket with elastic loops at each corner, its color was a faded and mottled red brick and dark gray, a close match for the colors of the surrounding volcanic landscape. Slipping a corner strap over one boot, then the other, he pulled the blanket up over his body, and in seconds effectively disappeared.

During his years as a U.S. Marine sniper, Charlie Dean had frequently used camouflage Ghillie suits, making them himself in the field from locally available materials. The tech-Ghillie was a high-tech wrinkle on an old idea. The surface color adapted to the local light levels, fading in strong light, darkening in shade. A ceramic weave inside the layers of fabric blocked infrared radiation—heat—rendering the tech-Ghillie effectively invisible under IR. That last made the things ungodly hot, since the wearer's body heat couldn't escape to the open air, but then the same was true of traditional Ghillie suits, which commonly inflicted temperatures of 120 degrees on the people wearing them.

The things were custom ordered for specific environments; the color scheme of these blankets had been based on satellite photos of the top of the Cumbre Vieja taken just a few days ago.

Dean could hear the stuttering *whop-whop-whop* of the helicopter now as it grew closer. Helicopters, he knew from his briefing, were being used to transport men and material up to the volcanic craters, but there was always that small chance that something had gone wrong, that the op had been compromised and the aircraft overhead was actively searching for them.

The thunder of rotors grew louder, then still louder. Dean hugged the ground, motionless. As the noise passed overhead, he raised his head slightly, risking a look. The helicopter, a civilian Puma, was flying over the rim of the crater ahead. As he watched, it circled to the left, hovered, then drifted slowly down, vanishing behind the lip of the crater.

"Green Amber One, let's move," Gunny Rodriguez's voice said over the tactical radios each man had strapped to his combat harness. "The opposition'll be busy watching the landing."

As one, four patches of brick red earth shifted, bunched up, and opened, revealing the four recon team members as they continued the climb up the steepening slope.

SAN MARTIN CRATER
MONDAY, 1424 HOURS LOCAL TIME

Ibrahim Hussain Azhar stood on the floor of the crater near the tents, watching the Marrakech Air Transport helicopter fly low above the caldera's eastern rim, then gentle in for a landing a dozen meters away. Feng, standing beside him, muttered something in Chinese.

"What was that?" Azhar asked.

"I said it's about time," Feng replied in his thickly accented Arabic. The man didn't speak Urdu, so Azhar's conversations with him were in English, which Feng spoke very well, or in Arabic, which he did not.

"For the weapon?" Azhar asked, shifting to English. "Or for the passenger?"

"Both, actually," Feng replied in the same language. "This is the last device from Tan-Tan. It's taken long enough . . . but we should be ready to go by tonight."

"We can have the weapon in place late this afternoon," Azhar said, "but the plan calls for detonating the weapons tomorrow, at thirteen hundred hours."

"Why such a precise time?"

"Because that will be eight hundred hours, eight o'clock on the U.S. East Coast. The cities will be filling with commuters driving in from the suburbs. In cities farther west like Houston and New Orleans, it will be an hour earlier, seven o'clock, but the highways will still be crowded. News that a volcano has exploded, that a megastsunami is rushing across the ocean toward the United States, will reach them when the bridges, the tunnels, the highways leading into their cities, and the narrow canyon-streets inside their cities all will be jammed with traffic . . . what they call 'rush hour.'

"The wave won't reach them until sometime in the afternoon, but for some six or seven hours, the panic will build . . . and build. Millions of people will be struggling to get out of the city death-traps, and when the wave does hit, with the highways and tunnels impassably blocked by fleeing people . . ."

"Ah!"

"We believe that this timing will increase the number of deaths tremendously, first in the panic, then as cars are swept from the highways, bridges toppled, and tunnels drowned later in the afternoon. We conservatively estimate between one and two million deaths as a direct result of the strike. A similar number, we believe, will die of starvation, disease, and food and water riots within the next several weeks."

"An ugly picture."

Azhar shrugged. "You want to see America's commercial and industrial infrastructure destroyed. We want to kill as many of them as possible, to drive home the message that this is God's judgment on a sinful people. The devices will serve both of our purposes."

"You put a great deal of trust in this megatsunami concept," Feng said. "The reality may be considerably less than you anticipate."

"Perhaps. We are aware of the Dutch studies that suggest nothing much will happen. We believe them to be mistaken."

"What makes you so certain?"

"First, science in the West has been so completely politicized, their researchers routinely come up with the the answers that fit their preconceived theories. They do not *know*. Look at their idiocies, the way they cripple themselves economically, with their politically correct beliefs about global warming.

"Second . . . have you ever been to the Hawaian Islands?"

Feng nodded. "Many times."

"One of the islands—Molokai—is long and slender, running east and west."

"Yes. A beautiful place."

"One and a half million years ago, Molokai was round in shape—an enormous shield volcano emerging above the surface of the ocean, much like the Big Island to the southeast. But half of the island or more broke away in a volcanic or seismic event. The debris spilled northward for hundreds of kilometers under water, leaving behind the sheer cliffs of Molokai's northern coast. Similar landslips have occurred off Oahu and the other islands as well. The geological evidence is that these underwater landslides raised catastrophic tsunamis that scoured much of the Pacific Rim." He smiled. "Of course, there was no economic infrastructure to wreck then, and no rush-hour commuters."

"So what is your point?"

"Simply that the computer simulations in Holland and elsewhere were calculating the waves raised by the *splash* of several hundred billion tons of rock as it struck the ocean. Those researchers pointed out that all of that rock would have to hit the water at one time to raise even a small tidal wave . . . say, thirty meters. But it's not the splash that causes the tsunami. It is the movement of vast quantities of rock underwater, the submarine landslide, that displaces the water and raises the tsunami."

"Ah. I read once that the Indian Ocean tsunami of 2004 was caused by a relatively small movement of the Earth's crustal plates."

"Exactly. In that case, a twelve-hundred-kilometer stretch of the fault line moved about fifteen meters. Here on La Palma, the fault line is only an estimated fifteen kilometers long—but all of that rock will be moving for hundreds of kilometers, displacing titanic volumes of water as it moves." He pointed west. "Out there, the sea floor drops sharply away from this island. Four hundred kilometers from here, the bottom is forty-eight hundred meters down, and it continues to drop. We expect that the landslide will generate a megatsunami similar to the ones caused by the collapse of Molokai in the Pacific." Azhar spread his hands. "It is possible that the megatsunami will be something less than the one- to three-hundred-meter wave we expect. There are many variables, including how efficiently the nuclear explosions split the rock from the fault line, and how quickly it actually travels along the sea floor. But even a thirty-meter wave would drown tens of thousands of people, from New England to the Texas coast."

"Not to mention England, France, Brazil, and other countries around the Atlantic coastlines. But . . . your point is taken. My objective is simply that America's economy be crippled."

"Tens of trillions of dollars of property damage. Millions of homes and automobiles destroyed. Their financial centers in New York wrecked. Their capital flooded and their government forced to relocate. Many of their military bases submerged. I think such a blow would cripple their ecomony to the point that they might well never recover."

"And the People's Republic becomes *the* dominant superpower in the world, both economically and militarily," Feng said. "And you have your global jihad."

"Allahu akbar," Azhar said, shifting to Arabic. "God is great. And with the Americans . . . *preoccupied* with their personal problems, they will no longer be a player on the world stage, not for many decades, if ever."

"Ah!" Feng said. "There is al-Dahabi."

The helicopter's rotors had stopped turning, and a man in a business jacket and checkered Palestinian kaffiyeh stepped off the boarding ladder carrying what looked like a doctor's bag. He was old, his face deeply wrinkled, and he was smiling.

"I still fail to see the purpose of bringing *him* here," Azhar said, speaking English again.

"The woman has information. She is CIA, I am certain of it. We *must* know how much the Americans know of our activities here."

"In another twenty-four hours, none of it will matter. America will have fallen, the woman will have been incinerated . . . and you and I will be busily engaged in the next phase of Wrath of God. What can you possibly learn in that twenty-four hours that will help us?"

"Whether or not the Americans know what we are doing here, for one," Feng replied. "Whether or not they are mounting some sort of attack. But . . . I admit that there are personal issues."

"What issues?"

"The woman defied me," Feng said. "She attempted to use me, and then she *defied* me. I will break her—and your man, there, will help me do just that."

"It would be cleaner to simply shoot her," Azhar said.

"You speak of killing millions of Americans as they drive to work, and you dislike the thought of torturing one woman?"

"Killing millions," Azhar said, "is war. The other, as you have pointed out, is personal. The two do not mix."

"But you are wrong, my friend," Feng said, walking forward now to meet al-Dahabi. "War is *always* personal in its effects—in terror, in pain, and in blood."

23

Charlie Dean held himself motionless, staring intently upward at the sharp edge where rock met sky. He'd just seen movement—the head of a Tango sentry making his rounds about the caldera's rim. The sentry vanished again and, after an agonizing wait, Rodriguez gave a hand signal and the four began crawling forward once more. The slope consisted mostly of loose cinders here, with a few chunks of larger rock, the hill rising now at a forty-five-degree angle. If any of them lost their footing, they would slide helplessly back down the slope, raising a billowing cloud of dust as they fell.

They picked their way forward cautiously, making certain of each step before they moved. They were only a few dozen yards beneath the crater rim now, and it was vital that they not be seen or heard by the sentries.

As the ground began leveling off, the four again unrolled their tech-Ghillies and secured them to ankles and wrists. Staying flat on the ground to avoid showing their silhouettes against the sky, they inched their way onto the edge of the caldera and had their first look down into the interior.

The view was much the same as the images transmitted by Lia

yesterday, but from the opposite side of the crater. The helicopter sat on a level spot near an array of tents. Within a deeper portion of the crater to the right, a drilling derrick rose from a tangle of support structures and struts, the rumble of pumps and generators filling the bowl with noise. Ten or twelve men were visible—workers around the derrick, and guards carrying AKs. Two sentries were on the crater rim, the nearest a hundred yards away.

Several unarmed men were walking away from the helicopter, following a curving path that led to the deeper part of the crater to the right.

Dean pulled out his binoculars and focused on the group. There were three men, and two he recognized from file photos transmitted to his computer during his briefing for this op. The Asian man was Feng Jiu Zhu, formerly a major in China's Ministry of State Security, now a vice president of COSCO, itself virtually a branch of the Chinese military. The other was Ibrahim Hussain Azhar, the Jackal, terrorist and cofounder of the Jaish-e-Mohammad.

He didn't recognize the third man, the one carrying a satchel, but he was wearing the black-and-white checkered headscarf that served as a unifying symbol of solidarity for the Palestinians.

"Art Room," Dean whispered. As he spoke, he reached down and removed the case containing his rifle's SOPMOD kit from his leg sheath, opened it, and began removing the four-power optical telescopic sight. "I've got both Feng and Azhar in view. I have a clear shot. Request permission to fire."

It was a long shot, he knew. The team's orders were specific—to wait and watch until word came down the chain of command initiating the assault—but Feng and Azhar both were high-priority targets. Capping them now, before the assault teams all had even gotten into position, would decapitate the Tango force, perhaps panic them, and certainly leave them without anyone telling them what to do.

"Negative on that, Charlie," Rockman's voice came back. "The boss is seeing POTUS now. Let's not drop him in hot water."

"Copy." He continued attaching the sight to his weapon's rail, however, using the marks incised in the metal to put it solidly in its presighted configuration. He'd practiced this a lot at the range back at Fort Meade; the sight might be a hair off, but at this range, less than two hundred yards, it wouldn't miss the aim point by more than an inch or two, making it plenty accurate enough for him to take a shot without needing to sight in the weapon anew.

With the sight screwed down tight, he brought the M4A1's butt to his shoulder and peered through the sight. He could see the backs of all three men as they made their way down a steep trail into the deeper part of the crater.

"Art Room. Targets are descending into the northern part of the crater, down where the derrick is."

"Copy that," Rockman replied. "Do you see where the wall between the two drops off sharply? Kind of separates the two craters."

"I see it."

"The drop is about thirty feet, straight down. There's a cave or a lava tube at the base of the cliff. That's where they took Lia."

Dean felt cold. "I copy."

He watched them as they walked down the trail. He was *very* much tempted to take the shot, regardless of his orders.

There was no telling how many guards might be with Lia now, though, or what they would do to her if a firefight broke out—and, far worse, the team hadn't located the nukes yet. If the bad guys panicked, they might set something off, and that would make it a bad day for everyone.

So Dean kept watching the three as they rounded a corner at the bottom of the path and he lost sight of them.

"Art Room. Have you been able to reestablish communications with Lia?"

"That's negative, Charlie. They took her into a cave, and we lost contact. We haven't heard a word since."

Dean studied the surrounding ground. He was currently at about the three o'clock position on the crater rim. If he could make his way over to about the one o'clock position, he would have a direct line of sight on the cave mouth, and he also spotted a broad, eroded gulley down the caldera's interior slope there. The ground was broken, with lots of boulders, escarpments of bare rock, and even a few pine trees. It offered a good route for descending into the caldera.

If he could make it without being spotted by Tango sentries or the workers near the drilling derrick.

Quietly, he told Rodriguez what he was planning, and the Marine nodded.

Akulinin said, "I'm in," and the two slowly began making their way counterclockwise along the crater rim.

LAVA TUBE
SAN MARTIN VOLCANO, NORTH CRATER
MONDAY, 1438 HOURS LOCAL TIME

Lia heard the clatter of footsteps at the cave mouth and saw her two guards hastily stand and take on a look of unremitting vigilance.

She had no idea how much time had passed since they'd brought her here. The lava tube widened slightly, creating an underground room perhaps fifteen feet across, and while enough light filtered down from the opening to illuminate her surroundings, she couldn't see the outside, or guess at the passage of time by the movement of shadows—especially now, with those two damned lights in her eyes.

She suspected that it had been at least two hours since she'd been brought here, which meant perhaps twenty-two hours or so since her capture. She hadn't been mistreated in that time, exactly, other than being tied to a chair, unable to walk or lie down. There had been some psychological abuse, though. An hour ago, several men had brought in the two bright floodlights on folding tripod stands and connected them to a long power cord leading in from the outside. Then they'd set up a folding metal table against the black rock wall nearby, a six-foot-long table with several eyes attached around the edge that looked like attachment points for ropes or straps.

After that, Feng had taken some delight in letting her know what was in store for her.

Twenty-two hours. The question, of course, was how long it would have taken the Art Room to put together an op of some sort—either a rescue op, or a military mission to swoop in and grab the nukes. She was pretty sure most of the nukes were already here on La Palma; earlier, she'd listened in as her guards, assuming she spoke no Arabic, had chattered on about how there was only one bomb yet to put into place.

Bill Rubens *must* be putting together a strike force. Hell, by now he might have the whole U.S. Marine Corps on its way.

Assuming he'd been able to get the President's support for military intervention, of course. She didn't like thinking about that part of things.

Three men entered the chamber, Feng, Azhar, and an older man in a Palestinian headdress. He, she thought, must be the "specialist" Feng had promised, a professional interrogator.

"Ah!" the third man said in English, smiling broadly. "This, I suppose, is our subject?"

"It is," Feng replied. He looked at his watch. "You have eighteen hours to break her."

"Now, now, these things can't be rushed. You of all people should know that, Major."

"Eighteen hours. I want her real name, who she works for, and in particular I want to know how much they know about our operations here." Reaching out, he cupped Lia's chin in his hand. "And then I want her to beg me to end her pain. Understand?"

The man sighed, but he was still smiling. "I'll see what I can do, Major. Although I really need more time with her than that for a *thorough* job."

"You should have no problem with this one," Feng said. "Americans are *so* squeamish when it comes to torture. Look at how they cripple themselves, unable to carry out the simplest interrogation for fear of violating a prisoner's rights! They expect the whole world to play by the *rules!*" He laughed, a harsh sound. "Do what you must, Doctor, but in eighteen hours we are leaving this island. Anyone who remains behind will die."

Releasing her chin, he stepped back. Azhar watched silently, scowling.

Walking to Lia's side, the interrogator placed his doctor's bag on the metal table and opened it. One by one, he began removing various implements, holding them up to the light, turning each as he inspected it. A bone saw. A pair of pliers. Several clamps. An olive drab canvas roll opened to reveal a dozen different scalpels and lancets of various sizes held in place inside small pockets, along with forceps and several long needles and probes. Surgical retractors. Several implements she couldn't even begin to name. He held up a wood-burning tool with a long electrical cord. "Do you have an electrical outlet in here?"

"Over there by the light."

"Good." He plugged the tool in and laid it on the table. "We'll just get that heating for now. Are you gentlemen going to stay and watch?"

Feng hesitated, then shook his head. "No. I must supervise the placement of the final . . . package outside. Call me if you get anything out of her." Turning, he walked out of the chamber, followed by Azhar. The two guards remained, half hidden in the shadows behind the bright lights.

"Well," the man said. Did that smile *never* leave his face? "Just the two of us, then. And the guards, of course. Now . . . we can be businesslike about this. You can tell me what I want to know, immediately, truthfully, and without reservation. If you cooperate, it is possible I won't even have to resort to the use of these various tools laid out for your inspection. You might even live. If you resist, you will die, and I promise you that it will take you a very long time to do so. Well . . . eighteen hours, at least, and, believe me, that can seem like a very long time indeed. So . . . we begin. What is your name?"

Lia had been trained to face torture, and she'd faced it more than once in her career with the NSA. That time in North Korea . . .

The important thing now was to spin things out as long as possible. The Tangos obviously were facing a deadline. They would push her hard, hoping to break her in a few hours.

Yet, if the interrogation went true to form, they would spend at least some of that time engaged in *psychological* torture . . .

They would do their best to terrify her, to try to get her to the breaking point simply through threats, suggestion, and terror. They probably wouldn't start the really rough stuff for some hours—and might also resort to drugs.

Her training had taught her that spinning things out, pretending to cooperate, even pretending to break, was the best strategy. Later, there might be nothing she could do but try to endure . . . but she could try to go along with her captors for now. The longer she could hold off the physical torture, the more time Rubens and Desk Three had to put together some sort of a rescue.

She had to believe that help was coming. *Had* to.

Lia knew that cooperation was her best strategy right now, but when she looked up into that obscenely grinning face, she found she couldn't do it.

"I asked you a question, woman. What is your name?"

"Go fuck yourself, asshole," Lia said.

PRESIDENTIAL BRIEFING ROOM
THE WHITE HOUSE, EAST WING
WASHINGTON, D.C.
MONDAY, 1002 HOURS EDT

Rubens checked through the final security point and walked past the Secret Service guards posted outside the massive red-oak doors. The room beyond was dominated by an immense mahogany table and a number of dark green chairs. General James, he saw, was already seated at the table. So were several other generals, Army, Air Force, and Marine, as well as a Navy admiral, several NSC staffers, the secretary of state and several members of her staff, the director of national intelligence, and a contingent from the CIA. Debra Collins, the Agency's deputy director of operations, watched him coldly as he walked across the luxurious carpeting and took an empty chair next to her.

"Well, Bill," Collins said quietly, sat, "I hope you realize just how much trouble you've managed to stir up these past few days."

"And what would that be, Debra?"

"Running gunfights in the streets of Dushanbe? Almost starting a war with the Russians? Kidnapping Russian nationals? Shooting down one of their helicopters? Shooting up one of their freighters on the high seas? Any of that ring a bell?"

"The helicopter, as I understand it, was shot down by Indian aircraft, and it was downed on the Afghanistan side of the border."

"They were in hot pursuit of *your* people, Bill. You provoked them."

"They were trying to kill my people, Debra."

"And your people managed to kill quite a few of them—twenty or thirty, we think, all told. They also managed to kill a Lieutenant Colonel Pyotr Vasilyev of the FSB Vega Group. He was on the helicopter."

"That's ancient history, Debra. Old news."

"Indeed. Today's headlines appear to be all about the United States invading Spain. What the hell are you playing at, anyway?"

"As you know well, *we* are trying to recover a number of tactical nuclear weapons now in terrorist hands. Ah! I wanted to thank you, especially, Debra."

She looked startled. "For what?"

"Letting us use your conduit into Somalia. That worked very well."

"I just saw the report on the *Yakutsk* affair this morning. The Russians are screaming bloody murder, you know that?"

"Let them. We have more serious concerns right now."

Further discussion was interrupted as a dark-suited man stepped into the room. "Ladies and gentlemen, the President of the United States."

Everyone around the table stood as the President walked in, followed by more suits who kept pace behind him. He looked angry as he strode to the chair at the table's head, slapped a manila folder on the table in front of him, and sat down. "General James? What the hell is going on? The pickle this morning says we're about to invade Spain! The last I heard, they were our allies!"

Technically, the term "pickle" was somewhat dated. Years ago, the President had received each morning a ten-page newsletter describing the overnight developments of five or six situations of concern around the world called the President's Intelligence Checklist, abbreviated as PICkl. The Executive Office bureaucracy had changed over the years, however. Since 2005, the Agency no longer reported directly to the President, but through the director of national intelligence instead. Even so, one insider's term for the CIA was still "the pickle factory" and special intelligence memos sent directly to the President were still refered to as pickles.

James cleared his throat. "Mr. President, we have evidence that foreign terrorists are about to launch an attack, technically a *nuclear* attack, against the continental United States. It is imperative that we capture and secure the nuclear weapons they control before they can carry out this attack. The details are all laid out in the briefing I delivered to your office yesterday."

"David?" The President looked at Admiral David Blaine, the director of national intelligence. "What do you know about this?"

"The intelligence was developed out of an ongoing operation carried out by the NSA, Mr. President. I was aware of some of the background . . . but these latest developments are all brand-new."

The President tapped the folder in front of him. "According to this, a small but secret bureau within the National Security Agency has been carving a path of destruction through south-central Asia, shot up a Russian cargo ship, and is now suggesting we carry out a Marine invasion of the Canary Islands. This is *unacceptable*! And I want the resignations of the people responsible on my desk this afternoon!"

"Mr. President," Rubens said, speaking into the sudden silence around the table. "There's more to this than you're hearing. There's more here than cover-your-ass politics. We are talking about the very survival of the United States."

"Who the hell are you?"

"I'm the man whose resignation you want. William Rubens, NSA. And you'll have my resignation, sir, effective the moment I know my people are out of danger. But, with respect, sir, you'd *damned* well better listen to what I have to say first."

There was no audible gasp from the others seated around the table, but the effect was much the same. The cold silence dragged on for long seconds. Then the President folded his hands on the table and leaned forward, pinning Rubens with a hard stare. "You *have* my undivided attention, Mr. Rubens. What do you have to say to me?"

Rubens took a deep breath and began speaking.

He left nothing out, though he restricted his statements to cold facts and ignored the speculation and theorizing that had followed the Haystack investigation from the beginning. Nor did he mention the problems that had dogged them—the interagency battle over limited satellite assets, for instance, or the delay resulting from the failure to get high-level clearance for the *Yakutsk* op. He did admit to the intelligence failure in Karachi, when the German deserter, Koch, had failed to tell them about the enemy flying nukes to Morocco.

He concluded with a detailed report based on Lia's recon along the Cumbre Vieja—of drilling rigs and helicopter flights from Morocco and something called Operation Wrath of God—along with a brief description of what the terrorists were probably trying to do.

That was the point at which he deliberately violated everything he'd ever held dear about intelligence work and started lying to the President of the United States.

GREEN AMBER ONE
NORTHEAST RIM, SAN MARTIN CALDERA
MONDAY, 1506 HOURS LOCAL TIME

Charlie Dean kept crawling, moving slowly, keeping flat beneath his brick red tech-ghillie. It was painstaking and slow, but he was making progress, moving at last into the rugged ground above the eroded gully leading down into the northern half of the caldera. Lying beside a car-sized boulder, he studied the crater floor and surroundings carefully with his binoculars, transmitting everything he was seeing via satellite back to Fort Meade and the Art Room.

From this vantage point, he could see the mouth of the cave Rubens mentioned in the briefing, all but invisible in the shadow of the overhang of the cliff above. The drilling rig itself was a good fifty yards north of the cave entrance. Even at that distance, the rumble of pumps and motors and the grind of the drill itself drowned out every other sound. They certainly wouldn't hear him coming.

With the sun well past the zenith, much of the crater floor was in deep shadow, which would make it easier for him to move to the cave mouth without the drilling workers seeing him. But he also saw a problem—two Tango sentries seated on a boulder ten yards from the cave. There was no possible way of reaching the opening without being seen.

He would have to eliminate those sentries.

That brought Dean face-to-face with a serious problem. Getting into that cave, grabbing Lia, and getting out . . . that was one thing. However, if he killed Tangos to pull it off, missing guards or dead bodies were certain to raise the alarm—and that would be deadly for the Marines now moving into position at each of the target craters along the Cumbre Vieja, deadly for Marine forces now at sea and preparing to land on La Palma, and quite possibly deadly for millions of people in the Americas and in Europe and Africa if the bad guys set off their bombs and those bombs did indeed generate a large tidal wave. Even if they didn't, a lot of people would die on La Palma—civilians, Marines . . . and Lia.

So Dean and Akulinin lay at the top of the caldera gully, watching. They attached certain SOPMOD units to their M4A1s, including sound suppressors screwed tightly over the muzzles of their weapons, and they snapped magazines loaded with special 5.56 mm subsonic ammunition into their receivers. They also swapped out the four-power telescopic sights for their SOPMOD ECOS-N CompM2s.

Technically, the M4 was a *carbine*, not a rifle, and was not intended as a sniper weapon because a carbine's short barrel length—in this case fourteen and a half inches—reduced weapon accuracy, but the CompM2 was a special, battery-powered sight that placed a red dot inside the sight directly on the weapon's aim point. The unit's accuracy would more than compensate for their not having a true sniper's rifle, like his beloved M24 or the newer M40A3.

Akulinin also attached his M203 grenade launcher beneath the barrel of his weapon. The CompM2 interfered with targeting with the 203's leaf sight, but in this situation—shooting down into what was effectively a huge bowl—that wouldn't be an issue. If they needed to start lobbing 40 mm grenades into the bottom of that hole, instinctive point-and-shoot would be good enough. *Close enough for government work*, as Ilya had said when they'd gone over the special-issue gear that morning at Rota.

By the time they were done modifying their weapons, the M4s were a lot heavier. A standing joke about the military's SOPMOD system had it that the basic unloaded M4 carbine weighed less than seven pounds . . . but by the time you finished attaching all the SOPMOD bells and whistles, the thing weighed more than an M249 SAW, a light machine gun weighing seventeen pounds. Not *entirely* true, Dean thought, hefting the weapon, rolling onto his belly, and taking aim, but amusing nonetheless. He was more concerned about the system's complexity. The more bells and whistles you added to a weapons system, the more likely it was that something critical could fail—and Murphy's Law ruled that a failure would always happen at the worst possible time.

He positioned the red sighting dot on the back of the head of one of the guards, adjusted the brightness level down a click, but didn't fire. *Orders . . .*

Dean tried hard not to think about what might be happening to Lia right now inside that cave.

PRESIDENTIAL BRIEFING ROOM
THE WHITE HOUSE, EAST WING
WASHINGTON, D.C.
MONDAY, 1012 HOURS EDT

Rubens reached the crescendo of his lecture. "We estimate, sir, that the tidal wave could be as high as three hundred feet and be traveling at something like five hundred miles per hour when it reaches the East Coast. The wave will easily travel inland as far as twenty-five to fifty miles. In places with narrow tidal estuaries or rivers to channel and focus the wave—places like the James River, the Hudson River, the Potomac—the wave could possibly become *much* higher and more powerful. Mr. President, we are looking at the complete destruction of New York City, Washington, D.C., and a dozen other major cities from Portland, Maine, to Houston, Texas. Millions of people could be killed. The damage will amount to the tens or hundreds of trillions of dollars. *Sir, we may not even survive as a nation!*"

He let those words hang above the table for a moment, then added, "Mr. President, we need to capture or disable those nukes before the terrorists detonate them, and we need to do it *now*."

After a moment, the President sighed. "Are you quite finished?" he asked.

Rubens thought over what he'd just said, then nodded. "Yes, Mr. President." The die, as Caesar had said, was cast. In his case, though, challenging the laws of Rome by crossing the Rubicon had merely placed his career, his life, and his army at risk. Rubens had just done all of that, and by challenging the President directly, by speaking out of turn this way, he might have put the survival of the country at risk as well. Rubens knew he needed to convince the man, not make him so angry that he ignored the true threat.

"I am concerned," the President said slowly, "that what you have just told us represents another intelligence gaffe. I'm sure you remember what our so-called *intelligence* agencies did to my predecessor in office."

He was referring, of course, to the celebrated failure of U.S. intelligence concerning weapons of mass destruction that had led to the invasion of Iraq in 2003. The comparison, though, was not really apt. The problem had been far more involved than the CIA telling the President that Iraq had WMDs, and the President sending in the troops. Intelligence work was always a shadowy and imprecise business, more art than science despite high-tech satellites and futuristic eavesdropping techniques. You found a piece of the picture here, another there, pulled in others from someplace else, and you hoped to fit it together into a coherent whole.

Coherence, though, was almost impossible when politics were involved—when agency directors were protecting their own turfs, when department heads were protecting their jobs, when *not* fitting neatly into the correct political orientation for a given worldview was tantamount to career suicide. *Any* given intelligence result had more than one possible interpretation, and political animals within the system tended to adopt the interpretation that made their superiors higher up the chain happy.

Of course, that same weakness in the system still existed now. The current political wisdom within Washington tended to downgrade the War on Terror to a skirmish, to downplay the threat of radical Islam in the holy name of political correctness.

Still, sometimes it was necessary to drop political correctness in the name of national survival.

The problem here, though, was not national survival so much as it was victory in this particular piece of the skirmish, and the survival of Rubens' people. Katie Walden had been pretty emphatic in her declaration that dropping half of La Palma into the Atlantic would *not* result in a three-hundred-foot megatsunami.

But, damn it, Rubens wasn't going to risk the possibility that the scientists might have gotten it wrong.

He also wasn't going to let Lia and Charlie and the rest twist in the wind, nor was he going to watch some tens of thousands of La Palma islanders get blown away in the name of political expediency. If he had to lie—or, at the least, to *overstate* the threat of a tidal wave scouring the East Coast down to bare rock—in order to save those people, then he'd do it, and damn the consequences to himself.

"My predecessor invaded Iraq because you people gave him bad information!" the President continued. "Now you're telling me to invade an island belonging to Spain. If I do this and you're wrong again, this will *not* be good for America's image overseas. They already see us as the world's bully, the tough guy going around knocking down the little kids."

"For God's sake, Mr. President," General James said. "This isn't some schoolyard scrap!"

"Perhaps," the secretary of state said, "we could turn this whole thing over to the Spanish authorities. Let *them* deal with it. Our hands stay clean."

"How about that, General?" the President said. "It doesn't have to be us putting our reputations on the line."

"With all due respect, Mr. President," Rubens said, "there isn't time for that. Sometimes you have to put *everything* on the line."

"What do the Spanish have in the area?" the President said.

The DNI was prepared with the figures. "Mr. President, local Spanish forces include one light infantry regiment—the 9th, the 'Soria'—deployed to La Palma along with a headquarters battalion. Two more light infantry regiments, an artillery regiment, and a helicopter battalion are all positioned on Tenerife, about eighty miles away by air."

"And frankly, sir," General James said, "they won't be able to do shit. Light infantry without combat experience? Artillery? That's exactly the wrong tool for the wrong job."

"And what is the right tool, General?"

"I'd say a U.S. Marine recon force deployed by helicopter, followed up by a Marine landing battalion. FORECON just happens to be in the area. And the *Iwo Jima* can be there in twenty-four hours."

"They 'just happen to be in the area,' huh?"

James met his stare with a level gaze of hs own. "Yes, sir. The *Iwo* was on her way to the eastern Med, and is currently four hundred and fifty nautical miles northwest of La Palma. We managed to preposition FORECON on the *Iwo Jima* just in case they were needed."

The Air Force general at the table cleared his throat. "Sir, acting on a recommendation from Mr. Rubens, we have deployed six aircraft of the 43rd Fighter Squadron out of Tyndall. F-22 Raptors with laser-guided JDAMs. Call sign Firestorm. Officially, and until you say otherwise, it's a routine training flight across the Atlantic to Rota and back." He looked at his watch. "They should be engaged in their second air-to-air refueling as we speak."

"You're suggesting an air strike?" the President said.

"The JDAMs will seal off the boreholes Mr. Rubens mentioned. If the nukes are already in position at the bottoms of those holes, the explosions will bury them, leaving no way to set them off. If the nukes are still on the surface but in the craters, the explosions will fragment them without causing them to detonate. There may be some radiological contamination in the area, but no nuclear explosions."

The President sighed. "So help me, people. If this is another case of bad intelligence—"

"This isn't a case of bad or misapplied intelligence, Mr. President," Debra Collins said. "We *know* this threat exists, and we're in a position to do something about it."

Rubens blinked. Collins was coming in on *his* side?

"Admiral Blaine? What is your assessment?"

"I don't see that we have any other choice, Mr. President. This looks damned solid."

"I ran this nonsense about tsunamis past my science advisor before coming here," the President said. He was looking directly at Rubens. "*He* says the danger from a large tidal wave is overstated. Pseudo-science."

Rubens continued worrying the bone. "And the people I talked to said we can't know for sure what would happen if those nukes go off. Maybe nothing will happen. Maybe the tidal wave will be thirty feet high instead of three hundred. But even that would drown a lot of people, Mr. President. It would drown New York and Washington, and it would kick our economy in the nuts so hard that we might never recover. The intel we have so far suggests that the Chinese are behind this for exactly that reason. They plan to step in and take over all over the globe when our economy goes under."

"Even if nothing else happens, Mr. President," Collins said, "no tidal wave, no Chinese takeover, we're going to look *very* bad if ten nuclear weapons are detonated on La Palma and a few thousand people are incinerated. We cannot afford to stand by and do nothing!"

"Fuck," the President said.

24

Fuck this," Charlie Dean whispered. "I'm going down there."

"Shit, man!" Akulinin said. "You trying to start a war?"

"No, but when we get the word to go, I want to be in position and *ready*. Now."

"I heard that, Charlie," Marie Telach said. "I recommend that you stay put! We should be hearing from the boss soon."

"Recommendation noted," Dean said. He was already crawling forward, the tech-Ghillie stretched over his back, shifting with each movement of hand or foot.

The descent was a lot tougher than the slow crawl around the crater's rim. He was moving head-down, and at times the ground was steep enough that he began sliding on loose gravel or cinders. Each time he did, he spread his arms and legs, bracing against whatever support he could find in the ground with his hands, and hung on until the slide stopped. Then he would freeze in place, holding himself absolutely motionless in case someone at the bottom of the pit noticed the slither of rock and cinder down the slope.

Then he would begin moving again. He didn't have to worry

about being quiet, at least. The drill was pounding away with a steady *thump-thump-thump*, and the air was filled with the rumble and chug of motors and pumps.

Ilya had his back. Watching from the top of the gully through his sniperscope, he would be alert for signs that Dean's crawl down the slope had been noticed, and take out any threat before the bad guy opened fire.

But the idea was to get all the way down without being seen.

Because once people started shooting, there was a real danger that the Tangos would set off their one-kiloton toys.

THE WHITE HOUSE
WASHINGTON, D.C.
MONDAY, 1035 HOURS EDT

Rubens emerged from the conference room, bemused and gratified. The President had given the necessary approval. Operation Mountain Storm was now officially a go.

"So why'd you do it?" he asked Collins, who was walking out beside him.

"Do what?"

"Go to bat for me in there. Point out that this time the intel was good. He didn't even ask for my resignation."

"He will if this goes bad."

"If this goes bad, he won't have to ask."

"We *are* on the same team, Bill."

"With all of the interagency politics, sometimes it's hard to remember that."

"You don't have to play stupid, you know."

"What do you mean?"

"You deliberately planted information about the *Yakutsk* through CIA assets in Ethopia and Somalia. You made sure those Somali pirates knew that the *Yakutsk* was a rich target for them. The *Constellation* battle group was shadowing that ship. As soon as the *Yakutsk* got off a distress call, your team went in."

"It wasn't my team." *Well, except for Charlie and Ilya*, he thought, *but she doesn't need to know everything.*

"It was a Navy SEAL VBSS unit you 'happened to have close by.'"

"Our ships and personnel are required by the law of the sea to respond to any distress call at sea."

"Uh-huh. And you were setting up the same thing in La Palma."

"Not the same thing at all. I just made sure that we had plenty of solid assets where they could be used when they were needed."

"You already have an assault force on the island, don't you?"

"Not exactly."

"A reconnaissance force, then. Marines? Black CAT? I notice that you didn't tell *him* that."

"I didn't want to complicate things."

"I admire your balls, Bill."

"You haven't seen them in years."

"That's not what I meant and you know it."

They reached the secure elevator that took them down to the underground visitors' garage beneath the White House East Wing. Rubens pulled his cell phone from his pocket and examined the screen. He still wasn't getting a signal—part of the White House's security system.

Rubens and Collins parted company in the garage. "Bill?" She called after they'd gone a few steps. Her voice echoed off the bare concrete.

"Yeah?"

"Keep me in the loop."

"Don't worry, Debra," he told her. "I'll tell you if this works. You'll know if it doesn't."

Still no signal on his phone. He got into his car, checked out past gate security, and pulled out onto East Executive Avenue Northwest. He was reaching for the phone again when it rang. He didn't bother checking the caller ID.

"Rubens."

"Bill? Katie."

"Katie! Yes. What can I do for you?"

"I just wanted to let you know . . . after our conversation Saturday?"

"Yes."

"Some of us here have been doing some digging. There *is* a danger."

"Really? What did you get?"

"Those Dutch studies were looking at water displacement from a large amount of mass striking the ocean. You remember? I was telling you it all had to hit at the same time."

"I remember."

"Well, I got to thinking about other examples of landslips we know. There was one off of Sicily, Mount Etna, that caused a devastating tsunami all across the eastern Mediteranean eight thousand years ago. Some scientists think that might have been the source of the biblical flood myth. And there have been a number of landslips in the Hawaian Islands. Molokai and Oahu, especially. There's evidence that those sent huge tidal waves all across the Pacific Rim something like a million and a half years ago.

"But those tidal waves weren't caused by the impact of all of that rock in the ocean, but by something more subtle. Those island-sized masses of rock moved, and they moved fast, sliding for hundreds of kilometers across the sea floor before coming to rest. It was the movement that displaced the water, generating the waves, not the splash."

"So what are you saying?"

"That there very well might be a danger to the U.S. East Coast if part of La Palma does break off and fall into the sea."

"How certain are you of the data?"

"Not very." He could hear the frustration in her voice. "The things are totally unpredictable. The size and strength of the wave would depend on the actual mass of the rock and on how fast it was moving. You might get a wave a hundred meters tall hitting the United States. Or it might be ten meters. Or less."

"Okay, Katie. I appreciate knowing."

"I'm sorry to give you bad news."

"Look at the bright side. I didn't just lie through my teeth to the President of the United States."

"I beg your pardon?"

He laughed. "Never mind. Thanks, Katie. I need to get off and make another call." He hesitated. "Are you thinking of leaving the area?"

"No, Bill. Too much to do here. And too many good friends."

"I understand. I'll keep you informed, okay?"

"Okay, Bill."

"Later." He switched off, then hit the speed dial button for the secure line to the Art Room.

He needed to let them know of the President's decision.

LAVA TUBE
SAN MARTIN VOLCANO, NORTH CRATER
MONDAY, 1535 HOURS LOCAL TIME

Lia's ears were ringing, blood drooled from her mouth and nose, and her left eye was swollen almost shut. After he'd spent all of that time showing her the nightmarish implements of torture in his bag, the beating the smiling man had given her with his bare fists had been brutal, direct, and startlingly unexpected. She'd thought she'd been beginning to understand Feng's interrogator, but his savage response to her defiance had left her shaken and uncertain, as well as hurting.

Then, after the beating, he'd begun puttering about the chamber, smiling, chatting pleasantly, attaching straps to the four corners of the table, and finally showing her once again each implement in his bag, carefully explaining what each was for.

The stress, the sheer terror, was building in Lia to a near-unbearable point, her heart pounding in her chest, her breath coming in sharp, short gasps, her teeth chattering in her bruised jaw.

"Now this . . . this is one of my favorites," the man said, holding up a lancet with a long, slightly curving blade that gleamed like oil in the light. He brought it to within a couple of inches of her eyes, turning it slowly in front of her. "A flensing blade . . . you understand? For skinning the subject. For example, I can use it to slice through your skin just . . . here . . ." Reaching down, he dragged his fingertip lightly across her upper thigh, from groin to hip. She flinched at the touch, and his smile broadened.

"I cut all the way around your leg, you see," he continued, "and then use just the tip of blade to *tease* the skin from the underlaying fascia. I work my way down your leg, peeling back the skin as I go, around and around, until I roll it in one piece from your leg, just like removing a stocking.

"The entire process lasts, oh, perhaps an hour, an hour and a half. The time depends on how often you pass out from the pain, and on how long it takes to revive you each time. And then, of course, we go to the other leg . . . and your arms . . . eventually we get to your face. It's necessary to proceed slowly to avoid having you lose too much blood . . ."

Her own pulse thundered in Lia's ears as the nightmare monologue dragged on, louder, it seemed, even than the sounds of drilling from outside. She told herself that this was part of the actual torture, a psychological softening up that would leave her more vulnerable to drugs or to the actual touch of a scalpel when it finally came.

Her training had emphasized going along with an interrogator, giving him what he wanted, if necessary. The important thing was to keep her wits about her, to resist going into shock, to keep alert for the possibility, *any* possibility, of escape . . .

"Please . . ." she said. Her lips were dry and cracked, despite the sweat drenching her face. "Please don't . . ."

"You have something you wish to tell me?"

"What do you want to know?"

"Your name, for a start." With precise, businesslike movements he replaced the lancet in the canvas carrier. "We've not been properly introduced, you see. I am Dr. Taysir al-Dahabi. Oh, yes! I am a medical doctor. The University of Cairo. It helps to be able to monitor my subject's condition as I work. And you are?"

"C–Cathy Chung," she said. Her voice cracked with the effort.

"Ah, yes. The name on your ID card we found in among your things. And you work for?"

"The U.S. State Department."

"I see, I see." He extracted a notebook and pen from the bag and wrote something with quick, flowing scribbles. "That matches the fact of the ID itself, of course. But why should I believe you? If, as my employers believe, you are CIA, that would all be part of an internally consistent story, a legend, as I believe spies call it."

"I . . . I *told* you I'd talk!"

"Yes, but you are nowhere close to being broken yet. Broken to the point where you are *begging* me to be allowed to tell me everything you know. So we will need to test those statements."

An inarticulate whimper escaped Lia's lips; she did it for effect, but she didn't have to reach down far to find it.

"I'll tell you what, Cathy. I'll call you Cathy for now, anyway, until we learn more about you . . . about the *real* you. I'm going to ask you to do something for me. How well you do this will tell me how willing you are to cooperate with me right now. Okay?"

"Anything . . ."

"Very well. I'm going to have one of the guards untie you and remove the handcuffs. You will then remove your hiking boots and place them under the chair. The other guard will have very specific orders. If you try to escape, if you so much as *look* as though you're going to try to attack me or them, the other guard will shoot you in the knees. The wounds will leave you helplessly crippled and in a *very* great deal of pain. Do you understand me?"

Lia nodded.

"Say 'Yes, Doctor.'"

"Y–yes, Doctor."

"Very well." Al-Dahabi turned and spoke rapidly to the guards in Arabic, too rapidly for her to understand most of it, though she caught the words for "shoot," "knees," and "be watchful."

Al-Dahabi stepped back from the chair and moved his black bag well out of reach. One guard leaned his AK against the tunnel wall and walked slowly toward her, keeping to one side so that he did not at any time block the other guard's line of fire.

The remaining man, smiling as broadly as al-Dahabi, raised his weapon and took aim at her legs.

SAN MARTIN CALDERA
MONDAY, 1537 HOURS LOCAL TIME

It had taken Charlie Dean more than twenty minutes to work his way down the gully, a crawl of perhaps fifty yards, made with exacting, slow, and painstaking caution. His eventual objective, the mouth of the cave, was still over a hundred yards away—and that was a straight-line distance, not the length of the twists and turns he would need to make to stay behind boulders and within eroded gullies in the crater floor.

There were those two sentries ahead as well, still perched on a rock. One faced the cave, his back toward Dean; the other, beside the first, was facing Dean. The two were chatting with one another, but every so often the guard on the right would look up and scan the ridgetop, the gully, and the bare slopes of the crater's interior.

Another guard, Dean noticed, was on top of the crater rim, over on the opposite side of the bowl. He was sitting on the ground, smoking a cigarette.

So far, the tech-Ghillie had worked as advertised, its photo-reactive surface darkening to the same tone as the shadows in the gully and at the crater floor. Dean, his face only partially exposed beneath the blanket, watched the guard on the right carefully, timing his movements for those moments when the man was talking to his friend, freezing motionless when he began scanning the hillside.

The two were perhaps a hundred yards away now, just ten yards in front of the cave mouth. The racket from the drilling rig, more or less muted up at the top of the hill, was in full voice down here, and the air was filled with a haze of minute particles of dust thrown up by the pounding.

They certainly weren't going to hear him with all that noise close by.

He began moving forward once more. The ground here was still broken and offered decent cover. Drawing on his old Marine sniper's training, he picked each new piece of cover before moving, then made his way toward it with slow, steady progress, stopping every few yards to check around him. He could see the drilling rig now off to his right. Two of the men he'd watched earlier were with them now—he thought they were Feng and al-Wawi, though he couldn't be sure with all of the dust in the air.

"Charlie?" Marie said over his implant. Even with her voice bone-conducted into his ear, it was hard to hear her over the pounding of the drill. "Charlie, do you copy?"

"I'm here, Marie."

"The boss just called! Mountain Storm is on! Firestorm is en route, ETA ten minutes!"

He wasn't sure he'd heard her right. He pressed his fingers into his ears, and said, "Art Room, say again, please!"

"I said, Mountain Storm is on. Firestorm is en route, ETA ten minutes!"

Dean almost laughed aloud. "Now *that's* what I call good timing," he said.

LAVA TUBE
SAN MARTIN VOLCANO, NORTH CRATER
MONDAY, 1537 HOURS LOCAL TIME

Lia sat barefoot in front of al-Dahabi, rubbing life back into her sore wrists.

"Very good, Cathy," he told her. "*Very* good. Now, stand up."

Awkwardly, she did so. Terror still gibbered at the back of her mind, and she was trembling. She *hated* appearing weak like this, but the obscenely smiling interrogator, she realized, was having an almost overpowering, mesmerizing effect on her, on her will.

The fact that she *knew* it was all part of the interrogation process didn't help one bit.

"Good," al-Dahabi said. He was still standing well back from her, too far for her to kick, even if she'd had the strength. One of the guards, ten feet away, continued to aim his assault rifle at her legs. "Next, you will remove all of your clothing, fold it neatly, and place it on the chair."

"What?"

Al-Dahabi sighed. "If you were a man, I would simply have my friends here rip the clothing from your body, a somewhat brutal demonstration that you are helpless. But working with a woman is different. You *know* you are weaker physically than a man, so the demonstration must prove that you are helpless psychologically. *Vulnerable.* Mine to command. You *will* do what I tell you, without argument, without hesitation. If you do not, I will find another and more unpleasant way to demonstrate your helplessness. Do you understand me?"

At that moment, Lia couldn't tell which emotion was stronger as it churned in stomach and chest and throat—fear or fury. Women, in this bastard's world, were *things* to be manipulated, toys, objects for psychological manipulation.

Several possible replies flashed through her thoughts, ranging from profanity to laughing in the little creep's face. His prejudice was a weakness, she told himself. There had to be a way to use it to her advantage.

Her eyes locked with his, she began peeling off her T-shirt.

SAN MARTIN CALDERA
MONDAY, 1537 HOURS LOCAL TIME

The noise of the drill stopped, the silence startlingly sudden. Dean froze in place, lifting his head above the edge of the gully just enough to see what was happening. All the pumps and generators, a line of blue metal boxes to one side of the drill site, appeared to have been switched off at once.

A moment later, a single diesel engine fired up again, and a heavy winch began grinding away as the workers started removing the drill stack section by section. Metal clashed on metal with clanks and shrill chirps, and he could hear the men shouting at one another in Arabic.

Dean saw movement beyond and to the left of the drilling rig and pulled out his binoculars for a better look. Two of the paramilitary types were coming down the path from the upper crater. One carried an AK; the other lugged something very much like a large, heavy suitcase.

Shit!

"Green Amber, this is Amber Three," Dean said, switching on his tactical radio.

"Three, One," Rodriguez's voice said in his earpiece. "Go."

"You see the two gonzos with the suitcase, coming down the hill to the drill site?"

"Negative. Not from this position."

Shit and *more* shit. The two bad guys had already moved around the bend in the descending path and were out of the line of sight of the two Marines on the hill above.

Maybe the damned timing wasn't so hot after all. Ahead was the cave where they had Lia. To his right, the bad guys were bringing down one of the nukes.

Lia or the nuke?

"Amber One, did you get the word on Mountain Storm?"

"Three, that is affirmative. We are preparing to light up the target."

Okay . . . so Rodriguez and Dulaney were going to be busy for the next ten minutes. The options sucked. If he took out the two with the suitcase nuke, he would start a firefight, the bad guys would sound the alarm, and any nuclear weapons already armed and in place elsewhere on the island might be set off—and a firefight would pin him down here, unable to reach Lia.

If he went after Lia, the bad guys would arm that weapon and put it down the hole, ready to fire. It was not exactly a comfortable prospect.

"Art Room," he said.

"Go ahead, Charlie."

"I have one of the suitcase nukes in sight. Looks like they're getting ready to put it down the borehole. If I engage, they may disappear with it, and they sure as hell will pass the word to every other Tango on La Palma. I'm going to go in after Lia."

"We concur, Charlie. Good luck."

"Ilya?"

"I'm here, Charlie."

"Target is the two Tango sentries outside of the cave entrance. I've got the one on the right. You take the one on my left. Do you copy?"

"I copy."

"Do you see another sentry at about two seven zero up on the crater rim?"

"The goldbrick with the cigarette. I see him."

"He's your number two target."

"Roger that."

Slowly, Dean eased his M4 out from under the tech-Ghillie and braced it in the prone firing position, left elbow supporting the muzzle, right hand closing about the grip. He checked to make sure the selector switch was on single-shot, then peered through the sight, adjusting the picture until the red dot was over the sentry's chest. The range was less than a hundred yards now, but he wasn't going to try for a fancy head shot and risk a miss. He would go for center of mass.

"First target."

"Sighted in."

Both of the guards had turned now and were watching the activity at the drill head. With luck, *everyone* in the crater would be watching them hauling up the drill pipe and planting the bomb, and they wouldn't notice the two sentries outside the cave getting capped.

"Okay, Ilya," Dean said. He held the target picture steady, took in a breath, released it partway. "On my mark . . . and *three* . . . and *two* . . . and *one* . . . and *shoot!*"

His rifle kicked against his shoulder, the sound of the gunshot muffled by the suppressor to a harsh cough. Both of the sentries jerked together, collapsing into one another and then tumbling off of the boulder.

Dean pulled the tech-Ghillie straps off his wrists and ankles, got to his feet, and started toward the cave at a fast trot. He was in full view of the people near the derrick now, but all of them were focused on the activity around the borehole.

"Target two sees you," Akulinin said. "Taking the shot . . ."

Dean glanced up at the crater rim to the west in time to see the lone sentry silhouetted against the sky, saw him raising his rifle . . . then toppling backward and falling out of sight.

"Good shot," Dean told Akulinin under his breath. He ran faster, staying in deep shadow and moving from boulder to boulder to minimize his exposure, but no longer staying out of sight. Speed, now, was more important than stealth.

"I've got the others covered, Charlie. *Get Lia out of there!*"

Reaching the boulder in front of the cave entrance, Dean stopped, checked to make sure no one was looking in his direction, then dragged the two bodies and their weapons around behind another boulder resting close to the side of the cliff. That might buy a few more minutes, depending on how frequently the bad guys checked up on their sentries.

Then, still in shadow, he started for the lava tube entrance.

25

LAVA TUBE
SAN MARTIN VOLCANO
MONDAY, 1538 HOURS LOCAL TIME

'm waiting, Cathy. If you prefer, the guard will put a bullet through
your right knee. It will then hurt a *great* deal more when we put you
on the table and forcibly undress you."

Lia evaluated her chances. If she dove for al-Dahabi and tried to
grapple with him, she *might* catch the two gunmen by surprise. If
she could get close enough to the interrogator, they might not be
able to shoot for fear of hitting him.

But then what? She was bigger than al-Dahabi, and younger . . .
but she'd spent the past twenty-some hours tied to a chair, and both
the adrenaline surge of the past few minutes and the beating had left
her shaking and weak. Even if she did take him down, she would be
no match, then, for the two armed Tangos on the other side of the
chamber.

Besides, she now noticed that al-Dahabi also had a gun, a holstered pistol on his right hip. Jumping him would be suicide.

She decided to keep stalling. If she could keep him talking . . .

The danger lay in the possibility that he would become impatient and move on to the next level of force in this psychological
game.

"No!" she cried. "Why should I make it easy for you, you bastard? You're just going to torture me anyway!"

"I *will* need to ascertain that you are telling me the truth. The process can be relatively brief, a matter of an hour or so as I ask you questions, then apply, shall we say, a certain measured amount of pain as I test your truthfulness. But if you force me to rip the truth from you, the process *will* be long and agonizing no matter what you tell me."

"You're still going to kill me!"

He shrugged. "Perhaps. But . . . cooperate, and I might see if I can intercede with Major Feng. He's not a monster, after all. I think he likes you. He might let you live."

The lie was so transparent she very nearly laughed in his face.

She battled to keep her face frozen, empty of expression. She'd just seen . . . was that *Charlie* slipping in through the tunnel entrance?

The two guards were watching her with wide, hungry eyes, their backs to the entrance.

"Okay!" she cried. "Please, please just don't hurt me!" She started fumbling at her belt.

LAVA TUBE
SAN MARTIN VOLCANO
MONDAY, 1538 HOURS LOCAL TIME

Dean eased into the widening of the lava tube, all of his senses at a heightened pitch. He saw Lia in the pool of light ahead, facing him, and felt a surge of relief. Her face was bruised and bloody, but she appeared to be standing on her own, at least. To the left was the Palestinian, an old man standing with arms folded beside a steel table. Directly in front of Dean were two guards, their backs to the entrance, watching Lia undress.

If he shot them, a convulsive muscle contraction might close a trigger finger and kill Lia.

"Hey!" Dean shouted, his voice echoing down the tunnel. *"Allahu akbar!"*

The two guards and the old man turned to face him.

LAVA TUBE
SAN MARTIN VOLCANO
MONDAY, 1538 HOURS LOCAL TIME

Lia heard Charlie's shrill yell, an echoing battle cry, and saw the startled guards spin to face him. Immediately, she launched herself at al-Dahabi, who'd also turned to face Dean and was groping at his hip for his holstered sidearm. Dean's rifle fired, a sharp chuff of sound, and the back of a guard's head exploded in a scarlet spray.

She struck al-Dahabi from the side just as he started to pull his sidearm clear, slamming him back into the portable table, upending it with a clattering crash, then continuing on until Lia, al-Dahabi, and the table all smashed into the light stand.

The light toppled, flared, and went dark with a loud pop.

There was neither room nor time for subtlety. Lia raised her arm, then slammed her elbow down against the side of al-Dahabi's head. The man beneath her screamed, dragging his pistol up, twisting beneath her. She elbowed his temple again, then again, but he turned his head and her last blow caught him squarely in the nose with a gush of blood.

She kept hitting him, kicking and kneeing him, slamming his head and face with her elbows and knees as the pistol hit the stone floor and clattered away into the near-darkness.

She felt a hand close on her shoulder and spun, still fighting.

"Easy, Lia! It's me!"

Her breath coming in savage, rapid gasps, she stared up into Dean's face for a moment, still ready to kill—

"Charlie?"

"It's okay, Lia. It's me."

She let him pull her back from al-Dahabi. Dean knelt and probed the interrogator's throat with two fingers. "He's dead. Nice hand-to-hand technique."

She shuddered. "Thank God you got here!"

"What's with the striptease?"

She glared at him. "Don't you dare even joke about that!"

"Sorry." Dean looked away, checking the darkened chamber. Enough light was filtering in from the entrance to to show shapes and dark shadows. Both guards, Lia saw, were dead, sprawled in growing pools of blood. She hadn't even heard Dean kill the second one. "Just those three?"

"Yes."

"Are you okay to walk?"

"I think so."

"Get dressed. We need to get the hell out of Dodge."

"That's the best offer I've had all day."

FIRESTORM FIVE
12 NMI NORTHEAST OF LA PALMA
MONDAY, 1538 HOURS LOCAL TIME

Lieutenant Colonel Randolph Farley saw two red indicators on his weapons panel wink on. "Firestorm, Firestorm Five," he called. "Signal acquired." He tapped an icon on the screen, watched another indicator light up. "I have target lock." A moment later, a second indicator winked on, his second target, illuminated at a slightly different wavelength. "Firestorm, Firestorm Five, I have *two* target locks."

"Five, Firestorm Leader. Copy. Arm the force packages."

"Roger that. Arming the packages."

Using the touch-screen controls, he told the computer on board his F-22 Raptor to arm the two JDAMs nestled into his internal bays and to open the bay doors. The Raptor was an extraordinarily stealthy aircraft—at certain angles it had the radar cross-section of a steel marble—and carried its munitions internally to maintain that stealth.

On the advanced touch-screen readout, the schematic drawings of both JDAMs switched from gray to green.

"Firestorm, this is Firestorm Five," he called. "Weapons hot, I repeat, weapons hot. Bays open. Ready to engage."

It had been a long flight. The six F-22 Raptors of the 43rd Fighter Squadron had lifted off from Tyndall Air Force base on the Florida panhandle nearly four hours earlier. At a supercruise speed of Mach 1.8, the coast of Africa was less than three hours' flight time from home, but they'd needed two rendezvous along the way with KC-135 Stratotankers for midair refueling.

Each aircraft carried two one-thousand-pound LJDAM-modified Mk 83/BLU-110 gravity bombs in internal bays; LJDAM stood for Laser Joint Direct Attack Munition, the kit that turned an ordinary dumb bomb into a precision smart weapon. Guided in by a laser designator on the ground, a Raptor traveling at Mach 1.5 could precisely plant one of those babies on a moving target from twenty-five nautical miles away and fifty thousand feet up. The weapons could also be precision-guided by onboard GPS units, but the mission planners didn't have precise GPS targeting data on all of the targets, and so the decision had been made to use laser guidance instead.

Old tech—but it would work just fine, so long as there were no clouds or smoke in the target area.

Six aircraft, twelve LJDAMs; the extra was along as backup in case of weapon malfunction or a problem with one of the aircraft. Firestorm Five's targets were the southernmost two in a line of ten. The Raptors were strung out now in a long line at forty thousand feet, angling toward the island of La Palma from the northeast at Mach 1.2.

"Firestorm, Firestorm Leader." That was the voice of Colonel Edward Mackelroy, in Firestorm One. "Firestorm is clear to engage."

Farley tapped the release icon for his port-side weapon—"force package" in the newspeak glossary of military terminology. The aircraft bounced higher as a thousand pounds of bomb dropped from its belly.

"Five, weapon one away." He tapped the second icon. "Two away."

Death hurtled toward La Palma through the brilliant blue of the Atlantic sky.

DRILL SITE
SAN MARTIN VOLCANO
MONDAY, 1539 HOURS LOCAL TIME

The assembly was almost complete.

The suitcase nukes purchased from elements of the Russian *mafiya* a few weeks earlier rested inside their cases in several pieces: the actual warhead, containing two masses of plutonium at either end of a forty-centimeter-long steel tube; and the firing mechanism, consisting of a shaped charge of plastic explosives inside a cylinder designed to fit snugly over one end of the tube; three detonators, which needed to be uncased and inserted inside the plastique; a battery; a timer; a length of electrical wire; and a small radio-receiver trigger device.

It took a matter of minutes to prepare one of the weapons for detonation. They were broken down so that they would fit inside the suitcase; assembled, one of the weapons was half a meter long and thirty centimeters wide at the widest.

In standard drilling practices, most rigs created a borehole just under twenty centimeters wide—about eight inches. The specialized drilling equipment they'd purchased from the Frenchman, Chatel, allowed JeM to drill boreholes thirty-five centimeters wide, including the thickness of the high-strength tubing necessary for keeping the boreholes open.

Each nuclear device had an eye ring soldered to one end of the plutonium housing; the boreholes were wide enough to allow each device to be lowered at the end of a long cable deep into the shaft. The electrical wire paid out behind as it was sent down the hole, attached to the reels of electrical cable flown in from Morocco. When the device was in place at the bottom of the borehole, the radio receiver was attached to the surface end of the cable and placed high up on the crater rim. A single radio signal transmitted from a safe distance would detonate the plastic explosives, which would drive the plutonium masses together, creating critical mass and detonating the bomb. The timers were included in case circumstances forced a change in plan, but the idea was to have one radio signal detonate all ten bombs at the same instant, something impossible with separate electrical timers.

Al-Wawi himself came up with the idea years ago, after seeing a documentary program on the BBC. Seeing the plan through, however, had been a monumental effort. Factions within both the JeM and al-Qaeda wanted to use the Russian suitcase bombs against American and European cities, or even simply to hold them in reserve as bargaining chips or for future blackmail efforts. The politics involved had been the most difficult part of the entire operation, harder even than drilling down through hundreds of meters of solid basalt. Al-Wawi had gotten his way at last only by giving up two of the recently purchased weapons for a Palestinian attack by Hamas against the Jewish government in Jerusalem.

The operation had been expensive. Not only had millions been paid for the weapons themselves, but the cost of the drilling operation itself, the bribes paid to Aramco and Petro-Technologique and the authorities in Santa Cruz, the cost of the helicopter charters out of Marrakech, all of those had amounted to several hundred million dollars. Only massive financial assistance from the Chinese had made the effort possible.

As for the technical difficulties, they had been almost insurmountable. Drilling over a hundred meters down through the solid basalt within the throat of each of the selected volcanos had been expensive, time-consumming, and fraught with breakdowns and delay. Along the way, the Aramco engineers reported that as the boreholes went deeper, they were approaching a magma chamber beneath the island. On the one hand, that was excellent news; the nuclear detonation might well trigger a massive volcanic eruption, and that, it was hoped, would hide indications that the explosion had been triggered by nuclear weapons, suggesting that it *had* been an act of Allah. On the other, however, the rock grew increasingly hot and plastic the deeper the drills went, until the drill bits themselves began to melt. The discovery had limited the depth to which the boreholes could be drilled.

Now, at last, everything was in place. The last borehole was complete, the last weapon about to be lowered into the depths of La Palma's volcanic ridge. After this, it *would* be Allah's wrath, in a way. Azhar was convinced that there would be a tidal wave, a megatsunami, despite the skepticism of some geologists. How big it would be, how much devastation it would cause, that would all be up to God.

"Al-Wawi!" a fedayeen standing nearby called. "Where are Abdullah and Nadhir?"

Azhar's head snapped up. A hundred meters away, the boulder where he'd posted the two guards outside of the lava tube rested bare and empty. The guards were gone.

They would not have simply wandered off. The fedayeen—the fighers—attached to JeM's La Palma operation had been extensively trained in Pakistan's Northeastern Territory, and most had fought the Americans in either Afghanistan or Iran. They were well disciplined and knew the penalty for deserting their post. If they were gone, it could only mean . . .

"Suhair! Amir! Get your men! Get them to the cave!"

His eyes flicked across the crater rim looming in every direction about the drill site. If the Americans had already infiltrated troops, they would be up there among those heights somewhere. He reached for his radio. "Shihadeh!" he called. "Do you hear me?"

There was no reply. Turning, he looked up at the west rim of the crater. Shihadeh al-Ali should be up there.

"What's the matter?" Feng asked.

"We may be under attack."

Feng smirked. "By who?"

"The enemy, obviously. The Americans. Three of my sentries are missing."

Feng's face went blank, and he drew his pistol from his holster. "What . . . are your intentions?"

Azhar knew exactly what Feng was asking. The final bomb was not yet assembled completely, but the other nine were, and they were planted, awaiting only the radio signal from a remote location. If those nine weapons were detonated now, everyone along the Cumbre Vieja would die—including Feng.

The Aramco employees had no idea what the boreholes were for, were completely unaware that their lives now hung in the balance. Azhar's fedayeen had sworn to die at his orders. Feng, however, wanted to live. Azhar suspected that if he said he was going to set off the bombs, Feng might well shoot him on the spot.

"We will fight, of course," Azhar replied. "The remote detonator is not yet in place."

He thought for a moment. He didn't trust Feng or Feng's associates. Operation Wrath of God would not have been possible without Chinese money and influence, but the man was in it for reasons of his own, reasons that had nothing whatsoever to do with uniting the Islamic world in jihad. He'd been using the Jaish-e-Mohammad for his own agenda from the start.

Which was fine, since JeM had been using him as well—and now, Azhar could use Feng to draw out the enemy. If American forces were already up there on the crater rim, they would never let the helicopter escape.

Azhar added, "You can, if you choose, escape in the helicopter."

Feng was looking about the crater rim wildly. "Yes. Yes. I could set off the weapons, if you wish."

Azhar reached into the nearly empty suitcase. Inside was a remote control with a single button.

"Very well. You will need a clear line of sight to all of the craters in the Cumbre Vieja, and you will need to be at least five miles away . . . no, make that ten, if *this* device is not yet buried. Minimum safe distance for a surface one-kiloton burst."

Nodding, Feng accepted the controller, turned, and began jogging up the trail toward the upper crater.

Azhar's men were running in from several directions now. Kneeling by the bomb, he pointed at the cave. "There! See if the enemy is there!"

His men charged toward the entrance to the lava tube.

LAVA TUBE
SAN MARTIN VOLCANO
MONDAY, 1540 HOURS LOCAL TIME

Dean raised his hand, stopping Lia at the entrance to the cave. "Wait a sec!" Carefully, he peered around the boulders framing the left side of the opening. A dozen armed men were charging toward them, running flat out. Raising his rifle to his shoulder, he flipped the selector switch to three-round burst, took aim, and squeezed the trigger.

One of the running fedayeen crumbled and fell. The others dropped to the ground, firing wildly. Full-auto rounds chirped and howled off rock above Dean's head.

"Ilya!" he called. He hoped the surrounding rock walls weren't blocking Akulinin's signal. "Ilya, do you copy?"

"Right here, buddy. Keep your head down. One forty mike-mike surprise package on its way."

A moment later, an explosion erupted fifty yards away, behind the attacking fedayeen and near the drilling rig. A few seconds after that, a second round detonated, this one squarely among the Tangos. Dean heard a shrill scream, saw a body flying with the gout of cinder, smoke, and fragmented rock.

He loosed another burst toward the attacking troops. "Ilya! We're inside the tunnel mouth! They have us trapped! Can you lay down some smoke, let us get out of here?"

"On the way."

Another 40 mm grenade burst on the crater floor, between the tunnel entrance and the drilling rig. White smoke erupted from the canister, boiling into the sky, creating a smoke screen between Dean and Lia and the attacking JeM soldiers.

"Let's go!" Dean told Lia, and the two darted into the open, hunched over, running hard.

SAN MARTIN CALDERA RIM
MONDAY, 1540 HOURS LOCAL TIME

Ilya Akulinin broke open the M203 grenade launcher attached to his M4 carbine, ejected the empty cartridge, and slipped a fresh blunt-nosed grenade into the receiver. The enemy was just about at the maximum effective range for the weapon—160 yards—but the shot was tricky because he was shooting *down* into the bottom of a huge bowl, and he had to correct for a tendency to aim high. His first round had been way over the target.

He didn't want to correct too far, however, or he would risk hitting Charlie and Lia. He snapped the receiver shut on the second smoke grenade, took aim, and fired. The weapon gave a solid thunk as it fired, and the round burst close beside the first. The bottom of the crater's bowl was beginning to fill with thick white smoke.

"Amber Four! Amber Four! Negative on the smoke! Repeat, negative on the smoke!"

Calmly, Akulinin reloaded with a third smoke grenade, took aim, and fired. As the round burst in the crater below, he said, "Amber One, this is Amber Four. Did not copy. Please repeat."

"Amber Four, cease smoke! Cease smoke! You're screwing the laser lock!"

Ambers One and Two, some two hundred yards south of Akulinin's position, were using a tripod-mounted GLTD II, a small and lightweight ground laser target designator, to illuminate the base of the drilling rig for the incoming Firestorm strike. Smoke, however, blocked the laser light.

Akulinin glanced at his watch. Firestorm was still seven minutes out. The smoke ought to clear within a couple of minutes.

Plenty of time . . .

INNER SLOPE
SAN MARTIN VOLCANO
MONDAY, 1541 HOURS LOCAL TIME

Dean knelt at the bottom of the gully, his rifle against his shoulder. A thick clump of pine trees and a tangle of large rocks provided a good firing position.

"Climb straight to the top," he told her. "Ilya's up there, among those rocks."

"Aren't you coming?"

"Right behind you. *Go!*"

White smoke drifted heavy and opaque at the bottom of the crater, like thick fog. A shadow, upright and moving, began to materialize ahead, and Dean put a three-round burst into it. At least, he thought as the shadow twisted and fell, he had the comfort of knowing that anything moving in that cloud would be a hostile. He didn't need to worry about inflicting friendly-fire casualties.

He heard the Tangos calling to one another—whether in Arabic or a Pakistani language, he wasn't sure. He stayed in position, listening to the sounds of Lia's clamber up the rugged slope fade. "Ilya?" he called. "Lia's on her way up the gully. Don't shoot her by mistake."

"Copy that, Charlie. I'm not shooting. I can't see shit in the crater. And Amber Four told me to stop making smoke."

"Just sit tight and take care of Lia."

"She okay?"

"Seems to be. Don't piss her off, though. I just saw her kill a guy with her bare hands."

"So much for rescuing damsels in distress."

"Roger that."

Another shadow appeared, and Dean shot it down.

Lia was well on her way up the 160-foot-high slope. Somewhere out there in the smoke, someone had a small nuclear weapon, but there was no way Dean could find him, or do anything about the nuke. That job was best left to Firestorm, now . . . six minutes out.

It was time for him to start climbing.

HELICOPTER
SAN MARTIN VOLCANO
MONDAY, 1541 HOURS LOCAL TIME

Feng Jiu Zhu, still a major of the *Guóānbù* despite his current technical status as a civilian, senior vice president of the China Ocean Shipping Company and, most recently, international terrorist, ran for his life.

It was that foreign woman, damn her. It *had* to be. The CIA must have planted her, must have organized an attack on the La Palma operation when she disappeared. Azhar had been right. He should have shot her yesterday—should have left the island and detonated the nine nuclear weapons already in place, rather than waiting for the final borehole to be complete. Nine weapons, surely, would have caused as powerful and as destructive a wave as ten.

His pistol in one hand, the remote control in the other, he reached the upper level of the crater floor and raced toward the helicopter. Feng couldn't fly the thing; he needed to find the pilot.

He spotted him, standing with his copilot near the fuel tank.

The Aérospatiale Puma had a range of 580 kilometers. The airport at Tan-Tan in southern Morocco was 650 kilometers from La Palma, which meant that with each helicopter flight between the islands and the mainland, they had to touch down at Lanzarote or Fuerteventura to refuel. As a safety measure, though, the operation planners had brought in a small store of aviation gasoline at each crater—about a thousand liters' worth for each—to give helicopters flying out of the craters a safety margin.

The pilot looked at Feng with wild eyes. "What is going on?" he demanded in Arabic. "We heard gunshots! And all of that smoke . . ."

Feng gestured with his pistol. "We're leaving! Now!"

The pilot seemed more than happy to leave the crater. He was a civilian employee of Marrakech Air Transport and knew nothing about the operation save that his company had been hired by foreign petroleum engineers to fly equipment and personnel in and out of the Canary Islands from Morocco. Gun battles had not been part of the contract. He and his copilot were in the aircraft's cockpit in seconds, as Feng scrambled on board behind them. Taking his position in the right-hand seat, the pilot began going through preflight.

Feng pressed the muzzle of his pistol against the side of the man's neck. "Go! *Now!*"

The pilot flicked a switch, and the main rotors began to turn. . . .

CALDERA TABURIENTE
NORTH END OF LA PALMA
MONDAY, 1542 HOURS LOCAL TIME

CJ and Castelano drove back up to the Taburiente Caldera from the Santa Cruz Airport as soon as Carlysle and Damlier were safely in the air. She'd originally planned to go back to the Hotel Sol at Puerto Naos, but the Art Room had pointed out that if the nuclear charges actually went off and the western half of the Cumbre Vieja did slide into the sea, the Hotel Sol lay directly in the landslip's path.

"Shouldn't we try to warn someone?" CJ had asked.

"To what purpose?" Jeff Rockman had told her over the phone. "If anything's gong to happen, it'll happen within the next couple of hours. The local police and military wouldn't even be able to begin to evacuate thousands of people—and that's assuming we could get in touch with the right people quickly enough, and that they believed us. No, we're just going to have to pray that the nukes don't go off."

It seemed damned cold to CJ. There were dozens of small towns, villages, and resorts along the coast between the southern tip of the island and Puerto Naos, with as many as twenty thousand people in the potential landslide's path.

Castelano, however, had agreed with the Art Room. "There's nothing we can do for them," he'd said as they drove up the mountain, "except make sure it doesn't happen."

During the entire drive, there was no sign whatsoever that a major military insertion was under way. Even so, she was conscious of the fact that the assassins who'd tried to kill Carlylse earlier might well have returned to the Taburiente overlook, and that they might have friends.

This time, though, there was a difference. James Castelano was a former U.S. Navy SEAL with combat training and experience, and he was carrying an aluminum case with an H&K MP5SD3 9mm submachine gun tucked into the foam cutouts inside. He'd asked CJ if she could shoot and she'd told him yes; he'd given her a pistol, a SIG SAUER P226 with a muzzle modified to take a screw-on sound suppressor.

"There *are* civilians up there," she told him as she drove the rental car into the Taburiente overlook parking lot. "We may be a bit conspicuous carrying guns around."

"If anybody asks," Castelano told her, "we're *policía* here on official business."

The parking lot was considerably less crowded than it had been a while ago, and she noticed that there were police cars parked in two of the spaces—summoned, no doubt, by the reports an hour and a half earlier of attempted murder and gunfire. They got out of the car and walked up the path toward the overlook, Castelano carrying his weapon inside the aluminum case, CJ with hers tucked into the waistband of her pants at the small of her back and covered by a tug on the hem of her sweater.

A police officer stopped them halfway to the overlook. *"Alto! Zona restringida."*

Castelano flashed an ID. *"Investigador especial,"* he said.

But CJ had already seen something farther up the path that turned her cold. The overlook tourist platform, where the assassin had tried to push Carlylse over into the caldera earlier, had been cordoned off with yellow *línea policía* tape. A bearded man in a *guardia* uniform and holding an H&K submachine gun stood guard in front of it; three men were on the platform behind him, one with what looked like a small remote control unit, two with binoculars raised to their eyes.

They were studying the mountainous vista toward the south.

Toward the Cumbre Vieja, where a small patch of white cloud appeared to be caught on the ridge top.

26

NORTHEAST RIM
SAN MARTIN VOLCANO
MONDAY, 1545 HOURS LOCAL TIME

Lia reached the top of the crater slope and looked around wildly. Ilya was *supposed* to be up here, but . . .

A patch of brick red ground a few feet away suddenly moved. "Get down, Lia! They'll see you!"

She dropped to the ground. "Ilya?"

A lumpy camoflaged sheet of material rolled back, exposing Akulinin's face, his M203, and a bandolier of 40 mm grenades. "The one and only. You okay?"

"Yeah." Her whole body was sore from the beating al-Dahabi had given her, and she was having trouble breathing through her bloodied nose, but . . . yeah, she was all right. The realization was only just now sinking in, and it left her as weak and trembling as the terror had earlier.

In the bowl below, the smoke was rapidly clearing, though tendrils of white fog remained in the deepest recesses of the lower crater. "What's happening?" she asked. "I've kind of been out of the loop."

"Two Marines down that way," Akulinin said, pointing south. "They have the drilling rig illuminated with a target designator, a laser. We jumped with a whole string of Marines. By now, there are two perched above every crater you and CJ identified, pointing their lasers at the drill sites. An air strike left the U.S. a few hours ago and ought to be on final approach. Thousand-pound laser-guided bombs. They should be arriving any minute."

"Ilya," Lia said with a dawning cold horror. *"Charlie's still down there!"*

INNER SLOPE
SAN MARTIN VOLCANO
MONDAY, 1545 HOURS LOCAL TIME

Charlie Dean ducked as rifle bullets plowed into loose cinders just above him. The smoke screen was dissipating rapidly, and he was now in clear view of gunmen down on the crater floor. He could see several armed men kneeling or standing near the drilling rig, aiming their weapons at him as they tried to pick him off the inside wall of the bowl.

If the air strike was on schedule, the bombs were already on the way. He needed to get out of the crater, and quickly, or a laser-guided JDAM was going to sweep him off this slope like a broom.

The trouble was, he'd moved around the inside of the crater counter-clockwise, hoping to lead the bad guys below away from the gully where Lia was climbing. He didn't have the gully's rough ground to aid his scramble up the hill. The ground here was bare rock, too steep even for the cinders that covered everything on the lower slopes, and he had to pick his way along carefully or risk sliding all the way back down into the pit.

Another burst of full-auto rounds whined off the rock just ahead, making him flinch back.

Bracing himself against the slope, taking aim, he loosed several bursts at the gunmen below. He didn't wait to see if he'd hit anything; he just wanted to make them keep their heads down, giving him a chance to move a bit farther up. The ground was so steep here that he couldn't move straight up but was having to navigate along the northern slope toward the west, trying to work his way uphill a few feet for every dozen yards that he traversed the inside of the crater rim. The top was still a long way above him.

"Charlie! Ilya!" sounded on his tactical radio. "Lia's here with me."

"Good." He didn't have the breath for extended conversations at the moment.

"You've got about two minutes before it gets very noisy down there."

"I know. See if you can distract those guys near the drill rig."

"I'm on it."

"No smoke. The bombs are probably already locked on."

"Copy that. Forty mike-mike HE on the way."

A few seconds later, an explosion thundered in the bottom of the crater, spewing a geyser of cinder, rock, and smoke.

He began climbing faster.

HELICOPTER
SAN MARTIN VOLCANO
MONDAY, 1545 HOURS LOCAL TIME

At last, the helicopter began to lift from the ground. Almost immediately, bullets started striking the aircraft, sounding like rocks thrown against a tin roof.

"Get us up!" Feng screamed. "Get us up!"

The helicopter rose faster . . .

NORTHEAST RIM
SAN MARTIN VOLCANO
MONDAY, 1545 HOURS LOCAL TIME

Akulinin heard the roar of the helicopter's rotors, saw the brightly painted civilian aircraft begin to rise above its makeshift landing pad.

He didn't know who or what was aboard that Puma. It might be

Tango leaders trying to make an escape, gunmen getting airborne to try to find the Marines at the crater rim, or even someone with a nuclear weapon trying to get clear of the combat zone.

Whatever the case, it wouldn't be good for the mission, and he wasn't going to let them get clear of the crater.

The range to the helicopter was about 250 yards, well within his weapon's maximum range, but farther than its effective range of 150 meters for a point target. He should be able to hit an area target at that range, though, and the general area of a helicopter was all he needed.

Snapping home another 40 mm grenade, he took aim and squeezed the trigger.

INNER SLOPE
SAN MARTIN VOLCANO
MONDAY, 1545 HOURS LOCAL TIME

Charlie Dean was almost at the top, racing along the inner slope. He went to ground again, though, when he heard the helicopter taking off. Bullets kept snapping and whining past him, but Ilya's grenade barrage had driven the Tangos to seek shelter, and their fire was now sporadic and confused.

He considered trying to take the helicopter under fire but decided that the Marines and Ilya would have that problem covered.

Dean continued making his way upslope, loose rocks and gravel spraying from beneath his boots with each step and avalanching down into the bowl. He braced himself with his right hand against the slope as he continued to move, cutting across the face of the slope to the east as he gained height.

How much time was left? He couldn't know for sure. He wasn't certain if the "ten minutes" Marie had mentioned eight minutes ago was how far the incoming aircraft were from releasing their weapons or how far out the bombs themselves were. He knew he could call the Art Room, but at the moment he needed all his wind for running.

He would assume the bombs were just a couple of minutes out, and use that time to get off the inside slope of the crater.

The slope was a lot steeper here. He slung his rifle over his shoulder in order to free his hands.

NORTHEAST RIM
SAN MARTIN VOLCANO
MONDAY, 1545 HOURS LOCAL TIME

Akulinin was loading another grenade when the first exploded. It hadn't struck the helicopter but had fallen short, landing close to the tents.

The explosion came in two parts—an initial burst followed by a much larger, much more powerful detonation that sent a towering plume of smoke and orange flame boiling into the sky. At first he thought he'd hit an ammo dump, then realized that he'd managed to touch off a large supply of fuel, probably avgas for the helicopter.

The blast, visible as the rising plume of smoke, caught the bright green helicopter and tilted it wildly to the side . . .

HELICOPTER
SAN MARTIN VOLCANO
MONDAY, 1545 HOURS LOCAL TIME

The helicopter lurched savagely to the right, throwing Feng against the side. Outside, a wall of boiling, oily smoke was engulfing the aircraft, which began turning sharply, out of control. They were going to crash, Feng knew it. He had only a few seconds left. Raising the remote unit Azhar had given him, he mashed his thumb down on the firing button.

Nothing happened. The helicopter continued to spin as it fell.

Panicking now, Feng hit the button again and again, then flipped the remote over and clawed off the plastic panel over the battery housing.

There were no batteries.

He just had time to realize that Azhar hadn't trusted him after all before the helicopter struck the floor of the crater in a burgeoning mushroom cloud of flame and black smoke.

FIRESTORM FIVE
12 NMI NORTHEAST OF LA PALMA
MONDAY, 1547 HOURS LOCAL TIME

Lieutenant Colonel Farley stared at the telemetry readout from his number two JDAM. *Shit!*

"Firestorm, Firestorm Five," he said. "One of my weapons just lost target lock. Switching to GPS mode."

"Five, One. Which target? Over."

"One, Five. The southern San Martin crater. It's now tracking on GPS guidance."

"Copy, Five."

Farley didn't know why their orders called for them to drop bombs on one of the Canary Islands. The whole thing was classified and compartmentalized, and no one talked much about it. For all he knew, it was another training exercise, one with live weapons.

He *did* know that the GPS coordinates loaded into those weapons were only approximate, gathered by someone on the ground and adjusted visually for distance. Under these circumstances the weapons would have a CEP—a circular error probability—of thirty yards or more.

He just hoped the people on the ground knew what the hell they were doing. This was a great way of scoring an own goal. . . .

DRILL SITE
SAN MARTIN VOLCANO
MONDAY, 1548 HOURS LOCAL TIME

Ibrahim Hussain Azhar heard the explosion and saw the green Mar-rakech Air Transport helicopter suddenly begin to rotate and fall. An instant later, another explosion rocked the crater as the aircraft crashed and burned.

He'd expected as much; the American forces on the crater rim wouldn't allow a helicopter to escape the trap, not when it might be carrying a nuclear weapon off the island. He had to assume that they knew about the suitcase bombs by now.

That either bombs or U.S. Marines were now on the way was a certainty. Gunfire continued to bark and crackle across the crater floor as high-exposive rounds dropped among his men one after another. As oily black smoke rose from the helicopter crash on the higher part of the crater floor, he knew he might now have only minutes left. There was no time to evacuate the crater, no time to attach the bomb to a cable and lower it into the laboriously exca-vated borehole.

He'd deliberately given Feng a remote control without batteries, knowing that he would have fired the bombs as soon as he came under enemy fire. Maybe that would have been the best possible alter-native, but Azhar still hoped the plan would work as originally designed. Shah and Chatel were up at Taburiente now, and as soon as they real-ized that the volcanos were under attack, they would trigger the bombs from there.

This one wasn't connected to a receiver yet, though, and couldn't be triggered down here, where the rock walls of the crater blocked incoming radio signals. But there was another way.

Scooping up the nearly completed weapon, he rose and dashed toward the lava tube entrance.

CALDERA TABURIENTE
NORTH END OF LA PALMA
MONDAY, 1548 HOURS LOCAL TIME

As Castelano talked with the policeman, CJ took a couple of steps forward, staring at the group of men on the tourist viewing platform. They seemed intent on something on the ridge to the south.

A moment ago, there'd been a wisp of white cloud above one of the craters visible in the blue haze in the distance. Now a black pillar of smoke hung like a storm cloud above one of the peaks. The men were arguing, one gesturing with what looked like a television remote.

Reaching behind her back, CJ pulled out the P226, raised it braced in both hands, and began squeezing the trigger. The guard in front of the police tape twisted and fell.

Advancing step by step, she continued firing. Behind her, the policeman reached for his holstered sidearm, pushing past Castelano, yelling at her in Spanish to stop. Castelano reached out and grabbed the officer, using his foot to lash out and trip the man into a headlong sprawl.

CJ kept firing.

FIRESTORM FORCE PACKAGES
MONDAY, 1548 HOURS LOCAL TIME

Ten bombs whistled softly through the afternoon sky, spreading out slightly as each vectored in on its assigned, illuminated target. They guided on beams of reflected laser energy, each beam set at a different frequency to avoid targeting confusion, their tail control surfaces adjusting moment to moment to keep the falling weapon centered on its target.

The first strikes were at the cluster of three northernmost peaks, at Volcán de San Juan and Birigoyo almost simultaneously, with a bomb striking the third crater seconds later. Gouts of smoke and cinders were hurled into the sky, as drilling derricks toppled and collapsed, as fuel stores erupted, as JeM personnel tried to take cover . . . and died.

The next two in line were Hoyo Negro and Duraznero. The explosions seemed to walk south along the crest of the Cumbre Viaja, explosion following explosion in thundering promenade as drilling rigs were torn apart, boreholes sealed, and radio receivers and electrical cables flung about and shredded by the blasts.

One bomb, the second released by Firestorm Five, lost its lock on its illuminated target when clouds of smoke blocked the laser light from the Marine position nearby. Operating now on GPS data as backup, it howled in low above the northeastern rim of the crater, missed the drilling rig by scant yards, and slammed into the upper portion of the crater floor.

The blast was akin to the crack of Armageddon.

NORTHEAST RIM
SAN MARTIN VOLCANO
MONDAY, 1548 HOURS LOCAL TIME

Akulinin saw the detonations of the other bombs off to the north. "Get down!" he screamed. Lunging forward, he knocked Lia to the ground, throwing himself over her.

An instant later, they heard the bomb shriek over the crater and strike among the tents close by the burning wreckage of the helicopter.

The explosion felt like a volcano going off, a heavy, massive *whoom* that literally shook the earth and slammed Akulinin's chest and belly with what felt like a hard kick. They were plunged into shadow as a vast column of black smoke and debris lofted itself above the crater rim; then, slowly and with a measure of grace, it began to collapse back into the pit.

It began to rain rock fragments and cinders, and all the two could do was cover their heads and necks with their arms and ride it out.

The ridge top was suddenly, inexplicably, and oddly silent.

Akulinin could see Lia shouting something . . . but he couldn't hear her words.

Dean had just made it to the top of the crater rim when the blast caught him from behind, lifting him up, flinging him forward, slamming him down. Lying flat, he covered his head with his arms as rock pelted him. As the cascade subsided, he rolled over and looked back at the crater.

The drilling derrick still stood. He couldn't see any signs of life, but the crater floor was filled with smoke and swirling dust from the explosion. The tent farm, the wrecked helicopter, the landing pad— all had vanished, replaced by a steaming crater fifteen yards across.

CJ's SIG SAUER clicked empty, the slide snapping back on an open chamber. She'd reached the yellow tape, now, stepping past the body of the Tango in the *guardia* uniform.

On the observation platform, Shah lay on his back, dead, the remote control device just beyond his outstretched hand. The other two were wounded, one clutching his belly in grimacing anguish, the other, Chatel, clutching his leg. With one hand, the Frenchman reached for the remote. CJ stepped up to him, the P226 still gripped two-handed, and aimed it at his face, point blank. "Don't," she said.

Chatel rolled back, his hands held up, palms out. His expression was one of glassy-eyed shock, and he didn't seem to notice that CJ's pistol was empty.

Castelano reached her a moment later, followed closely by an angry and confused Spanish police officer.

"These are the ones," Castelano told the officer in Spanish. "You'll need to take them into custody, keep them under heavy guard."

To the south, pillars of black smoke were rising above the line of volcanic craters.

WESTERN SLOPE
SAN MARTIN VOLCANO
MONDAY, 1550 HOURS LOCAL TIME

His ears were ringing loudly, but Dean could still hear. "Art Room!" he called. His own voice sounded distant, almost muffled, and it cracked as he spoke. His mouth was parched and felt like it was coated with dust.

"We copy, Charlie," Jeff Rockman said.

"The strike went down. I don't know about the other targets, but this one missed. The derrick is still standing. I can't see it, but I think the borehole must still be open."

"That's okay, Charlie." Rockman's voice, too, sounded distant. Dean had to work to pick the words out from behind the auditory ringing. "Marines from the *Iwo Jima* are on their way in. You may be able to see them now."

Dean was standing on the northwestern slope of the crater, a good 280 yards from the top of the gully where Ilya and Lia were sheltering. He couldn't see them, and hoped they'd found cover on the outside slope of the cone. They were close over there to the spot where the bomb had struck.

Turning, he looked northwest and saw the helicopters coming in.

The helo in the lead was an MH-60S Knighthawk, painted pale gray and sporting Navy markings.

"The Recon Marines will be in soon to secure the area," Rock-man was telling him. "That lead helicopter is there to pick up you and the Green Amber Marines."

"Roger that."

He could see Ilya and Lia now across the crater, standing side by side, waving. He saw Rodriguez and Dulaney as well, farther south, their forms barely glimpsed, shimmering, through the haze of smoke filling the caldera. The helicopter flew past Ilya and Lia, vectoring in on the Marines.

Dean was feeling a bit exposed on the crest of the ridge, so he moved over the top and started down the western flank. A bike path was there, winding its way from crater to crater along the top of the ridge.

The rifle shot ricocheted off a boulder two feet to his left, and Dean hit the ground. Lia's report had mentioned Tangos manning road-blocks along those bike paths; some of the bad guys must still be out there.

Crawling around behind the boulder, he tried to see where the enemy fire was coming from.

Another shot struck the rock close by his face, close enough that fragments stung his cheek.

LAVA TUBE
SAN MARTIN VOLCANO
MONDAY, 1550 HOURS LOCAL TIME

The massive explosion had thrown Azhar to the floor of the lava tube and showered him with rock breaking loose from the ceiling, but he was still alive. He'd dropped his flashlight, saw it yet gleaming in the dusty air nearby.

The bomb was intact, thanks be to Allah.

This, he thought, was deep enough. The Cumbre Vieja, he knew, was riddled with lava tubes like this, some of them winding through the depths of these mountains for miles. He didn't know how deep this one ran, wasn't even sure how far down he'd come. At one point during the planning for Wrath of God, they'd considered using this lava tube, and others, rather than drilling boreholes. The far more costly expedient of drilling wells into the throats of these volcanos had been adopted in the end for the simple reason that doing so guaranteed placement of the bombs as deep beneath the mountains as possible, to lift the maximum mass of rock from the flanks of the Cumbre Vieja and hurl it into the sea.

This would do, though. The explosion moments earlier *might* have been the other nukes all going off together . . . but he didn't think so. He hoped he was wrong, hoped the bombs had detonated, but if they had, they should have taken this section of rock along with them on the long slide to the sea. More likely, the blast had been an American bomb, and that meant that the plan had almost certainly failed.

There was still a chance, however. One bomb was not ten, and a lava tube some hundreds of meters in length was not a borehole sunk four hundred meters directly down into solid rock, but it was *something*. He would detonate the weapon, and the resultant landslide might be enough.

At the very least, he would blow the top off of this mountain and wreak a measure of revenge against the enemy forces that had brought his plan for Islamic unity to ruin.

He still needed to connect the battery. Holding the flashlight between his teeth, he began working on the final steps to arm the device.

NORTHEAST RIM
SAN MARTIN VOLCANO
MONDAY, 1555 HOURS LOCAL TIME

Lia watched as the Navy helicopter came closer. It had picked up the two Marines on the west flank of the crater, and now the aircraft was coming after her and Akulinin. Four more Marines from the FORE-CON Green Amber team were arriving as well from nearby craters. As the helicopter touched down, rotors still turning, they formed up in an orderly line and began filing aboard, clambering into the side cargo hatch.

The Marines were brisk and businesslike; Lia had expected that they would have been jubilant at their success, bringing in nine out of ten blockbuster bombs to annihilate the terrorist threat on La Palma. A nuclear holocaust had been averted, as had a potential doomsday threat to the U.S. East Coast. She'd have thought they'd all be whooping it up.

Maybe they were as numb as she was.

Maybe the celebrations would come later.

Ilya helped her up into the helicopter. "Is that all of you?" a crewman yelled at her over the clatter of the rotors as the last Marine came on board.

Her hearing had been gone for a moment or two there, but the ringing in her ears had been steadily growing louder over the past couple of minutes. She realized she could hear again, though the ringing made it touch and go.

She shook her head and pointed west. "One more!" she yelled. "Other side of the mountain somewhere!"

The roar of the rotors increased, and the helicopter lifted off again.

LAVA TUBE
SAN MARTIN VOLCANO
MONDAY, 1558 HOURS LOCAL TIME

In the darkness far below, Ibrahim Azhar looked up toward the ceiling of the tunnel.

He believed in Allah, the merciful, the compassionate. He believed that God had spoken through His Prophet, bless his name, and that God would judge the universe. That belief, of course, was as much a part of the image of radical fundamentalist Islam as was hating the

Jews and demanding an end to the Jewish state. Yet . . . sometimes the faith wavered, something he rarely admitted even to himself. What just and merciful God would allow the injustice and poverty of so many people, while their rulers enjoyed such opulence?

Though God alone was what united a billion Muslims, He seemed curiously unwilling to assist His people in regaining their rightful place in this world.

So, if God refused to show Himself, what remained was only . . . *politics*, his passionate yearning to see his people united under a single leader from Morocco to Indonesia and the Philippines, from central Asia to sub-Saharan Africa. To see the western oppressors humiliated and overthrown. *Especially* to see America brought low.

Operation Wrath of God yet might work.

It was possible. God might act after all. Azhar could yet be that God's avenging right arm. Perhaps God had brought him here to this darkness for exactly that purpose.

"*Allahu akbar!*" he cried. "God is great!"

He brought the bare end of one wire down on a battery contact.

And darkness turned to Light . . .

WESTERN SLOPE
SAN MARTIN VOLCANO
MONDAY, 1558 HOURS LOCAL TIME

Dean saw a Tango leap up from cover and dash forward up the hill, racing toward his position. He raised his rifle, but the man dropped again behind cover before Dean could squeeze off a round. There were several bad guys down there among the pine trees and boulders, and they had him pinned here, unable to move. That helicopter wasn't going to be able to come in to dust him off if hostiles were firing at it from a hot LZ.

Then the earth moved.

It started as a vast and powerful, deep rumble, an eruption from far, far below the surface that became louder and more powerful moment by thunderous moment. The boulder was actually trembling, and loose stones and cinders on the ground were dancing about wildly as the earthquake grew in strength.

The side of the mountain was *lifting*, rising toward the sky . . .

NAVY HELICOPTER
NORTH OF THE SAN MARTIN VOLCANO
MONDAY, 1558 HOURS LOCAL TIME

The helicopter lurched suddenly as though swatted by a giant hand, tipping wildly to starboard. Lia clung to a handhold as several of the Marines around her cursed, some of them pitched to the deck.

"What the hell is going on?" one demanded.

Sparks burst from a bundle of electrical wiring attached to the overhead, spilling foul-smelling smoke into the compartment. The Navy crewman yanked a fire extinguisher from a wall bracket and doused the fire with CO_2.

Below, half of the mountain appeared to be rising, pushing upward atop a pillar of black debris, rising and falling outward, toward the west.

"Hang on, everyone!" the pilot yelled above ongoing thunder and shouting Marines.

The helicopter began climbing.

WESTERN SLOPE,
SAN MARTIN VOLCANO
MONDAY, 1558 HOURS LOCAL TIME

He tried to stand up but couldn't. The boulder that had been his cover shifted suddenly, then began rolling and bouncing down the hill. The Tangos, fortunately, were too busy hanging on to take advantage of Dean's sudden exposure.

All he could do was hang on. Above and behind, the top of the mountain appeared to be exploding into the sky, a pillar of smoke and blackness that must have been a mile high, perhaps higher, and *still* it continued to grow.

The side of the mountain to which Charlie Dean was clinging continued to rise . . . and then it was falling, dropping back again, slaming against the ground, but the ground itself was no longer solid but a fast-flowing avalanche of rock and gravel and dirt.

Dean guessed that he was riding a single block of stone, a chunk of mountainside perhaps a hundred yards long and fifty wide. The nearest edge, toward the north, was crumbling away as he watched, bringing the edge closer and yet closer. Beyond, the ground was a hellish churning of tumbling rock and debris, an avalanche hurtling down the western side of Volcán de San Martin, racing toward the sea.

A lone Tango a dozen yards away made it to his feet, swaying as he rode the mass of basalt, and then the rock lurched and pitched and he fell over the side and into the thunderous slide. As bigger and bigger chunks broke from the northern edge of the rock, Dean managed to get to his feet and scramble south, putting some distance between himself and the edge.

The rock slab was pitched forward nearly forty-five degrees. Dean could look down the slope at green pine forest and banana plantations, at sheer cliffs and, beyond, the sparkling blue of the Atlantic. There was nothing to stop the landslide now, *nothing* between millions of tons of falling, sliding rock and the ocean.

Charlie Dean was falling with it.

NAVY HELICOPTER
NORTH OF THE SAN MARTIN VOLCANO
MONDAY, 1559 HOURS LOCAL TIME

"There he is!" Lia cried, pointing. "In the middle of that big rock!"

The helicopter swung around out of the north, descending. Somehow, *somehow*, the pilot brought the aircraft under control after the shuddering impact of the shock wave, and now he came in low above the avalanche.

"Ain't no way I can land on that, miss!" he yelled.

"Just get us fucking closer!" Lia yelled back.

WESTERN SLOPE

SAN MARTIN VOLCANO

MONDAY, 1600 HOURS LOCAL TIME

Dean was staring at the fast-approaching ocean. There was no way he could survive falling off those cliffs ahead, a sheer drop of hundreds of feet into the sea.

"Charlie!" Marie Telach yelled in his skull. "Do you hear me?"

"I hear you!" He had to yell, too, just to hear himself above the roar.

"Turn around! Look up!"

He did so. The light gray belly of a Navy helicopter was pacing the sliding rock, twenty feet above him and a little to one side. He could see someone leaning out of the open cargo door, pointing at him.

It was Lia.

"Ilya just patched a call through to the Art Room," Marie told him. "You weren't answering your radio!"

His tactical radio, he realized, had been lost in either the first explosion or this second, far vaster blast. His implant was still working, though, and his link with the Art Room.

A length of rope came looping and falling toward him, uncoiling as it dropped. It wasn't *quite* long enough, and the winds roiling above the slide right now made it twist and snap unpredictably . . .

The huge slab of rock struck something, jolted hard, and it began fragmenting, falling to pieces beneath Dean's feet, lurching again skyward, and hurling him with it. Desperately, he reached out and snagged the trailing rope one-handed. The wind tore at him, but he managed to grab it with both hands, clinging to the end of a twenty-foot line as the helicopter began rising, rising, hauling Dean up and away from the deadly torrent of crumbling, hurtling, thundering rock.

Then he was out over the ocean as the landslide spewed out over a hundred-foot cliff. He saw the mass of rock, half a mountain's worth of basalt, strike the sea in a titanic explosion of whitewater and spray.

He was far too weak to climb. All he could do was cling to the rope, his lifeline, as the Marines on board the helicopter used a winch to haul him up.

Among those who grabbed hold of him moments later, arms clutching him and dragging him up and over and onto the Knighthawk's cargo deck, were Lia and Ilya.

Behind them, a volcano erupted beneath a black umbrella of smoke, sending gouts of molten rock, glowing orange-hot, roiling high into the tropical sky.

SAND BEACH
ACADIA NATIONAL PARK
MAINE
6:08 P.M.

Sand beaches are uncommon along the rocky coast of Maine. On the entire island of Mount Desert, within the boundaries of Acadia National Park, there is exactly one, a 350-yard stretch of white sand facing south into the Atlantic. The chill waters of the Gulf of Maine are too cold to tempt any but the hardiest souls, even in late summer, but tourists flock to the beach to watch the waves, to hike the nearby trails, to play in the sand and photograph the picturesque headlands, the rocky islands along the coast, the lobster boats plying their trade just offshore.

The La Palma Landslip, as geologists would later refer to it, had indeed raised a tidal wave as it slid into the sea three thousand miles from New England, creating a swell within the ocean that raced out across the Atlantic at five hundred miles per hour. Unseen in the open ocean, it was a wave in the physics sense, a transmission of energy rather than a visible moving crest. Only as it passed into shallower water did the physics begin to manifest as something visible.

The wave rippled across the Atlantic in six hours; Mount Desert was the northernmost stretch of U.S. coastline not sheltered by the loom of Nova Scotia just over a hundred miles away. On Sand Beach, Brad and Tammy Matheson were sitting on the beach, watching Ryan, their nine-year-old son, building a sand castle between the high and low tide lines. He'd been at it for nearly three hours and had erected a labyrinth of towers and walls that would have done Camelot proud. The tide was coming in now, but Ryan still had perhaps an hour before his edifice faced a serious marine challenge.

The rogue wave caught them all by surprise. It surged up past the high-water mark, a white swirl of foam and froth that kept coming . . . and coming. It engulfed the sand castle as Ryan squealed, toppled ramparts, washed away walls, and continue climbing the gentle slope of the beach, forcing the Mathesons to scramble to snatch up towels, blankets, clothes, and beach bags.

"Not yet!" Ryan screamed at the implacable elements. *"It's not ready!"*

Then the wave receded once more, streaming down the beach and back to the sea, taking the sand castle with it.

EPILOGUE

Lia, Dean, and Akulinin had gathered at the Hotel Sol after the helicopter had brought them to Puerto Naos the day before. Hours later, they'd been joined by CJ and Castelano. The two had been detained by the authorities, but Rubens' intervention and a call from the U.S. State Department had gotten them released. Now the five of them were on the patio near the hotel's swimming pool, the blue waters of the Atlantic crashing against the rocks far below.

"Yeah, so then this Spanish general turns to me," CJ was telling them, "and he says, 'Do employees of the U.S. State Department *always* go about so well armed? It gives me a new respect for your Hillary Clinton.'"

They all laughed.

In the background, black smoke continued to stain the morning skies above the Cumbre Vieja.

The nuke had indeed triggered a minor volcanic eruption. The Marines off the *Iwo Jima* landed the evening before in what was now being called a humanitarian mission, helping to evacuate islanders threatened by the unexpected eruption of the San Martin volcano. The chain of savage concussions from the top of the Cumbre

Vieja startled everyone on the island. Today, as San Martin continued to erupt, sending streams of lava down the scar gouged in its western flank by the landslide, hordes of volcanologists were descending on La Palma. Men in silvery reflective suits protecting them from the heat were seen investigating the lava flows, and U.S. Marines helped the local *guardia* and military move residents out of harm's way.

Although a final tally was not in, estimates suggested that as many as five people had died when the landslide swept past the tiny village of El Charco on its way to the sea. Three Spanish tourists who'd been at Zamora Beach to the south were still missing as well, but the landslide missed a large banana plantation on the top of the sea cliffs, missed the village of Casas de Remo, missed the enormous luxury Teneguia Princess resort hotel at Fuencaliente, missed Puerto Naos and the Hotel Sol to the north . . .

For a time, late last night, there was talk of evacuating the entire west coast of the island, but the eruption was already subsiding.

Things could have been a *lot* worse.

"So where to next?" CJ asked.

"I'm headed stateside," Akulinin said, grinning. "Masha's in New York, waiting for me!"

"Tell her hi for me," Dean said. "*I'm* thinking that I might be able to persuade the boss to let us have a couple of days here on La Palma to . . . you know, wrap up loose ends. Did you know that the nickname for La Palma is La Isla Bonita? The beautiful island. I figure we're due a bit of vacation time—assuming they don't find any radioactive contamination up there and decide to evacuate the place."

"*Was* there any radiation from the blast?" CJ asked.

"Apparently not," Dean told her. "Our NEST people have been all over up there, Rubens says, and they haven't found anything. It was an underground burst, so whatever radioactivity the bomb released was mostly kept underground, and what wasn't was spread out and buried by the lava. I guess it's not a problem."

"Being underground kept down the EMP, too," Akulinin pointed out. "I thought we were goners when that wiring caught fire from the electromagnetic pulse."

"Apparently all of that rock blocked most of that as well," Lia said. It had been close, though. The helicopter's Navy pilot had just been able to make it to a field above Puerto Naos before the engine died.

"So far as anybody else is concerned," Dean said, "it was just a natural volcanic eruption—not even as big as the Tenaguia eruption in '71." He chuckled. "A tidal wave all of ten inches hit the East Coast. A bit of anticlimax, that."

"What about the prisoners?" CJ asked.

"Tough call," Lia told her. "Technically, no American laws were broken, so it will be tough to extradite them. Chatel may face trial in France, since he was misdirecting his company's assets for personal gain. The State Department may try to put together an indictment, but conspiracy is going to be damned tough to prove."

"The Marines picked up a few dozen Tangos and Aramco employees fleeing the drill sites," Dean added. "They'll probably be shipped back to their own countries, mostly Pakistan and Saudi Arabia. Unless Spain decides to put them on trial."

"Maybe for trespass and vandalism!" Akulinin suggested, laughing. "The important thing is . . . we stopped them!"

"The one that worries me," Lia said, "is Feng."

"I don't think he got away, Lia," Dean told her. "He was either in that helicopter, or he was caught inside the crater by the nuke. We'll never know for sure, but we do know he can't hurt you anymore."

"It's not *that*," Lia said. "It's the whole Chinese connection. Was Feng working on his own? Or was the Beijing government behind it?"

"Well," Akulinin said slowly, "we know Feng wasn't the only PRC officer on this op. Kwok Chung On, in Dushanbe. Remember him?"

"You know," Dean said, "we just might need to pay a follow-up to those guys in China, to try to find out if Wrath of God was a scam Kwok and Feng dreamed up . . . or a first strike, an act of war."

Lia leaned over and slipped her arm around him. "In the meantime, Charlie, I think your idea about a tropical vacation is *perfect*."

Together they watched as the rising sun cleared the top of the Cumbre Vieja, filtering through the black smear of volcanic smoke in a dazzling display of light and shifting shadows.